TWO DOORS AWAY

Also by Elle Spellman

Running into Trouble

TWO DOORS AWAY

Elle Spellman

ORION

First published in Great Britain in 2022 by Orion Fiction,
an imprint of The Orion Publishing Group Ltd.,
Carmelite House, 50 Victoria Embankment
London EC4Y 0DZ

An Hachette UK Company

1 3 5 7 9 10 8 6 4 2

A CIP catalogue record for this book is
available from the British Library.

ISBN (Mass Market Paperback) 978 1 4091 9157 5
ISBN (eBook) 978 1 4091 9158 2
ISBN (Audio) 978 1 4091 9159 9

Typeset by Born Group
Printed and bound in Great Britain by Clays Ltd, Elcograf S.p.A.

www.orionbooks.co.uk

For Dad

Prologue

Why now? Why tonight, of all nights?

I don't want to hear it. Not that song, not now. But as the opening piano notes grow in familiarity – in volume, in confidence – I have no choice but to listen, to feel my world collapse all over again.

I turn on the taps in a hasty attempt to drown out the sound, but the song is still there, echoing around the bathroom, making it feel as though the walls of this already tiny box are closing tightly, tightly in.

Every night, at exactly 10 p.m., my next-door neighbours sit down to play the piano. Number 26, the neat house with the glossy red door and the hanging baskets filled with bright geraniums. On the other side of the wall they play, loud and beautiful, the nightly melodies drifting into my own little world. Not all noisy neighbours are annoying, inconvenient – sometimes, they're a blessing. They can unknowingly brighten your day. They can give you something to look forward to of an evening, to sing along to, make the world feel that little less lonely.

Until now.

Now, I just want it to stop. I want that song to go away. That particular tune comes complete with a memory I don't want to relive.

Gripping the side of the bathtub, I haul myself out and don't bother to dry, leaving puddles in my wake as I head for the other room. It's much louder in there, the song gathering intensity with every note. My musical neighbour is on a roll tonight.

'Stop!' I shout, tapping lightly against the magnolia wall. The music continues.

'*Stop!*' Louder this time.

I hit harder, shout some more, until I'm screaming, pounding my fists against the hard plaster, the barrier between us. I hit and hit until my hands are red and numb.

'Stop! *Please.*'

I'm tired. I'm exhausted. I can't take this.

Why now, why this song, why tonight of all nights?

'For fuck's sake! Shut. The fuck. *Up!*'

My legs give way for the second time today and I crumple in a heap, a naked, wet heap on the cold floor of my bedsit, angry tears streaming down my face.

The music stops.

On the other side of the wall, there's a distinct thump of a piano lid closing. Then silence. It falls like a blanket over my tiny room.

And suddenly, I wish I could take it all back.

STEPH HIGGINS

Facebook Memories

#MadeTheMove #NewHome #NewCity #NewLife

Hi, gorgeous people! Sorry for the week of radio silence. But – drum roll – it finally happened. I've moved. Hello, glorious new home. Hello, Bristol!

You know when I said America was an unforgettable adventure? It was. But while there I realised things need to change. It came as a mild epiphany during a crisp, early morning jog through Central Park (you've got to try it once!). Which, I'll admit, was after one too many cocktails.

Anyway, something became astoundingly clear: I didn't want the excitement to end. I need to be away, visiting new places, trying a new life on for size. It's always been the way for me. So after some time, and some soul-searching (and apartment-hunting – my God, I have stories!), I can confirm I've left Weston.

I need the adventure. So let the fun commence.
And the unpacking!

Comments:

Jack: Good luck, Steph! Although why you didn't
take me with you will remain a mystery. We shared
so well at uni! I miss our pub crawls. And how you
always did my washing-up. (You know I love you.)
Have a great time.

Amanda: Yaaay! I'm so happy for you. And excited. Not that I'm surprised. When we were kids you were barely able to sit still for longer than five minutes. I'll call you tomorrow. X

Alisha: When did you get back from the States?! We need to meet up! Let me know when you're back home. Gutted I missed you before you left. I want to hear all about that guy from the bar on your Insta . . .

Claire: Where are the pics of this new place of yours then??

Amanda: Yes, we require photos! Also, 'apartment'? Babe, you were in America for a mere five months. It's a *flat*.

Miles: This is great news, Steph. I'm glad to hear you're doing so well after . . . well, after what happened. I hope your new home is amazing and everything you hoped for. Would still love to talk to you. Call me at some point? X

TWO YEARS AGO

From: Steph Higgins
To: Amanda Higgins

Subject : Re : Moved !

Hi, Mand!

It's been two weeks since moving and I'm loving every minute! There are some serious perks to having your own space. Behold:

PROS OF LIVING ALONE:

1. The bed's always half-empty, so you can have the entire thing to yourself. Miles would always conduct an entire bed takeover during the night, inching his way closer and closer to the middle, and I'd wake up holding on to the edge of the mattress for dear life. Now? I can spread out like a starfish Every. Single. Night. It's utter bliss.

2. You can leave clutter wherever you damn well please. OK, so I'm currently typing this with a newly organised colour-coded wardrobe behind me, but . . . well, you *know* me. We shared a room for years, so you know I'll soon have the dreaded 'chair pile' that used to drive Mum mad. But now, nobody's here to judge me and my sordid, messy, cluttered ways.

3. You have free rein of the fridge and bathroom, and therefore don't need to succumb to the needs and bad habits of others. (Case in point: Jack from uni.) Also, I can cook what I like, when I like. If I want to eat Coco Pops for dinner, that's my choice. No judgement, besides you – you'll be rolling your eyes as you read this, I can tell.
4. Total peace and quiet. Everyone needs 'me time'.

See? Not at all scary.

Love you! Missing you and Stevie and little Poppy as always. I'll see you soon, promise. All is well. You don't have to worry about me, honestly. Xx

S xx

Chapter 1

Steph

It's one of those broken mornings, I can tell.

One that will inevitably lead to one of those broken *days*. Where one disaster, however slight, leads swiftly into another, and soon you can see the entire day panning out like a vicious domino rally of disappointment in which everything is spoiled.

Take this morning, for example. Having had approximately three hours of sleep after last night's neighbour debacle, I woke late, feeling the distinct jab of my broken sofa bed digging into my side, only to make it halfway down the street before realising I'd left my umbrella at home. I stood, frozen in time, for a second that felt like forever, mentally debating whether to jog back and grab it, or carry on and get the bus on time. Overhead, the gloomy sky threatened an imminent storm, the strange September humidity causing my clothes to stick to my skin. I chose the latter, rushing for the bus stop against a downpour of sheet-like, sniping rain, only to see the bus pulling away. 'Wait!' I'd yelled, to no avail, watching as it vanished into the distance without me.

When the next bus pulled up in the city centre, depositing me a four-minute run from the office with only one minute to spare, I realised I'd had my top on inside out the whole time.

Cons of living alone #148: There's no one around to say 'Steph, your top's on inside out.' Or hand you the umbrella before you leave the house, in that loved-up, wide-eyed way, your fingers brushing as you realise how lucky you are.

Thankfully, nobody seems to notice I'm a few minutes late. The open-plan office of Everly Cope Associates is quiet besides the tapping of keyboards from the overly keen early birds and the dull roar of the kettle from the communal kitchen. I slip through, heading straight to the toilets in a bid to tidy myself up; putting my top on the right way, wringing out my hair and trying to salvage my make-up. Less 'drowning raccoon', more 'dewy'. I even take a selfie for good measure once the transformation is complete.

'Steph! *Oh my God*, you're here!'

OK, *someone* notices.

Saskia accosts me the minute I enter the brightly lit office. Her voice is almost a shriek, startling our colleague Jeff as he walks in carrying an overfilled *Star Wars* coffee mug. I watch the dark liquid slosh over the rim as if in slow motion, landing on his shoes with an almighty *splat*. He lets out a disgruntled sigh.

'Steph,' says Sas. 'You're just the person we need!'

A flutter of panic works its way up from my stomach to my throat as I wonder what outraged client Saskia will bestow upon me today.

I look at her, taking in her pristine blouse-and-skirt ensemble, her blonde hair styled into enviable waves, and hurry to my workspace, dropping my rucksack and bright pink unicorn-themed lunch bag on the desk. I turn on my PC.

'Oh?'

Saskia looks at me. Really *looks*. There's a hint of concern etched into her doll-like features.

'Are you all right?' she asks me. 'You look a bit . . .' She points at my eyes with a beautifully manicured finger that puts my own stubby nails to shame.

'Me? Oh, yeah. I'm fine.' Clearly, my concealer didn't do the trick. 'I just didn't have much sleep, that's all.'

'Ohhh!' she says, her eyes alight with glee. 'I see.'

She says it coyly and I'm momentarily confused until I realise what she's getting at. She thinks I've been kept up all night in the *fun* way.

'No, nothing like that . . .' I begin, ready to burst her bubble.

To Sas, my sloppy appearance is undoubtedly down to a night of mind-blowing sex. Alas, that's not the case, even though I wish it was.

As it happened, my sleepless night mainly involved a lot of crying. And shouting at my next-door neighbour, for which I feel mildly guilty.

I'm about to elaborate but stop myself. Admitting the truth would make me sound even sadder. Maybe going along with it would be worthwhile, even though it would be an outright lie. For starters, she and the others might finally cease trying to convince me that dating apps are amazing, because I'm single and therefore obviously *need someone*.

But I can't bring myself to lie. I've done that all too often recently.

'I just wasn't feeling too great,' I conclude.

'Anyway!' Saskia continues. 'We need your opinion on something. Can you come and help us?'

I trot behind Sas like an obedient puppy, wondering why she seems so desperate for my expertise first thing in the morning. It can't be good.

'Does this have anything to do with Mr Chambers?' I ask, groaning at the thought of yet another phone call with the argumentative client who wouldn't let me get a word in edgeways. 'I thought that had been resolved.'

'What? Oh, no. It's not work-related.'

Breathing a massive sigh of relief, I arrive at the other end of the office to see the other account managers poised around their little hub. Behind them, a sliver of morning sunlight peeks in through the big window that overlooks the Floating Harbour. The sky is still a looming grey, but the glint of the sun is present, edging its way out from behind the clouds like a positive affirmation.

Unlike Saskia, I'm not an account manager here at Everly Cope. I'm a complaints handler. Which means I know a thousand ways of politely telling someone to fuck off – a universal skill, if you ask me – and a million ways of saying sorry. But that's hardly useful when it comes to their roles, unless some of their angry clients land in my inbox. Curiously, I peer bleary-eyed at Saskia's screen and I'm greeted by a picture of a sprawling country manor house.

'Caz got engaged,' Saskia says, now looking serious.

'Caz? Who's Caz?'

Saskia's head whips round, surprised. 'Caz? From the fourth floor? About five foot three, blonde hair? Everyone knows Caz.'

I don't know Caz.

But I nod anyway as I conduct an identity parade in my head.

'She's thinking of having the wedding *here*,' Sas continues, jabbing at the dreamy historic manor on the screen, 'but as you already know, Tamzin here was planning on booking that venue. Quite rude, if you ask me!'

Nods. Nods everywhere. *Shame on you, Caz.*

'Wait,' I say. 'When did Caz get proposed to?'

'Last night.' Sas stops for a moment, opening Insta. 'She posted at around 8 o'clock.'

'And she's booking the venue already?'

'Things move quickly, Steph.' *Don't you know?*

It's too early in the morning for this.

'Anyway, now Tamzin has to change her venue and we were thinking . . . *here.*'

She clicks and up comes a huge Gothic hotel, incredibly charming, set among sprawling, lush green fields. To be fair, it's stunning.

'I can't fucking believe it,' Tamsin herself interjects, through a mouthful of croissant.

'What do you reckon, Steph?' enquires Sas, as if I'm the fount of all knowledge. Even though I'm the only one who's single.

I laugh. 'Why are you asking me, of all people?'

'Because you're sensible,' confirms Tamz, picking apart the remaining half of her buttery pastry.

Sensible. I don't know whether to feel grateful or offended.

'Should I lose the deposit and change the venue, or just keep the booking?' asks Tamz. 'I have to decide *today.*'

'Can't you just . . . both get married at the same place?'

Both women look aghast at the suggestion.

'Caz is looking at early June,' says Tamz, who's on the verge of frantic tears.

Sas gives a solemn nod. 'Tamzin's wedding is in July. 'It'll look like *she* copied.'

I have absolutely no interest in people's pending nuptials, but if I admit that, they'll just think I'm bitter. Nobody wants to be bitter.

'Um, OK, so . . . I think you need to make a pros and cons list. That's what I always do. For example, does it *really* matter who does it first? I mean, it's *your* special day, right? Both weddings will be so different . . .'

'I guess we *could* try to bring the date forward . . .' says Tamz thoughtfully.

'No, you don't need to!' I say, perching on the edge of the desk, looking at the website on Saskia's screen, imagining having that whole luxurious place to myself for an entire day. 'If you give up the deposit, how much would that set you back? Is it worth it overall? How do you . . .'

I trail off, because my attention is caught by something on the site. As they stare at me like some sort of guru, awaiting my next *sensible* suggestion, my gaze falls on the price list on the right-hand corner of the screen. I lean forwards to read the elegant text: Prices start at £20,000. Find out more about our full wedding packages . . .

Suddenly, I feel a bit sick.

'I don't really care about the deposit,' says Tamzin, who's turned the page of her notebook and has started jotting down her list already. 'It's not about the money.'

Twenty thousand pounds.

Who can afford just to wave away twenty thousand pounds? I mean, Tamzin's husband-to-be is a doctor. She makes no secret of the fact they're doing very well. That amount is probably nothing to them. It would maybe mean one less extravagant holiday. But just . . . I can't even formulate a response.

My mind races. I think of my overdraft, where I'm currently hovering in that frightening in-between of red and black. I checked this morning, saw the numbers slipping dangerously into warning territory, reminding me to be careful. I think of the council tax bill pinned, threat-like, to the corkboard in my tiny bedsit. I think of the home I've always dreamed of owning but is unlikely ever to happen, every curious peek at Rightmove ending in abject misery.

I think of my parents who had their wedding party in their garden. Their marriage may not have lasted, but that's not the point. At the time, they loved each other. They were happy, and they didn't care that the buffet was served on paper plates, that the cake was an off-the-shelf selection that Gran decorated. Mum's dress was second-hand, taken in to her measurements and topped with a beautiful veil made by Gran. She looked amazing.

To my parents, back when things were promising and wonderful, all that mattered was the two of them. That they were in the company of everyone they loved.

'We should try to find out what Caz's bridesmaids will be wearing,' Sas suggests, a glint of mischief in her eyes. 'Would be a shame if you outdid her.'

I'm suddenly warm. Warm and too tired and too damp and too annoyed, and my knuckles are red from hitting the wall last night. They glow, an unattractive reminder, and I quickly tug my sleeves down to conceal them. I want to be home, sleeping. Or in the bath, singing along to my neighbour's piano like I usually do because it brings me some kind of weird comfort. It's nice.

Except for last night. That song. *That* wasn't nice.

After feigning some excitement for Tamzin (which isn't entirely a lie – she's lovely and I'm genuinely happy for her), I suggest that she works on the list and goes from there. It's a start. Then I hurry back to my desk, where I gulp down water and try to focus on my daily tasks. A headache lingers behind my eyes, pounding slowly, the result of my lack of sleep. Hopefully, my neighbours will play something much happier tonight.

I work through my emails on autopilot.

So incredibly sorry for our oversight . . .

I am so sorry to hear of your experience, but we will be working to put this right!

> . . . please accept our sincere apologies for any trouble
> this may have caused you . . .

I laugh at my own false sincerity as my fingers fly across the keyboard:

> Apologies for your First World problem, knobhead . . .

I am the queen of apologising.

There's a sudden tap on my shoulder and I jump, just as my email disappears.

'Done it!' Tamzin trills, and in a moment of sheer horror, my life as I know it flashes before my eyes.

Please say I didn't send that, please say I didn't send that . . .

'Steph?'

I'm frozen in terror but manage to click back to Outlook. Where, thankfully – *oh so thankfully* – the email remains unsent. I'd simply clicked it away.

Phew.

'I finished my list,' Tamzin says proudly, handing it over. I can sense Jeff watching me, listening in.

'Can I take a look later?' I whisper, pointing at my screen where ten unanswered emails sit waiting impatiently. 'It's just . . .'

'Sure! Thanks. It really helps to get the reasons down on paper. Perspective, you know?'

'Tamz!' At that, Saskia rises from her seat, calling halfway across the office. 'Caz just messaged. We're going to that nice new bar after work – a little impromptu engagement do! You coming?'

'As if I'd miss it,' says Tamzin.

There's much excitement and, for a moment, I feel strangely left out. Steph, the single, sensible one.

Tamzin must read my expression, because she lingers

at my desk for a little too long, clutching her notepad. I catch *'miniature fountain in grounds much better for photos, other venue only has archway'* scribbled in pen, beneath the heading of 'Pros'. Perspective.

'You should come, Steph,' she says.

'I'm sorry, I can't,' I say. 'I'd need to change . . .'

I gesture apologetically at my clothes, the stripy, faded top that's now sporting some unfortunate deodorant streaks and black jeans, still half soaked from the rain. As someone who doesn't need to go to client meetings, I don't exactly have to dress up.

'Oh, don't be silly,' says Tamzin. She looks at me kindly, up and down. 'We're not going till later. You can buy something new on your lunch break.'

See? Everything is broken.

Phone Notes

Cons of Living Alone:

1. The bed is always half-empty.
2. There's nobody to tell you off jokingly about the clutter.
3. There's nobody to make breakfast for.
4. It's so *peaceful* and *quiet* that my only company is the noise from my next-door neighbours.

And I've never even met them.

Chapter 2

Steph

The bar is already busy. It's dimly lit, filled with noise; chatter emanates from every table and there's a faint sound of soft music being piped through the speakers, subtle against the soft clinking of glasses. I can't help a secret flush of pride, walking into this chic, expensive place behind Saskia and the others, relishing the curious glances being thrown our way. We shrug off coats before they're whisked away by smiling staff. I am *Mean Girls*' Cady Heron to Saskia's Regina George.

Then I feel like a terrible person for basking in it.

Caz, the blushing bride-to-be, is already here, tucked into a table at the back with people I vaguely recognise from work. Caz is noticeably on what appears to be her second bottle of champagne already.

'Heeeyy!' Caz says, louder than necessary. She gets to her feet, stumbling slightly. 'Thanks for coming, everyone!'

There's a flutter of congratulations and squeals of well-deserved excitement. Caz looks in her element. I don't think I've seen anyone smile so widely. I reach over to give her a hug, even though she probably has no idea who I am. I've seen her a few times when she's come down to talk to the accounts team, but to her I'm probably just someone she's seen around. She's polite about it, anyway.

'Thanks, love,' she says. 'Help yourself to bubbly!'

Obviously I do, even though I'm tired. I'm totally knack-ered, already counting the hours until I can get home, microwave a curry, have a bath and sleep like the rock star I am. Part of me is ashamed that I fell victim to the fear of missing out; I should have said no, that I'm only existing on three hours of sleep, thanks to a metric fuck-ton of caffeine, but *no*. I let it happen. Which means that deep down, I *actually wanted to*.

Besides, I need to get some use out of the dress I picked up on my lunch break and changed into at work. A plain black £5 sale-rail find, though if Saskia asks (she won't), it's some designer 'old thing' I already had at the back of my wardrobe. Paired with my office flats and some tights, it looks nice. Understated. Passable.

I pull out a seat next to Tamzin, whose inane grin undoubtedly conceals the sheer fury of this morning. I know she's only here to try to get some intel on the wedding itself.

'You all right?' I ask.

Tamz nods and gulps back the contents of her glass.

Another reason I'm glad I came? The gorgeous setting of this posh bar is perfect for photos. Leaving my workmates deeply engrossed in work-related goss, I discreetly take a few snaps of the table. The candles, set in cute little wreaths of decorative faux roses, glimmer beneath the cosy light. The glasses, champagne and floral décor, set on polished oak, look so good they barely need a filter.

I upload them quickly – *Celebrating! #OutWithTheGirls #Engagement #Friends* – along with all the other hashtags that float to the forefront of my tired mind. I also upload the #toiletselfie from earlier, after swiftly altering the lighting, pulling up my face-edit app and tweaking my make-up a little. To make my eyes look a little brighter. Make my hair look less frizzy. Lose the fine lines that have started to creep along my forehead.

'So, are you seeing anyone yet?' Tamzin asks, turning to me.

She's halfway through another glass and I catch her peering nosily at my phone, at the selfie.

Saskia leans forward in her seat next to Tamzin. 'She's single. Aren't you, Steph?' She turns to Tamz. 'She says she's waiting for the right person. You should get yourself on those dating apps,' Saskia helpfully suggests, for the thousandth time since I started working at Everly Cope. 'Everyone's on Tinder, aren't they? Well, except us, of course.'

She catches my unimpressed look as I drain my flute.

'What I mean is,' Sas quickly confirms, 'if I *was* single, I'd be on there, too.'

'Nice backtrack there,' I hiccup. 'But no. I'm not ready for that yet.'

Tamz is incredulous. 'Why?'

'It's just . . . I think I'd rather meet someone in person. I don't want to search for a relationship, I want it to just *happen.*'

'That's romantic,' says Saskia.

Tamz gives me a nod of approval. 'So you're an old soul, in the romantic sense. How old are you, really?' she asks, as if I haven't told her before.

'Twenty-eight.'

'Oh! I thought you were younger. There's still plenty of time!'

I groan inwardly, her compliment spoiled by the ever-looming threat of *not having enough time*. Like there's a giant clock hanging over my head and it's ticking, ticking. I glance back down at my selfie. At the fine line I've just edited out, exposed and glaring like a neon light in Vegas.

'Use that picture,' says Tamzin, nodding at Instagram, where my #FeelingCute photo has just been posted. 'You'll get *loads* of interest.'

Tamzin's fiancé, Patrick, is gorgeous and kind and successful. Tamzin has all the luck. As a result, she has no need for Tinder. And neither do I; at least, I don't *want* to apply for love. Or sex, for that matter. I'd much rather leave it to chance, and risk having none at all than something fleeting that comes with a side helping of anxiety and first-date nerves.

I want love that's accidental. That's what I keep telling the girls at work, and my sister, and everyone else who's seemingly intent on thrusting a phone under my nose when they discover I've been single for the best part of three years. As if my soulmate is just somewhere out there, ready and waiting, and all I need to do is write the best profile or submit the best photo, as if it's a competition. No random occurrence, no magic, no Fate.

I met my ex, Miles, purely by chance, at a train station. He was heading to his platform and I caught a flash of orange as his ticket fluttered from his pocket and out onto the floor. He strode on ahead, oblivious. I sprinted after him to return it.

Hardly the most romantic of moments. But it was random and sweet and surprising.

Saskia grins and sits up, her blonde head surveying the bar. 'You never know,' she says, frowning as she hones in on someone, squints, says 'hmm' then looks away. 'There could be someone here. In fact, there are plenty of nice-looking men in this very room.' She *hmms* again. Then she stops. Her eyes go wide over the rim of her champagne glass and she taps Tamzin's arm with enthusiasm. 'Isn't that Alex?'

Tamz and I follow her gaze to the end of the long table, where a few more stragglers from work have turned up, deep in conversation. I notice a few familiar faces, yet more people I've seen in passing. Except for one: the tall man with the sandy hair, dressed in a black shirt that, I observe, clings quite nicely to his toned body.

'Alex?' I ask.

'Alex Jessop. He's new,' says Tamz. 'Started last week. He's one of the managers from upstairs. Causing quite a stir, apparently. Ffion can't shut up about how gorgeous he is.'

'He . . . looks nice,' I comment, going back to my champagne.

The table is filling up now. In fact, the entire place is getting busier, thriving with the buzz of the post-work crowd.

I'm tired. So *tired*. I peer down at my phone and notice that the selfie has already racked up twenty likes. Oh, and that it's almost 7 p.m. already.

Tamz gets up to talk to Caz, probably to interrogate her on the sly about bridesmaids' dresses, and Saskia goes to grab another drink, stopping to chat on the way. I watch as she throws her head back in laughter, wishing I could be as perky. It's warm and I'm knackered and I need to get out of the crowd.

I get to my feet and trudge awkwardly to the toilets, weaving my way through the throng of people chatting, laughing, drinking, following the welcoming beacon of the ladies as if it's a star. Cool air hits me as I enter, along with the vague scent of bleach, and I'm grateful to be away.

It's 7.03 p.m. Suddenly, the lure of home is too powerful. The noise outside the door is loud, too loud; I hear it again when someone breezes in, heading for a cubicle. In the mirror I look glamorous, all besides the eyes, where my lack of sleep is evident. All because of last night.

Because of that song.

Hearing the shuffle of a dress in the occupied cubicle, I quickly take a photo in the full-length mirror opposite. The lights in here are nice, as well. I'll upload it later once it's suitably edited.

I pee, wash my hands and head out into the new-found obstacle course that is the bar. I don't want to be here any more. I curse myself for coming out – it's not like I can afford to have much more to drink, anyway; when the last bottle of fizz reaches its bitter end, so will my emergency credit card. Standing by the toilets, watching our long table erupt in laughter in the distance, I contemplate leaving.

Everyone's immersed in conversation. I could slip out.

But I should stay – that's the polite thing to do. I wanted to come out, didn't I? Now I'm faced with the prospect of awkward goodbyes and those gasps of faux panic. *But it's not even late!* they'll protest. *Stay for one more?* They'll think I'm a party pooper, The Serious One, the *sensible* one, even with nobody to go home to, *how absurd*.

I should at least say sorry.

I say sorry countless times a day. I don't know how many 'sorry's I rack up each month. But now, I'm faced with the potential head-tilt and the excuse and the feeling of being too serious, even though I was never the serious one until . . . well, I'd rather not think about that. Instead, I think about getting an Uber. The queen of apologies wants to lose the crown for just one night.

Glancing back, I'm almost lured towards the table again, but the decision is made. Instead, I retrieve my coat and step outside into the cooling air to wait for the Uber. It's almost delicious.

In the car I sit back against the plush leather and I feel a hint of guilt, soon settled by the calming tunes of the radio and the warm glow of Instagram. In the dim light, my feed illuminates the car. My Uber driver is silent. My feed is not. Saskia's just uploaded a photo of a colourful cocktail. I swipe – there are more drinks, bright and *#perfect*, arranged artfully on a tray. Then a group shot. Glasses raised, huge smiles.

#Engaged #Celebrate

Leaning back against the leather, I wait for the telltale ping of a WhatsApp message from the team questioning my whereabouts, a flurry of words drunkenly mistyped: 'Steph, where did you go??' 'Did anyone see Steph get back from the loo?'

By the time the cab pulls up outside my house, there's nothing.

Nobody has noticed I left.

At 9.55 p.m., I'm waiting; fresh from the bath, comfort show on Netflix muted, newly washed hair pinned in a bun. Slumping down on the bed, I listen for the clunk of the piano lid as my neighbour takes a seat. There's a moment of anticipation as I wonder what song they'll play today, what tune will creep beautifully through the wall.

The other night it was 'Eternal Flame'. Hardly one I could forget – my sister Amanda and I performed the Atomic Kitten version at the Year 7 school concert. Yet, even with all the embarrassment attached to the memory – Amanda and I warbling it out in pastel pink crop tops to an echoey hall full of amused students, deeply regretting it the very moment we stepped onto the stage – nothing stopped me from belting it out right there, in my tiny living room-slash-bedroom.

What'll it be tonight?

I watch as the minute ticks over: 10 p.m. I listen. Nothing.

I move closer to the wall, press my ear against it. There's nothing but silence.

For the first time since I moved into Chapel Gardens, my neighbour at number 26 isn't playing the piano.

And I feel terrible.

Chapter 3

Eric

I hear the noise before I reach the door. High-pitched screams that escape from the perfect pale-brick house before me. Music thumps from inside those walls, beating like a pulse, and I know that once the door opens, there's no going back.

I reach out to press the doorbell, strangely anxious. Around me, in the quaint little cul-de-sac, identical homes stand like oversized doll's houses. The English equivalent of a white picket fence.

All is quiet besides the thump of the music. And then the door swings open to reveal Tim.

Tim, my best friend, loud and cheerful and, it seems, ever so slightly drunk. The way he stumbles over the doorstep is a giveaway.

'Eric!' he yells, over the background noise.

Now that the containment is broken, the sound from inside intensifies sharply. His house is full of toddlers. Screaming, happy, laughing, excited toddlers. His living room has been transformed into a colourful pop-up soft play. I'd be on my fourth beer by now, as well.

'Hey, Tim! You OK?'

'You made it! You found the place all right, then?'

Smirking, I point to the door, which is festooned with clusters of balloons in silver and pale blue. A holographic banner reading 'Happy First Birthday!' takes pride of place on the window. 'What could have given it away?'

'Sadie went all-out. Now come on in.'

I follow Tim inside. The narrow hallway is full of tiny shoes. Some in neat little pairs, others stacked haphazardly, thrown off in all the excitement. Tim's wife, Sadie, pops her head out to say hello, quickly escaping from the cacophony of noise and destruction behind her.

'Eric!' she says, bouncing Harry, the birthday boy, on one hip.

I reach down to ruffle his little mop of fine blond hair.

'Long time no see!' says Sadie. 'How have you been?'

'Good, good.' The usual stock answer. Not that Sadie's really listening; her attention has been grasped by Harry, whose curious gaze is now fixed firmly on me. His small, chubby hand reaches for my shirt and he lets out a small noise in greeting. There's no denying it – he's adorable.

Despite our friendship, which began at university, Tim and I haven't seen each other for months. Tim and Sadie moved into their new house and life just became busy and all-consuming. Mainly for Tim. Which is understandable.

'Wow, he's exactly like Tim,' I comment, watching Sadie's eyes light up. 'He's a miniature Tim. A clone.'

Harry laughs as if in agreement. 'God help him,' Sadie jokes. Her gaze trails to the gift I'm holding, wrapped in shiny paper. 'Thanks for coming over. And it's really sweet of you to bring a present! Go on through and get yourself a drink.'

The gift is still in my hands, but she walks away, arms full with Harry and a nappy bag. I carry on through to the kitchen, unable to stop myself from peeking in at the carnage in the living room. The room is huge, separated by a big archway, and the floor is covered with colour; an array of toys and activities take up every inch of space. There's even a ball pit. The sofa, and the beanbags arranged around the room, are all occupied by parents, glossy and happy as they talk and play and do silly dance moves with the kids to the repetitive child-friendly pop track playing in the background that will now be stuck in my head for the next two decades.

'Here he is!' says a voice I recognise.

Joe's here, with Lukasz. Aside from Sean, who's currently on a weekend break with his girlfriend, the whole uni gang is present, squeezed into Tim's kitchen as if it's a secret apocalypse bunker.

There's a collective cheer as I walk in and I join them, hearing joy in my voice that I don't recognise.

I look at my friends. There's change – there's definitely change. I see it in the tiny streak of white hair above Joe's left ear. And the way he stands there, leaning against the worktop almost rigidly in his charcoal-grey shirt, a far cry from the band T-shirts he wore at uni, always so faded and worn out. It was only after he started seeing Tess that the shirts began to disappear mysteriously. One by one, they vanished from our shared house in Filton; one morning they'd be draped over the radiators, the next – gone. A total mystery.

I wonder how they see me now. I know there are differences – I have lines, too. They cluster beneath my eyes and then spread out like tiny branches. Clarissa used to love them. She'd run a soft, elegant finger over them in bed and tell me how sexy I looked when I smiled. There's already some telltale grey in my dark hair, too. Well-concealed, but it's there. I've noticed it in the mirror – a flash of silver under a particular light. One strand, two strands, glistening and visible. But that's just what happens – the passage of time. We grow, we acquire new tastes, new shirts, new partners, families.

For them, anyway.

'I found Eric on the door, clutching a present, looking like he was turning up for prom,' says Tim. He snatches a bottle of beer from the neat line on the worktop, pings the lid off with expert precision and hands it over, giving me a strong pat on the shoulder. 'It's been ages, mate.'

'I know. Hey, I brought this,' I say, accepting the bottle and proffering the gift, a perfect cube wrapped in blue-and-silver paper. A football pattern.

Tim's expression is almost comical. 'Nice one! You didn't have to. Just dump it on the side there.' His face lights up with incredulity. *Dump it on the side.* As if I didn't dedicate an entire afternoon to trawling the toy shops of central Bristol to find a gift. *The* gift, something special, seeing as Harry is one whole year old. Something that both he, and his dad, would appreciate, not just the first piece of colourful tat I laid my eyes on.

A whole year. I remember Baby Harry in those initial pictures, fresh from the hospital, cheeks big and adorably puffy, his face contorted into a crying ball of rage. I remember his newborn photo shoot, a few weeks later; a reel of images with pastel backgrounds, a tiny, oblivious, curled-up Harry posed in plant pots and knitted hats – and in one, a little pumpkin outfit, because it was Halloween. 'My amazing son,' Tim had captioned. 'My world is whole.'

The photo shoot is seared into my brain because that Halloween was also the night Clarissa ended it. The stream of baby photos had arrived on my phone just minutes after she'd got up from the table in the pub and wove through the busy throng of people all oblivious and happy on their spooky night out. I watched her as she squeezed past a sexy witch and a killer clown, dodging capes and a low-hanging pumpkin garland before striding out of the pub and out of my life.

I sat there for two hours, alone, while she packed some things in the flat. She'd stay with her parents for a few days, she said. I didn't know where else to go, so I stayed put, watching the killer clown get increasingly tipsy and determinedly attempt to sip Thatchers Cider through a latex mask. He wasn't successful. I drank as people danced and talked and laughed and kissed. It was just me, happy strangers and – as my phone lit up to inform me – Harry, the latest addition to my best mate's happy life.

As Michael Jackson's 'Thriller' blared out around me for the fourth time that night, I stared into Harry's tiny face, at his curious frown. Another of my friends had joined the dads' club. Happiness engulfed me yet, at the same time, I was devastated. Clarissa had gone, no matter how hard I'd tried to change things. Witnessing Tim's joy only made the knot in my stomach tighter, made the noise around me louder, made the walls close in until I could barely take it any longer. So I left the pub and walked home slowly, counting almost every step as I staggered into the night, taking out my frustration on some unsuspecting neighbour's lovingly carved pumpkin because its lopsided grin was taunting me.

Dutifully, I push the gift onto the worktop.

'Is Sean not coming, then?' Joe asks. He takes a swig of beer.

'It's Kate's birthday, so they've gone away for the weekend. Left this afternoon.'

I know this because I live with Sean. We've been house-mates for almost a year.

'Anywhere nice?'

I tell him Sean mentioned it, but I'd since forgotten. A cabin somewhere, I know that much. The conversation descends into a discussion about holidays and other such matters, punctuated by parental woes.

'Try boarding a plane with two toddlers,' Joe adds. He's silent for a second, as if reliving an awful memory. 'We want to take the girls to Disneyland, but not for another year . . .'

'I can imagine,' says Tim. 'Sadie was thinking about camping next summer, but I think a caravan would be better.'

I zone out, only listening in as Lucasz tells us about his recent trip to Prague. I pick up a metallic conical party hat from a small pile on the worktop, feel the elastic twang painfully against my skin as it snaps on. Hey, at least I look the part.

Tim turns to me. 'So, how's things?' he asks. 'Still at the bank?'

'For my sins,' I reply, laughing in a way they hope is genuine.

Nora, one of Joe's four-year-old twin daughters, bursts into the kitchen to request a beaker of squash. She stares up at me, unimpressed.

'That's a kids' hat,' she says matter-of-factly. She shakes her head before running back to rejoin the screaming masses in the living room.

'And still . . .'

'Single? Yep.'

Joe looks away. Luk's beer bottle is suddenly so very interesting; he's been with his partner, Dave, for almost two years.

'Ah,' says Tom. 'I saw Clarissa the other day. She's . . .'

There's a sudden silence. So instant, so fleeting. I notice it; the looks shared, darting so hurriedly across the room.

'She's what?'

'Oh, nothing. So, how's it going on *that* front, anyway, mate?'

It's unnerving, the way they're looking at me, as if seeing me for the first time with new eyes. Yes, I'm still in the house share. Yes, I'm still single. And *yes*, I'm still working at the fucking bank.

It's as though they can read my future – I've dropped a tarot card from a deck and it's bared all. It's glaring, a huge red beacon of failure lighting up the already bright kitchen and casting a shadow over the loud, noisy, cluttered perfection. Just glancing around the room, I see it all – all the contentment nestled among the evidence of busy life. *Family* life. There's a picture tacked to the fridge with a duck-shaped magnet – three handprints, immortalised in poster paint, slapdash and messy. Three colours; Harry is yellow, Mummy is red, Daddy is blue.

I try to picture Tim dipping his hand in paint. I imagine him trying to take it seriously. Years ago, he'd have cringed at the thought of doing something so wholesome. Tim, the leader of our uni group, the guy who would outlast all of us on a night out. Whether it was football, drinking, chatting up the girls at the students' union – Tim was the one who had put us all to shame. Now, he turns down invites to the pub because he has to put the baby to bed. Sometimes I wonder if he's the same guy.

But he is. We've just all grown up.

I pull myself out of my reverie to notice they're all looking my way, expectantly.

'Please tell me you've got someone on the go now,' says Joe. *Pop* goes another bottle cap. 'How long was it since Perfect Clarissa? Must have been what . . . a year ago now, wasn't it?'

'Perfect Clarissa?' I ask.

They laugh.

'*Perfect Clarissa?*' Luk almost splutters. He puts his empty glass down on the worktop, picks up another. He passes one to me, too. 'Come on, mate. If she was that perfect then they'd still be together.'

'You know what I mean,' says Joe. 'She was the whole package, wasn't she? A bit too over the top if you ask me, but still. She was nice. Had that good job, drove that nice car . . .'

'You mean she was hot?' I force myself to laugh along. 'Come on now, just admit it.'

'Well . . .'

'I know you liked her.'

'Most people thought she was hot,' Joe admits.

'Eric, mate, you were punching well above your weight,' says Tim, his drunken volume rising a few decibels.

Laughter erupts in the kitchen. I grip my bottle tightly. Maybe I'll just keep drinking until I no longer care.

'Come on now, guys,' says Luk, shaking his head.

But Tim's on a roll now.

'Next time, Eric, go out with someone who doesn't know every single answer in the pub quiz. It's great that we always won, but Clarissa put us all to shame.'

More laughter. More reminders of my old life, of group nights out, time spent in pairs. When Clarissa was no longer part of the group, we kind of dispersed. Odd numbers just don't work in that kind of dynamic. So I stopped going.

'Eric, you need to get on those apps, mate,' Joe remarks. 'And please, tell us everything. We can live vicariously through you. Make the most of it. Live it up before you get tied down.'

There's the sound of a balloon bursting in the other room, followed by the loud, siren-like chorus of a dozen startled babies.

Tim chuckles. 'You've got all this to look forward to.'

Again, they laugh. They laugh like they used to when family homes and fatherhood were mere 'what-ifs' in the distance.

They laugh, but it's a shared moment, caught in time – one that I'm not part of.

They laugh because they know they wouldn't change it for the world.

After four hours, five beers and a paper plate stuffed with the remnants of a kids' buffet, the taxi pulls up outside number 24 Chapel Gardens.

'Just here,' I say as we pull around the delicate corner and I point out of the window at the black door with its faded paint, with the unkempt patch of weeds, rising and multiplying shamefully beside it.

There's a damp scent in the air, a faint stickiness from the morning's rain that lingers as I amble towards the front door, being careful to step over the cracked paving slab. The jingle of my keys entices our cat, Freddy, out from his hiding place. He sneaks out from beneath the hedge that borders the adjoining house and hurries towards my feet.

'Where have you been, then?' I ask. As if he can answer me. 'Shitting in next door's flower beds?'

Freddy meows enthusiastically – or impatiently, given how eager he is to get in the house, where all the food is.

'That's a yes, then.'

Freddy isn't exactly *our* cat. Officially he belongs to Lloyd; a third-year computer science student who occupies the top-floor room. Lloyd tends to keep himself to himself – he's the kind of guy you barely see besides in passing. Freddy's often referred to as housemate number four; quiet, unassuming, out for most of the day and generally only appearing for food. Much like his owner.

The door creaks open and I'm faced with darkness. The air inside is cold. Freddy slips out from between my feet and darts off towards the kitchen. The entire house is empty, so I flick on the light and make my way down the hall. It's eerily silent.

The house may be empty but for me, but something's missing. I stand in the near darkness, listening, and then I realise.

I can't hear next door.

Stepping into the living room, I listen for the sounds – the noises that usually travel through the walls. Sounds I hear even when Sean is watching TV. Faint chatter, or the clink of cutlery as the family next door, at number 26, sits down to eat. A woman's voice that travels in from the open window as she prepares food in the kitchen. And every night at ten o'clock, the tinkling of a piano that filters through my open bedroom window. I don't block it out. I never do. I've heard it every night for as long as I've lived here.

Tonight, there's no sound.

Freddy lets out a loud meow.

'Have some bloody patience!' I laugh, reaching to stroke his ginger fur.

It'll be ready meals for the both of us tonight.

I've never met the family next door, the ones with the boxy hedgerows and neat little lawn and hanging baskets on either side of the glossy red front door. Never seen them, never really looked out for them. I've never noticed.

Yet, somehow, now that I can't hear them, and the house is still, their absence is more noticeable than ever.

Chapter 4

Steph

Here's the thing: I've never actually met my next-door neighbours.

Which sounds strange, now that I really think about it. Shamefully, in the eight months of living in Chapel Gardens, since hauling boxes of my possessions from the small rented van up the rain-soaked path en route to my brand-new life in Bristol, I've yet to so much as glimpse the residents of number 26.

I pondered this last night, curled up in bed on the side that wouldn't make my back ache in the morning. There were no soothing piano notes – only silence. I waited, only to be greeted by rain softly hitting the window, like a child's xylophone. All I could do was lie there and listen, watching ten o'clock come and go, feeling that door – the door to an hour of fun memories surging through the wall – close sharply before me.

Are they late? I wondered. Have they moved the piano? Have they gone out?

And then it occurred to me: *they have never gone out*. Every night they've played, right as the clock ticks over to ten. They've been a soundtrack to my evenings for as long as I've lived here. A welcome noise – something else to hear besides the frantic sounds of the city beyond the window.

And now it's gone. Because of me.

But then, who *does* know their neighbours that well nowadays? Is it really that strange? It's just how we live, how society has changed, adapted. People live in their own little worlds, just happening to coexist alongside one another. Gone are the days of chatting over garden fences, of gossip in the post office queue, of the days where 'we'd always leave our doors unlocked!' as though serial killers weren't even a thing.

Granted, I know *of* my neighbours – some of them, anyway – I just don't know them personally. There's the guy at number 30; a light-haired, middle-aged man who lives with his wife and two teenage children. His house is neat-looking, with a stained-glass rose in the front window and red curtains, behind which is a cosy living room full of bookshelves and plants and a huge TV.

I only know this because he kindly takes in parcels for me now and again because number 26 never answer their door. 'You all right?' he always says, friendly enough, smiling pleasantly as he hands me whatever won't fit through my own letter box. He offers the usual trinity of neighbourhood politeness: a hello, a nod, a 'no problem'. That's it.

I don't even know what his name is.

I don't know anything about number 30, just like I don't know anything about the woman who passes me each morning, taking her child to school the moment I'm scurrying towards the bus stop. Blonde, shoulder-length hair, blue parka. She walks briskly, pushing an infant in a buggy as her young, uniform-clad daughter hurries behind her, carrying a book bag. We briefly exchange glances. That silent, unspoken 'good morning'.

But we don't *know* each other. She probably forgets about me the minute I'm out of her sight. We're not friends.

Should we be friends?

I question this as I browse the huge rack of greeting cards before me, in search of the right kind of message. I pick up a blue card bearing the word 'sorry' just as my phone rings.

'Hiii!'

'Amanda! Hey.'

'Is this an inconvenient time? I can hear people. Are you out? I can call back.'

There's that uncertainty in my sister's voice. She always seems to think she's interrupting something majorly important. I pull the greeting card from its place, to reveal: *For your loss – we are here for you.*

OK. It's pretty, I'll give it that, but not what I'm looking for, unless I want to look sinister.

'Not inconvenient! I'm just out shopping.'

'Oh, OK.'

I select another card, this time with a cutesy illustration of a star: Sorry you're leaving!

'Why are there no "sorry I fucked up?" cards in shops?' I ask. 'There's definitely a market for them.'

'What?' Amanda's tinkly laugh travels down the line. 'Why would you want one of those? Have you fucked up?'

'I don't know.'

I walk along the aisle, scanning for anything that might be appropriate. My basket already contains a box of chocolate truffles as a peace offering for next door.

'Hey, Mand, remember when we lived at Mum's – we knew the neighbours really well, didn't we?'

There's a pause.

'Yes, we did!' Amanda says. There was Zahra who lived next door. She was always at ours, talking to Mum, sitting at the little kitchen table drinking tea and gossiping.'

The memory is sweet.

'Yeah! And there was Sylvia, upstairs, with the noisy

grandkids. Could barely sleep if they were over, but they were really nice.'

'And Dana!' Amanda adds, voice full of joy. 'She was the best. She babysat us loads, remember?'

'Yes! Dana!' I pause for a moment, remembering. 'I could never forget Dana.'

'I saw her just the other day, actually,' says Amanda. 'She asked how you were doing.'

My heart soars. Amanda still lives in our home town, just a stone's throw from Mum's old place. Memories flash. Polaroid snapshots of people I haven't thought about in a long time. Sylvia with her grandkids, the incessant *thump thump thump* of footsteps from the floor above. Baking cakes with Dana. Amanda would pour the mixture with intense concentration, being careful not to lose a drop.

'Don't worry about it,' Dana would say in her soft Jamaican accent, expressing a giggle at Amanda's dedication.

I, on the other hand, would be scooping out mixture with vigour, all haphazard excitement.

'What if they burn?' Amanda would ask nervously, refusing to take her eyes off the cakes through the glow of the oven door, while I'd be on my third round of Scrabble with Dana.

All these people. People who also just coexisted alongside me. They were special.

'Why are you asking, anyway?' Amanda asks as I move down the card aisle, selecting one with a picture of a dog.

Do the people next door even like dogs? They might not. They might have a houseful of snakes, for all I know.

'Because I think I've been an *asshole*.' I put on my faux American accent, which is utterly terrible and winds my sister up.

'What did you do to make you think you're an arsehole? Wait. Did you have a loud party again?'

I've never once had a loud party in Chapel Gardens, but anyone who looks at my Instagram would think otherwise. It's not *exactly* a lie. A party on my own, with drink and headphones, counts – right?

'I just . . . I think I pissed them off.'

'How?'

'I just know I did.'

There's no point in telling the truth. About what had happened that evening before I started pounding at the wall with my bare fist. All Amanda would do is worry. So I do what I normally do: gloss over the truth. Or better still, not tell her at all.

Thankfully, she doesn't ask me to elaborate.

'And now you're feeling shitty?'

'Super shitty.'

Stepping further along the aisle, eyes drifting over more rows of pastel cuteness, I pass the birthday cards. Nosily, I pick up the loudest glittery ones, the ones with glorious round badges attached. The kind Mum used to get us when we were small. We'd pull off the badges and wear them proudly all day; to school, followed by the usual kids' party. Or some years, when we didn't have big parties, Mum would take us bowling and we'd pin them to our tops, enjoying the attention.

There's a man standing by the birthday cards. Tall with blond hair, clutching a basket containing a microwave meal and a bottle of red wine. He peers intently through thin-framed glasses, as though he's trying to crack the code for a bank vault, not selecting a card that'll be looked at and, at best, hidden in a drawer for years.

He is, I notice, rather handsome.

My own mission somewhat neglected, I move closer, wondering what to say. This could be it, the start of something new and wild and random. Like Miles but possibly better. More spontaneous.

'One sec,' I tell Amanda, stepping closer, eyes on the selection in front of him. 'Hmm,' I begin, brow furrowed, as though this is the hardest task ever.

He catches my eye. Smiles slightly, awkwardly, and edges forwards.

I'll talk first.

'Hi!' I say, offering a grin.

It's supposed to be friendly. Seductive, even. He smiles again, wider this time. He has a nice smile.

See? Random attraction still works. It's still a *thing*. We aren't all robots, impatient and ever-picky, forced to rely on the intricacies of algorithms and online dating. The old songs that my grandma used to listen to are right, after all. Real love is spontaneous. If this happens, right here in the card section surrounded by glitter and cutesy missives, I'll be immensely happy. Not only will I get to prove a point at work on Monday, but it'll also be a great story to tell our future kids. *We locked eyes adoringly between "Retirement" and "You're 80!"*'

'All right?' he says kindly.

Still clutching my phone, I hear Amanda's fretting.

'Steph? You still there? *Steph*?!'

'Yep!' I manage. Under the harsh light of the shop, the man's hair looks brighter. 'It's always difficult, isn't it?' I say. 'You want to pick the best one . . .'

He moves in slightly. Excitement builds – he really is good-looking. It's only then I realise he's trying to edge round me. I follow his gaze to the card he's reaching for and my heart plummets. Hope is lost.

'Happy Birthday, Darling Wife' it reads, in swirly font above an illustration of boutique shopping bags.

Fuck.

'Sorry,' he mutters before shuffling off, out of my way. *Wonderful.*

At least, I tell myself, he has shit taste in cards. Or am I bitter?

I must be bitter.

'Steph, please say you're still there.'

'Where else would I be?'

'I don't know . . . in a dark alley? In the van of a serial killer? You can never be too careful. It takes *minutes* . . .'

'Mand! Calm down. I'm in a busy shop. Stop listening to those podcasts before bed. I was just . . . momentarily distracted.'

Annoyed now, I grab the first greeting-free card I see – a plain mint-green square bearing the words 'You're Amazing' in glitter before taking it to the checkout.

'If you say so. You know I worry. Anyway, about the neighbour. Whatever it is you did, just say sorry. That's what I'd do. We *had* to, once.'

'Why?'

'Stevie's brother came over for a barbecue and accidentally set their fence alight. I sent Stevie over there, grovelling. The neighbours found it funny, once we'd agreed to pay for it.'

Sometimes, just sometimes, I wish I could be Amanda for a week. Or even just a day. She and her girlfriend, Stevie, and their little daughter, Poppy, are just the epitome of perfect. Even if they set fire to a fence, it sounds charming.

'So,' I ask, suddenly realising the time. Amanda rarely calls me in the middle of the day, unless it can't wait. 'What's up?'

'Nothing much,' says Amanda, which I know is a lie – I can tell by the way her voice falters.

I wander to the self-checkout, scanning the chocolates and the card.

'Nothing *much*? Come on, Mand. Spill.'

'Well . . .'

My stomach knots. I brace myself for impending doom.

'Are you having another baby?'

'What? No! Bloody hell, one's enough. It's not *my* news, it's . . . look. Remember Natasha? Nat?'

There's silence. Because there's no way I could forget our cousin Natasha – that overbearing, unstoppable force that makes it practically impossible to banish memories of her from anyone's mind. It would take a whole lot of brain bleach to accomplish such a feat. That, or an exorcism. Which is a mighty shame, because we have her wedding to look forward to soon. I tell Amanda as much.

I picture the 'Save the Date!' card pinned to my corkboard and shudder.

'Well, there's a hen do,' Amanda continues, slowly, until she delivers the final blow. 'It's next week. And we've been invited.'

What joy.

'Wait. Isn't Nat already booking a spa week for her hen do? She was organising it last week.'

'How do you—'

'Instagram. She followed me first. I can't unfollow her now. It'll be . . . weird.'

Amanda sighs. 'Well, I think *that* party might be for her best buds. This one is friends and family. She said she sent you an invite, too, but it must have got lost in the post. I just wanted to let you know *your attendance at this event would be greatly appreciated*. I kid you not.'

Beep! goes the checkout again and I stuff the card and chocolates in my bag before escaping into the cool air.

'Do I have to? I'm surprised she even wants me there. After—'

'Yes,' says Amanda. 'She does. Maybe she's finally grown up.'

Vague memories surface – vague because I distinctly recall knocking back about six rum and Cokes the last time we had the misfortune of a family gathering, simply to grant me the ability to deal with her presence. That was before I shouted. Before I swore. Before Amanda had to pull me out of the packed hall with a quick heartfelt apology and load me into a taxi as everyone stared in shock and amusement.

Nat and her endless questions. The competitiveness. The judgement. The pity in her eyes.

Truthfully, I don't want to see Nat. I absolutely hate family events and all their forced niceties. Amanda knows this.

She practically reads my mind. We've always had a tendency to do this – a shared bond.

'I know you won't want to be there. But just come?' she pleads. 'It won't be that bad. You could stay with us. We miss you, Steph. Plus, you could come and see Mum. I know she misses you, as well. It's been a while.'

Outside, free from the humid grasp of the store with its overly bright lights and piping music, I take a deep breath, letting the cool breeze hit me.

'Fine,' I say with obvious reluctance. 'I'll come.'

An hour later, I'm back at Chapel Gardens, traipsing up the garden path clutching a bag containing a baguette – soggy from the bus ride, which took longer than usual. Music floats from the first-floor windows, belonging to the only neighbours I *have* met. Sarah and Ash live upstairs – yet more people I only know well enough to say 'hi' to as we pass on the communal stairway, normally as they head out for morning runs. Yes, they're the kind of couple who go running together. Infuriating.

Rummaging in my bag for keys, I sneak a glimpse over the small hedge and into the front well-kept garden of number 26. The tiny card feels like a lead weight, a symbol of guilt. I remember the first day I moved in, when I carried all of my belongings into my bedsit and took a quick look over at next door and wondered if the residents were nice.

It was raining that day, the sky an imposing blanket of grey, but in my mind it was clear and blue and cloudless. And the rainwater seeping through my shoes didn't bother me one bit – it just propelled me to finish, to get my boxes in and out of the rain, pile them up like a solo game of Jenga. I'd looked at my excited, marker-pen scrawl on the neatly packed cardboard, this stack of promise in front of me. I didn't care that the bedsit was tiny. 'Studio in prime city location!', the ad had boasted. 'Perfect for professionals!' I saw my future, my new home, the first adventure of many.

I'd done the rounds, checking out properties riddled with mould or that had carpeted bathrooms or suspicious stains on the original floorboards, so when 28a Chapel Gardens came up, I leaped at it. Yes, there's a window that doesn't open and the place sometimes gets cold, and I have to eat, sleep and cook my food in the same space, but it's mine.

It didn't take me long to unpack – besides two boxes that I've stuffed in the corner, next to my wardrobe. And I'll get round to them.

I've promised myself I'll get round to them.

I look at them now as I pull the card and the chocolates from my bag. Taking a pen from the kitchen worktop, I write 'I'm sorry!' on the front of the card, under the swirling glittery missive. I open it up:

> I'm Steph and I live next door. I recently shouted at
> you through the wall and asked you to stop playing
> the piano. I'd had a bad day and . . .

The pen hovers above the card, as if I'm ready to elaborate. Hastily, I decide against it.

> I didn't mean to shout. I love the music. It makes me
> happy. You're amazing at it. Please play again!
> Love,
> Steph (28a)

Grabbing my keys, I hurry outside and down the path, up towards number 26. *Just say sorry.* For once, I'm going to take my sister's advice. I ring the doorbell, hearing the opening chimes of 'Oh My Darling Clementine' echo through the house, but nobody comes.

I try again. Knock until my knuckles sting. There's nobody home.

Carefully, I slot the card through the letter box, watching it hit the mat at an angle, the pink envelope visible against the frosted glass.

I trudge back to the comfort of my flat to make a cup of tea and run a hot bath, not before snapping a photo for Insta:

> A warming tea and lavender bath – just what I need
> after a long day! Never underestimate the
> importance of self-care: #metime #relaxing #bullshit.

Obviously, I delete that last bit.

Later, lying in bed, eating the truffles I bought for next door, I await the music.

It doesn't come.

Chapter 5

Eric

Perfect Clarissa. *Perfect Clarissa.*

Joe's words roll round and round in my head. They've been doing so ever since Baby Harry's birthday party on Saturday. It's now Monday and they're still there, taunting me. Ringing in my ears, following me on the drive to work. Repeating on me like some dodgy 2 a.m. kebab.

It wasn't exactly a secret that they'd given her that moniker. Perfect Clarissa was always their nickname for her, because let's face it, they were right. Back then I laughed along, my cheeks warm with contentment as I wondered if, deep down, my friends were jealous. I'd notice their gaze flick towards us, sat closely together in the local pub. The fact that the guys saw her as some higher being, someone so wholly out of my reach, clearly meant I'd done something right.

I realise now I'd been just as smug as Joe. But our group, settled and decided less than a week after we all arrived at Bristol Uni armed with ambition, freedom and a dire need for change, had always been the same. Tim and Joe jostled for the top spot in our little group, but as for Lukasz and me, we were happy to take a back seat. We fit seamlessly into the dynamic, watching their happy, almost comedic rivalry from afar, content to blend into the background.

At least, I did. I was hardly the most confident. Which is why, when I met Clarissa on a night out, I didn't think she'd actually want to see me again.

But she did.

Sadly, now it just feels like another in-joke I'm no longer part of. After managing to haul myself out of bed for work this morning, last night's thoughts whirled around in my head again. *She was perfect, Eric. Why did you fuck it all up?*

I didn't think Joe's innocent comment would feel like a nasty gut punch. Last night, with the house bathed in an unexpected silence, all the thoughts and memories decided to resurface. Lloyd was out, leaving me with the place to myself, so I listened to music, but it didn't help. TV didn't, either – nothing could keep my attention. I even pulled out the screenplay I've been slowly working on since uni all those years ago, but reading four pages made me want to burn the entire thing.

There was no noise from next door. No audible chatter as the neighbours moved from room to room – the kind that, strangely, left me with a sense of comfort. Without the background noise, out they came, an onslaught of ghosts that linger in the dark, so loud I could almost see them, even though my eyes were closed. Images of Clarissa, lying in bed next to me at our old flat. A soft sliver of light beaming through the pale blue curtains onto her bare shoulders. I'd reach out and touch her, feel the warmth of her skin as she snored quietly beside me.

I returned to the screenplay, staring at the screen for ten minutes, waiting for the words to come. They didn't. Reading over it made me shut the laptop in frustration; the setting too generic, the dialogue too stilted. All I could think about was Clarissa.

It's your fault, Eric.

I'm at work now. The harsh lights of the bank glare down on me like a spotlight as I stand, smiling and welcoming, beneath them. I feel exposed.

Why did you fuck it all up?

My boss, Joshua, loudly clears his throat behind me. I hear his shuffling footsteps along the glossy tiled floor before he appears at my side by the front desk. Where, admittedly, I've been trying to conceal my phone.

A photo of Clarissa beams out from the screen. I turn it off, but not quickly enough.

Joshua is the kind of guy who fusses as if he's always a little too hot, always a little too daunted. He moves with the air of someone who thinks the world will end at any second and he has to be on constant alert. Right now, his ultra-quick glances dash from me to my phone and then the door, where the lack of customers is prevalent.

'Eric.'

'Yeah?'

'Could you . . .' He's staring at the phone now. 'That,' he says, pointing cautiously to it as if he's just discovered a bomb and doesn't want to raise too much panic. 'Could you put it away? You know you're not to have it on show. If you want to browse Tinder or whatever, do it on your break.'

Joshua is at least a decade younger than me, which makes this whole situation even more soul-destroying.

'Sorry, mate,' I say. 'It was urgent.'

'Really? Didn't look urgent to me.'

The lone customer nearby, waiting for her mortgage appointment, peers up at the impending drama. I lower my voice to a whisper.

'It wasn't Tinder.'

'Right.'

'Seriously. Do you think I'd be perusing that in here?'

'Maybe. I caught Lisa on it the other day. Thinks she's hidden, sitting behind that desk over there. Like I don't have eyes.'

'Well, I wouldn't.'

'Are you all right?'

The question surprises me. I look at him as I stand at the desk, aware of the warmth of my face, not helped by the harsh lights above us. Joshua's tall and perfectly put together. The kind of person who doesn't leave the house until everything is in order. His blue suit, a standard staple of the bank we both work at, looks professionally tailored compared to my off-the-rack effort. His brow furrows, as it always does. Part of me wants to tell him not to worry so often. He was only promoted two months ago and clearly thinks it's all going to go wrong. I don't know what's worse – a first-time manager on a power trip or one who's convinced the sky is falling.

'I am indeed. Why do you ask?' I grin at him in an attempt to feign jollity.

'You look tired. And . . . who is that, anyway?' He nods discreetly towards my phone again. 'New girlfriend?'

My chest tightens as I reach for the phone, knowing that when I press that button, Clarissa will appear once again. I don't want him to see. Apparently, I have one of those faces. 'Too much expression,' my mum always joked. Incredibly easy to read. Which means I'm utterly rubbish at lying. Joshua will catch my expression the moment I see the photo. He'll watch my face fall and awkwardness will ensue.

'So?' he prompts.

'Clarissa. She's not my girlfriend. She *was*.'

Sighing as quietly as I can, I let the picture appear on the screen. There she is, in that summery red dress. It's one of her favourites. She wore it when we went to Brighton; one of our earlier dates. An impromptu September getaway, a seaside B & B, an evening stroll along the sea, after which Clarissa took off the dress mid run, discarding it on the sand before leaping into the freezing water, shrieking as the waves lapped at her feet. I thought she was crazy. I followed her in.

I don't tell Joshua any of this.

'Oh, yeah. I remember her. Sorry, mate.'

He walks away towards the cash machines, then stops. He comes back, confusion etched on his face.

'Wait. Clarissa, you said? Didn't you guys split up ages ago?'

Over a year ago. 'Yeah.'

Confusion lingers on his face for a moment too long. I know exactly what he's thinking, what he wants to ask. *Why are you looking at her photos, Eric?*

Instead, he shrugs. 'Ah. In that case . . . go on Tinder.'

'Er . . .'

'But just do it on your break.'

The woman nearby fails to conceal her amused smile. I go to put the phone in my pocket but stop. Just one quick, final look.

I know I shouldn't have kept the photos. But I didn't have the heart to delete them. A reel full of happy times, a curse as well as a blessing, because in the weeks that followed the break-up, all I could do was look back on all those memories and wish things were better. Lukasz had deleted the thread of text messages, the entire story of our relationship from start to finish. Thousands, gone, just so that I couldn't use them to wallow. I managed to stop him before he got to the photos.

'Eric!'

The sound of Joshua's hissing takes me out of my reverie. He's trying to be inconspicuous. A couple of customers are heading my way. Normally, I'm not this distracted. Being the first smiley face you see as you enter the bank is probably not the greatest role for me today. I'd much rather sit in the glass-walled office doling out 'expert' advice on mortgages and loans and the best ways to save, delivered by a thirty-something man who lives in a houseshare, who's struggling to scrape together a deposit for the tiniest of flats. But they don't see that. They read the name badge and see Eric Fisher, this pinnacle of financial wisdom.

They approach, entering the bank as if it's Harrods at Christmas. They're a starry-eyed couple. In their late twenties, perhaps. He's tall, professional-looking. She's blonde, with a wide smile. Their hold hands tightly.

'We're here for our two-thirty appointment!' the girl says, giddy with excitement.

They share a look; fleeting but easily read. Their world has stopped turning and they're the only ones in it. We are merely bystanders.

I think of Clarissa in her red dress, sandals in hand, heading confidently towards the sea.

'We want to buy our first house,' my customer tells me.

He says they're looking for their starter home, their own little place, for the family they're planning. A world of firsts.

And I realise I could have had it all, too.

The phone suddenly feels heavy in my pocket. Prominent. Inviting. Tempting.

What if it isn't too late?

Chapter 6

Eric

Freddy isn't waiting outside to greet me tonight. I cast a glance around the darkened street as I pull up in Chapel Gardens, easing into the nearest parking space I can find, in search of his reflective collar. I half expect him to dart out from next door's hedge again, the quick flash of his eyes as he follows me to the door, but he's not there. Judging by the flicker of our TV behind the window and the faint laughter escaping from the living room, it's clear as to why. Sean and Kate have returned from their minibreak, so Freddy's obviously found someone else to do his food-related bidding.

There's something different about the scene, though. I notice as I stand on the doorstep, fumbling for my keys. Chapel Gardens looks as it usually does on a Monday evening: quiet, unassuming, the recent arrival of cold weather forcing everyone indoors. The Victorian houses stand tall on either side of the silent road, cosy light beaming out from bay windows, some half concealed by hedges and flowers and small, neatly preserved lawns.

Yet, something is amiss, and it's not the latest cluster of weeds that snake up from the broken path, claiming it as their own, or the faint beat of music coming from a passing car. It's next door.

There's no light coming from number 26.

52

There's *always* a light on in number 26. They have beige curtains and once, through a gap, I could make out the shape of an old-fashioned table lamp that cast a glow around their living room. The same sight greets me each day as I get in from work – the familiarity of that light behind the hedge. Of that presence. Today, it's not there.

Then I remember they've gone away, because I haven't heard them like I usually do. There's no noise, no piano.

Inside the house, I kick off my shoes in the hallway, grateful to be back inside. My shoulders instantly loosen. I head straight for the kitchen, where Lloyd is tentatively trying to retrieve a steaming Tupperware tub from the microwave.

'Ouch,' he hisses, noticing my entrance. 'Left the bloody thing in too long.'

The kitchen smells like chicken korma and it's heavenly, only I'm not hungry. My body is hungry, but my appetite is shot. Probably something to do with my phone, sitting like a ticking clock in my pocket as I await a vibration that could alter the course of my life.

Sure enough, Freddy sneaks out from the hall and pads into the kitchen as if to join in the conversation. I reach down to give him some fuss, but he heads straight for Lloyd, wrapping his bushy orange tail around his owner's leg.

'Hey, where's the loyalty?' I joke.

'All right, Eric?' Lloyd asks.

I watch as he empties the steaming curry into a dish. Despite the fact we have a dining table, albeit tiny, Lloyd rarely eats downstairs. His method is mainly batch cooking on the weekend, then hiding in his room the rest of the time. I shrug off my jacket before heading to the fridge, pulling out a cold beer. I stocked up yesterday.

'Do you happen to know the people next door?' I ask.

53

Lloyd's focused on the curry, brow furrowed in slight irritation as he stirs it. He takes his attention away from dinner prep to give me an inquisitive look.

'Sorry?'

'Next door. Number 26. Do you know anyone who lives there?'

Lloyd thinks for a moment. 'Which side?'

'That side . . .' I nod my head towards the wall. The wall through which, on a regular evening, I can hear the faint sounds of laughter. 'Red door?' I prompt. 'Hanging baskets?'

Clearly, this means nothing to Lloyd and I suddenly realise how truly sad that sounds. The only thing I know about my next-door neighbours is the mundane details of the exterior of the property. They are 'the house with the hanging baskets'.

'Christ,' I say out loud.

'What?'

'Just thinking. If I don't know them well enough even to describe them, what do they think of me? Us? Are we "those blokes next door"? Should I be more neighbourly?'

Another shrug from Lloyd. 'Why would you? You're neighbourly enough. Besides, they probably know you as that bloke who got stuck outside in his pyjamas.'

'You're talking as if I'm some kind of street celebrity.'

'Maybe you are, you just don't know it.'

'Brilliant.'

Once. Just *once* I thought I'd be fine to nip outside and put the bin out late, seeing as I'd forgotten the night before. At the first sound of the recycling vehicle, its loud roar mixed with the clinking of bottles, I'd leaped up from the sofa to get there just in time. And, in the process, locked myself out.

And it was raining.

It took Sean two hours to come to my rescue with his key, by which time I'd already attempted to scale the walls à la Spider-Man – the fact I was wearing a pair of Spider-Man pyjama bottoms only added to the hilarity.

'Can honestly say, I haven't a clue who lives there,' Lloyd admits finally.

'You've never seen them?'

'Just trying to think . . . There's the guy a few doors down with the grey Land Rover. His partner does yoga.'

'And you know this because?'

His lips curl into a sheepish smile. 'She does it in the living room every morning.'

He notices my raised eyebrow.

'In my defence, the curtains are wide open. I have to walk past her *house*, Eric. Plus, she put a leaflet through the door about classes. I might go. In any case, I'm pretty sure that's number 18. Oh, and there's the woman who walks past the window every day. Dark hair, bright pink bag? She usually rushes past me as I'm leaving the house. But again, I'm sure she's not next door.'

'Hmm.' I'm vaguely familiar with Pink Bag. I've seen her a few times, on the rare occasions I've left for work early. The flash of a dark ponytail, the fierce thud of trainers hitting pavement, a stark contrast to the rest of her smart outfit. Blink and you'll miss her. In fact, she was probably the only one who didn't notice me on the day I got locked out. So immersed in her own world, she didn't bat an eyelid. For which, let's face it, I was overwhelmingly grateful.

'Why do you want to know, anyway?'

'Because,' I begin, and then stop. The words escape me and I try to think, try to pull them back, before realising there weren't any in the first place. Because *I don't know*. 'Their lights are off. For the first time in ages.'

'Right.' There's a moment of silence before he bursts into laughter.

'What's so funny?'

'You know people can turn their lights off, right? There's nothing unusual about that.'

'I know. But . . . it just feels *odd*. They *always* have a light on in the house.'

'Why does it matter?'

'I'm just nosey, I guess.'

'OK,' Lloyd chuckles, filling a glass of water.

This is probably the longest conversation I've had with him in a week.

I flick on the kettle for a cup of tea, feel the phone nestled in my pocket. It's usually on silent, but not now. Not when Clarissa could reply, when her words could be making their way to me at any given moment.

I pull out the phone just to check, just to make sure I haven't made a mistake. That I didn't miss that telltale buzz.

There's nothing. Yet.

'Doing much tonight?' I ask.

There was a time, at the beginning, where Sean, Lloyd and I would hang out together. Just sit around, watching TV, eating a takeaway. It was almost like the student days hadn't ended, only with Lloyd as a new addition. Lloyd who is distinctly younger, yet still good company. Back then, when I moved to Chapel Gardens, *I* was the new addition, the outsider welcomed with open arms.

After the break-up, I moved out of the tiny flat in Knowle that I shared with Clarissa, into Sean's houseshare. Where, as luck would have it, his other housemate had decided to move out, leaving a vacant room. The ground floor room that was once a dining room, with its view of our unkempt garden and blinding sun that pours in on summer mornings.

I didn't mind. At the time, it was perfect, because after all, it was only meant to be temporary.

'I'm going out in about half an hour,' Lloyd announces. 'It's Sophie's leaving do.'

I have no idea who Sophie is, but I don't want to tell him. Perhaps he's mentioned her before and I've forgotten.

'Nice,' I say instead.

'What about you?'

It's my turn to shrug as I look down at my phone, distracted by the message that hasn't arrived. I frown at the device, as though willing it to give me an answer.

Maybe Clarissa's thinking about what to say.

Glancing at the screen, I read the message I sent for the tenth time. I tapped it out meticulously during my second break of the afternoon, hunched over the table in the chilly break room, even though I'd agonised over the words for the best part of the day. I must have typed out the message a hundred times, thinking I'd finally perfected it. What *do* you say to someone who's been out of your life for a year?

Hey. It's been a while. Just wondering how you're doing. X

OK, it's basic. Not perfect. But better than previous attempts, including 'Hey, what's up?' (too 'young') and 'Hi, Clarissa, hope you're well. It would be wonderful to catch up again soon.' (Way too formal. All that's missing is 'warmest regards'. Which we all know is sarcasm. I'd have sounded like a total prick.)

'I don't know. Had a long day. Might try to write later. Or watch a film.'

I know I won't write. My head's not in it, I'm not in the right mood. Tonight will likely end with copious amounts of beer and a horror movie. Technically, it's research.

Lloyd merely nods.

Dropping a teabag into my mug – white, emblazoned with the letter E, one half of a pair Clarissa and I bought when we first moved in together – I hear the noise from the living room come to an abrupt halt, the sounds of on-screen cheering shushed into a silence. Sean appears in the kitchen doorway, followed closely by a smiling Kate.

'Hey,' says Sean.

'How was the cabin?' I ask.

'Brilliant,' says Sean. 'Just what we needed.'

Kate's wearing a strange expression, one I can't quite place. Since she started dating Sean, Kate's been a regular fixture in our house. She's great – funny, smart, considerate, and gets all of Sean's jokes. Someone has to.

There's a cautious air of silence, broken only by Lloyd.

'See you later,' he says before disappearing with his food, leaving the three of us remaining in the kitchen bathed in the faint aroma of chicken korma.

'Good day?' Kate asks.

It's forced, almost. Convenient small talk. Something is going on.

It's confirmed when Sean says, 'Can we chat for a minute?'

'Sure. Is everything all right?'

I finish the tea, stirring for longer than is necessary, aware of a strange cloud present in the kitchen. The mood has shifted, somehow. Sean heads through to the living room and I follow, plonking myself down on the armchair. They both take the sofa.

Sean flicks off the TV. We sit in silence until he speaks.

'So,' Sean begins. 'You might have guessed already, but, well . . .'

'We're moving in together!' interrupts Kate, barely able to conceal her joy.

I look to Sean and then Kate. They're glowing – Kate especially. Her big brown eyes are aglow with love. She reaches for Sean's hand and they gaze at each other, seemingly forgetting that I'm also in the room.

I clear my throat loudly, jolting them back to the present. As they're in their happy love bubble, I'm perched in the armchair opposite, feeling like a naughty child. Sean remembers where he is and turns to me.

'We talked about it while we were away. We've been together for a while now—'

'Six months, isn't it?' I ask.

'Yes,' says Sean.

Kate rests her head on Sean's shoulder.

'So Kate and I figured it's about time we took the plunge.'

Kate and I. Of course. I've been there. I've been in the throes of early-days excitement, where it's all picnics and weekends away and fantasising. And gawping at each other with looks that make old ladies sigh with happy nostalgia and your friends uncomfortable. That's all part of the process.

It's then that the realisation well and truly dawns, and my stomach lurches, as if I'm in an elevator and I've been dropped a hundred feet.

They're kicking me out. Kate's moving in so *they're going to kick me out.*

'Shit,' I say. The words are out before I have time to stop them.

'Well, congratulations would be nice, mate,' says Sean.

'Sorry . . . I panicked.' I rub at my temples. 'It's just . . . you want me to move out, don't you? How long do I have?'

'What?'

They regard me with confusion. I feel childlike. They sit before me on the leather sofa, knees touching, hands held as they deliver the blow. They're giants, towering over me, pitying. They'll talk about this later and go 'poor Eric' and 'oh, bless' while they pour a glass of celebratory champagne and pick out their new furniture.

I hope everything you want is out of stock, I think bitterly, then chide myself for being an awful friend.

Sean sits up as realisation hits. 'Eric, we're not kicking you out. We're moving in together. *I'm* moving out. We've found a place up by Victoria Park. We'll be moving in next month. So you can either stay on and take the rest of the rent, or you can find a new housemate.'

There's absolutely no way I can afford this place on my own, especially when Lloyd departs next year.

'A new housemate. Right.'

'I can help you find someone,' Sean offers. 'Of course I'll help. But essentially *you'll* be living with him or her, so ideally you should be the one to choose.'

A new housemate. A new stranger to get to know, to live in the house, to share my space. I knew this would happen eventually, but it's still a shock.

I throw them my best smile. 'That's no problem. I'll put up an ad this week.'

As I get to my feet, I catch the look that passes between them. Brief, nothing more than a flash, but it was there. A look of pure relief. Kate stands to give me a hug, as if that'll make it all OK.

'Congratulations, both.' I say, trying my best to sound happy. 'This is great news. I'm going to miss you, though. Everything's changing so quickly, isn't it?'

'Mate, nothing's changing. We're just moving. We'll still see each other all the time. Can't live like students forever, can we?'

'No. We certainly can't.'

With that, I step from the living room and into a whole new world.

Chapter 7

Steph

'We are now approaching Weston-super-Mare.'

The cheery announcement that blares through the carriage pulls my attention away from the glare of my phone, where I'm mindlessly scrolling through Instagram. I've already uploaded a photo. In it, I'm gazing artfully out of the train window as if contemplating the complexities of life itself, green fields rolling to a blur behind me, beneath a muted filter. It's already got fifty-seven likes.

> #Home is where the heart is. Isn't that what they say? Sometimes, heading back to the place that shaped you is an adventure in itself . . .

Home. The one place that makes my heartbeat quicken – the low rumble of anxiety makes its presence known as the familiar platform comes into view beside the pale brick station. The train finally slows to a halt alongside eager passengers who stand in wait. The doors open with a hiss and I'm deposited into the chilly air, wheeling my miniature suitcase towards the exit.

All around are the sights of home. Or at least, what home *used* to be. Bristol is my home now, with its colourful scenery, its sense of fun and opportunity. Yet, there's something about going back to your home town that makes you nostalgic and morose in equal measure. Even the smell is familiar, that all-encompassing mood that you can't find elsewhere. Here, it's as if I've stepped back in time, leaving behind the bustle of the city, the promising blue of the sky.

I drag my suitcase outside. It's floral with a broken front wheel and makes a loud trundling sound as I haul it behind me on the pavement. As soon as I make it out of the station, I spot a flash of pink in the distance. A familiar red-haired figure in the brightest cardigan known to man is waving at me alongside a red Vauxhall Corsa.

Amanda.

'Steph! *Steph*! Over here!'

My sister is waving as if she's shipwrecked.

'Hey, Mand!' I call, dragging the case across the road. 'What are you doing here?'

'I'm here to pick you up. Thought it would be a nice surprise.' She gestures to the car as though it's a fairytale carriage.

'You didn't have to. I could have got a taxi.'

Amanda hurls herself at me for a hug. Her migraine-inducing pink cardigan is itchy against my bare arms, but I pull her tight, close. Her hair smells like coconut. Some things never change.

'Look, if I offered, you'd have said no. I know what you're like. You'd have gone, "Don't worry about it, Mand, I'll take an Uber." But come on, I haven't seen you for ages.'

She can see me start to protest and laughs. Her smile is wide, revealing her slightly crooked front teeth – just like Mum's.

'And no, before you say it, video chat doesn't count.'

'Ha! Fine.'

'I miss you. I wanted to drive you home. Is that so wrong?'

Home. The word doesn't go unnoticed.

Amanda smiles hopefully as she pulls the handle of the suitcase from my grasp before shoving it into the boot of her car.

'Get in, loser,' she squeals excitedly. 'Poppy can't wait to see you. She's been talking about you non-stop for the past three days. It's all Auntie Steph this and Auntie Steph that.'

I'm suddenly overcome by a wave of love for my adorable five-year-old niece. Love, and guilt. I know I should see her more often. Glancing across at Amanda as she pulls out from the station and towards town, my eyes drawn to the cluster of freckles around her perfect nose, I can sense she wants to say the same.

Instead, she says, 'So, how is the world of finance? Congrats on your promotion, by the way. I'm surprised you didn't post about it on the 'gram. I was looking forward to the party photos. You have the right to brag, you know.'

Shit. The promotion.

Of course, there was no promotion. Just something that unexpectedly came out of my mouth while on the phone to Amanda two months ago. Amanda asked me how everything was going, how my new life plan was being put into action and 'Is it everything you thought it would be?'

Also: 'I'm so proud of you.' The very words that can undo me in a matter of seconds. Or at least, cause me to lie monstrously. So I blurted out a whopping fib.

'I got a promotion!'

I rack my brains, trying to recall the exact details as I attempt to rearrange my expression into something humble yet also Oscar-worthy.

'Oh! Yeah, it's going well. I didn't want to make too much of a fuss about it. Some of my colleagues were in the running for it, you know? Didn't want to rub it in. Plus, it wasn't a party as such. Just a little get-together.'

This is also a lie – someone came to my flat to check the boiler the other day, resulting in the two of us awkwardly edging around each other for a whole half-hour. 'Not enough room to swing a cat' is an understatement. There's no way I could host a get-together at my place – it's physically impossible. Luckily, Amanda doesn't have to know this. Our lives are separate. Different. A world away.

'Ah! I totally get it. It was the same with Stevie. Did I tell you she was promoted, as well, to Head of English?'

'Yes! You went out for dinner at that nice sushi place. How's it going?'

'She's loving every minute.'

Stevie, Amanda's girlfriend of two years, has been a teacher since she left university. It's how they met. When Amanda was sent to work with the school as part of a new reading initiative for her children's charity, it was love at first sight. I love them both to bits, even if I *am* a little envious at how perfect they are for each other.

Amanda turns at the roundabout by the town hall, heading down the familiar side streets, past antique shops and fish and chip places and the wind-beaten façades of hotels. From here I can see the sea and I open the window a little, to feel the slight chill of the breeze on my face, through my hair, as it all falls into view. I can almost hear the sound of the arcades ringing in my ears – their loud, repetitive tunes an imprinted memory – and suddenly I'm pulled back to a world full of hope and teenage worry. Of penny machines and bright colours and awkward dates, of hope sprinkled with salt and wrapped in paper. Times when things were so easy. When they were wonderful, but I didn't realise. When it wasn't enough and I couldn't wait to get away.

I'm enthralled and saddened in equal measure. Now, with the sky tinged grey, the sea doesn't look as inviting. It looks icy, as if it would freeze your toes. I peer out of the window in the hope of glimpsing the Grand Pier, but we're veering away now, and I realise this isn't the way to Amanda and Stevie's house that's just outside the estate we lived on as kids. We're heading in a different direction.

'Where are we going?'

Amanda is quiet now. 'Well, I thought we could go and see Mum first.'

'Right. So *that's* why you came to pick me up. So that I couldn't get out of it.'

'Pretty much, yeah.'

'Mand . . .'

She lets out a sigh as I slump against the seat, arms folded, defiant. It's as if this place brings out the teenager in me. A vision of Jake, my then boyfriend, and me hand-in-hand by the pier flits into my memory. I was seventeen. I wore knee-high socks in a brazen attempt to be sexy. It was freezing, so I was filled with instant regret. His kiss tasted like vinegar with the faint bitterness of smoke from the cigarette we'd daringly shared. We'd kissed to the clattering rhythm of a two-pence machine delivering a decent bounty.

'Steph,' she says matter-of-factly, the same tone she uses with Poppy when she's just about had enough.

Amanda has a lot of patience, but not with some things. Sometimes, there's a point of no return. There's a hint of Mum in her voice. Maybe I'll sound like that too, if I ever have kids.

'You have to see her at some point.'

'No, I don't.'

'Don't you want to?'

It's a difficult question, one I don't want to answer. Just thinking about it makes me remember the song again, the piano tune drifting through the wall. Instead, I plug in my phone and open Spotify in search of a different earworm.

'Early 2000s Hits!' I say, perked. 'Just what we need.'

'Brilliant.'

I put it on and a familiar tune fills the car.

'So, are you ready for Nat's party?' Amanda swings into a small car park near a row of shops. 'The Natstravaganza?'

'Is anyone?' I laugh. Christina Aguilera blares out through the half-open window and I belt out the intro to 'Dirrty'. 'But I'll be on my best behaviour.'

Amanda pulls up outside a little florist's.

'I'm just popping in to get something for Mum. You coming?'

I consider this but shake my head, preferring to stay in the safe confines of the car with my phone than listen to Amanda nervously deliberate over what colour flowers to buy Mum. Not that it matters; Amanda gets different ones every week and Mum doesn't care. Instead, I open up Instagram as if it's second nature. I head straight for Nat's feed. Nat was first to add me, inviting me as some reluctant voyeur to her grid full of rose gold and filtered faces. In the latest photo she's standing by a pink-and-white balloon arch with a bride-to-be sash and matching tiara. For Nat, it's strangely understated. Below the image is a stream of congratulatory messages liberally peppered with wedding ring emojis and brides. I'm lost in them, scrolling, only jolted back to the present at the sound of the car door.

'Back!'

Amanda has returned, bearing a bunch of carnations. She opens the door and places them oh-so carefully on the back seat, as if the bouquet is a tiny swaddled baby.

'Ready?' she says.

She already knows the answer to that.

Chapter 8

Steph

The cellophane crinkles beneath Amanda's shaky grip. She looks at the flowers with a strange kind of longing, poking the petals softly, straightening them. She treats them as though they've been presented to her by a new lover, rather than a cheap bouquet she's picked up on the way here. Not that it matters, because the love in her eyes is immeasurable.

'Hey, Mum!' she says, and her happy, chirpy voice carries on the breeze.

Mum's grave is the seventh along, four rows from the beginning of the footpath. I have it committed to memory, like a sinister crossword. The headstone is black marble, with pretty gold lettering, sitting between the grave of an 88-year-old woman called Maud and a much-loved father of four called David. David's grave is decorated with a bright array of flowers and a little collection of small pebbles, painted and glossed by a child's hand.

Maud, Mum and David all died in the same year – one I wish never happened. One I'd do anything to change.

Amanda arranged the funeral, chose the hymns, picked out the headstone. She selected that gold lettering from a list of fonts and colours, as if such details are remotely important when you're wading through grief. Amanda sorted it all.

My sister is ahead of me now, traipsing down the well-trodden path that leads between the rows of headstones. She kneels on the ground, her red hair glowing like fire in the sun, her thick pink cardigan dragging along the earth, the brightness a welcome sight in the sombre greyness of the place. She tugs last week's offering, now crisp and wilted, from the little grave vase.

'Let's get rid of these old ones, shall we?' she asks, staring into the black marble, where there's nothing to greet her but her own reflection behind the letters, the facts.

I amble up behind her, looking at all the stones and wishing I hadn't left my jacket in the car.

'In loving memory of Deborah Jane Higgins. Mother, sister, friend. Aged 52 years. Until we meet again.'

'She can't hear you, Mand.' I can't resist pointing it out.

'Maybe she can. Who knows?'

'She's not there, though, is she? You're just talking into the void. Mum's not there. That's just her body.'

I hate the way it sounds. I shudder, but not because of the cold, and I see Amanda flinch, too. *Mum's body.* Her tall, strong, beautiful body that we loved so much – the body that gave us hugs, that pulled us closer on the sofa as we snuggled together. Her scent, of strawberry shampoo and Dove soap and the faint smell of coffee that would linger in our bedroom long after she'd said goodnight. On the days when our teenage worlds felt like they were caving in, blown apart by unrequited love and broken friendships, Mum was there, arms open for hugs and reassurance. She'd tell us everything would be OK. We'd look out of the window of our tower block, watching over the buildings, seeing everything so small on the ground below, feeling as if nobody could get us.

Until she wasn't there anymore.

I thought she'd always be there. I thought I could go away and come back and she'd always be there. But I was wrong. Now, Mum's in a box, below this ground that's hard and cold, and Amanda is busying herself unwrapping the cellophane and filling the vase with fresh water she's brought in a bottle. For weeks after Mum's death I thought of her, lying cold and alone and decaying in a locked box beneath the soil, and I couldn't sleep. Sometimes, I still can't.

Amanda is silent as the puts the last of the flowers into the little round slots, arranging them with care.

'I like to talk to her,' she says, her back to me. 'I at least like to think she's listening.'

'If she could, do you think she'd hang around here?' I ask. 'She's not here, having a tea party with Maud and David, Mand. She's gone.'

'Steph . . .'

'She is. She's gone. You know, if her spirit were really living on, she'd be over at Nat's, popping that bloody balloon arch.'

This, at least, raises a smile.

'Sorry,' I offer. 'But you know how I feel about all this. I can't romanticise this like you do. And you *did* bring me here against my wishes.'

I hate this. I hate the way I feel about this, about Mum. It's as though coming here makes me remember how I'm a terrible person. Amanda and I are so different – we've always known that.

Amanda finishes the job. She stands up, brushing the dirt from her jeans, her cardigan. I feel as if I've spoiled a special moment, that I've cut her conversation with 'Mum' short.

'We can't all be like you,' she says finally.

'What do you mean?'

'You know.' She gestures around at the expanse of grass, dotted with headstones, all in lines. Lines and lines. 'Move around, travel, go and live a life full of parties. Consider yourself lucky that you can distance yourself.'

She points at the headstone again, as if to prove a point. The only thing I see is stone, new and reflective, fuelling the fire that is Amanda.

'Mum was always proud of you for being the independent one,' she continues. 'I always wondered, should I be the same? And I tried, but I just couldn't. I just couldn't be like you. I like familiarity. But how you see things, and how I see things . . . well, it's different. I like talking to Mum, OK? It brings me a bit of comfort when I've had a shitty day. I like to think she's still listening.'

With that, she takes the cellophane and the remnants of the old bouquet and walks past me, head down. As if we're teenagers again.

Amanda's usually perky mood is partially restored when we arrive at the house. Stevie's bustling in the kitchen making a pasta bake, her long black braids swishing behind her as she moves from cupboard to cupboard in search of plates and glasses.

'Ten more minutes!' she tells Poppy, who has taken over the small dining table, which is covered in paper and glitter.

'Auntie Steph!' she yells, leaping off the table and hurling herself at my legs, which are now boasting enough sparkles to rival a unicorn at Christmas. 'I made you a painting. And some cookies.'

'She's decorated them,' Stevie confirms, leaning in to whisper. 'Some of the gingerbread men look like they've been the victims of a brutal murder. Don't laugh, though.

She takes criticism seriously.' Stevie winks and I look down at Poppy's hopeful, gorgeous face.

Amanda looks the most like Mum in our family. The same red hair, the same grey-blue eyes. Her height; Amanda is tall, I'm average. Which is *kind* of annoying when your baby sister towers over you, but we can't all be lucky. I have Dad's thick chestnut brown hair and long, straight nose – not that I can remember him that well, seeing as he left when we were small. He's never even met Poppy, who's seemingly inherited Mum's features, too. She's a miniature Amanda, which in turn is a miniature Mum. Much better than being the spitting image of Amanda's shitty ex, Jason, her boyfriend of a year who fled straight after Amanda broke the news she was pregnant.

Now, Poppy's big blue eyes gaze up at me, her smile bright and happy, and I pick her up for the biggest hug I can manage.

'How are you, Pop?' I ask, breathing in the soft smell of her curly hair. 'I've missed you.'

Poppy proceeds to tell me about the park she's visited today and the cookies she's baked.

'I'll get some for you!' she says excitedly. 'Mummy Stevie, can we have the biscuits?'

I look to Amanda, wide-eyed. '*Mummy Stevie?*' I whisper.

'She asked,' Amanda replies. Her eyes are full of unmistakable joy. 'She said she wanted to call Stevie Mummy, as well.'

'That's amazing,' I say, teary. 'I'm so happy for you. I want to cry.'

'Don't cry,' says Stevie, passing me a cup of green tea and a plate bearing a gingerbread man who might just require a 'graphic content' warning. Stevie wasn't wrong.

'Oh my God, I see what you mean.'

'We only had red icing pens left,' explains Stevie, trying her hardest not to laugh.

'Do you like them, Auntie Steph?' Poppy asks proudly.

I pull her up into another cuddle. 'Of course I do. They're brilliant, just like you,' I say before Amanda pulls her away.

'Bath time!' she says, leading a contented, glittery Pop away to the bathroom.

Stevie takes her own tea and joins me at the table.

'So how are you, Steph? Congratulations on the promotion.'

Instantly, I feel terrible. Again.

'Thanks.'

I'm about to offer the same congratulations to Stevie, but she pulls up a chair, peering at me excitedly through her trendy round gold-rimmed glasses.

'Amanda told me about your neighbour. Did you work things out in the end?'

Being in Amanda and Stevie's house feels like being enveloped in the warmest, cosiest hug. The walls are bright. The fridge is full of colourful magnets and Poppy's pictures, happy paint-splashed faces gazing out at me. The place is cluttered, but beautifully so; it's lived-in. It shows their personality. It gives off the feeling that only good things happen in this house. Nice things. Nightmares can't get you here.

'Not exactly. I left them a card, to try to say sorry. It's a start. It's not like I burned down their fence or anything.'

'Amanda told you about that, then? Typical.' Stevie laughs.

'Of course. It's great that they forgave you. I think that's what makes me feel most guilty . . . I haven't spoken to my neighbours. I haven't apologised *in person*. I don't even know them. But hopefully, they'll get my card and all will be well.'

'Wait. So you haven't spoken to them?'

'I've never even met them.'

Disbelief flashes across Stevie's face, so quick it almost doesn't happen. I guess it's different here, in this little neighbourly bubble. I imagine Stevie knows everyone. She's just that kind of person. Friendly and sweet and always quick to offer advice, a helping hand.

'It'll be fine,' she says, tapping my hand while offering me a smile. 'I'm sure they'll understand.'

Outside, the street is dark, lit only by the street lights and the glow of headlights from passing cars. On the other side of the house, something else illuminates the darkness, something I don't want to see, yet at the same time, I still do.

Later, in my pyjamas, clutching a freshly poured Rioja that Amanda had been saving, we step outside into the blackness. The soft grass of the well-kept garden is cold against my thin socks, but I don't care.

In the distance, the tower block rises above us, standing watchful overhead, its lights bright against the sky. Even from the ground I can make out shadowy figures as they move past the windows, flashes of blue from televisions as people hide inside, away from the cold, together.

Eight up, three across. Another puzzle that will always be stored in my mind. I see it, high among the stars, the large window standing out as it always did, only this time with a new light: yellow behind pink curtains. Someone else's light, someone else's home. I take another sip, appreciating the liquid warmth, craning my neck to see, as if the ghostly silhouette of Mum, or a younger Amanda, or even a younger me, will come out to greet me.

'That was us,' Amanda says, pointing skywards.

While I moved away to escape, Amanda stayed close. Too close, in my opinion, but I don't air this. I never have.

'Remember when we used to look out of the window at night?' asks Amanda.

'All the time,' I say. Sometimes, I remember wanting to fly. 'When we were kids it felt great, living at the top of a tower.'

We stay for a while, just chatting, wrapping blankets around our shoulders and drinking the last of the wine. Part of me loves reminiscing. Part of me wants to run far, far away.

And part of me wishes I'd never left.

Chapter 9

Eric

The time comes at exactly five minutes past seven on Sunday evening. The time to make *the call*. I pause *The Shining*, leaving Jack Torrance in hasty pursuit of his terrified family in the Overlook Hotel, freeze-framed. The phone is in my hand, finger hovering over the call button like it's a question: *Call? Do you really want to do that?*

I have to.

Miraculously, I'm saved by the sound of jangling keys. In bursts Lloyd, laden with his oversized sports bag, straight from the gym.

'All right, Eric?' he says, dropping the bag to the floor. 'I have some news you might be interested in.'

'Oh?' I put down the phone and listen.

I have no idea what news Lloyd could have for me – but when I hear it, my heart sinks.

'I was talking to Hugh today. He's looking to move closer to work and I told him we've got a room going.'

Hugh. Why is that name familiar?

'Eric?' he asks, jostling me out of my trance.

Lloyd's gaze lands on the empty plate on the coffee table.

'It smells like toast in here,' he says. 'Did you have toast for dinner?'

'Yeah.'

Lloyd is incredulous. 'Why?'

Because I'm tired. Because I just couldn't be bothered to do anything else. Because it's effort I don't have the energy for.

'Just fancied it,' I shrug. 'Had a big lunch.'

'Ah, right. Anyway, Hugh. His lease is coming to an end soon, so he's hoping to get somewhere to rent quickly. What d'you reckon?'

He's expecting an answer, one where I might go 'Yes, that's brilliant! He can move in right away' and the house-mate-hunting problem will be rectified quickly. And as much as I'd like that, something doesn't sit right.

The name Hugh rings a bell, and not necessarily a good one.

Then I remember.

'Lloyd,' I begin cautiously. 'Which one is Hugh, again? I distinctly remember *a* Hugh. He came on that night out with us. Last December.'

I have a vague recollection of a work do in the city centre last Christmas. The kind of night where everything melds and suddenly you've lost all of your actual colleagues but everyone else is there instead. And you vow to see your new best mates again but never do because when you're not all pissed, you have nothing in common. The memories them-selves might be hazy, but there was something unforgettable about the evening: a loud, lanky auburn-haired man belting out explicit Christmas carols, whipping off his trousers and swinging them round his head.

'Is that the same Hugh? The one who got us kicked out of that bar?'

Lloyd sighs. 'The very same. He's a bit of a dick on nights out, but he's a nice enough bloke once you get to know him. He's fun. That night-out stuff, it's just his way of letting off steam.'

76

'Fun? He was pouring vodka into Andrew's lemonade when he wasn't looking.'

'In Hugh's mind, he was being generous.'

'Andrew's a recovering alcoholic.'

Lloyd frowns, lets out a breath of discomfort. 'I didn't know that.'

'I'm not sure if he's the right fit,' I say finally.

'Does it matter? He'll be at work most of the time. It's not as if you'll be cooped up together constantly.'

'Hmm.'

'Hmm?'

I tell him I'm not sure, that maybe we need to go through our options.

'Look,' says Lloyd. 'I have to go. Got a night of undisturbed gaming planned with the guys. I've told Hugh you'll think about it and will let me know. He's desperate to find a place.'

'Will do.'

Lloyd takes his bag and heads upstairs, leaving me staring once again at the TV, accessing the mental library once more to slot something else inside. Hugh, a potential housemate I don't want. I feel bad for turning him away, for being undoubtedly cruel to someone in need.

The trouble with sharing is that people grow. They move from one story and into the sequel. For me, it didn't work the same way. Home was with Clarissa, now it's here – a room in a terraced Bristol street while everyone else's worlds enlarge and change for the better. I've gone backwards.

I need to find someone new, someone else to share this space, this predicament.

But please, God – anyone but Hugh.

With Lloyd gone, I turn to the phone again. Press Call.

My parents are awake; I know that much. Their evening schedule hasn't changed since I lived at home: dinner at seven, then a few hours in front of evening quiz shows while Mum reads and Dad gets on with some paperwork and catches up with the news. 'Background noise,' he insists, because he doesn't like anything 'mind-numbing', even though he'll shout out answers to the quiz questions at least six times.

I know where Dad will be at this very moment: settling into the sofa post-meal – it's Sunday, so I'm guessing roast beef – next to the little table where the landline sits, the chunky 'cordless' relic. At the sound of the dial tone, part of me hopes they won't answer. Maybe they've chosen tonight to meet up with their friends at the little country pub down the road. Maybe they're visiting Nan at the care home. Maybe they think I'm calling to ask if they're interested in a new TV and broadband package, so they'll let it ring out.

They don't.

At the eleventh ring, there's a shuffling noise as Dad picks up.

'Hello?' he asks, ready to tell me where to stick my broadband or life insurance.

'Dad!'

'Eric!' His tone instantly softens. 'How are you? Everything OK?'

I hear Mum's call of 'Hi, Eric!' in the background as if delighted to hear from me. I love hearing their voices, which makes me feel a tad guilty. I haven't called them in a while, because life has been . . . well, life. Yet at the same time, I don't want to be calling tonight. Correction: I don't want to be calling for *help*.

I ensure Dad that yes, all is fine. I ask about Mum – she's also fine, he says; she's next to him on the Laura Ashley sofa, her nose in a book about Bonnie and Clyde.

'*Syndrome*,' I hear her correct Dad. '*Bonnie and Clyde Syndrome*. It's when people have an attraction to those who have committed atrocious crimes.'

'Hybristophilia,' I say.

'What?' asks Dad.

'People who fancy serial killers.'

Dad doesn't hear me, or chooses not to. As he regales me with the long-winded account of his recent MOT, my heart beats faster, because I know the question's coming.

'How are things at work? Promoted yet?'

And there it is.

'It's . . . all right,' I say. Because what *can* I say? 'And no, I haven't been promoted.'

'Why not? You've been there long enough!' He chuckles. There's hope in his voice.

I shift position on the sofa, make myself more upright, as if Dad can see me slumping. Luckily, he's not really into the whole video call thing.

Each time we speak, there's the same agonising conversation. It doesn't help that I'm phoning for a favour today. A favour, all bundled up in niceties.

'The thing is, I've been concentrating on other things.'

I hate lying, but I do it anyway. I know that once you start fibbing, there's no going back, but who's to say it isn't more exciting? It would beat Dad's reaction to the truth, anyway. I don't tell him that my lack of advancement is partly to do with there not being many jobs and partly because I'm just not interested right now. I don't know *what* I'm interested in job-wise any more. Any excitement I had for it disappeared with Clarissa. It's hard to admit to Dad – the man who so kindly funded my economics degree – that my education hasn't exactly 'paid off'. (His words.)

'Things? Oh, are you talking about the film you were writing? Have you sold it? Is that why you're calling?'

I picture him, voice rising with excitement as he clutches the phone tightly to the sound of quiz show applause, waiting for that ultimate 'Yes!' so that he can pop the champagne and tell everyone in their quaint little cul-de-sac that his son works 'in film'. Sadly, he won't be doing that for a long, long time. If ever.

'Er, no. I haven't . . .'

'Have you finished it yet?'

The answer hangs in the air, in the distance between us. All I want to do is steer the conversation back to general pleasantries, or tyre changes, or Bonnie and Clyde Syndrome – anything but say no. Anything but go 'No, Dad, I haven't.' Along with everything else that hasn't worked out.

'Yes,' I offer instead of the real reason. 'Yes, I've finished it.'

The room suddenly feels very small. I get up and pace but I can only do so for so long until it feels smaller still, like I'm a hamster in a cage, going round and round. So I pad through to the kitchen, pull a beer from the fridge and sit outside. The air is cold, but it's nice. It whips against my face, bringing me back to the present.

'Brilliant! Nice to see something you've stuck with. Hopefully, you'll have some success. Did I mention Mike's daughter, Arianne? She works for the BBC and apparently, she's up for an award . . .'

As Dad talks, I sit on the outside step, peering over at next door. There's still no light from number 26. Their wheelie bin is still on the pavement – the only one. They must have put it out before they left for their holiday. Taking a gulp of beer, I put my glass on the wall, deciding to do the neighbourly thing and drag it safely inside the front garden.

'. . . should watch it. A really good crime drama, by all accounts. Krakatoa!' Dad shouts.

'What?'

'Krakatoa! That's the answer.'

Tense music can be heard from the TV.

'If she doesn't get that one, she's a bloody idiot,' Dad continues.

I sigh.

At that moment, the phone vibrates in my hand and as Dad berates the contestant on-screen, I take a look.

Clarissa.

Bracing myself for the worst, I swipe to open the message. Just because she's replied doesn't mean it's positive. She could be telling me to piss off. Compared to what she said when she dumped me, that would be polite.

Hi, Eric! Long time no see. Things are great, thank you – busy, though! It would be lovely to have a catch-up. So much to talk about! X

The world has shifted.

I leap up from the sofa and punch the air. She's replied, *and* she wants to see me. Which means there's hope, after all. There's hope – it's not all bleak.

'Where do they get these people?' Dad asks, at the television rather than me.

'Dad, I have to go. I'll call you soon, OK? Love you both!'

Picking up my beer, I head back inside to the warmth and the light and the rest of *The Shining*, feeling suddenly lighter.

Chapter 10

Steph

I'm woken by a pounding on the bedroom door and the high voice of Poppy calling from behind it.

'Auntie Steph! *Wake up!*'

What time is it?

Light floods through the window of Amanda's tiny guest room, illuminating the small round rug, pink and fluffy and stained with make-up, which I recognise from our bedroom at Mum's. I rub my eyes, watching the room come into focus, only just remembering where I am, what I'm doing in yellow pyjamas and a single bed that's more comfortable than my own, with a mouth that tastes as if something's crawled in it and died.

I'm at Amanda's, and last night we had wine. Wine, copious amounts, followed by a PlayStation session on Crash Bandicoot which, I have to admit, I aced, considering the level of tipsy. Just thinking about it makes me remember the days at Mum's, in the flat, our small, gangly bodies filling my top bunk. Amanda insisted on having the bottom bed because there would be 'less chance of getting overly tired and falling out'. We'd grab snacks, climb up onto the top bed and play all weekend, each wanting desperately to complete the game, passing the controller over when a level was complete or, of course, when one of us lost a life.

'Auntie Steph? You awake?' Poppy calls again, rapping on the wood three times like a restless spirit.

I get up and pad over to the door, readying myself for the hugs that will ensue. I lift Poppy into a massive cuddle and I smell the fresh fabric conditioner and the waft of a cookie she's been eating.

'Will you play on Crash with me? You can do all the hard levels.'

'Maybe.'

A door opens from the landing and out steps Amanda, already looking glam in a green mid-length dress, which she's accessorised with brightly coloured jewellery. She's brushing her red hair back from her face, blindly pulling it into a bun.

'I think not! Auntie Steph has to get ready.'

Poppy pouts and slumps off.

'Jesus, Steph, we're leaving in two hours.'

'What? This is a hen party, Mand. Don't they usually take place in the evenings? Not . . .' I pull out my phone, where I notice not just the time, but also more Instagram notifications. Maybe those pretentious, arty selfies are the way to go. 'Two o'clock in the afternoon.'

'Mate, this is *Nat*. This is merely hen party numero uno. This is just a family thing.'

'How do you get away with having *two* hen parties? Like . . . why?'

'Who knows? But I'd start getting ready, if I were you. Stevie can't come – she's hosting a workshop in Cardiff – so I've got to take Pop round to my friend's before we go.'

My sister looks at me, taking in my face – the make-up, I can tell, that's lingering, ink-like, around my eyes. I forgot to take it off last night. I blink away tears.

'You all right?' Amanda asks.

'Yeah. Just . . . tired. I'll go and get ready.'

I don't know what's got into me, but seeing as I'm due my period in a matter of days, I put it down to that. Hormones. Rather than the possible reality – that spending the evening with my sister and her perfect family has brought back so many memories. Our old home peeks out from behind the curtains. I tug them shut.

I take a quick shower then rush back to the guest room, where I drag my suitcase onto the bed and unzip it in search of my black dress, the one I wore to go out with Tamzin and Saskia the other day. I pull it on in front of Amanda's curved mirror, shimmying into the cheap fabric. As I hoist up my tights, I catch sight of the shelves on the far wall. Shelves of toys, standing in a weary line: bright plastic ponies and dolls in hues of blue and pink; My Little Pony and Polly Pocket and Sky Dancers. My heart swells as I walk closer, carefully scooping a pony from its place and turning it round in my hands, running a finger through its pink mane.

We spent hours playing with these as children, although Amanda was careful; her ponies would be thoroughly looked after, kept in perfect condition. While my toys would be scattered all over the floor of our small living room, Mum complaining that it resembled an obstacle course, Amanda's would be placed in a perfect line along the coffee table, or safely tucked away in our bedroom.

Amanda must have taken all the toys when she cleared out Mum's. Because, just like everything else, she did that, too.

I think of the two boxes tucked away in my flat and suddenly, I want to be anywhere but here. I want to be back in Bristol, curled up in my own bed, singing along to whatever tinkly rendition of an old pop song number 26 is playing. I'd rather be in work, typing out my 1000th arse-kissing apology. Anywhere but here. It's not Amanda's fault, it's mine.

I place the pony back on the shelf, but not before giving it one final touch. I can even smell it, that sweet, plasticky scent. It brings back a host of memories: playing on the little square of grass outside the block with some of the neighbours' kids. Playing Scrabble with Dana when Mum was at work. Spending hours in our flat, looking out over the town as sheet-like rain pounded against the windows, reading *Goosebumps* books and eating too many sweets.

Today, I can't be seen to be upset. I need to get this family event over with.

My phone pings with a notification just as I'm applying my make-up. It's from Instagram: a new follower. Intrigued, I click on the little image that takes me to their page.

And I stop cold.

Miles. My ex, Miles, has just sent me a message on Instagram.

Chapter 11

Steph

The last time I saw Miles was three years ago, as I collected the last of my things – a Sainsbury's carrier bag stuffed with random bits; a couple of odd socks, shampoo, a toothbrush, a drinks bottle, three books, one earring and some herbal tea that Miles didn't like – from his flat in Hengrove.

That was two weeks after the night it all went wrong.

It had been a usual January evening, cold but comfortably so. The best kind of cold, which makes you venture out in a scarf and nice boots and the breeze is calming against your skin, especially when you're walking down a street full of people, watching their breath on the air, hearing their laughter against the soft waves of the harbour.

Everything was nice and normal. Until it wasn't.

It took less than an hour for everything to unravel.

Miles and I had been together for two and a half years at that point, ever since the day I hurried after him at Temple Meads station to return his nearly lost ticket. We both had ten minutes to spare, so we went to get a coffee in the busy station, chatting in the line that snaked round towards the little booth. He was living in Bristol, on his way to another part of town. I was heading home after a job interview. We exchanged numbers and went out two days later.

For weeks afterwards, I wondered what the catch would

be, how I somehow managed to find this man, who was so perfect for me. It was the kind of love that people used to write songs about back in the day; songs about finding love in bus stops and under the boardwalk, and dancing with someone one night, being unable to forget them later. Mum would sing them as well, hum them round the house.

I grew up pondering how I'd find the right guy. Would it be a night out, or some strange, fated occurrence, like just chatting to someone at the bus stop? At a party? At the cinema? I watched romcoms with a sense of hope. I stayed up at night with Amanda, whispering into the early hours as we made fortune-telling devices out of paper.

Ultimately, meeting Miles showed me that I didn't need apps or digital intervention when it came to finding someone perfect. I'd been right all along.

Two and a half years. Two and a half years of being bliss-fully content. On that particular night, the night it all went wrong, we left the cold evening air, hurrying into a nearby pub, where we sat snug in the corner. I shrugged off my jacket, curious about the smile Miles had plastered on his face the whole way there. It was mischievous, as if he had something planned. For a brief moment I wondered if what he had planned was *the proposal*. The inevitable moment many of my friends had already succumbed to. But I knew Miles and I knew he wouldn't choose a humid, crowded place to pop the question; there was barely space to get down on one knee.

Plus, he knew my stance on public proposals. Which is an all-out *no*. I'd want it to be intimate and private, not some forced scenario that would make me look terrible if I dared to say no. I'd always teased him about it: 'If you ever did that, I'd say no anyway.'

'You wouldn't.'

'Try me.'

Oh, God. Surely he wasn't *actually* going to try?

Miles got up, cautiously picking his way towards the bar and returning with two pints of cider. We talked about the usual, the normalcies of life: a video of baby Poppy that Amanda had sent and the news that one of my best uni friends had started a new job with a theatre company in London. It didn't take long for Miles to blurt it out, the reason why he'd brought me there, the sole reason for that grin of his. He could barely contain the excitement as soon as it left his lips.

'Steph,' he began.

I braced myself, heart hammering, waiting for him to reach into his jacket pocket and pull out a box.

He didn't.

'So remember that job I went for a while back? Well, turns out there was a delay in the recruitment process. Main hiring manager went sick. I've . . . well, I've got it.'

'What?' I leaped up from my seat, causing the table to wobble and cider to slosh out of my glass, but I didn't care – I needed to hug him.

He'd been pinning all of his hopes on that job – he was working in marketing and had been trying to get on the next step for months. Especially since we'd decided to start saving for a house.

'That's absolutely bloody amazing!'

'Isn't it just? The thing is, it's in Birmingham.'

'*What*?'

'And it starts in two months' time.'

I froze.

Surprisingly, my smile stayed pinned to my face, as if being held there by invisible hands.

'Birmingham? I thought you said it was going to be based here in Bristol?'

Miles shrugged. Took a giant sip of cider.

'Change of plan. The Birmingham office is bigger. There are more staff and it looks like they'll need me more up there. I couldn't exactly turn it down, could I?'

'Well, no, but . . . it's quite a trek to Birmingham. I can come and see you on weekends—'

'Weekends?' Miles put down his glass, half-empty. 'No need to worry about that. I've got us sorted. The company have put me in touch with an agency. I'll rent a flat for six months while we get settled in and look for something more permanent. I'll be moving there next month, so you can come. I'm sure you'll find a job in no time. Then we can maybe look for a place of our own.' His excited smile grew wider. 'I really want us to move forwards, make this work . . .'

The pub had started to fill, bulging with people in suits who'd clearly escaped the nearby offices. There we were, Miles and me, squashed in the corner, clutching pints and trying to hear each other through a haze of other people's noise. Suddenly, my cider tasted more bitter than sweet.

'It's just got me thinking,' he said enthusiastically, his hands as animated as they could be without whacking the person on the next table in the face.

Usually, I liked that about him, how excitable he got over the simplest things. Not now, however.

'Miles.'

'And if things work out there after a year, I—'

'*Miles.*'

He stopped talking, gazing at me like a rabbit caught in headlights. He could tell that I wasn't enjoying this fantasy as much as him.

'Miles,' I continued. 'I'm going to America, remember?'

'What?'

'America. I'm going to America for three months.' It came out like a croak. How could he have forgotten?

America. My dream trip. There were tickets waiting in my inbox, tickets for the trip I'd saved for ages to buy. Saving everything I could through an array of vastly unglamorous, often shitty, temp jobs. I was leaving in May. He knew this.

'But after that, we can move things forwards,' he continued as if he didn't hear me.

As if I hadn't been waiting for this trip for most of my life.

'. . . finally be together. And maybe, in a couple of years . . .'

He trailed off, looking at me with a strange expectant gaze. No doubt awaiting some joyous response, where I'd grin and say 'Oh-my-God, this is wonderful,' and not think about the trip I'd worked incredibly hard for, and the fact that oh, maybe I didn't want to move miles away.

His face fell when he realised this wasn't what he was about to get, when I shook my head and looked into my pint glass as if the answer to the meaning of life itself was in there.

'No,' I said. 'Not yet.'

'Why?'

He regarded me as if I were unwell, a confused expression on his gorgeous face, which rates highly on the 'Saddest Things About the Miles Predicament' scoreboard. He was so lovely, so perfect in almost every way (because who is perfect in *every* way?). But now, that frisson of love I felt every time I looked at him had started to wither. It made me panic.

In that humid, cramped pub, I thought of the breeze outside and how I wanted to get out, how I craved the cold on my face. It suddenly felt as if the pair of us had been walking around with some kind of rose-tinted filter superimposed onto our life and we couldn't see the faults.

I wasn't ready.

'Why?' he repeated. 'Steph?'

'Because I'm going to America, Miles. Because I don't want to decide on anything permanent yet.'

'I know. You haven't stopped talking about America, so it's hardly slipped my mind. Sorry, I just thought you'd be excited that we finally have a plan.'

'I haven't stopped talking about it because it's been my dream *for years*. It's finally happening. And *you* have a plan. You've just decided it for me. What if it's something I don't want?'

'Don't you? I thought you wanted us to get a place and actually do things.'

'Do things?'

I could read his expression. *Do the things that everyone else is doing.* Proposals. Weddings. Baby showers. All the things to tick off the 'life list'. Suddenly, I felt trapped, trapped in the pub, unable to see the escape route over all of the people.

'Come on, Steph. You're getting a bit over the top. You can still go to America. It's always there. It's a couple of months in a few cities. Hardly a once-in-a-lifetime thing.'

We stared at each other across the table. We'd never disagreed on something this hard. Never. We'd bickered over *some* things: movie franchises; TV shows that should have ended sooner than they did; the best American novels and, of course, the washing-up. Simple things. Nothing big. Nothing life-changing. Nothing like this.

'Am I, though? Being over the top?'

'You're being stubborn.'

There was a noticeable, serious shift in his expression. The cider swirled around nastily in my gut, making me feel woozy. I knew deep down it had nothing to do with the alcohol. All of a sudden, I felt sick.

Because in my head, I was greeted by a vision of me in a beige living room, with a plush carpet, the kind your feet sink into but is also never practical, clutching a tiny gurgling baby at my breast, making baby talk in its direction. I pictured myself in a loose floral dress, fuck knows why, and pulled myself away from Miles' worried gaze to my own faded Batman T-shirt, poking at the logo as if the dreamlike image would come true and it would transform into a massive daisy.

What I saw wasn't *me*, but I saw it anyway. I saw a big house, painted that pretty lemon colour. A preened garden, a porch with plenty of room to store the pram. An office for Miles. Miles hadn't exactly been subtle in his plans for the future; I knew what they included. The job, the ambition, the money, the home. That tiny, bawling mini Miles. Or mini Steph, for that matter. I sincerely hoped for the former, because nobody needed another wailing bundle of me, miniature or otherwise. He or she would be better off taking after Miles, with his adorable smile and bright blue eyes. And his brains and his drive, and the ability to keep everything in order.

It was like I'd slipped into the future for just a moment, seeing what was to come, and I was frightened. *Frightened*.

'I don't know what the problem is,' said Miles. 'You've always said you want to do things properly. The job, the security, not struggling like . . .'

I glared at him, because I knew where this was going. He didn't have to say it.

Not struggling like your mum.

A feeling of love and fear and defence overwhelmed me. Yes, Mum had struggled once; there was no denying that. But at the same time, she wasn't to blame. She'd done everything right. Mum once had a husband and a nice house with the pretty garden and a good job in hospitality. It wasn't her fault her marriage ended. It wasn't her fault Dad left, that she lived in a tiny flat, a single mum trying to work two jobs to feed us.

But then I saw the alternative. Life with Miles. Miles the boss, with the obligatory wife and kids, with the family dog and the annual holiday, the family portrait above the mantelpiece, all beaming smiles. The plush carpets and the 'nice bit of patio' and the *structure*.

I thought I wanted it. But faced with the stark possibility, I wasn't sure. 'Do what makes you happy,' Mum always said. Would that life make me happy?

'Miles, you can't just assume everything will go the way you plan,' I said, slowly this time. 'Mum works harder than most. What, you think just trying hard enough can save you when your life goes to shit?'

'You know what I mean, Steph. I thought you'd be happy. You said you wanted to move away, try new places.'

I got up. Or at least tried. It's kind of tricky when you're packed in so tightly you're squished between the table and the wall.

'Yes, I want to try places – on my own. I want to travel for a bit, see what life has to offer. I want to make sure whatever I do is my choice as well as yours. Bit bold of you to think I'll just follow you wherever you go.'

'So what are you saying? *No*? Because I've told them I'm going, Steph. If I don't take the job—'

'Take the bloody job. I'm not saying no. I'm saying *not yet*. I'm going to the States first. Maybe then we can re-evaluate. Maybe then I'll consider it. I just need time.'

93

I knocked back the remnants of my drink before pulling my jacket back on and weaving my way through the crowd and into the cold.

Miles left for Birmingham. We kept in touch, our communication getting less frequent as he was tied up in work, and even more so when I reached the States, our messages time-delayed and fragmented. We planned to meet up again as soon as I returned, maybe get back to how we were. Maybe I'd follow him to Birmingham, after all. Because I loved what we already had. Freedom. Time. *Us*.

Maybe later, I'd feel differently.

But then, Mum died.

Chapter 12

Steph

Now, I stare at the image in front of me, squinting to see every detail in the little square of black-and-white Instagram perfection, of this man with the neat hair and the brilliant smile and the woman standing next to him in trendy sunglasses. It doesn't compute.

'Who even *is* this?' I ask nobody in particular, but seeing as Amanda is next to me, having decided that now, in the back of a taxi that's going way too fast for my liking, is the best place to apply lipstick, she has the lucky prize of being my sounding board for the afternoon.

She takes her eyes off her pocket mirror to peer over my shoulder. 'That's Miles, isn't it? God, he looks different.'

'In what way?' I pry, knowing she's right.

My sister shrugs. The taxi driver turns up the football commentary. I learn that Stevenage FC are playing Newport County later this afternoon.

'Like he's evolved somehow. Miles 2.0. The older, glossier version. With expensive shirts.'

Amanda is of course correct, but that doesn't stop me from feeling a little sad, the dry toast I'd shoved down my throat as we rushed out of the house repeating on me. I feel it in my stomach, threatening to reappear. Hopefully not in the cab.

Miles *is* glossier. And he definitely has better taste nowadays, as evidenced by the dozen or so photos he's posted. He only started the account a month ago, it seems. There he is, on a beach, lying back against a backdrop of sun and sand. Another, all dressed up, looking gorgeous in a waistcoat and tie, on a stage at some formal corporate awards bash. And again, on what appears to be the top of a mountain, beautiful hills of green rolling in the background. The woman in his profile photo – the new girlfriend, obviously – plants a kiss on his cheek.

My stomach does another unpleasant flip.

'Ah, the typical mountain photo,' comments Amanda, still peeking over my shoulder with interest. 'Very coupley.'

She does a vomiting motion. I know she's trying to make me feel better, but it's not helping.

I sigh. 'It's just . . . wow.'

'It's like guys on Tinder and their fish photos,' adds Amanda. 'Jasmine at work is trying the whole Tinder thing. *So* many pictures of fish. And penises. You know what they say about sexuality not being a choice . . .'

'Yeah, well, you're lucky, then.'

She smiles smugly. 'You know I'm only kidding. But don't keep looking, you'll drive yourself mad.'

'She seems outdoorsy,' I reply. 'Her name's Vikki. They probably go trailing up mountains all the time. Not that I blame them. It's actually really fun. You get hooked.'

'If you say so.'

'I'm serious!'

'When was the last time you went hiking?'

'Er . . .' *America*, my tired brain confirms. And before that . . . with Miles. 'A while ago.'

'My point exactly.'

Obviously I don't, *can't*, voice what's actually hurting. It's not the message he's sent – the sweet, polite, quick missive:

> **Hey, Steph! I know we haven't spoken in ages. Hope you don't mind if I drop you a message, but I could see from your latest photo you're heading home. Hope things are going well! Give the family my love.**

No. It's the fact that for ages, I hadn't thought about him at all, and now here it is, this glimpse into his new and improved life.

The life I could have had.

As Amanda fumbles in her handbag for her phone, I do a sneaky click on Vikki's Instagram feed, like my own little form of self-torture. Curiosity really is a killer sometimes, but I just have to accept that. There's no way I'm *not* having a quick nose around her page.

As expected, I feel all the worse for it. There are the customary loved-up shots with Miles, including one where they're peeking out from beneath the bedcovers, all cute and coy. Then I see the caption:

> First night in our new home! Who knows what the future will bring? #homeowners #newadventure.

Of course.

Vikki updates way more than Miles and a virtual, albeit filtered, tour of their new home is fully available. I scroll through, enraptured, staring with envy at the brand-new monochrome kitchen and the half-finished living room, a snap of Miles up a ladder, his paint-splattered T-shirt riding up slightly as he reaches to work on the ceiling.

Why do I even care?

And does he look even sexier now?

Yes. Yes, he does.

I look again and wonder why I'm feeling so shitty and then realise that I'm feeling this way because *that could have been me*. That could have been us, with the hiking and the new house and the cutesy pictures, and I turned it all down.

I don't have time to dwell on it for much longer, because the taxi has slowed to a halt, pulling up near the seafront. The sight of the sea greets me outside the window, dark and rough beneath a dismal grey sky.

'We're here,' Amanda almost sings.

Sometimes the only way to let go of one nightmare is to walk straight into another.

Natasha has chosen to host her hen party at one of the seafront hotels. We were expecting a moderately sized function room, something pleasant with a semi-decent buffet. As it happens, Amanda and I find ourselves walking, totally flummoxed, into a restaurant area decked out in full-on engagement décor. The place is huge.

On the plus side, the food is more than decent. Not to mention the bar.

'What the hell?' I mutter, nudging Amanda in the ribs as a member of staff takes our names for the guest list.

Around us, circular tables boast huge cake stands, on which are *very* generous selections of gorgeous pastries, arranged beautifully and accentuated with faux floral arrangements that surround a framed, 8 x 10 portrait of Nat and her husband-to-be, Lewis.

'Each table has a different photo,' says Amanda.

'*Why*, though?'

'This is just how Nat is.' She laughs quietly. 'Do you remember when we had that joint swimming party? I was six and you were eight, and Auntie Grace made sure Nat's birthday bash that summer was even bigger. They've always been like that. Anyway, what does it matter? We're here, and there are free drinks. We can basically get blitzed and forget about it. Let's just go and say hello and thank Auntie Grace first.'

She turns to me suddenly, as if remembering something highly important.

'If you *do* decide to get sozzled, however, stay away from Nat. Stay. *Away*.'

Amanda has reverted to serious mode, her grey-blue eyes baring into mine with a warning, just like Mum's used to.

'I don't want a repeat of last time,' she adds.

I open my mouth to protest, but she's already off, dragging me by the hand towards the round table at the top of the room, where all the important people are sitting, such as Auntie Grace, Uncle Darren and Nat herself, like royalty overseeing their kingdom. I spot Nat, who's looking as glossy and made-up as ever, sporting the rose gold 'bride-to-be' sash and an *actual* tiara. I put on my biggest forced smile and give in to Auntie Grace's quick, polite hug. I want to get the formality over with so I can find a table in the corner, drink and spend the entire event obsessively and painfully scrolling through Vikki's Instagram.

'It's lovely of you to come,' says Auntie Grace.

She's wearing a glittery gold top that wouldn't look out of place at a Christmas party, narrowly missing Nat's apparent 'rose gold' theme. There are balloons everywhere and a huge banner is draped across the main wall. There's what looks like a DJ set-slash-karaoke at another end, and the gold-and-white balloon arch with a walkway of red carpet which, it now occurs to me, is for photographs.

'Welcome to my afternoon tea,' says Nat primly, as if she's Kate Middleton. 'It's lovely that you made it.'

I notice her give Amanda and me a brief once-over.

There's a massive cake stand on Auntie Grace's table, too.

'Ooh!' says Amanda. 'Macarons. Don't mind if I—'

'No!' Before Amanda's fingers can make contact with the delicate treat, Nat slaps her hand away. 'Not yet. Not until we've taken the pictures.'

'Right. So we have to take photos before we can eat anything?'

'Yeah?' she replies, as if it's obvious. Then it all makes sense.

Nat's party is clearly, deliberately, Instagrammable. Which, let's face it, is exactly my jam, yet at the same time I can't help but think it's ever so slightly bizarre.

Nat takes a little business card from a neat stack on the table, handing one to Amanda.

'Be sure to use that hashtag,' she says, her blue eyes hopeful and wide, pointing a long, light pink nail at the card itself, which bears a professional-looking photo of Nat and Lewis on one side. On the other, fancy text reads #NatsHenPartOne.

'Lovely!' says Amanda. 'Congratulations again, Nat.'

But Nat's already scuttled off to a nearby group of friends.

'You know,' says Amanda, 'this is nice, Auntie Grace. You've done a really good job arranging all this. An elegant, sophisticated-looking hen party.'

Auntie Grace shoots her a look so defensive I'm almost expecting lasers to emerge and vaporise my sister.

'Why wouldn't it be?'

'Well, you know. Hen parties can sometimes be . . .'

'Raucous?' I offer.

'Exactly. Yet here, there's not a plastic willy in sight. Makes a nice change.'

Auntie Grace's small face falls in a brief flicker of panic that tells me there are *definitely* bags full of tacky plastic willies somewhere in the vicinity, ready to be unleashed later when we're all a few wines in.

Auntie Grace sneers and says, 'I guess you're right. They wouldn't be *your* thing, anyway.'

I stare, waiting for Amanda to unleash her wrath, but then remember she doesn't do that sort of thing. *I* am the family troublemaker, apparently.

Instead, she just grins and says, 'Thanks for inviting us!' and leads me straight to the bar.

'Mand,' I say, half shocked, half giggling. 'You're going to let her get away with comments like that?'

She shrugs. 'Meh.'

'Mand, I'm serious. She can't . . .'

My sister stops as we pass the bar, watching a member of staff fill a row of empty glasses with champagne.

'Honestly, Steph, it doesn't matter.'

'Why?'

'Seriously? Grace is comedy gold. Have you seen what she posts online? Her opinions are so bizarre they go past the point of offensive. It's just so . . . sad. She once commented that there's no such thing as bisexuality because "it's not natural".'

'So why do you let her do it?'

Amanda takes me by the shoulders and exhales loudly. 'Steph, listen. There's no point. She's obviously unhappy in her life and I'm not. I've tried to educate – politely, might I add! – but she doesn't listen. So I live in hope that one day she'll out herself and her shitty views will go viral, and she'll have to deal with the consequences. Do I wish public humiliation on simply anyone? No. Do I wish it on Auntie Grace and smug Uncle Darren? Yes. Yes, I do. But until that happens, I no longer care. I'm just here for the free booze.'

'And familial obligation.'

'Don't spoil it. I have a child-free day and I'm going to

enjoy every bloody second.'

We pluck a couple of champagne flutes from the bar and find a table as far away from the main crowd as possible. We've arrived a little earlier than most. Guests are still trickling in through the main entrance, squealing when they see Nat. Then her bridesmaids appear in a group, having stepped out of a limo, wearing white and what appear to be angel wings.

'This is batshit,' Amanda says, downing another flute full of champagne.

It's undeniably crazy and over the top, but that doesn't stop me from taking the opportunity to take photos. I snap as many creative pictures as I can: our topped-up glasses of fizz, a sisterly selfie, the charming décor of the hotel.

The party games commence. There's a quiz about Nat and Lewis. We get four out of ten correct, and that's only because a couple of other girls, colleagues of Nat, have joined our table. I drink, I play the party games, all while barely taking my eyes off the online presence of Miles and Vikki.

Amanda has already told me off for looking.

'You're just torturing yourself,' she reminds me again.

'Better to do it here when I'm already being tortured – two birds with one stone and all that.'

'You're verging on drunk, Steph. You'll end up acciden-tally liking one of her photos if you're not careful. Wouldn't that be mortifying?'

'Point taken.' I drop the phone on the table like it's on fire.

'Know what's sad?' Amanda pipes up.

She's slurring now. We're only two hours in. This is rare for Amanda – she hardly ever lets her hair down.

'If one of us gets married, Mum won't be there to walk us down the aisle,' she says. 'Like, I know she'll be *there*, but not literally there. In person.'

The dark, draining feeling in the pit of my stomach returns.

So does the image of Miles and Vikki, their contentedness, their bliss. Mum loved Miles. Amanda's just a bit drunk and doesn't realise that to me, it all feels like a nasty smack in the face.

I go to offer a response, but there's nothing I can say. Nothing that can realistically make the situation better. Mum will *not* be there. Mum is gone.

The room is full of laughter. The room is warm. Uncomfortably warm.

I get up, snatching another drink on the way, and hurry out through the main door, where the seafront stretches ahead. The Grand Pier is all lit up in the distance, bringing back more memories. All that youthful naivety, that fun, that hope. Part of me wants to be back there. I don't want to revisit my teenage woes again. I don't want the acne or the rejection or the silly crushes that deep down I knew were no good for me. All of that can stay in the past. But I just want to return to that bubble, with Mum, where the sea always seemed bright and clear.

'Steph?' Amanda's voice calls behind me.

She finds me perched on the front step, looking out at the view.

'You OK? They're about to play another round of pass the parcel in there. The previous prize was edible underwear.'

'I'm fine. I'm just thinking.'

'About what?'

'Stuff. Old stuff.'

'Such as . . .?'

The breeze whips against my face and I twirl the champagne flute in my hand. 'Do you remember Jake from school?'

'God, yes! Isn't he the one who dumped you?'

'I dumped *him*. Because he cheated on me, but yes. *I* had the upper hand.'

'I thought you dumped him because of his hairstyle. I

would have.'

'Everyone had that style, Mand. It was hot.'

'If you say so. Why are you thinking about him, anyway? I'm sure I saw him a few weeks back, in town. Pretty sure he's married.'

'I was just thinking about when we were kids. And Mum.'

Amanda stumbles a bit but manages to sit herself down next to me.

'You always get like this when you come back,' she says. 'I'm sorry I kind of forced you here. I don't even know why we were even invited. What's the point? Oh, I remember – it's because Grace wants to show off to as many people as possible. And she has to pretend to be nice to us in front of other family. We're the sisters everyone feels sorry for. You know I'm right.'

'I'd sell my soul to get one more day with Mum, Mand. Even one of the mundane days, you know? Nothing special. Just one more. I could have had more, and that's what hurts.'

Amanda sighs. She reaches out to rub my back and I appreciate the comfort it brings, if only temporarily.

'OK, Steph. Listen to me. Mum was proud. She was happy you went to America, OK?'

'But if I hadn't—'

'Steph, this is grief talking. Don't be silly. She loved you.'

They told us how grief comes in waves. I never thought how disarming they'd truly be. How they don't just sweep you up – they fill your lungs and make you flail about and struggle. And when your head is finally above the surface, they throw you for miles. You're suspended in it, unable to move or be normal.

Before Amanda can continue, there's a click-click of

heels behind us. Auntie Grace has retreated outside for some fresh air, also clutching a champagne flute.

'All right, girls?' she says.

We nod dutifully.

'You're missing the games.'

'I just needed to get outside for a bit,' I say.

Auntie Grace takes a breath. She looks out at the view, at the darkened sea, as if it's all hers and she's proud.

'So, how are things with you two? Got a boyfriend yet, Steph?'

I shake my head and give her what I hope is a polite, cheery smile. 'Not yet.'

Auntie Grace simply nods. 'There's still plenty of time.'

Why do people keep saying that?

'Deb would have loved this,' she comments.

In my tipsy state, I initially I think she's talking about the pier, but then quickly realise she's not.

I turn round fast enough to give myself whiplash.

'What?'

'Your mother. She'd have loved seeing Natasha all ready for her big day. It's a shame that she . . . well . . . '

'That she what?'

Auntie Grace exhales into the cold air. 'She told me once how she'd have loved to see you girls walk down the aisle. I think all mothers do.'

'Do they?' Amanda asks with a hiccup. She shoots me a look of theatrical confusion. 'Mum never mentioned it.'

'We'd talk about it,' confirms Auntie Grace, slurring a little. 'It's a shame things didn't work out with that . . . what was his name again, Amanda? Jason?'

As tipsy as she might be, Amanda still manages to flash me another fierce warning glare. Too late, however. I'm already on my feet. My phone clatters from my lap to the floor. I hear it, hear the *clack* as it hits cold pavement, but I really don't care.

'Are you insane?' I snap.

'Excuse me?'

'Get real. Mum would have *hated* this. All this . . . fanfare. This' – I gesture wildly, drunkenly, towards the hotel door – 'is just to show off. And please, do *not* bring Mum into this.'

'Calm down. Don't get into hysterics, *again*. I was only saying, it's a shame she never got to see it. We never do know what's round the corner, do we?'

I'm angry now.

'Mum would have laughed. She'd have thought the whole thing ridiculous. You should know. You're her *sister*.'

Auntie Grace gives a little huff. Sighs as though I'm nothing, just another annoyance. Which is probably true, considering how she's never really liked us. Or even Mum, for that matter. They'd always had a rocky relationship; Auntie Grace was the competitive type. Since they were kids, just three years apart, everything Deb did, Grace would have to do better. Grades, dance classes, boyfriends, marriages. Kids. I suspect she was elated when Mum's marriage to Dad ended. In Grace's strange little world, she'd won.

Amanda's right. The only reason she invites us to these things is because she feels she has to.

'I take it we're going to have another little performance this evening?' Grace says slowly.

'No. We're going to leave now.'

'Are you sure? Are you sure you don't want to swipe at me again for trying to be nice to you? For trying to include you in family events you clearly don't want to be part of?'

The words burn. Amanda's gripping weakly at my arm, knowing what's to come. I could shout; I can feel the words coming, threatening, ready to burst out of me all over again.

Because *last time* was at Mum's wake.

Mum's wake – the last 'family event' that saw all of us together, cooped up unpleasantly in too small a place. The false niceties, the promises, the sorrys. So many *sorrys*. So many that I wanted them to end. I never wanted to hear that word again.

There was Grace and Nat and Uncle Darren; Grace's head tilted in that rehearsed, sympathetic way, her hand reaching out to touch mine softly, as if she'd learned how to be nice from the television. And then, when I'd gone to the loo to cry, away from the audience of apologetic faces, hunched over the toilet in the tiny cubicle with peeling walls as if it were the safest place on the planet, I could hear them enter. Their heels, their strides on the tiles.

'That Steph, no wonder she's in such a state. Swanning off to America when her mother was dying of cancer. Guess the guilt's coming back to bite her.'

And that's when I lost it. Stormed out from behind the cubicle door, overcome with strength I never knew I had. My eyes were wet, my vision hazy with the tears I thought would never stop, but I caught Nat's smug, pitying look. I'd had enough of pity. There was no longer room for pity.

Shaking, I grabbed Nat by the collar of her black dress and hurled her across the room. There was shouting. So much shouting – and it was coming from me. There was Nat, backed into a corner, cowering and sobbing beneath a hand dryer, and me, my words fierce and loud and unfamiliar. I can vaguely recall Amanda breaking through a crowd who had gathered outside the toilets to come and pull me away to safety, away from Nat. I was drunk, I was angry. I didn't care.

Because I hadn't known.

I hadn't known Mum had been so ill. I didn't know she was dying.

I didn't know.

Now, Grace and I stare at each other as if outside a Wild West saloon.

'No,' I say. 'We're going to get our coats and go. Aren't we, Mand?' With that, I grab my now-silent sister by the arm and she totters inside behind me. 'Let's go home.'

The karaoke has started. A couple of Nat's bridesmaids are on the makeshift podium, warbling out 'Daydream Believer'. My neighbour was playing that last week, on the piano. I sang along loudly, eating a Tesco lasagne for one in my pyjamas, and right now I want to relive that memory, rather than have the song ruined by this one. I want to be safe in my flat with the covers pulled up to my face, singing along.

I want to go home.

Chapter 13

Eric

'Read this,' I say, pointing at the screen. 'What do you think?'

Lloyd stops at the kitchen table. I turn the laptop round for him to see. He reads. Frowns.

'It says you're looking for someone "quiet, discreet and professional". What are you advertising for – a hitman?'

I take another look at the advert I've spent the past forty minutes trying to create. I'm failing so hard it's funny – at least to Lloyd. How is this so bloody difficult?

'Is it really that bad?'

Lloyd nods. 'Not horrendous, but it's a *little* bit dark web. You might want to tweak it slightly.'

'What's wrong with it, exactly?'

Lloyd sighs. We both stare at the screen. Finally, he releases his verdict.

'I mean, the wording is fine, but it just sounds too . . . serious.'

'Is that such a bad thing? I'm looking for a housemate. Someone to *live with*. This has to have some degree of seriousness. We'd have to get along with each other.'

'Is that why you're not keen on Hugh? You think you won't get along?'

'Do you want my honest answer?'

'He's all right. Honestly. He's a good guy.'

109

He's a twat, I want to say. I know that's unfair, given that I've only met him a grand total of once – perhaps twice – but first impressions and all that. His demeanour doesn't instil the confidence that he'd be a decent housemate.

I mean, I could be wrong. He could be perfect. But do I want to take that risk?

'He's still interested, by the way,' Lloyd adds. 'I've told him we'll let him know by the end of the week.'

Shit. 'Can we see how this goes first?' I nod towards the computer screen, where the four lines of my apparently awful advert stare back at me. If *this* is so terrible, there's no hope for my screenplay. 'I'm not ruling him out, it's just . . . it's nice to have some options.'

Lloyd flops into the chair opposite mine. 'Why don't you put a picture up?' he asks.

'I have. Sean took them.'

'Not *just* of the room, I mean. Of you.'

'Why would I do that? I'm trying to attract a housemate.'

'I know. But you might find someone really *nice* who wants to rent the room,' he says coyly.

I sigh and wonder just how desperate people think I am lately. Either they're urging me to get on Tinder like it's some kind of last resort, or . . . this.

'Lloyd,' I say. 'I'm searching for a housemate, not applying for *Love Island*. Or *Big Brother*.'

'How old are you, mate?' He laughs at me.

Ancient, apparently. 'I want someone nice and respectful. Not a situation that could turn out to be painfully awkward three months down the line.'

Lloyd holds his hands up in mock surrender. 'It was merely a suggestion. Right, I'm off. I'll probably end up staying round Sophie's tonight, so could you feed Freddy later?'

'You know I will.'

Once Lloyd's out of the room, I consider throwing my laptop against the wall. Even Lloyd is getting lucky and here's me, festering in my room, landed with the responsibilities of finding a housemate. But if I don't, what are the alternatives? It's simple: either I find a suitable person to share my living space, or I find the rest of the rent myself, admit full defeat and move back in with my parents or . . . well, invite Hugh to move in. All options are excruciating.

I wander to the kitchen and take another beer from the fridge. There are now only three left, so I'll have to get more tomorrow, along with more milk. Sean finished the last bottle and hasn't replaced it, which is against the rules he wrote.

The rules are pinned to the corkboard – a neatly typed copy. This is something I'll have to be clear on when the new person moves in: our house rules.

If we run out of milk, replace it.
Text other housemates if you're bringing home a guest.
Always put stuff in the dishwasher.
Adhere to the fortnightly housework rota.
Recycle.

Cracking open the bottle, I remember when the rota started. When the rules were first introduced. Sean handed me a copy one evening as I lay in front of the TV on a Netflix binge, cocooned in a fleecy throw I'd taken from the flat. It still smelled like Clarissa. I remained a pitiful ball, getting rum-fuelled and merry and swiftly losing track of time.

'We've decided to change things up a bit,' Sean said, trying his best to be friendly, not fully catching my eye as he said it. It was as if the grey carpet held something particularly interesting. 'We've all got to chip in with the house stuff. Starting today.'

My phone beeps with a new message and I rush to answer it, placing the beer back on the side as I fumble in my pocket. Since Clarissa's initial reply, we've exchanged a few messages, my heart leaping with a sense of joy each time that familiar ping comes through. Each one from her is upbeat, polite, teetering on the informal, playful tone that was there a year ago, as if she doesn't want to overstep some kind of boundary. I've done the same – trying to figure out how to respond as though I'm on some sort of secret mission, rather than talking to the woman who used to know me better than anyone in the world.

If I want to see if she'll give it another go, I have to take it slow. I have to show her things have changed for the better. Seeing her words, my heart soars.

> I'll be in town next Wednesday if you fancy meeting up. Are you still at the bank? There's a place just around the corner. We could get a coffee or something, if you like? X

I'm ecstatic. I want to leap around the room, punching the air. I settle with a quiet little 'Whoop!' that nobody else can hear. I reply:

> Of course. Let me know what time and I'll meet you there! X

While Clarissa's messages have brightened my day, the SpareRoom ad hasn't. Beer in hand, I look back at the screen, trying to summon some inspiration. I delete the words and try again.

Looking for a housemate! Spacious double room available from next month. We're two friendly guys – one student, one full-time professional – looking for someone to share our home in Redland! Ideal housemate would be quiet, respectable and must like cats . . .

Freddy chooses that moment to enter the living room, announcing his arrival with a loud meow. He leaps onto the sofa beside me and heads straight for my lap, his ginger paws padding over the computer, in total disregard for its presence.

'Knew you were being talked about, did you, mate?' I ask, rubbing his head and feeling his soft, rumbling purr against my chest.

It's going to be a shame when Lloyd leaves and takes Freddy with him. I'm going to miss this little guy.

Taking another swig of beer, I reread the ad. There's not much else I can add that'll make it, make *us*, sound that inviting. Defeated, I upload the photos Sean sent me of the room and hit Post. Finally, it's done. One less thing to worry about.

Then, with Freddy still curled up on my lap, I open the screenplay.

Clarissa wasn't a fan of the screenplay. Then again, she wasn't too big a fan of horror, which would instantly put her off.

'Why would you want to see *that*?' she'd say when I suggested we curl up and watch something scary. 'There's enough of that going on in the world. Real horror.'

She'd look momentarily angry, her face scrunching in the most adorable way, and I'd love her for it. We'd choose something else. We'd compromise. She wasn't too interested in reading my work, but who could blame her? It's fucking awful.

FREYA stands before the tall wooden door of the lake house, suitcase in hand. She reaches out for the brass knocker and tries again, three times. Mist descends on the woodland behind, coating the vast lake with an air of mystery. Her face is clouded in worry at the absence of anyone else. The door clicks open . . .

I close the laptop.

The living room is quiet. Too quiet. All I can hear are the sounds outside the window, the quiet whoosh of traffic, the wind pounding against the old bay windows. The distant beep of a car horn. Something's missing. I contemplate putting on some music, but just as I do, I notice the time. It's 10.04 p.m.

Usually, the music from number 26 is already in full swing.

I pick up the beer again and my movement startles Freddy, who leaps from my lap, affronted. He swishes off towards the kitchen, the bell on his collar tinkling. Setting the laptop aside, I walk towards the wall. Carefully, I press my ears against the coldness of it, listening for any sound. There's nothing.

On the coffee table there's an empty glass, one I was drinking from earlier. I grab it, placing it between my ear and the wall, and listen.

Complete silence.

I can't concentrate. I need to find some inspiration. *Any* inspiration. So I take my beer, head for the door and sit outside.

Until something – some*one* – catches my attention.

There's someone outside number 26.

Chapter 14

Steph

The bedsit is cold when I get home.

> Cons of living alone #149: You arrive to an empty
> house, where nobody is waiting for you with a cup of
> tea, or a much-needed cocktail. Nobody to ask how
> everything went, and to let you vent for hours about
> your terrible cousin's party and everything in
> between. Sometimes it's nice to have a sounding
> board. One who isn't always your sister.

Pulling my suitcase behind me, I feel around for the light
switch, peering around with a hint of fear as if there's a
knife-wielding murderer lurking in the shadows of my pokey
home. As it happens, there's nobody, just the sounds of
laughter and footsteps from Sarah and Ash's upstairs. They
obviously have some friends over again.

The overhead light flickers on and gets brighter, illuminating my place, this little space in the city that I've grown
so used to. I whack on the heating and lift the case onto my
bed, pulling out everything that I need to put in the wash.
I switch on the fairy lights around my bed, something I
put there to make the place feel cosier, and drop the dirty
clothes into the laundry hamper.

After the semi-disastrous weekend, I'm grateful to be back in my little sanctuary. My little studio with its bay window, under which I've put a storage box and some pillows to make a little 'reading nook', even though I rarely use it. A mantelpiece full of photos and candles and plants (fake, of course – I'm terrified I'd kill them). A bookshelf stands in one corner, and then my wardrobe and clothing rail. Beneath the rail, concealed beneath long cardigans and light coats better suited for the summer, are the boxes.

Mum's boxes.

Zipping up the now empty suitcase, I go to the rail, lifting up the garments one by one. My heart races as I make sure the boxes are still there, present and untouched. My whole body calms when I glimpse them.

Nobody has entered my home and taken them – not that anyone would. Some things are valuable only to me.

I run my hands over the top of the cardboard, feeling the corners, soft and slightly dented with age and wear. I move a finger along the layer of packing tape that's yet to be broken through. Mum's careful packaging. Her handwriting in black pen loops along the top: *For Steph*.

Amanda gave me these boxes shortly after Mum died. I've never opened them.

Just thinking about doing so makes me panic – cutting through that tape, lifting the lid, unleashing all those memories again. I've never had the courage. So I put them aside, knowing that I will.

One day, I will.

The soft thump of music pulsates through the ceiling from the upstairs flat. I shuffle through to the kitchen, edging past my bedside table and a chair full of clothes I need to put away, and take a tin of tomato soup from the cupboard, pouring it into the smallest pan. Uninspired, but it'll do. It's been a long day.

Suddenly, there's a loud thump at my door.

I jump up, startled. The pan flies from my grasp, sending hot tomato soup flying over the worktop, the floor and – as I notice with horror – my sleeve. The warmth seeps through the fabric of my shirt.

Panic rises in my chest. Who could be at my door at gone nine in the evening? I rarely have visitors. In fact, the last person to visit was the landlord for the six-month inspection. I lean against the door, cautiously peering through the little spyhole, to find it's just Ash from upstairs. Relieved, I pull the door open.

'Hi, Ash!' I say brightly, aware I smell like tomato soup.

Ash grins, a wide, perfect smile on display, before his gaze travels to my stained red sleeve.

'Soup,' I clarify. 'It's just soup.'

'Ah. That's a relief!'

He stands in the doorway, a dark T-shirt showing off his toned body, from all the running with Sarah. He's holding some envelopes which, I soon notice, are all addressed to me.

'So, er . . .' He steals a quick glance at the first envelope on the pile, then quickly looks back at me. 'Stephanie.'

Out in the communal hallway the music is louder still. There's laughter and a delicious smell of food wafting down from the big flat upstairs. My stomach rumbles.

'These are yours.' Ash hands me the letters with a smile. 'We have a new postman. He must have put them in our box by mistake, so here you go.'

He hands them over as if passing me a gift, not a stack of bills. The logo for the energy company is stamped on the front of the first one. Fantastic.

'Thanks,' I say, bestowing upon him a grateful smile.

'It's no problem! Would have just put them in your box, but it's full at the moment. Lots of menus and leaflets hanging out.'

'Oh? Er, thanks. I was away for the weekend. I'll go and see to it.'

Ash smiles again and for a brief, fleeting moment I wonder if he's going to ask me upstairs to join the party. A sudden sense of embarrassment engulfs me at the state of my room, how it looks like an H&M and a Deliveroo bike had a collision right here in my living room-slash-bedroom. How it's now in full view of my neighbour, who occupies the lovely big flat upstairs, which is probably all tidy with matching cushions and his and hers mugs. And treadmills.

He points to the ceiling. 'Oh, seeing as you're here . . .'

Hope rises in my chest. He's going to invite me to the get-together where all the fun is happening! Where he'll lead me up the stairs and say 'Hey, everyone, meet our neighbour, Steph!' And they'll all raise their glasses in a cheery hello.

'We've got some people over, but we'll turn the music off by eleven. We won't keep you up!' And with another friendly grin, he's gone.

Flopping onto my bed, the place is bathed in silence once more and I realise what the time is. It's piano time – and my neighbours still aren't playing. I press my ear against the wall and listen, desperate to hear any sound, any hint of them moving around the house.

Nothing.

I move along the wall, desperately seeking out any faint noise.

Then I remember – the card. I sent them a card.

The small stack of letters from Ash is on my pillow, so I grab them and take a look through, to see if they've slipped me a note in return. Besides the energy bill, some supermarket offers and a new local takeaway menu, there's nothing.

So I take my key and head outside. The night is crisp, the air cool against my skin. Outside the door, the little mailbox creaks as I free the stack of menus and glossy flyers that have been shoved inside. There's nothing other than advertising; no note, nothing from number 26.

I set off down the long front path and through the gate of the house next door. The lights are off again, shrouding the pretty Victorian house in shadowy darkness. It's uncharacteristic, spooky even, its darkness a contrast against my own building, where music and light emanates from Sarah and Ash's upstairs window. I make my way towards the front door, the hanging baskets swaying ghostlike in the breeze, already anticipating the answer.

Just as I'm about to knock, I glance down at the small pane of frosted glass in the front door. The little pile of mail is just visible in the darkness. Crouching, I look closer, spotting the pale pink envelope pressed up against the glass, the same one I'd pushed through before I went away. It's still there. They haven't even seen it, let alone opened it.

Getting up, I turn to head back to my flat, but something stirs behind me. A noise.

I'm not alone. Beside me, there's a rustling in the hedgerow, and from a small gap I can make out the shape of a person. A man. A pair of eyes stare back at me from behind the foliage. I almost leap out of my skin.

'Hello?' the man says.

Taking a step back, I contemplate running, retreating into my flat, but I'm frozen to the spot, my trainers glued to the concrete step.

'Um, hi?' the voice says again, and the eyes disappear.

Then there are footsteps and suddenly, the man is standing at the bottom of the path. He's tall, with dark curly hair and thick dark stubble. In one hand he's holding a bottle of what appears to be beer. Moonlight bounces off the bottle as he takes a sip.

'Sorry, I didn't mean to frighten you just then.'

'It's OK, you didn't.'

'Really? Because you jumped a mile.'

His smile is kind and I relax a little. 'OK, you did. You startled me, that's all.'

He holds up his free hand in apology. 'I didn't expect to see you either, to be honest. Do you live here?' he asks, pointing towards the house.

I shake my head. Who is this man and why is he familiar? 'This house? No.'

'Then do you know the people who do?'

'Sadly not. I wish I did.'

He looks at me strangely, and no wonder – I'm hanging around outside this apparently empty house and I don't know the owners.

'Sorry. I'm just . . . I'm not doing anything dodgy.'

'I didn't think you were.' He's smirking now.

'Look,' I say, 'I live next door, on the other side. I haven't . . . well, I haven't heard the neighbours in a while. I usually hear them, every day, but lately . . .'

'Lately, there's nothing and you're wondering if they're OK.'

'That. Exactly that.'

He nods as if he understands. He takes a few more steps up the path. In the faint light, I can make out his jeans and faded T-shirt, over which he's wearing a dark, thick cardigan.

'I get it. I've been wondering the same, too. I'm Eric, by the way. I live in number 24. I hear the neighbours every day, but it's been quiet for a while.'

'I'm Steph.'

'Well, it's nice to meet you. Have you ever met *them*, by any chance?' He gestures towards the door of number 26.

'Never. Have you?'

Eric shakes his head. Takes another quick swig from the bottle. 'Not once. I've seen food deliveries. And someone comes to do the garden every now and then. But never the residents. I don't think I've seen anyone visit. Or maybe I just haven't noticed.'

We look at each other and our gazes lock. I can feel my face drain of colour at the sudden worry. All the horror stories, the people being discovered dead in their homes weeks, months later.

He must see it, too, because he says: 'Oh, don't worry, I think they're just on holiday. They put the bin out before they left, so I brought it back round. And the lights are off. It's all good.'

That, at least, is comforting.

'Um . . . should I be calling an ambulance or something?' Eric stops, lowering the beer, suddenly staring in alarm.

Then I realise why. The sleeve of my cream shirt is soaked in thick, red soup.

'What happened?' he asks.

'This? Oh! This is just soup. I know it must look worse in the dark.'

'It really, really does.'

'I was just about to change and then decided . . .' I stop. There's no point in over-explaining. 'Know what? I'm glad we met. I thought I was being a terrible neighbour.'

'You're definitely not a terrible neighbour.'

He offers another smile before starting off down the path again. Then he turns round, brushing a hand through his thick hair. There's something about him that's sweet. Nice. Why haven't I met him before?

'Hey, you wouldn't be looking for a room by any chance?'

'Whoa, you move quickly.'

He laughs, as if only just realising how awkward that sounded.

'Oh, God, sorry. That sounded weird. And extremely forward. And creepy, maybe.'

'Very creepy.'

'What I meant to ask is are you looking to rent a room, or do you know anyone who is? It's just . . .' Eric gestures to his own house. 'I'm trying to find a new housemate. That's why I'm outside – I needed a break from looking at houseshare sites. If I leave it any longer, some guy, Hugh, is going to move in and, well . . . let's just say I'd rather find someone else, asap.'

I shake my head, even though I'm invested now. I want to know more about this Hugh character.

'Sorry. I'm not planning on going anywhere anytime soon, but if it helps, I could pin an ad to the noticeboard at work.'

'That would be great, actually. Shall I pop some details round tomorrow?'

It's cold out here, the wind getting stronger by the minute, settling in for another blustery September night. I should get back inside, make another attempt at dinner and watch something to blank out the weekend. It's been a weird evening. My eyes wander to Eric's beer. He sees me looking.

'I've got two more,' he says kindly. 'Want one?'

I'm tempted, but it's cold. I want to be somewhere indoors, somewhere cosy, full of warmth and chatter where I don't feel like an outsider with my face pressed against the window, looking in. My evening has veered off track and suddenly I want to be home, yet at the same time I want to be anywhere *but* home. So I suggest the next best thing.

'There's a pub round the corner, the Cambridge Arms. Do you want to get a drink?'

Eric's dark eyes seem to light up at the suggestion.

'That would be nice, actually.'

'I'll just pop in and get changed. I'll be right back.'

Hurrying inside to find a clean top, I feel a frisson of promise. Although Eric's wrong about one thing: I *am* a terrible neighbour.

But I'm going to make the effort. Because I don't *want* to be a terrible neighbour.

Not any more.

Chapter 15

Eric

The pub isn't as busy as expected, so we find an available table, nestled at the back. Steph insists on getting the drinks because, she says, it was her suggestion – and she really needs some chips.

'I'm starving,' she says. 'Are you sure you don't want anything to eat? Absolutely sure?'

I shake my head and watch as she moves towards the bar, pulling her purse from the pocket of her jeans. She's changed from the soup-stained blouse into a black jumper, which sparks a vague memory – of course, she's Pink Bag. The dark-haired woman I've sometimes seen hurrying past the window in the early morning. Blazer, small black rucksack, vivid pink lunch bag.

Steph returns to the table with two ciders, then hurries off to retrieve the basket of chips. I take a sip of cider, but only a small one. I've been drinking already this evening and this is enough. Enough to keep me light and merry and talkative in the presence of my new-but-not-new neighbour.

'These smell absolutely divine,' says Steph, pulling a face that suggests these hastily cooked fries she's doused generously in vinegar are the epitome of bliss. Though, judging by the aroma, she's not wrong.

'You can have some if you want,' she says, tapping the basket on the table in front of me.

'Oh, go on, then. Thanks for this,' I say.

'For a chip? You're easily pleased.'

I wave a hand round our surroundings. 'For the invite.'

Steph shrugs. 'It's just nice to be out of the house.'

'Oh? Bad day?'

'Bad weekend.'

I watch as she takes another chip and looks out of the window. There's a pause, as if she wants to elaborate but thinks better of it.

'I only got in an hour ago and, to top it all off, managed to spill my dinner everywhere. But at least the weekend's almost over.'

'Unless something goes wrong while we're here.'

'Hey! Don't.'

She's laughing now, and I'm glad.

'For that, I'm no longer sharing,' she teases.

'Hey, I did nothing wrong.'

'You tempted fate,' she says playfully. 'And to think I was worried.'

'Worried?'

Steph nods and despite her vow, proffers the chip basket.

'You can have one, because I'm nice. But yes – worried. I was all hyped for a moment, when you agreed to come here – and then I thought, what if I'm pulling you away from a nice pre-planned evening? What if you have other stuff to do? I thought, is he too polite to say no?'

I laugh. I can't help it.

'Planned evening? OK, you're expecting too much. Although Freddy might be a bit annoyed that I've left him in order to spend time with you.'

'Freddy?'

'My cat. Well, he's my housemate's cat.'

'Little ginger one? Always looks a little angry?'

'That's him!'

'I've seen him around. He's been in my garden a few times. I've opened the door to say hi, but he just stares at me until I go away. As if he owns the entire street.'

'Oh, that's definitely Freddy. I'd say he's less angry, more fed up with the world. If he's been digging up your flowers or anything, I can only apologise.'

Steph shrugs, smiling as she concentrates on dipping the chips into the little bowl of ketchup. Suddenly, she looks up.

'Wait. I've seen you before. Aren't you the man who got locked out of his house once?'

Oh no.

'In the Spider-Man pyjamas?'

She's laughing now, pointing at me as realisation dawns. 'You are!'

'Don't remind me. Is there anyone in Chapel Gardens who didn't witness that?'

'Apparently not.'

I sit back, folding my arms as her expression changes. She's trying not to laugh, but she's unsuccessful, letting out a splutter of giggles just as she's about to take a sip of cider.

'Hey!'

'I'm sorry. There's you, being all nice, and I'm making fun.'

'Don't worry. Even if you're laughing, you've done me a favour. A change of atmosphere is exactly what I need; I've been sitting inside for ages trying to write a bloody room advert.'

'Did you do it?'

'Eventually. I know it might sound odd, but . . . the next-door neighbours help. I guess I'm just used to hearing them all the time. It's strangely comforting.'

Is it just me, or does Steph look worried all of a sudden? There's a shadow of unease across her face. Beneath these cosy lights, I realise she looks tired. Not unlike me.

'Do you hear the piano?' she asks.

She takes a sip of her drink, eats another chip, dips it in the ketchup for a little too long this time.

'I do. I hear it every night. I used to find it annoying when I first moved in, but now I'm used to it. So used to it that it's weird without it. Now the place is too quiet.'

'I'm guessing you have housemates, then? Seeing as you're renting out a room.'

The change of subject jolts me out of my reverie. My mind had started to drift towards the recent past, of evenings holed up in the bedroom, listening to the quiet lull of the piano notes as I tried to focus on my work. It was either that or listen to the constant creaking from Sean's bedroom above.

'Yep. My friend Sean. He's finally moving in with his girlfriend, so . . . yeah. Bit of an unexpected change, but I'm sure it'll be fine.'

Steph nods. Tucks a stray bit of dark hair behind her ear. Beneath the light, there's a tinge of red in her shoulder-length locks.

'So, what do you do, Eric?'

'I work at a bank.'

'Nice!' she says, and for a second I assume she's being sarcastic.

Then it hits me. She thinks I'm *in finance*. One of those men with a tailored suit and a great car, like Clarissa's friends.

'Oh, nothing fancy,' I confirm, waving away the mere idea. 'I work in one of the branches. Customer service. Mortgage advice. Loans.'

'Do you enjoy it?'

'Well . . .'

'You don't enjoy it, do you? You paused when I asked you. That's a giveaway, right there.'

It's a question I haven't been asked in a long time. Another memory surfaces, this time of Clarissa, sprawled on the sofa with the laptop, her glossy hair tied back as it was every day when she'd returned from the gym. She'd lit a scented candle. It sat on the coffee table, filling the room with the aroma of cherry.

'I'm job-hunting,' she'd said. 'For you.'

'Why?' I'd asked.

'You don't enjoy it where you are, so I'm seeing what's out there. There's a great new position that's come up in Bath . . .'

Maybe I should have listened to her, let her find me something instead of refusing.

But I can't change that now.

I shrug, turning my attention back to Steph. 'It's all right. What about you?'

'I also work in finance. At Everly Cope, down by the harbour. I deal with complaints. Not the most glamorous job, but it gets me by.'

'I never wanted to work in the bank,' I confess. 'I always wanted to write.'

Steph's eyes grow wide with interest. 'Really? That's brilliant. I used to write – well, I had a travel blog years ago. It was more about all the places I wanted to visit and all the tips I'd learned more than actual travelling. What do you write? Novels? Short stories?'

Amid the cosy comfort of the pub, my face feels warm. I swipe another chip from Steph's basket.

'Not exactly. I wanted to write films. I'm writing one now, actually.'

'Let me guess – action?'

'Horror. Supernatural horror. I'm trying to get the story right.'

'Oh my God. I love horror.'

'Really?'

'Yes! Especially the classics: *Friday the 13th, A Nightmare on Elm Street, Night of the Living Dead* . . . my sister and I used to watch them in our early teens.'

'Which one was your favourite?'

'*Poltergeist*. Amanda and I – Amanda's my little sister – we'd borrow them from one of our neighbours; her big brother had them all on tape. The fact they were on VHS and were so well-worn just added to the creep factor. When Mum was in work, we'd turn off the lights and watch them. Amanda would be hiding behind cushions and I'd be shrieking at all the jump scares.'

'I used to do that, too! My dad hated it. Said I shouldn't be watching them. He said that the world was scary enough already. My ex thought the same.'

Steph nods thoughtfully. 'You could see it that way, I suppose, but for some of us, it's what takes us *out* of the real world and all the bad stuff. Those old movies . . . we know that ghosts, haunted houses and killers who chase you in your dreams aren't genuine threats. I mean now, everything's different. Fear exists everywhere. We've got so much to be genuinely frightened of as adults. Homelessness, empty bank accounts, cancer, losing people we love . . . watching those films is an escape.'

I look at her in awe and mentally curse myself for not making an effort before. I'd seen Pink Bag many times, hurrying down Chapel Gardens, but never thought to reach out and say hello.

'Finally! Someone who agrees.'

'Real-life horror is much, much worse,' she continues, and for a moment her expression darkens.

Something tells me she's had experience, but I don't want to pry.

'I'd take a rampaging killer doll any day,' says Steph. 'You know that's not a *real* threat.'

'Or so you think . . .'

'Ha! Well, I'll tell you a secret – I had a doll once, when I was little, which I was convinced would come to life and kill me in my sleep.'

'Seriously?' I can't help but chuckle.

'Hey! It's not funny. Her name was Cecilia. She was pretty, with a pale, porcelain face and big eyes, but a painted mouth that made her look constantly unhappy. My grandmother bought her for me, obviously with the best of intentions, but that doll scared the crap out of Amanda and me. I kept hiding Cecilia under the bed, but she kept reappearing. Obviously, Mum used to put her back on the shelf every time. Stop laughing, Eric.'

I hold up my hands in surrender. 'I'm sorry! But that's half funny and half adorable. Why didn't you tell your mum?'

'I thought it would hurt her feelings. To be honest, I wish I still had that doll. My gran died two years later – it was one of my last gifts from her. Doesn't make it any less terrifying, though,' she adds, her smile bright, bringing the conversation back to light territory once again.

When we wander back down the darkened street to Chapel Gardens an hour later, our faces pink with the flustered warmth of much-needed company, there's a flicker of hope in my world. Tiny, but just big enough to extinguish the impending worry.

I realise I haven't looked at my phone in all that time. Pulling it from my pocket, I catch sight of the notifications. A steady stream of emails already coming in from SpareRoom.

There are applicants already. There's hope with Clarissa. And I've been sitting in a pub talking about movies with someone new, enjoying the company of someone I don't already live with.

Things might be looking up. Finally.

Chapter 16

Steph

Miles is being friendly.

That's the only reason, so I've uncovered, for his recent decision to get back in touch.

> M: Really glad everything's going well! Yeah, things are good with me. The job's fantastic and I'm with someone – her name is Vikki. You'd really like her! We've just bought a house.

> S: Woo! Serious then, I take it? :)

> M: You could say that! We're talking about adopting a dog. Not sure what breed yet. Vikki's set on a small dog – they're easier, she says – but you know how much I loved Jasper when I was a kid! She loves Labradors too, so might be convinced. We'll see! How are things in Bristol?

They're getting a dog. A *dog*. This signifies that things are *very* serious. A shared responsibility, a living being to nurture and train and care for. Miles and I always used to joke that getting a dog together would be preparation, the start of something more permanent. We'd tease each other about it, playfully suggesting it during those lazy summer weekends that sprawled ahead. We'd walk in the park enamoured by all the dogs bounding around, playing fetch, trotting lovingly behind their owners.

There's no real reason for the sudden communication besides Miles being caring, which is enough to stab me in the heart all over again, because Miles was – *is* – a genuine and caring guy. He simply saw my Instagram and thought he'd say hello. Because I was on the train home. Because he knows that's kind of a sore subject. Because that's the kind of sweet, considerate person he is.

Obviously, I can't tell him the truth, so I tap out a reply:

It's great! I went home to pay Amanda, Stevie and Poppy a visit. I don't really get much time. Busy life! I'm seeing someone as well, but it's early days yet . . .

I hate myself more with every lie that spews forth from my fingers. Then again, he doesn't have to know I'm *not* seeing anyone. I'm about to type 'and I run marathons for charity', but stop myself before hitting Send. There's only so long I could keep that little lie up: five whole minutes.

I'm spending my lunch break in Castle Park, using my coat as a picnic blanket on the cold grass, enjoying the hot, buttery taste of a jacket potato. It's one of those nice wintery but sunny days, the kind that vaguely remind me of Christmas. When you can feel the cold on your face as you wrap up warm, but the sun pokes through the trees, gracing everything in its path with a golden hue. Bare branches, a welcome mist. People cosy up in cafés, toasty and warm. They clutch takeaway coffees in knitted gloves and the scent of cinnamon wafts in the air.

I have claimed my own little space on the ground along with others who have momentarily escaped the bustle of the city centre. I wanted to be anywhere but the office – it had become stifling, stuffy, so before I could allow Tamz to rope me into calling boutiques in search of dresses in a bid to one-up Caz's bridal party, I quickly made my getaway.

I sit, not far from the old church, near a large group of friends. Strangers to me. They laze on the grass, chatting, blissfully unaware of my presence, totally not noticing me pull my coat a few inches closer, edging slightly into the confines of the group.

They don't notice me lift my phone and when I'm certain no one is looking, snap a quick photo. In fact, they don't notice me at all.

In the picture, I'm glancing slightly to the side. Pleasantly startled. As if someone's just called my name, stealing my attention away from all of my friends. Pulling up my app, I do a quick editing job, blurring everyone besides me, and select an artsy filter.

'Lunchtime in the sun with friends,' I caption, along with a flurry of hashtags. There you go, Miles, I think to myself, smug. Look how popular I am!

The colourful grid before me makes me smile, the all-important feed that documents my life. My virtual scrapbook. Even the photos from Nat's hen do make Amanda and me look great; the negativity has been stripped away, leaving only smiles. There's just one thing missing from the grid – a snap from last night, with Eric. I didn't think to take one.

Last night was strange and unexpected, but Eric was a welcome distraction from everything else. He's nice. Plus, he has great taste in movies. I've spent the entire morning consumed by a weird sense of regret, that he's been there for months and I hadn't even talked to him. If only I'd got to know him sooner.

And if only I'd got to know number 26.

The office is quiet when I return, silent besides the tapping of keys and Jeff's incessant slurping of coffee. Even Tamzin and Saskia are hard at work, their brows furrowed in concentration at their screens. Then again, the six-month reviews are upon us, which might have something to do with it. Sure enough, our boss Ciaran is sat at his desk behind the glass walls of our office, the overseer.

I sit at my own desk, which is conveniently situated out of Ciaran's line of vision, so he can't witness me casually scrolling through Insta. From the time it took to walk from Castle Park to the office, my photo has already garnered forty-six likes, blessing me with a fuzzy feeling of joy and accomplishment.

My phone rings, abruptly pulling me from my scrolling. It's Amanda. I swipe to answer, picking up my pink 'Best Auntie!' mug adorned with photos of Poppy that Amanda had specially made, and go out to the small communal kitchen.

'Hey,' she says. 'You OK?'

She's still being cautious about the past weekend. All the tension that she doesn't want to unleash again, even though I have a sneaking suspicion as to why she's calling. I tell her I'm fine.

'So, I just had a call from Auntie Grace. She said she'd like to invite us to Nat's wedding, *but* she's concerned that you're going to cause a scene. She's asked you to ensure you're on your best behaviour. Too funny.'

I sigh, almost throwing the spoon into my mug. I want to pick up the big tub of cheap communal coffee and hurl it at the door, watch the grains spread all over the tiles.

'Take a deep breath, Steph,' says Amanda calmly, as if she can see me.

'I'm not going. I think it's best if I don't. What's the point?'

'She's family.'

Amanda and her politeness. Amanda allowing herself to take any crap because of some dutiful familial bond. As if by keeping up the pretence, she can somehow still be in Mum's presence.

'Mand, you know, don't you, that the only reason I yelled at Nat at Mum's wake was because of what she said.'

'I know. You don't have to explain. She was in the wrong, but maybe . . .'

I can sense her easing carefully into the suggestion. She's probably pacing her own office right now, slowly, one step at a time.

'Maybe we could use some more sisterly time. It's going to be in a nice hotel. Stevie and I could do with some time away. You should come. Take a date! We could make a secret bingo card to see how showy everything is. I bet she'll be releasing doves.'

'Is that still a thing?' I make a mental note to ask the experts, Tamzin and Saskia.

'Look, I have to go,' says Amanda suddenly. 'I have a meeting in five minutes, but I just wanted to give you the heads-up. Speak soon, OK?'

She hangs up.

I stir the coffee and take a sip. It's too bitter, but I've lost the ability to care. I'm too angry. Picking up the mug, ignoring the burning sensation as some of the liquid escapes, dripping onto my hand, I head back out towards the main office, but before I make it through the door, someone else hurries through at the same time.

There's a thump and I stagger backwards. Coffee sloshes out of my mug and onto the carpet.

'Shit! Sorry,' says a voice.

Glancing up, the heat of anger rising in my cheeks, I

open my eyes in readiness to snap. To tell him to be more bloody careful. To watch where he's going. But when his face falls into view, I withhold the sarky comments.

The guy who's just aimlessly barged into me is none other than Alex Jessop, the manager from upstairs. Alex with the sandy hair and the nice suit, from Caz's engagement do.

He turns to face me after inspecting his smart trousers for any coffee spillage.

'Are you all right?' he asks.

'I'm fine.'

'I am *so* sorry. Really.'

His voice is deep and soothing. Refined. Every inch of him seems refined. Clutching my now half-empty mug, all I can do is nod.

Alex puts a hand on my shoulder and it's as if all the frustration I felt seconds ago evaporates into the cool air.

'I was in a rush,' he explains. 'I didn't see you and—'

'It was partly my fault. I should have been more careful.'

He smiles and my body feels hot.

'I'm Alex,' he says. 'I don't think we've met officially, but I do remember you! Weren't you at Caroline's engagement party?'

'I was. I'm Steph.'

'Ah! Lovely to meet you. I was going to speak to you, but when I was finally free, I couldn't find you.'

Fuck. I went home early and missed out on Alex!

Behind him, in the office, Saskia makes no secret of watching our exchange. Her blonde head peeks nosily over the top of her monitor.

I can't move. Something's keeping me here, rooted to the spot, like a tree with clumsy branches, and all at once I remember what pure attraction feels like, as if it's never happened to me before.

Of course it has. It's just been a while.

'That's a shame,' I reply in a naff attempt at being flirty. 'I went home early, but had I known, I'd have stayed.'

I can feel Saskia's gaze burning into my skin, her presence hovering in the office as she tries inconspicuously to listen in. I sneak a glance behind me, to find she's giving me a coy little thumbs up.

'Well,' says Alex. 'Worry not – we have a team night out happening next week. Just a few drinks in town, only a casual thing. I'm new, you see, so I'd love to get to know the wider team.'

His gaze lingers on mine. He's even more attractive than I remember.

'Sounds good!' I say, at which he beams delightedly.

'I have to get to a meeting, but I'm sure I'll catch up with you soon.'

With one final, fleeting smile, he walks away.

A random encounter – two people brought together by mere chance. Isn't this exactly what I need?

Walking to my desk, Saskia beckoning me over in excited glee, I feel genuinely, unironically, #blessed.

Chapter 17

Eric

'This is completely unexpected. What am I meant to *do* with all these?' I pass my phone to Sean.

He stares blankly at it, scrolling, his expression changing from confusion to one of amusement.

'Eric, this is *good* news.' He stops to check, peering through his glasses. 'You have . . . eighty-four people who are interested in the room. *Eighty-four*! Which means you can fill it. Quickly.'

Sighing, I take the phone back and my insides contort with dread. *So many messages*. In the three days since posting the advert, responses have been flying into my inbox so rapidly that I've barely had time to read the latest, when more start pouring in. It's going to take me more than a whole evening to respond to them all.

Granted, some are verging on ridiculous. Last night I tried to make progress by sifting through, only to be greeted with such comedic genius as:

Hi! We're a couple looking to move to the area and *love* the look of the room! We're expecting twins in three months' time, but we wouldn't be too much trouble . . .

While I don't have a job right now, I'm certain that
God will bless you for your duty by providing me
with free shelter.

Hi, I just got a job in the area, looking for a place to
live. I'm twenty-two, professional, active social life –
will be bringing people round a lot, if you get what I
mean . . .

The ad didn't specify a garden. Do you have a
garden? If so, I do nude yoga outdoors, so some
privacy would be welcome – that is, unless your
neighbours are fine with it. My current neighbours
aren't. Hence my response to your post.

'Well, there *is* a garden,' says Sean, laughing.

He continues to scan the kitchen, pulling open the
drawers and searching the communal cupboards for any
stray utensils he might have forgotten.

Since announcing his move, Sean's barely been in the
house. He's spent most of his time at Kate's, occasionally
popping in to collect a few more of his belongings.

'People clearly aren't reading the ad properly,' I say, justifi-
ably annoyed. 'It specifically states: no couples, no children,
no pets . . .'

I think back to an email from a girl called Rosie, who
seemed absolutely perfect. I had my hopes up until she
casually mentioned her three greyhounds.

'This isn't a dog-friendly house,' I had to remind Rosie,
picturing the scenes of destruction – Freddy being chased
around the house by three dogs, fur flying everywhere. Or,
more realistically, the dogs backed into a corner by a hissing
Freddy. It wouldn't work. At all.

At that moment Freddy enters the kitchen, strutting past Sean and I in search of his food bowl. I bend down to stroke his soft ears. 'Look at Freddy's little face,' I say. 'He totally agrees on the no-dogs rule. Don't you, Fred?'

'What about that Hugh bloke Lloyd mentioned? Move him in – it'll save you the hassle.'

'Maybe,' I mutter. 'But I do think we need to be a bit more thorough. To make sure we see the best candidates before we make any hasty decisions.'

Sean picks up a pizza cutter from the drawer, turning it round in his hands, inspecting it as if it's a rare antique vase.

'Correction: *you* need to be more thorough,' says Sean. 'Lloyd's happy with Hugh. You're being too picky.'

'I just want to avoid naked people in the shared areas. Is that too much to ask?'

Sean shrugs. 'Is this mine?' he asks, pointing the pizza cutter at my face. 'Pretty sure it is.'

He drops it into the cardboard box he's carrying, along with everything else he supposedly left behind. He's already made off with the majority of the saucepans, some of which I'm certain are Lloyd's.

'Look, I can help you go through all the applicants if you want, mate. But not tonight. Tonight we're dismantling the last of Kate's furniture. Let me know if you need me though, yeah?'

With one final glance around the kitchen, he gathers up the clattering box and he's gone, the sound of his keys jangling in the hallway.

In the living room, I get out the laptop and open the responses, starting from the top. Sean's right – at least there's interest. One thing's for certain, the potential stress of finding the remaining rent has now diminished. Now, all I have to do is find a good candidate to live with us; someone who's clean, friendly and preferably doesn't want to salute the sun with their bare arsehole right outside my window.

One by one, I tackle the list of applicants, firing off the politest responses I can muster until I've compiled a list of the most serious candidates. Freddy purrs from the sofa cushion next to me, my disgruntled guardian, as I send email after email, inviting them to an interview in the flat next week. That'll be one nerve-racking predicament out of the way.

The next? Clarissa.

I wait for Clarissa in the café, on the second table from the window. It's a chain café, nothing special, but it's not far from the bank and, I remember fondly, one we used to frequent when we met up for lunch. *Our* café.

The night I met Clarissa is still clear in my memory. I revisit it sometimes. I lie there and summon the thoughts, as though the memory itself has been extracted, stuck pristinely into a scrapbook of perfect cherished snapshots of the past. I distinctly recall the night – a summer post-work drink with the guys that turned into many. It was warm, muggy, the smell of smoke hanging in the air, the kind of scent you'd bring home that would linger on your clothes. I weaved through the throng of people milling about and chatting outside, clutching their drinks as if life depended on it, excusing myself a thousand times until I could shuffle to the side to find a place to stand.

I was grateful to be out, to inhale the fresh air, to look to the sky, a dusky blue. Evenings in summer can go on forever, stretching out until you no longer realise the time, or how late it is, or that you're working tomorrow. You just don't care. I'd left my friends inside, grouped together by the bar for fear of losing their place in the boisterous crowd. It was too hot in there. Too confined. So I eased myself into the corner as people piled out into the street beyond, chatting and singing, enjoying the summer heat.

And then I saw her, heading out through the door. She looked around, as if in search of a free spot. Tall and confident, flicking back auburn locks of glossy curled hair that tumbled down her back. She turned, caught sight of me, asked if she could join me.

'My ex is in there,' she explained, leaning against the wall. She shuffled closer, her red-and-white summery dress snaking up her legs. 'I'm just trying to avoid him until he leaves.'

That was it. We got talking – and a week later we were officially dating.

Now, I watch Clarissa walk past the window, in a similar flouncy dress, only this time she's paired it with thick tights and a winter coat. She pushes open the door, spotting me almost instantly.

'Eric!' she says, her small face brightening, and reaches over to give me a hug.

It's not the hug I'm used to from her, where we'd almost melt into each other, never wanting to let go. This is more . . . professional. Quick.

'How are things?' she says, slipping into the seat opposite mine.

I tell her the usual, a spruced-up version of what she already knows. I'd ordered her a coffee, but she'd prefer a water, so she goes up to order.

'I can't stay out long,' she says when she returns to her seat. 'But I wanted to see you. It's been ages.'

'So you missed me, then?' As soon as it's out of my mouth, I want to cringe so hard I turn inside out.

Clarissa makes a 'heh' noise. *Shit.*

143

'I'm kidding,' I say.

I smile, unsure. I need to show her I'm not the same person she walked out on last year. I need to demonstrate how everything's different. How I've changed.

But then she says, 'In a way, yes. I don't want things to be awkward any more. I've been thinking, let's be better about these things. Let's be amicable.'

We talk. We catch up. The bank, Sean and Kate, the break-up: how it wasn't pleasant. Sitting here talking to her pulls me back in time, as if this is us, this is normal. We're just together like we always were, filling each other in on the regular, mundane pieces of our lives.

Her hand is resting right there on the table, so close to mine. I'm tempted to reach over, to place my hand casually in hers. She'll look up at me with all the love in her eyes and grip it tighter and all will be OK.

I decide to be brave.

I edge my hand closer, but before my fingers can brush against hers, she pulls away, picking up her phone from the table and tapping out a message.

'So you're doing OK, then?' she says.

She peels her eyes away from the screen to look straight into mine, and for a second I think I catch a flash of pity.

'I was worried, you know. When we split . . .'

'Why?' I ask.

'You didn't take it well.'

'Because you didn't let me explain.'

'Eric . . .' Her voice is stern now.

'You didn't need to be worried.'

There's that look again.

'I did. It was lucky that Sean invited you to stay with him.'

I'll be forever grateful to Sean, there's no denying that. But that's not what I'm here to talk about.

'Anyway,' she continues, glancing at her phone every few seconds, as if she has somewhere else to be.

Ping, ping goes the message tone. Nervous, I take mine out, too, put it on the table. I see the notifications already – more messages from SpareRoom.

'It was nice you got in touch,' she says. 'I was going to drop you a message.'

My heart soars with momentary joy. 'Great minds, et cetera.'

'Guess so! But yeah, I heard from Sean about the house. Obviously you know Kate and I are friends. I think they're planning on a house-warming party and I didn't want things to be awkward.'

The joy deflates like a dud balloon.

'Why would it be awkward?' I ask.

She shrugs. 'You know. *Us.* You didn't speak to me for weeks after we split.'

'I tried! You wouldn't listen to me. I sent you messages, I tried to call . . .'

I stop, slumping back in my seat, defeated. My heart feels cloudy. Heavy. As if it's being held in some kind of invisible vice.

'Look, Clar, I didn't come here to argue. I just wanted to speak to you, have a proper conversation. Show you I've changed. On the day we split, I didn't know what happened at first. I didn't understand why you were so angry.'

Across the table, Clarissa lets out an irritated sigh.

'But I've had a lot of time to think about it,' I add.

'I was angry because I asked you a question and you stalled. The way you *looked* at me, Eric. It was like . . . shock mixed with fear and . . .'

'Maybe it was. I was kind of put on the spot. If you'd just . . .'

'Why is it my fault?'

Her voice grows higher, louder, but she's trying to keep things civil. She doesn't like to make a scene. A few of our fellow customers are looking in our direction. They're not being subtle.

Then again, isn't that what *we* used to do? Clarissa and I, when we went out. We'd reside in our own smug bubble, listening in on other people's conversations as though it were our own personal soap opera. Back when things were normal and the days, weeks, months – even years – that we knew we'd have together spanned wildly ahead of us, all enticing and wonderful.

'We can talk about it, I promise,' I say. 'I want you to know I've thought about it. You were right, I was just having a moment.'

Clarissa's brow furrows with apparent confusion. 'What do you mean?'

'Being away from you for an entire year has made everything clear. What I want to ask is . . . would you consider giving things another go?'

My heart is racing. The place is warm all of a sudden, growing warmer by the minute. I take a sip of my coffee, the artistic, foamy leaf on the top now distorted and spoiled, trying to conceal my shaky hands as they grip the mug.

Clarissa's face takes on a strange transformation. The confusion has vanished, replaced by something I never wanted to see. Sadness and pity.

Finally, her hand moves towards mine. I jolt at the touch, her soft skin against mine. Something I craved so badly just moments before, but now it's all wrong.

'Eric,' she says softly. 'I thought you knew. I'm seeing someone.'

I catch the woman on the table behind Clarissa glancing round, listening. Go on, I think. Listen. Take it home. Tell your friends about the drama. Tweet it.

'You are?'

Obviously, I'd expected it. Clarissa is, what Sean would call, a 'top catch'.

'Yes. Um . . . this is really awkward, but I honestly thought you knew. I'm pregnant, Eric – three months pregnant. It's all been a bit quick, a bit of a whirlwind, but I'm happy. *We're* happy.'

Yet again, the bottom has fallen out of my world. All because of one moment, one simple mistake.

Pregnant.

Clarissa is pregnant.

We sit, silent, until the place feels cold again and the awkwardness makes it impossible to continue. Clarissa pulls on her coat, softly tugging her silky hair from beneath the collar, and picks up her bag.

'I'll see you soon, Eric. OK?'

She gets up, weaving through the tables, and I watch her leave my life for a second time.

There's nothing more to be said.

This time, it's well and truly over.

Chapter 18

Steph

It's been a whole week and not a sound from next door.

My card is still there, the envelope propped against the glass within the growing pile of mail. I tried again, jabbing the doorbell, the seaside tune echoing from inside the house. Nobody's home.

I think about this on the journey to work, my mind on autopilot, guided to the office by familiarity and habit. I wonder if they'll come back. *When* they'll come back. Eric misses them, too – is it strange to miss someone you've never even met?

Once I reach the office, however, all thoughts of number 26 disappear, because a message from Alex pops up on the screen.

Still on for tomorrow?

The team night out is tomorrow, and if there's one thing that can distract me from Miles and his wonderful new life, it's an evening with Alex. He's funny and successful and attentive, not to mention gorgeous. We've exchanged emails for a couple of days, bravely testing the waters before jumping into messages, quickly venturing from 'professional chat' into 'mild flirting'.

It's kind of nostalgic. That excitement of waiting for the next ping of a message, all flustered and giddy, like we've regressed to our teenage years, where you'd sit in front of chunky desktop computers eagerly awaiting your crush to pop up on MSN Messenger and see how cool you are with your song lyric username that made you sound so deep and profound.

I cringe at the memory.

Of course. Wouldn't miss it. Xx

I want to let out a massive scream of joy. I'm tempted, but instead I rummage in my unicorn lunch bag for a cereal bar, because I didn't have time for breakfast. Suddenly, it hits me how quiet everyone is, just as Tamzin emerges from the corridor and into the office, her cheeks flushed a faint shade of pink.

'You OK?' I ask as she passes me and Jeff's little pod.

Her heels move softly on the carpet and she tucks a strand of chestnut hair behind one ear. There's something about her I can't quite place.

'Yes. I just had my review. It seems Ciaran's going to be . . .' She glimpses Jeff, then lowers her voice to a whisper, as if she's telling me a secret at the back of the class. '*Letting people go*. Everly Cope is downsizing.'

'I can hear you, you know,' says Jeff, not looking up from his monitor.

Tamzin ignores him and lets out a sigh. I can't tell if it's one of relief or nonchalance. Either way, it's obvious she's not feeling what I am feeling. Which is complete and utter dread.

Letting people go.

The words repeat themselves over and over in my head. I drop the cereal bar in the bin beside me. Suddenly, I'm not hungry.

'I think I'm OK,' Tamz confirms. 'I *think* I'm safe. Ciaran will let us know by the end of the week. He wanted to give us a heads-up, some warning to start looking elsewhere. Just in case.'

My heart is thudding too quickly in my chest.

'What are you going to do, Tamz?' I ask, swivelling round in my chair, trying to arrange my features into a normal, worried expression and not look like I'm absolutely fucking terrified. 'I mean, if it's *not* OK. What will you do? You've got a wedding coming up!'

I've seen the plans, the pros and cons list that's now transformed into the blueprint of the most extravagant event of next summer.

Tamz pauses, then shrugs. 'Who knows?' she says, looking dreamily towards the window, where light bobs prettily on the waves of the harbour.

Playfully, I click my fingers in front of her face.

'Tamz! Earth to Tamz. This is serious shit.'

She gathers herself before perching on the edge of my desk, moving aside my mug and the little framed photo of Amanda and me at the zoo three years ago. In it, Amanda's wearing a birthday-girl sash and holding a parrot with a terrified grimace, and it's never been more relatable.

'Well, to be honest, I've been thinking of leaving for a while. Seeing what my options are. Or maybe I'll take some time out and see where things lead. I could go travelling!'

Now she's laughing, seeing all the possibilities. The freedom.

Tamz is in danger of losing her job and she's *laughing*.

'I'm so lucky I have Patrick. It could be much worse.' She throws a sympathetic smile into the distance.

So much worse.

'Good luck, Steph,' Tamz says, giving me sisterly pat on the shoulder before heading back to her desk.

I'm glued to my seat, feeling all the colour drain from my face, feeling my hands tremble, my breathing rise and fall, rise and fall, too quick, *too quick*.

Suddenly, I'm very warm. Sweat seeps through my blouse. I have a meeting scheduled with Ciaran at eleven.

Wondrously, I manage to quell the panic just long enough to utter a question.

'Jeff?' I ask, whispering across the desk. 'When did this happen? Why are we downsizing?'

'Didn't you get the email?' he asks. 'Last week? It was high priority.'

I vaguely remember an email. An email with the subject heading of: *Very Important One-to-Ones Next Week! All to Attend!!!!!!* Six exclamation points and everything.

In my defence, there were *eight* exclamation points when the email went round asking us not to feed the seagulls outside because they were starting to attack people. And there were a whole *ten* on the one advising us not to steal other people's milk from the fridge: *There will be repercussions!!!!!!!!!!*

So I *could* be forgiven for not realising just how important these one-to-ones are, that this is apparently DEFCON 1 and that maybe I should have read it properly rather than clicking 'accept' on the invite and filing it away.

Shit, shit, shit, *shit*.

'Ciaran does tend to overdramatise sometimes,' I say simply, as if it explains my stupidity. 'I didn't think it was *that* serious.'

Jeff shakes his head. Jeff has no need to panic. Jeff, like Ciaran, is in his mid-forties and has been at Everly Cope for the best part of two decades. Jeff is also one of Ciaran's best mates, which helps greatly in ensuring his arse stays firmly put. It also helps in ensuring I behave myself, because who knows what office gossip Jeff might drop at his next dinner round at Ciaran's.

Unlike Jeff and Tamz, I don't possess the ability to stay chilled through all of this. My mind is in overdrive. I have enough savings to last me three more months in rent and bills and that's it. Just three.

'There's been talk of a restructure for a while now,' says Jeff, leaning forwards into the gap between our screens, and I'm hit by a waft of his coffee breath. 'Not surprised it's finally happening. Saskia's team has lost someone already - Connor's been let go.'

'But how can they . . . wait. Connor? *Connor* has been let go?'

Jeff nods slowly, as if proud to be the one to divulge. I get up to peek round to the other side of the office in some thinly veiled attempt at hope. It swiftly deflates. Sure enough, Connor's desk – which usually boasts an array of little cacti in decorative pots hand-painted by his son – is bare.

'Already?' I mutter.

'He didn't take it very well. He stormed out first thing this morning. Never heard so much swearing from Connor.'

'Fuck.' If *he's* gone, there's no hope for me.

'I know. Terrible,' Jeff confirms.

'But Connor was great.'

'Wasn't performing as well as one would think.'

I'm tempted to ask Jeff, workplace oracle, how he thinks I'm doing, but decide that maybe I don't want to know. I have until eleven before my fate is revealed.

The office is too hot. I can smell the faint scent of sweat and it's coming from me. All the concentration I had ten minutes ago is no more and when I click on an email, open it, the words are there but nothing goes in. Everything is fuzzy.

Think happy thoughts, think happy thoughts. It's a fucking stupid mantra, but I need something – anything – to distract me. Maybe that's why so many people dedicate so much time to pasting 'inspirational' quotes onto sunset pictures for social media; maybe they need a distraction and even *that's* a godsend. Like, if they look at it long enough, they'll believe it. It all makes sense now.

At quarter to eleven, I'm in the toilets. Bag at my feet, I'm dabbing at my armpits with a balled-up tissue. Nerves make me sweaty and I've gone overboard with the roll-on deodorant, so I'm trying to even things out. Nerves also make me pee, which I've done three times already, as well as cried. I'm surprised there's any liquid left to come out of me, but even so, I've vowed not to leave this cubicle until I'm presentable.

Looking up at the ceiling, I take another deep breath, get up from the toilet and head for the mirror. I don't like it in here; it reminds me of *back then*, after Mum died. I went back to work after a month because work was a helpful distraction, only to find myself hiding in the toilets, fighting the urge to cry at the slightest reminder. Being out of sight, I quickly discovered, was better than being around everyone else – the colleagues treading on eggshells around me. Some didn't talk to me at all, just passed me with an awkward smile as if losing a parent was contagious. *Be extra kind to Steph, she's lost her mum.*

I wash my hands and rummage in my bag for my emergency mascara and concealer. The mascara is clumpy and needs to be replaced. I try not to care.

Heading towards Ciaran's office at the far end of the long corridor, I try to calm myself, to keep my heart from racing. I concentrate on my breathing: in, out. Slow, slow. I keep my eyes on the path ahead, the grey carpet, doing everything in my power to stay calm. If I'm going to get fired, I'll do so with dignity. With a smile.

I'm outside Ciaran's door.

He smiles when he sees me – the calm before the storm. I take a seat opposite as he clicks away at his laptop, drawing out the moment as if I'm some TV talent show finalist and the eager audience awaits.

'Steph Higgins,' he says finally.

I recall sitting in this very chair on the day I was interviewed, shuffling with nerves as Ciaran and Saskia asked me all the questions: Why do you want to work here? What makes you the right fit?

I told them I needed a new challenge. I conveniently left out the part where I was grieving and needed something to get me away from everything, from all the ghosts at home. Here, I could be someone new and different – the quirky, adventurous Steph, not 'Steph who lost her mum, bless her'.

Ciaran gives me the same smile now as he turns to face me.

Breathe, breathe.

'I know there's talk in the office about what's going on. So I'll be straight with you – we're restructuring. Sadly, I have to let people go.'

Breathe. Do not cry. Breeeathe!

He pauses before continuing. 'Ultimately, this wasn't my decision – orders from above. I'm trying to retain as many as possible. Having to . . . well, it breaks my heart.'

'Having to sack people?' I ask.

Ciaran sits back, surprised. I feel a pang of pity. He's always been nice to me, with nothing but praise in my one-to-ones. But let's face it, I'm the least likely to be needed here. I know what's coming.

'The thing is, Steph . . .' he says, 'your job is safe, but it's going to be merged with a few others. Essentially, you'll be asked to take on more responsibility. I know it could be worse.'

'Very. So I get to stay?'

He nods and relief floods through me.

'Thank fuck,' I say.

Thankfully, he laughs.

'The thing is, you're great at what you do. I don't think there's been a month where you haven't hit your targets. You get on well with everyone and I know you're wasted here.'

'Sorry?'

'You're too good for the role you do.'

'But I just do my job the way I'm supposed to do it.' What's so good about that? I wonder. I do my job, to the best of my ability, *because I need my job*.

He nods. 'Yes, but personally? I think you've outgrown the role. You've proven you can take on bigger tasks, bigger projects. I don't want to get rid of you, even though, frankly, you'd be better off in a different job where you can really thrive.

'There's a vacancy in the Manchester office,' he continues. 'That's who we're merging with; it'll be the main hub of Everly Cope. They need a team leader. It's a new role – you'd be managing a team of six administrative staff. It's an eight grand salary increase and there are better prospects for career advancement. They need someone to start asap, so if you want it, it's yours.'

His words fall and land.

'You don't want to sack me. You want to *promote* me.'

'I don't want to sack anyone, Steph. But yes. You're the best fit.'

The shock, mixed with relief, makes my hands tremble.

'Right,' I say, suddenly still. And then: 'Manchester?'

'Yes. The job will be in the Manchester office, not far from the city centre. You'll love it.'

The room spins. Manchester. I'll have to move to Manchester.

Ciaran's looking at me expectantly, awaiting my response. Manchester. A new city, a new job, a new life. Better still, I won't have to lie any more.

'What do you think?' he asks.

I wanted a new adventure and it's fallen straight into my lap.

'Yes!' I shriek. 'Oh my God! Yes, I'll take it.'

Chapter 19

Eric

A prospective housemate is looking at me, awaiting a response. His name is Daniel.

'So you're all right with the Saturday thing then, yeah?' he asks again.

Behind him, Lloyd is nodding. *Just say yes!* he mouths, tapping at an imaginary watch.

Daniel is about six foot tall and in his late twenties. He arrived early, parking his bicycle outside. He seems pleasant. Professional. He'd stepped into the house, glancing everywhere, taking in the kitchen and living room as though measuring them up in his head. The bedroom is big enough, he'd said. Perfect, actually. Until he let out an uncertain sigh.

'The thing is, I have my rugby club over for drinks every Saturday,' he explained. 'Do you think the living room is big enough?'

Now, he's waiting for my answer. Lloyd glances from Daniel to me, a hint of warning in his eyes. He knows this is ultimately my decision and he knows how I'd feel about a team of rugby players descending on the quiet house every Saturday without fail.

Normally, I'd be upfront. I'd tell him that no, that is not all right and that perhaps we're not the best match. But the trouble is, Daniel is by far the most promising candidate we've seen all day.

Finally, I tack on my best smile. 'Perfectly fine! But we're still interviewing, so we'll give you a call when we've made our decision.'

I watch him cycle off down the street five minutes later. When I turn back into the hallway, Lloyd's waiting.

'Seriously? Come on now, Eric. He's allowed to have guests.'

'An entire rugby team? On a Saturday? I like to chill out on Saturdays. They might be loud.'

Lloyd shoots me a look.

'Fine, he was probably the best of the bunch. How many interviews is that now? Nine?' I consult the list on my phone.

'Yep,' Lloyd confirms. 'And two no-shows. There's still time to call Hugh.'

Snatching a beer from the fridge, I slump onto the sofa, my T-shirt warm against my body. It feels hot, even though outside there's a noticeable chill. We haven't left the house all day, just showing potential new tenants around the various rooms and asking the same questions over and over. Showing them everything, from the kitchen sink to the windows and the one creaky stair, as though it's all vastly important. I'm exhausted.

Someone, *someone* in the ninety-odd responses I've had so far has to be a good match. I send a silent prayer to whoever might be listening. The Patron Saint of Housemates, perhaps.

'What do you reckon, then?' Lloyd asks. 'So far we've interviewed eleven people . . . that's nowhere near the number of applicants we have. We'll need to set up another interview day. Or five. Unless we can choose someone asap.'

The beer is cool and bitter against my throat, much-needed. 'I guess we'll have to. Daniel seemed perfect, if it wasn't for the Saturday thing.'

I sit back, almost sinking into the couch, mentally assessing the candidates.

There was Charlie, the 22-year-old, who turned up late, took one look at our chore rota and scoffed, claiming, 'I do chores, but when I'm in the right mood, yeah? My head's really got to be in it.'

Then there was the guy who brought along his girlfriend who would be moving in with him. 'I know you said no couples, but I thought if you got to know us first . . .' he'd said as his girlfriend pulled out a tape measure and started pointing at where she'd put their sofa.

'Oh,' she'd said, wrinkling her nose at my framed *Ghostbusters* poster. 'Could that, like, be moved elsewhere?'

'What about Ruby?' Lloyd asks, snapping me out of the awful memory.

On paper, Ruby, like Daniel, was another perfect candidate; twenty-nine, worked in the civil service, loved sixties jazz and roller derby. She showed up early, her dazzling smile instantly lighting up the room – until she laid eyes on Freddy.

'Ruby hates cats. I could see it – the minute she saw Freddy, it was like her whole face changed. She didn't want to go near him. She insisted she was all right, but . . . no. Not the right fit.'

'True. You can't live here and not get on with Freddy. He's part of the furniture.'

'Exactly! It was his home first. I just want someone we both gel with, you know?'

Lloyd nods. 'I still reckon you're overthinking this. We'll try again tomorrow.'

'Right.'

'I'm going to bed now – I've got a training course in the morning. We'll find someone, don't worry. And like I said, if the right housemate doesn't show, we have Hugh on standby.'

Sighing, I reach for the remote and flick on the TV, vaguely searching for something to watch. I'm thirty seconds in before I realise I'm just mindlessly flicking through, not taking in any information. I hate this feeling. Sinking. As though I have a hundred things to do but can't bring myself to do any of them.

Things are changing. My home is changing; soon, there will be someone new. Everything is changing, but I'm stuck.

My already fruitless search comes to a halt at the clink of keys outside the door. Hushed voices outside, voices that grow louder in the hallway. Sean and Kate come almost tumbling through into the living room, laughing, holding on to each other as if they're sixteen again, their cheeks flushed pink by the cold.

'Hey!' says Kate. 'How did the interviews go? Did you find anyone?'

'Not yet. I'm still holding out hope.'

I turn to Sean, fixing him with a stare. 'So, did you know about Clarissa?'

'What about Clarissa?'

'That's she's pregnant.'

There's a silence. The jollity has gone, replaced by an awkwardness that's fallen like a sheet, coating us all. Kate slips onto the sofa while Sean stands there, looking shifty.

Kate pipes up first. 'I thought everyone knew.'

'Well, I didn't.'

'Eric, what's this about?' says Sean carefully. 'Why does it even matter?'

'It matters to me. I went to see her.'

'Why?'

My heart pounds, faster and faster, and I know, judging by the looks on their faces, that I've done something horribly wrong.

'Because being the idiot I am, I thought there was a chance we could get back together.'

Kate's expression is unreadable. 'Eric . . . Clarissa's been seeing Ade for months.'

'I thought you were well over her,' adds Sean. 'Besides, I'm pretty sure Luk brought it up last week in the group chat.'

The group chat. The chat I muted, because I was fed up. Fed up with all the baby milestones. The playdates. The pictures of days out. The playful competitiveness and little jokey comments about 'the other half' that ooze love. Moments shared among husbands, dads and actual adults – a club from which I'm excluded. Yes, the group chat – the chat in which I'm invisible.

'Well, I'm fully aware now.'

'Where did this all come from?' asks Sean.

He's acting all concerned, but I know they'll be discussing this later. I shake my head. I don't want to be in this room any more – it's stifling and it's hot and it's cold at the same time. The walls feel as if they're closing in, just like they did in the pub last Halloween, when I watched Clarissa leave.

I could have tried harder. I could have chased after her, tried to persuade her to come back, to talk. I didn't.

Suddenly, I want to be anywhere but in the stuffy house.

'I'll see you later,' I say and head for the door, grabbing my cardigan as I go.

I don't know where I'm going, but I head down the path, grateful for the breeze. I turn left down the street, beneath the trees that line Chapel Gardens, then stop.

Outside number 28, lugging a hefty bin liner down the garden path in a pair of fluffy bear-shaped slippers, is Steph.

Chapter 20

Steph

I clutch the phone, awaiting the inevitable line: *Mum would be proud of you*. There's a pause, as if Amanda stops herself.

'We're so happy for you,' she says instead. 'Has it sunk in yet?'

'Kind of. It's starting to feel real. I went through all the pros and cons immediately after the meeting.'

Which is true. Walking back from Ciaran's office, light-headed from the shock, I sat down to write the list. Pros: better job, more money, brand-new city, new people. Cons: further from Amanda, no Alex. I explain everything to Amanda.

'There will plenty of Alexes,' suggests Amanda helpfully. 'I hope you're celebrating tonight.'

'Already got it covered!' I laugh before we say goodbye.

I don't have it covered. The bin is heavy and leaves a thin trail of juice as I hurry through to the front door. I'm in my oldest (yet most comfy) pair of pyjamas and teddy bear slippers and my hair is in dire need of a wash. I *should* celebrate though, somehow.

Cold air hits me as I open the front door and as I pad down the path, I see him.

Eric from next-door-but-one is walking along the street, head bowed towards the ground. He stops when he sees me.

'Hey!'

Seriously, he really needs to stop running into me when I'm looking like shit. I flip the lid of the wheelie bin open, stuffing the bag further and further inside. I tug my pyjama top down; I know the bottoms are so old they're see-through.

'Hey! How are you?' I ask. 'Did you manage to find a housemate?'

'Sadly not. Still looking.' He runs a hand through his dark curly hair and releases a breath of frustration. 'It's an arduous task.'

Eric looks slightly different from when I last saw him. More stubble. It suits him. He's wearing a cardigan over a black T-shirt with an image of a B-movie poster on the front. Faded yet still bright. I ask him if he's going anywhere.

'I was going for a drive,' he says, shrugging. 'Just need to get out for a bit.'

'The housemate search *really* not going well, then?'

'It's not that, it's . . . well, it's kind of that.'

From above, the lights of Sarah and Ash's flat come on, bathing us in a soft spotlight. Music starts to thump down onto the newly illuminated path, only serving to make number 26 seem cloaked in darkness, spooky behind the hedge.

'Looks a bit creepy, doesn't it?' Eric asks, following my gaze.

He's right. The only other light comes from passing cars – orbs that momentarily light up the old brick, casting faint, moving shadows. From where we stand, the house seems imposing. Empty.

'They must still be on holiday,' offers Eric. 'Anyway, how are things with you?'

My pink teddy bear slippers feel cold against the path. Eric's noticed them. I catch him smirking.

'Present from my niece,' I explain.

'Excuses,' he chuckles.

'Leave my terrible fashion sense out of this. My slippers are great. As for me, I'm good. Wonderful, actually. Had some good news today!'

'Oh?'

'I got a promotion. Signed the contract this afternoon. I'll be moving away, a whole new start.'

Eric stuffs his hands in his pockets. I can hear his car keys.

'Moving away? That's a shame.'

'A shame?' I fold my arms jokingly.

'To see you go, I mean. Sorry. That came out all wrong.'

'Ha! I knew what you meant. Just winding you up.'

'That's amazing news, though. Congratulations!'

He hesitates, smiling, his dark eyes meeting mine. I know they're hazel. In this light, they appear more brown than green.

'Well . . .' says Eric. 'I was going to go for a drive, but seeing as you're here, *and* you've been promoted today, how about we go for a drink round the corner? My treat.'

'That would be nice, actually. Um, I need to change.'

'Nah, you don't. Wear the slippers. I dare you.'

'Funny.'

'I'll buy all the drinks if you wear the slippers.'

'Nice try. No. Come on in if you like – I won't be long.'

Eric follows me up the path and into the flat.

'I love the slippers really, you know,' he says. 'They're cute.'

I kick off the bears and hurry to wash my hands before grabbing some clothes: skinny jeans from the chair pile, a black woolly jumper that's hung on the rail. I spray on some dry shampoo from my half-empty can, and slip on my trainers.

I notice Eric glancing around my little sanctuary.

'Your place is nice,' he says. 'Cosy.'

'Tiny, you mean.'

I'm suddenly embarrassed at all the clutter. Another thing to add to the list of pros: I can be different in Manchester. I can be tidy and notoriously organised.

Leaving Eric perusing my bookshelf full of now outdated travel guides and cherished favourites – possibly the only thing I *do* keep meticulously in order – I hurry to the bathroom to change.

A couple of minutes later, I emerge dressed and suitably spritzed with perfume. Eric stands by the clothing rail, his gaze fixed on the boxes.

'Started packing already, then?' he asks.

Something in me, something protective and fearful and embarrassed all at once, makes me stride over and hide them again, pushing them further back, concealing them safely behind two coats.

'Not yet. They're just something I've been putting off.'

He shrugs and it's forgotten. 'Ready?'

The Instagram photo I've just posted is very creative, if I do say so myself. It's of two large glasses of Pinot Grigio, courtesy of Eric, in muted tones, with a filter that brings out the sparkle:

Onwards and upwards! #Promotion #Celebrate #NewAdventure #Proud.

Thirty-three likes.

Eric returns with the second round of drinks and places them on the table.

'Typical,' Eric says. 'I finally meet a nice neighbour and she moves away.'

'Now I *know* you're just saying that.'

'Why would I make it up?' He smiles again.

'Because you're being nice and polite and neighbourly.'

He shrugs. I kind of share the feeling – I mean, I finally make a friend in the street and it's time to leave him behind.

We're at the same table as we were last time, by the window; Eric seemed drawn to it. I like it – it's perfect for people-watching. I don't recognise anyone in here despite the pub being so close to where I live and I glance around as if I'm going to see the man who takes in my parcels, or the mystery family of number 26, even though I have no idea what they look like.

'Know what?' I say. 'I hope the people in number 26 come back before I move. I'd love to see them.'

'Why?'

Eric leans forwards, his eyes bright beneath the low light. They're greener now. I watch as a stray curl flops over his forehead. He pushes it away. I didn't notice before just how attractive he is. But maybe that's just because I'm in a good mood and the wine is nice and I have a tendency to overthink.

'I feel bad about them just vanishing.'

'They didn't vanish – they're just on holiday. They've turned all their lights off. That's what people do when they go away for a few days. I'm almost jealous. Wish I was sunning it up somewhere.'

I take another sip. I know I should be spending tonight thinking of Manchester and being all self-congratulatory, but something's weighing on my mind.

'I'm just not convinced.'

Eric shoots me a kind look. Kind, or concerned?

'Why?' he asks. 'You don't know them, they don't know you.'

That's the problem, I think bitterly.

I put down my glass, ready to explain.

'I feel a bit responsible, that's all. The other night, the

night before they apparently left . . . well, let's just say I wasn't too nice.'

Eric looks confused now. He pauses from taking a drink, his eyes locked on mine, and I feel bad all over again.

'What do you mean? I thought you said you didn't know them?'

'I'd had a bad day. And they were playing something on the piano, something I didn't want to hear. I knocked on the wall to get them to stop. I knocked really hard, and shouted, and they *did* stop eventually. They just haven't played since.'

'Oh,' is all Eric says.

'See? That's why I feel responsible.'

He shrugs. 'It's probably not as bad as you think. Maybe they just thought you were annoyed, so stopped. Some people are just . . . well, they live in their own little worlds and don't realise how much noise they make.'

'What if they're super nice people and I've offended them?'

'And what if they're not? They could be lovely, *or* they could be awful. They could be mean, for all we know. Or they could be the nicest people you meet - they could cross your path again . . . unexpectedly, like in *The Five People You Meet in Heaven*'.

'I see you paid attention to my bookshelf.'

He grins. 'I always snoop on people's bookshelves. How can you not peek? I find it hard to resist. It reveals a lot about someone.'

'And what does my collection reveal?'

'Hmm. Travel, the classics, thrillers, a good dose of para-normal young adult . . . and top marks for Stephen King. I find you very interesting by your choices alone.'

I reach across the table, poke him in the arm. He sits back with a fake gasp.

'Hey!' he says. 'I'm saying I like it. It shows you're fun. Our tastes are similar. *Five People* is one of my all-time favourites.'

'Really?'

'Yep. I've read it six times. But in any case, I think you're worrying too much about this next-door thing. I'm sure all is fine, it was just a misunderstanding.'

'But after that night, there was no more music.'

Eric looks at me, smiles again. I peer into the glass of wine, swirling it like the professionals do, watching the liquid move round and round.

'So you'd had a bad day,' he says. 'If you don't mind me asking, what happened?'

Chapter 21

Steph

The memory of what happened makes my skin prickle uncomfortably, my recollection of the evening hazy, as if my mind is doing everything in its power to stop me from revisiting it.

But Eric is sitting there, waiting for me to elaborate, his eyes searching mine for the answer.

The pub seems like the strangest place to be talking about it, but the chatter, the clinking glasses, the company of these unknown people, is somewhat calming.

'I was in Tesco,' I begin. 'I'd finished work and went to pick up some dinner.'

I remember that part clearly, the *before*, when I felt normal. Trainers shuffling along the tiled floor, wandering the aisles on autopilot. Loading food into my basket: vegetables, pasta, fruit, a bottle of the cheapest wine.

'I went to queue at the checkout and then I saw her.'

'Who?'

'My mum. Only it *wasn't* my mum. She's been dead for three years.'

Eric runs a finger along the side of his glass. Up and down, up and down – I watch, mesmerised.

'Wait,' he says. 'What are you saying? That you saw a ghost?'

I shake my head. 'No, it was just a woman who looked like her. *So* much like her that for a second I thought it was her. And . . . well, I panicked. I freaked out.'

Just thinking about it makes my heart race, makes my limbs shake all over again, just like they did at Mum's funeral, when I watched her coffin being lowered into the ground. I had to watch, helpless, unable to do anything but look and scream and cry and try everything not to throw myself in, as well.

Tesco was busy, the queue was long. As I looked up from the phone I was mindlessly scrolling through, numbing my tiredness with other people's reels of life, I saw her. Her appearance caught me off guard, made the breath catch in my throat.

She was further ahead, stepping from the queue and towards a self-checkout. *It's her*, I thought. *It's Mum.*

She had Mum's hair – red, just past her shoulders, with a hint of copper, like the dye she used to cover her sneaking, beautiful greys. A black jacket and jeans, not dissimilar to Mum's own. And when she turned to get the attention of an assistant, I saw another flash of her pale face.

Mum's face.

I tried to move, but my limbs didn't comply. I stood there, frozen, aware of customers tutting and sighing behind me, hearing the collective hiss of their displeasure as the robotic voice of the next self-service checkout announced its freedom with a booming thank-you. But all I could see was Mum.

She's right there, I was saying in my head, maybe aloud – *she's there and I can reach her.* But my feet were heavy and unmoving and the lights were too bright and the noise all-consuming. I could feel the line of people growing behind me, so many people, a snake made of flustered faces and tired eyes and annoyance. They glared at me, the woman who wouldn't move.

I watched her as she swiped her groceries. Swiped her card, collected her shopping, smiled – the way Mum always smiled. Someone pushed past me – a woman; her arm dug into my shoulder, but I barely felt it.

She said, 'Well, if you're not fucking moving . . .'

The shop blurred before my eyes: the bright lights, the blue, the people, the faces. The basket fell from my grip, sending the wine crashing to the tiles, erupting into a blood-red pool of liquid and glass. An apple rolled beneath a magazine stand. I watched it escape.

Then my legs gave way.

'That's when it all gets hazy,' I tell Eric.

I tell him about the fall, the people, the vague bits I've remembered and pieced together as if it wasn't really me, like I'd stepped outside of myself for a moment, my body hovering, moving weightlessly through my surroundings. He nods, understanding. Even though now it sounds so silly and weird.

'So the woman was just a stranger?' asks Eric, intrigued.

'Definitely. Just a random woman who happened to look like Mum. At least, she did in my head. I mean, I knew it wasn't *her*. Mum's dead. And the woman was buying quinoa, for starters. Mum never liked that. And brandy. Mum hated brandy. She had too much of it one night when she was eighteen and it made her incredibly sick.'

Eric laughs, and I'm glad.

'I must have just caught the similarity and went into panic mode. It made sense later.'

Eric smiles kindly as he sits back in his seat. 'I've heard that happens a lot. We might see someone who looks like a lost loved one. Or we might hear someone with a similar voice, and it's a shock to the system. Maybe that's what ghosts *are*. Maybe that's where the whole idea evolved from.

Memories and emotions stored up until we see something that triggers them.'

'You might be onto something there. After Mum died, it was strange. I was caught in this weird limbo of time and for months afterwards, I'd just forget she was gone, you know? Some days it wouldn't register. I'd wake in the morning thinking I was going to see her soon, or wondering what she was up to, but then reality would all come flooding back and I knew I wouldn't see her ever again. I wondered why I was being punished like that.'

'The human mind can play awful tricks on us,' says Eric. 'It's not a punishment, it's normal. It's your brain trying to process the grief.'

'I don't remember much after collapsing,' I continue, 'apart from being outside afterwards. It was cold. I was sitting on the ground, propped upright against the wall. There were people surrounding me, keeping me safe. I remember a man with a beige coat and a kind face, who rubbed my back slowly, telling me it was going to be OK. Someone called an ambulance and I was taken home. I was still in shock, I think.

'And then . . .' I look down at the table, because I feel terrible and don't want to see any judgement in Eric's kind eyes. 'Later, after I'd slept for a while, I had a bath and waited for next door to start playing the piano like they always did. I hoped it'd be something fun, something to take my mind off everything. And then the music started and it was possibly the worst song I could have heard that evening.'

'What was it?'

'"Sealed with a Kiss",' I tell him, trying not to let the tune back into my head, to stop it from filtering through and infecting everything happy. 'It was one of Mum's favourites. She used to sing it to us when we were kids. It was played at her funeral.'

She was sick.

She was sick and I wasn't there.

'Steph,' says Eric, and he reaches across the table for my hand, the scratchy sleeve of his cardigan brushing against my skin.

His touch is warm, comforting as his fingers close around mine, and it suddenly occurs to me how long it's been since I last held someone's hand.

Miles. Miles was the last time I experienced real human connection. No wonder it feels like electricity is fizzing through every nerve right now.

'Honestly, you don't have to talk about it if you don't want to,' says Eric.

Nodding, I take another sip of my drink, grateful for it, for this place, for company.

'I don't mind,' I tell him. 'It helps.'

'So what happened after that?'

'I shouted for next door to stop. They didn't. So I yelled some more. I punched the wall – kept hitting it and screaming and swearing until they finally stopped. Look . . .' I show him the fading red marks on my knuckles. 'The music stopped abruptly. I thought someone was about to come round to tell me off for the noise – or at least the swearing. But nobody came. There was nothing. Just silence. Since then, there's been no music.

'I wanted to say sorry, but the next day, nobody was home, so I posted a card. But they just seem to have upped and left. I can't help thinking I had something to do with it.'

Eric's eyes widen. 'OK. I understand why you'd think that way, but honestly? It's probably pure coincidence.'

'Is it? They've been at that piano every day for as long as I've lived here. To stop like that . . . at that very moment? They stopped because of me.'

'Why would they? It's happened to all of us. I think we've all pissed off a neighbour at some point. When my ex ended things, it was Halloween and I brutally attacked someone's pumpkin because I was angry and upset and drunk.'

'You *what*?'

'Yep. Kicked it, watched the pieces of its stupid smiley face get pummelled into the pavement. Did I feel guilty the next day? Oh yes. I felt *terrible*, so I went over to apologise like a child.'

I'm laughing now. Wildly. 'That's so bad.'

'Hey! Not my proudest moment. But it happens. We get on with life. Look, number 26 might have stopped playing for a host of reasons. They might have thought you were banging on the wall because you were trying to sleep.'

'And after that? They haven't played since. Explain that away, Mr Holmes.'

Eric smirks. 'Holiday. I can guarantee it. You probably just reminded them to pack their skis.'

'I don't believe you, but I'll accept it. For now.'

'We'll find out soon,' Eric says. 'When they come back.'

Sighing, I gaze out into the dark street. 'I wish I'd bothered to get to know them. That's what I hate about all this – all I want to do is say sorry, but I don't know how. They've lived on the other side of me since I moved in, so why are we strangers?'

Eric shrugs, the question hanging in the air. Suddenly, he sits up.

'How about this? How about we make a promise – that when the residents of number 26 return, we get to know them?'

'That sounds good. I just hope they get back before I move away.'

Disappointment flickers briefly across Eric's face, so quick I almost miss it.

He looks at the table before smiling back up at me. 'I'm sure they will.'

'I can be a good neighbour,' I say theatrically, declaring my resolution with eyes full of determination and resolve. That's a lie – my acting is, quite frankly, rubbish. 'I *will* be a good neighbour. I can . . . invite them round for drinks. Do a barbecue! I can make some cookies and take them round in a neat little basket, like they always do on those American TV shows.'

'I'm a neighbour and I like cookies,' Eric hints.

I throw a beer mat in his direction. He manages to duck out of the way, laughing, and places it back on the table.

'So, how's that for a plan?' he says. 'New mission: get to know number 26.'

'I like that idea,' I say. 'I really do.'

I spend most of my days apologising, yet the one time I mean it, I'm unable to. Which was probably the worst thing about seeing the woman I thought was Mum in the supermarket.

If she really *was* a ghost, at least I could have told her how sorry I am.

An hour later, we scramble out of the pub and cross the road towards home, lost in conversation of movies and childhood nostalgia. My heart is full with a new sense of promise, thinking of our new pact – that I, Stephanie Higgins, vow to be a better neighbour to number 26 Chapel Gardens. And not just number 26. *Everyone.* Everyone in the world.

OK, so I might be a little tipsy.

Eric's busy describing the plot of his screenplay.

'There are various spirits, who attach themselves to each of the new residents,' says Eric, who has also had one too many, so he's veering off somewhat and it's funny. He smiles a lot when he talks about his work.

As we round the corner into Chapel Gardens, dusky light filtering through the trees and onto the pavement, Eric frowns. 'There are just some little bits I haven't worked out yet. *Why* do they attach themselves to each resident? It may be a haunted house, but it's different. As if it's not the house itself, you know? It's like . . . like . . . something deeper, maybe.'

Our houses are close and our footsteps slow in unison as we talk, as if not wanting the evening to end.

I've been dropping him suggestions for the past hour, dissecting scenes from our favourite horrors. I've been busy trying to convince him to set it a few decades earlier.

'No phones!' was my reasoning. 'So many plots can be spoiled by GPS and tracking apps.'

'Maybe it's the nineties,' he says now. 'I like that idea.'

'Early or late? I mean, there could be . . .'

I trail off. We're standing outside Eric's gate now. Behind him, standing before his front door, is a figure, cloaked in darkness.

Eric follows my gaze, turning. The man is tall, his outline dark in the limited light, against the pale front door.

'Um, hello?' says Eric tentatively.

At the sound of Eric's voice, the figure jumps, startled. A man. A man with chin-length hair and a brown jacket. He bounds down the path out of the darkness, deliberately leaping over the last step as if competing for the long jump.

'Hey!' he says brightly. 'Are you Eric?'

Eric nods.

'Brilliant! God, I'm *so* sorry. I should have been here hours ago but I left work late and I didn't have your number and . . . I've really screwed it now, haven't I? Anyway . . .'

He holds out his hand for Eric to shake and shakes mine, too, with enthusiasm, offering us both a beaming smile.

'I'm Jude,' the man says. 'You're probably wondering what I'm doing here at this weird hour. I'm sorry to have turned up on your doorstep like this so late, but . . . I'm here about the room.'

Chapter 22

Eric

There's an abundance of hope in this man's eyes that's hard to ignore. He stands there on the path, searching my expression as if I'm about to throw open the door and suggest an impromptu party.

'It's gone ten,' I tell him. 'We did the interviews earlier.'

'Ah, dammit. That was my fault. I was late from work. Rushed here and before you know it, my phone's dead and I'm lost in Redland. I must have walked past this street twice and never realised. Tucked away, isn't it? Kind of nice.'

I stand here in the cold, watching our breath on the air, faced with this awkward predicament. I can't exactly turn him away now. Steph is beside me, and I see all hope of inviting her inside diminish in a puff of smoke.

'How long have you been standing there?' she asks.

'About fifteen minutes, maybe. I knocked but there was no answer. I thought I'd hang about for a bit just in case, *et voilà*, here you are. Never give up, as they say! Worked out for the best, I reckon. We must share some kind of psychic bond.'

'That's a good start,' says Steph, who's smiling broadly, clearly charmed – if not a little amused – by the presence of Jude.

Jude. I think back to the list earlier, the spreadsheet that I made containing all the details of the SpareRoom candidates, or at least what they were willing to share. Which included Jude Harris; thirty-five, a bartender, likes music, books and, most importantly, cats. To be fair, he answered the ad pretty thoroughly.

Jude glances from me to Steph. 'Ah, I get it,' he says solemnly. 'The room's gone already, hasn't it?'

'It hasn't, actually,' pipes up Steph. 'Has it, Eric?'

She's grinning at me. Seriously? He's just arrived and already he's charming the socks off Steph. And then I wonder: am I jealous? Do I fancy Steph?

She's my neighbour. I repeat that in my head. *She's just my neighbour and we were just out for a drink.* Steph's lovely. Steph's great. Steph has been some company on a night when I've been feeling terrible. Steph isn't Clarissa.

Jude is still on the path, rearranging the mustard-coloured scarf he's wearing, tucked into his brown jacket. He's smart, casually so, and makes me look like I've just hauled myself out of bed and rolled into some clothes. Which, let's face it, isn't too far from the truth most days.

'Catch you later, then!' Steph says, a playful look in her eyes before she heads up the path to number 28.

I turn to Jude.

'Sorry, mate,' he says loudly as Steph searches for her keys.

They jingle, the only sound in the quiet street . . . besides Jude. His loud voice carries over the bushes separating us from number 26.

'Did I interrupt what was meant to be a romantic night? Shit. I did, didn't I? I can go if you want. I can come back tomorrow if you two were about to . . .' He curls his hands into a gesture I'm sure he assumes is erotic and I can't find my own key fast enough.

'*Just get in the house*,' I hiss.

The door swings open and I almost push him inside.

'Sorry, mate. Was only checking.'

He's been here less than a minute and I'm already irritated, no doubt because I'm tired, and a little tipsy . . . and Steph has made her escape. I'll offer Jude a cup of tea, usher him quickly around the house and tell him we'll be in touch. No harm in that, surely.

In the hallway, I switch on the lights, illuminating the long corridor with its high ceilings and old Victorian features. Over the years they've been painted over, modernised, but there's no mistaking the soul in the house, the years of history deep within its bricks.

'This is a great house,' says Jude, looking around as if it's a museum, taking in the details as though he can't see the threadbare carpet, the chipped paint on the skirting boards and the bad paint job in the hall. As if it's all invisible. 'Really nice. Old bones, you know?'

'That's my room,' I say, pointing to the door at the far end of the corridor. 'Here's the kitchen, clearly. I'll show you Sean's room – he'll be leaving soon.'

He follows me upstairs, the old wood creaking beneath us, and I push the doors open to reveal Sean's spacious double room. His stuff has already been packed into neat little boxes, piled to one side.

'It's a good size,' I say, reeling off my spiel. I've been uttering this stuff all day and can guarantee I'll be saying it in my sleep. 'We do have an additional bedroom, but it's tiny. We use it for storage and extra desk space. Anyway, the big window's nice, too – plenty of light in the house.'

As Jude gazes around the room, at the glare from an outside street light beaming in through the naked window, my phone pings with a text: Steph.

He seems very nice!! Looks like you've got your new housemate. :)

My stomach gives an unexpected lurch.

'I love it,' says Jude, with such excitement that I feel bad all of a sudden.

He's so friendly, yet at the same time, I want him out. I'm undecided.

'So, if I *was* successful, when could I move in?'

'Do you want a cup of tea?' The question leaves my mouth before I can stop it.

'Yes! Bloody hell, yes,' he says enthusiastically. 'I'm parched. Strong with two sugars, please.'

We head back downstairs to the kitchen. I reach for two cups and whack the heating back on as he peers around the kitchen, at our ancient dining table (the landlord's), the fridge (also the landlord's), which he opens nosily. I briefly describe our system: the cleaning, the rota, the fridge organisation.

'Sounds great to me,' he says. 'My current place is a bit like that. Dedicated cleaning rota and laundry days. Works well, if you ask me.'

As the kettle lets out its soft roar, Jude shrugs off his jacket, revealing a faded band T-shirt. He hangs the jacket on the back of the chair and wanders into the living room, followed by the tinkling sound of Freddy's bell.

'So, *this* is what you meant by "must love cats"!' says Jude, ecstatic. He reaches down to fuss Freddy behind his ears. The purr can almost be heard over the kettle. 'What a little charmer!'

'He's just testing you,' I say, watching Freddy squish his face into Jude's hand.

I'm shocked. It usually takes Freddy more than a minute to get used to someone new. Normally, he'd leap away from any unwanted attention, maybe even hiss. Not now, however.

I fetch the tea, placing the mugs on the coffee table, noticing that Jude has already sunk into the sofa, making himself at home.

'Thanks, mate,' he says. 'So, who was that?' He nods towards the door. 'The lovely lady you were just with.'

'That's Steph. She lives two doors down.'

Jude reaches for his mug and we sip in silence. Jude is most definitely a character. I take in his outfit: the beaten-up black trainers, the dark jeans and the T-shirt. He's fashionable, yet somehow old-fashioned; an aura, Clarissa would say, that's hard to place. Not that I believe in that kind of thing.

'So,' Jude says. 'Interview time. What would you like to ask me?'

'Um . . .'

I think for a moment, wondering which of the many generic questions that I've asked a million times to bore him with first: What are your hobbies? Do you go out a lot? Do you smoke, or do drugs? Do you do nude yoga, or own six dogs? Are you planning on building a meth lab in the box room?

I wish Lloyd was here to do this. All I want to do is sit down and watch something. Or maybe try to write. Set myself a goal. Just one page, perhaps. Talking to Steph has ignited a spark of creativity and I'm itching to get back to it, make the most of it before it dies out.

I take a sip of tea. Strong, with one sugar. Clarissa always said I had my tea too strong. It always stained the nice mugs.

Clarissa. I wonder what she's doing tonight. Gazing around her new nursery, I expect, snuggling up to Ade and getting ready for her new life to begin. And here I am, pointing out our crap garden with the rusty, defunct barbecue in the corner, in this temporary home.

Is she happy? Is she happier now than she would have been with me?

'OK. So I guess my first question is, why do you want to live here?'

'This is a great brew,' says Jude, inspecting the mug. It's covered in little cartoon dogs. I have no idea where it came from.

'Well, the landlord's putting up the rent. Which is to be expected, I guess, but I live with four other people. It's great, but I need more space.'

'Right.'

'Plus, I'm looking for somewhere new, you know? Maybe a different area. New people, new focus.' He pauses, looking dreamily towards the closed curtain. 'And no, before you ask, I'm not on the run or anything like that.'

'That's exactly what someone who's on the run would say.'

'That's what the last interviewer asked. I kid you not.'

'OK.'

'Plus, this place is closer to work. And it's nicer.'

'You work in a bar, right?'

Jude nods enthusiastically, as if delighted I remembered. I look at this man, wondering what brings him here, to this houseshare. He's two years older than me. Surely he wants more than a shared space and a collection of mismatching furniture gathered from the fast-moving tenants of yesteryear.

Then again, we all have our own little mysteries.

'Lloyd's usually here,' I say. 'He's the other housemate – lives upstairs.'

'Is he Welsh?'

I nod. 'Lloyd will be moving out next year, once he graduates,' I explain.

'I love Wales,' says Jude. 'Have you been there? Gorgeous beaches, rolling hills . . .'

He bursts into a monologue and I wonder whether or not he's going to leave any time soon. He catches my look, clearly realising I'm not paying full attention.

'Right,' he says. 'I know I'm prattling on a bit! It was lovely to meet you, anyway.'

He gets up, takes his empty mug and, to my surprise, carries it out to the sink. Definite potential.

'When are you going to let the successful applicant know?' Jude asks.

I'm tired. *I'm exhausted.* Just thinking about another day packed full of interviews is enough to wear me out. Lloyd isn't even here, but despite Jude's talkative nature, I'm warming to him. He seems genuine and considerate.

Is he slightly annoying? Yes. But there's something about him.

But it's my decision. And at this rate, out of all of the potential housemates we've seen today, Freddy's mortal enemy, Ruby the Cat-Hater, seems like the clear winner.

What if I'm left with a choice? Ruby or Hugh?

'Are you sure you'd want to live here?' I ask.

'Why wouldn't I?' Jude reaches for his jacket. 'Like I said, it's a great place,' he says. 'You seem sound. Look, all I want is a place to relax after work, with some nice housemates and my music. That's it.'

I look at him, suddenly realising the answer to my impending housemate problem could essentially be solved. *Right now.*

Before I take the time to think it through fully, the offer is already out.

'Then the room's yours. Obviously, I'll need to see your references – oh, and a deposit. But if you could get those to me by the end of the week . . . well, welcome to Chapel Gardens.'

Jude's smile is so wide it's almost blinding. He looks like a kid on Christmas morning. Rather unexpectedly, he pulls me in for a hug – that quick, brotherly sort I'm not used to – slapping me on the back with gusto.

'You're a star,' he says. 'I can't wait. To new beginnings! OK, so I don't have a drink, but if I did, I'd be raising my glass right now. For once, being late has paid off. Thanks, mate.'

Then he's gone, and the house is quiet again.

Chapter 23

Steph

I'm getting dressed, pulling my tired limbs into my last remaining pair of ladder-free tights, when Amanda rings.

'I'm sorry for calling so early!' she trills.

She sounds elated, her voice high with laughter, undoing the knot of dread that instantly forms at any phone call that comes before 8 a.m. Amanda *never* phones before 8 a.m.

'Poppy insisted. She's refusing to do anything this morning until she's made the world aware of Wendy. She wanted to show Auntie Steph.'

'Wendy? Who's Wendy?'

Tights on like silky armour, I rummage through the chair pile for a suitable work top. One that will also be acceptable – OK, *perfect* – for an after-work team night-out-slash-date with Alex. OK, so not an *actual* date, more of a sneaky one under the helpful guise of a works do. Clothes-wise, I'm short on options, and the basic black dress is no longer one of them. I'd be like a female celebrity in the *Daily Mail*, exiled for wearing the same dress to two – *two*! – events. The horror.

I can hear Poppy's sweet voice in the background.

'She's our guinea pig!'

'Wendy? You called it *Wendy*? Bloody hell.'

'I chose the name!'

I can hear Poppy's tone in the background, potentially shifting from ecstatic to destroyed, and then it occurs to me that Amanda must have me on speaker. Whoops.

So I give Poppy a quick video call, watching as the furry little ball called Wendy nuzzles into her little hands before scrabbling to break free. The pride on her face is adorable.

'She's wanted one for ages, so we finally gave in,' Amanda whispers, her face filling the screen. 'She was up at six wanting to feed Wendy. Let's see how long that lasts.'

'I'm surprised. You hate guinea pigs.'

'Shh! I do not.'

'You did when we were kids.'

'Because I thought they were boring. I wanted a horse.'

Laughing, I rummage further, upending the pile onto the floor – a helpful accident. A sliver of teal peeks through the pile of various fabrics, making itself known: a blouse I bought three years ago that I sometimes wear for formal events. It'll do. I managed to avoid the snooze button this morning, getting up twenty minutes earlier to try to make more of an effort with my make-up. Or at least look less tired than usual, even though the flat is freezing and outside will be even colder, turning my expertly applied mascara into tiny icicles that'll later thaw and stream down my face in the office.

The additional prep doesn't escape Amanda's attention. On the screen, her eyebrows rise inquisitively.

'And what are *you* getting all dressed up for? Big meeting?'

'Not exactly.'

'You're smirking. Who is it? Who?'

I indulge her, putting her on speaker as I finish getting myself ready, giving her the low-down on Alex. Before the small bathroom mirror, I tease my hair into some semblance of style, pulling my winter hat over it. While I'm jostling for space in the tiniest of flats, my sister's family is getting (ever so slightly) bigger, her life fuller. There's an ache somewhere, and I can't place where it's coming from.

'He sounds lovely,' says Amanda, but I know that's just code for 'until I find out more'.

Which normally means mining social media for enough info to make (almost) sure I'm not dating the next Ted Bundy, pretending she isn't and then slipping up about it later. She passes the phone to Poppy, so that she can tell me more about Wendy and all the adventures they're going to have, as I spritz my hair with some coconut-scented shine spray.

Amanda finally prises the phone from Poppy's excited hands, pleading, 'Auntie Steph has to go to *work*, Pop!' as my niece shuffles away, new pet in hand. 'Maybe now she'll eat her breakfast,' Amanda says. 'She tried to sneak Wendy into her school bag this morning. Oh, I was thinking, I know it's still early, but do you want to come and spend Christmas with us this year?'

Christmas without Mum is a strange experience. The first one was torture, and it hasn't felt right since. When it comes to thinking about how I'm going to spend it, I'm torn. There's my sister's house full of happiness and festivity and the scent of Christmas cookies, and an excited Poppy, which should be amazing, yet I can't help but feel sad. As if I'm sat in a dark cinema, watching all the happiness play out on the screen like an old memory. And spending it alone is just as painful, but at least I won't have to put on a brave face. I can start on the booze at 9 a.m. and watch as many cheesy Christmas films as I can find before scrolling through everyone else's lives on social media with a bottle of gin I won't have to share.

At least this year I have a decent excuse. Surveying the detritus on the floor, the contents of the chair pile now a pool of fabric at my feet, I remind her about the promotion. About Manchester.

'So what? Come home for Christmas!'

'I'll think about it.'

She doesn't argue, because I say the same every year.

I pull my knitted scarf from the chair where I'd left it yesterday, just as a bright flash moves past the window. I notice it from a gap in the curtain. It moves again – a flicker of white.

I pull the curtain open, peering out onto the darkened, foggy street. October has arrived after a seemingly too long summer, pulling everyone into their homes, bringing with it cosy nights and colder mornings, making the row of plane trees that line Chapel Gardens bare, exposing the road beyond. There are footsteps and a figure is visible on the path – the postman. The light bounces off his jacket, with its fluorescent stripes.

I'm startled by the piercing sound of the buzzer.

'Gotta go, Mand!' I say, promising to call her later about Christmas.

She knows I won't.

Outside, the postman clutches a bundle of letters and a square-shaped parcel.

'Any chance you could take in something for upstairs?' he asks.

Sarah and Ash went out half an hour ago, jogging into the morning darkness in unison. I nod, accepting the parcel, and my gaze falls on the letters.

'This one's for you,' he says, plucking one from the stack and handing it over. I groan when I see it; the thick ivory envelope with my address beautifully written in gold. It's emblazoned with a wax seal, a perfect 'N & L'.

'Fuck,' I say out loud.

The postman gives me a sad look. And then, glancing down, I notice something. The light from the hallway shines on the first letter in his hand. A bill, by the looks of it. I can make out the address on the front. But it's not for me.

It's for 26 Chapel Gardens.

And there, disappearing with the postman as he wanders back down the path, are the names of my next-door neighbours.

The rest of the day goes by in its normal haze of routine, helped by liberal bursts of 'I'm leaving!' excitement. The evening, however, is better.

Alex sits beside me on a black leather sofa tucked in a corner at the far side of the bar, bathed in a neat glow of exclusivity. Saskia, Tamzin and a few of the others are with us, perching on the accompanying sofas, clutching flutes of champagne. I have a gin and tonic. Even Jeff turned up, but left an hour later, heading home to his family, leaving us behind to drink the night away. Saskia's already suggested leaving in an hour to go somewhere else before 'seeing where the night takes us'.

'It's a Monday, Sas. *A Monday*. We need to be up tomorrow, don't we?'

'So what? We're out, it's a nice night and we're celebrating.'

Saskia waved off my complaint, because she's obviously blessed with the ability to stay out all night and still look immaculate the next day. That, or her tiredness is well-concealed beneath her layer of perfectly applied foundation that magically stays put all day.

'Fuck it,' she said through her dark MAC lipstick, waving her initial fizz-filled glass skywards. 'You've got a new promotion. Tamz is getting married. There's lots to drink to. What's one hangover?'

Painful is what it is, but I didn't say anything. Instead, I nodded vigorously but died a little inside. Still, it feels nice, because Alex is with me. Alex with his dark shirt that clings so perfectly to his toned frame. Edging closer to him, he smells fresh; a hint of lime shampoo, as if he's stepped straight from the shower, which instantly takes my mind to certain places. Such as the shower.

I cross my legs on the sofa in a bid to look less squashed-in and awkward. I want to look sexy. Effortless sexy. I shuffle in my seat to face him, leaning against the low-backed sofa, focusing my attention on him and only him. He seems to like this, his fingers grazing my knee as he reaches for his drink.

I can be popular. I can be *hot*.

After all the emails, the flirtatious messaging at work, all that small talk – here we are, *out* out. He's brought up the promotion, the fact I'm moving far away, but I'm trying not to let it bother me. 'Have fun!!' Amanda texted right before I left work, and I plan to.

Tamz has taken the hint and has left us alone, winking at me every time she catches my eye.

'Really is a shame,' says Alex as the others are immersed in conversation. 'Now that you're moving away.'

'Aren't you happy for me?' I laugh.

'Of course. I just haven't had the chance to get to know you. Not properly.'

He moves closer, his fingers trailing softly along my shoulder, away from everyone's view.

'What are you suggesting?'

I feel elated, wanted, *in*. Sitting here with these people, admiring the bright lights of Bristol outside as we're bathed in warmth, slightly dizzy on account of my third – or was it fourth? – gin, I'm in my element. Snapping some quick photos of our drinks, I select one to upload to Insta – a sneaky shot of my oversized, decorated gin. My legs are in the photo – my sexy legs, which look deceptively long in these tights and heels – cosied up against Alex. I upload it, along with a caption: *Great people, great night, great company . . . x*

'Maybe we should make the most of it.'

I sit back against the leather. The lone butterfly that was fluttering around inside my stomach has now morphed into a whole swarm, frantically moving and spinning in want of escape. *I've missed this feeling.*

I don't want to leave. I know I'll have to go to the toilet, but I don't want to *leave* leave. I don't want to get up, put my jacket on and face the cold night as we all totter towards the next venue as is Saskia's plan, which will probably be full of people and no comfy seats. Maybe, just maybe, Alex will have other ideas. Perhaps I can convince him. He *is* lovely.

'Basics?' Amanda asks via text.

I quickly type back:

Surname: Jessop. Age: 31. Has two siblings. Plays football on the weekends. Gym three times a week, clearly shows. Don't stalk.

I feel his hand on my shoulder, pulling me close. His fingers start again, tracing faint circles around my shoulders through the fabric of my blouse. Tiny shocks of electric, fierce and comforting all at the same time.

But what if I like him? What if I end up falling for Alex Jessop? What if it turns out we're really great for each other? I'm moving away. In a matter of weeks.

Alex pulls me closer still. I feel another jolt of excitement. Taking a sip, I tell myself *fuck it*. That this is what I've been waiting for. A chance to meet someone at random. Alex is sweet, he's charming and he's downright sexy. I thought it before, but right now it's more obvious than ever.

Shouldn't I just be having fun?

Alex excuses himself, breaking the spell, and I reach for my phone like it's second nature. On Instagram, I check my likes hungrily (eighteen). I see what Nat's up to (pedicure; soft pink glitter). I scroll through the other lives I'm now only connected to by a follow and the occasional comment. How often do I tell Amanda I've met up with my uni friends? All the time. How often have I actually met with them? Almost never.

The pictures scroll by in a whirl of colour as if they're moving themselves but I'm doing it, moving this magical stream of pictures for my own amusement and dread. My university friends were close, but not when we left; some are lucky to have that super-close, best-mates-forever dynamic, the kind I've always envied as they follow each other into further walks of life. As for my group, we've all moved on; Erin works in stage design at a popular theatre, James has now settled in Plymouth with a family, Ty also has two kids and Paloma works for a local housing association while running a TV review blog about old soap operas.

Alex reappears, scooting in beside me again with a fresh drink for both of us. Saskia's talking to a man I vaguely recognise from work; Tamzin's been swept into the crowd by the bar – I can just about see her designer jacket.

'So, where did you say you lived?' Alex asks. 'You did tell me, but I don't recall.'

'Redland.'

He raises his eyebrows, impressed. 'Very nice! Got your own place, then?'

'Kind of.'

'Kind of?' All of his attention is on me.

'Well, it's my own in the way that I live there, alone. I rent it.'

'You rent?' He looks at me, incredulous.

I sip more gin, nodding. 'Yes. It's tiny but nice. The whole place is mine, you know? Granted, it's small – a bedsit, really – but it's cosy.'

Alex looks confused all of a sudden. 'You rent a *bedsit*?' Then he laughs. He actually laughs.

My face is still and unmoving.

'Wait, you're not joking?'

'Why would I be joking?'

Now it's Alex's turn to be still.

'Why would you waste money renting a bedsit?'

'Um . . .'

Alex places his drink on the table, his hand on my shoulder, guiding me close, and now it feels *too* close. There's no more room on this sofa to edge away.

'The trouble when you rent is that the place is never *yours*. You might as well take all that money and drop it straight into a fire.' He sits back, clearly thrilled to be imparting his financial wisdom.

'So what do you suggest?' I say sarcastically, looking all doe-eyed and eager in my need for sage advice, because obviously I've been doing something wrong all these years.

He doesn't realise I'm kidding.

'I take it you've asked your parents to help out? Mine did.'

'*What?*'

Any excitement I felt minutes ago evaporates into the humid air. I feel the colour, the comfort, the *fun* leave my face, my body, as if liquid. Alex's confident smile has been swept away by confusion.

'I mean,' he continues, in all seriousness, as though I didn't hear his question, 'have you asked your parents to help out with a house deposit?'

I stare at him. It feels as if the room has been turned upside down and all the sanity's fallen out of the bottom. This man is serious. He is *actually* serious.

I don't tell him that my mother is dead. I don't tell him that, following my trip to America, what remained of my savings went to living, surviving in a world without Mum. The therapy. The sessions I had to pay for because the NHS waiting list was too long. I don't tell him that I came to Bristol as soon as I could.

I don't tell him that I haven't seen my dad in over twenty years, that I probably wouldn't recognise him if he walked into this very bar. I've seen photos; we share similarities – his jaw a little too wide on my own face. My nose a little too rounded, our eyes a little too pale to be described as sea-green. The only time I ever think about him is when I'm doom-scrolling at night, panicking over some symptom or other – heart palpitations, a strange mole – then wonder, shit, is it genetic? How would I know? That's about as serious as our relationship gets.

The words come out like a croak. I'm sitting upright now; I can't remember when I changed position.

'Do you think we all have that option?' I press, my anger surprisingly contained. 'To simply ask Mum and Dad?'

His face falls again, but in a second it's back and he chuckles, pulling me in for a hug. I move like a doll in his grip.

'Ah, I'm sorry,' he says. 'I've pissed you off, haven't I? You know I was just kidding. I didn't mean anything by it, Steph. I just thought . . .'

I wave it off. 'It's fine. It's *fine*.'

Yet I'm frozen to the spot, clutching my drink as if the glass will break between my fingers. I had an inkling that Alex was well off, but I just didn't realise how different we are. Or, how different *I* am from those sitting around me.

'Do you forgive me?' he asks, and there's genuine concern on his face now, in those eyes that were, just moments ago, enticing me.

His hands venture to my back again and something inside me loosens, this live wire of anger that's just been cut. I sigh, drinking, wondering if staying here, trying to enjoy what's left of the evening, would be so bad, after all.

Alex *is* nice, I tell myself. He can't help it. He doesn't understand.

'Sorry,' he says again, wounded.

He can't help it, I tell myself again and again. He just doesn't know any better.

Chapter 24

Steph

'OK, so hear me out,' I begin. 'What if the neighbours are hermits?'

'*Hermits?*' Eric proffers a bag of crisps he's just brought back from the bar and looks thoughtful.

I take one.

'Yeah. You know, people who really keep themselves to themselves.'

'Hmm, I don't see it,' he says, amused. 'Even if they *were*, we'd still hear them like we always have.'

I swipe more of the snacks from Eric's bag. He doesn't seem to mind.

'What about witness protection, then?' I helpfully suggest. 'Or . . .' I raise my hands to set the scene. 'Murderers. They've killed someone – accidentally or otherwise – and so they just upped and left, escaping justice.'

Eric laughs so hard he almost chokes on a crisp.

'Fine,' I tease. 'Don't believe me.'

We're in the Cambridge Arms yet again; I texted Eric to see if he fancied coming out. I needed company – and I finally have the names of the elusive residents of number 26. He replied seconds later:

Readily available! X

This time, however, both of us have decided to get coffee instead of our usual tipple of choice. Eric's tired from working on his screenplay into the early hours and getting things ready for Jude's imminent arrival, and my head's still pounding from Monday's work do. Granted, I didn't stay out as long as Saskia and the others – who, by all accounts, wafted home at about five and were back in the office all sprightly for eight, still glowing as ever. I'd left the next bar at 1 a.m. and headed home to wash away the smell of the gin that was starting to seep through my pores.

But not before I'd kissed Alex.

It was unexpected. And strangely wonderful.

He waited with me outside the bar for the Uber he insisted on booking for me, the two of us nestled together on a bench. Just talking, giggling like naughty students at the fact we had to be in work the next day. We moved in closer, snuggling almost, as if trying to shield ourselves from the cold but knowing full well the real reason – need. Excitement. A different kind of warmth.

Before I knew what I was doing, we were kissing, his hands cupping my face as we unleashed all the frivolous urgency we'd been harbouring over the past weeks in the office.

'Steph, I think your suggestions are great, but aren't they a little OTT?' asks Eric now. 'I completely maintain that my "holiday" explanation is the most obvious one.'

Eric grins. It's nice when he does that, when his smile is wide and he leans back a bit in his seat, as if shy. He's had a tiring few days judging by the dark circles around his eyes, but he's shaved recently. His usual short stubble had been getting longer, though admittedly, it suits him.

'Your ideas are pretty wild,' he comments, and I give him a theatrical bow. 'Fancy writing my screenplay for me? I can't pay you in money, but I can pay you in tea.'

'How's that coming along?'

'It's not. I spent three hours last night just staring at the screen, waiting for inspiration to come. Did it? No. Not a jot.'

'The dreaded writer's block?'

'Pretty much.'

He runs a hand through his curly hair. He's shrugged off the cardigan, revealing another movie T-shirt. I think I recognise the image from *The Shining*.

'I'd read through it for you, if you like. I'm no expert, but—'

'But you're a horror aficionado and that would be amazing. Really.'

'In that case, I will. You seem to trust my judgement.'

Eric seems ecstatic at the prospect, but then his expression changes. It's almost as if he's puzzled.

'Wait. You'd *actually* read it? I warn you in advance, it's dire.'

'Aren't first drafts *always* bad?'

'Trust me, if you saw this draft in its current state, I'd be so embarrassed. No way are you seeing it before an edit.'

'Relax. You should have read some of my A-level poetry.'

'Was it that bad?'

I nod. 'I wonder what happened to all that. It was in Mum's cupboard. Maybe Amanda has it somewhere. Reams of paper full of my desperate, angry scrawls about pain being like razor blades searing through my very soul.'

'Oh, if you ever find it, you have to let me read *all* of it. How about we swap?'

'No way.'

'Why?'

Part of me feels like I *could* show Eric all of my terrible poetry. That's one of the things I like most about him. I never feel embarrassed around him. I can be *me*.

'Not a chance. I'm keeping you well away from my emo phase. Deep down I'm praying Amanda threw it all out.'

He holds up his hands. 'Not fair. But I'll take your help. Maybe it'll give me a push to get the next scene written. Writing can be lonely. I look for inspiration and end up feeling like my own work is terrible in comparison. Like I'm a massive fraud. Doesn't help that my dad keeps asking about it, wondering when it'll make me rich.'

I knock back the remnants of my coffee, watching the foam gather in the bottom of the mug. 'Oh?'

'I started it for fun. I've always loved watching films. I used to run a blog in my early twenties. Then, I thought, you know what? Maybe I'll give it a go myself. My dad . . . well, he's one of those people who's done really well for himself and can't seem to understand why I'm not following in his footsteps, why I'm not all about the career. If I enjoyed something, there always had to be a reason.'

'Surely he has hobbies, as well? Things he finds fun and rewarding.'

He shrugs, absent-mindedly stirring his coffee. 'Golf, mainly. And a bit of travel. Loves history. He's not creative and tried to steer me away from it. I can't fault him – he means well. Just wants the best for me, you know? It's just grating. He wants me to be successful. He's just trying to be encouraging.'

'Sometimes it's good to do things just for fun. Why does everything need to be some kind of side hustle? My mum always said whatever you want to do, do what makes you happy. She was always encouraging. When I wanted to play the recorder in school, she bought one, before we both swiftly realised I wasn't at all musical.'

'Not at all?'

'Honestly? You have heard *nothing* as bad as me on a

recorder. Actually, I'm wrong – violin was worse. I tried one class and I'm certain it's what Hell sounds like. The noise of me scraping along as everyone's burning.'

'Dark.'

'True, though.'

Just make the most of life. That's what Mum used to say. The last time she said that was before I left for America. Recalling that day makes the world cloudy again, makes everything taste bitter.

Did she know? When she was helping me to pack, placing newly ironed clothes in my suitcase, waving off my offer to let me be an adult and do it myself – did she know just how sick she was? By then, how far had the cancer spread?

'I'm sorry,' says Eric. 'I shouldn't complain. Not with . . .'

He trails off, his dark eyes gazing into mine, and for some reason, I feel safe around him; safe to talk, safe to share.

'It's OK,' I tell him. 'I was just remembering something.'

He doesn't know me, not really. He doesn't see the altered version, the one bathed in a filter that the rest of the world sees. Just me, the woman from number 28a.

'So anyway,' I say, and my sudden smile makes Eric sit up with interest. 'I finally uncovered the names of our next-door neighbours.'

It's as if this simple information is the resolution to a decades-old case, but I guess to us, it feels that way.

'Oh?' he says, intrigued. 'Who are they?'

'They're a couple. The Robertsons. Laurie and Malcolm Robertson.'

*

The photo is generic but happy. The couple in it, contained in the pretty summery image, grin back at the camera.

They're both wearing sunglasses. She's in a hat; a straw beach hat with a wide brim, her thick, flyaway hair in blonde waves, brushing against her shoulders. Her arms are around him, this tall, broad man with his happy face, pink from the sun, his dark hair greying at the sides. It's not a selfie; someone else must have taken it for them as they stood proudly before beautiful green hills together. I look closely, scanning their faces for any recognisable features, deciding whether or not they match anyone I've seen in Chapel Gardens. They don't.

'Are you sure that's them?' asks Eric. 'The Robertsons?'

We've ordered more coffees. The pub has become livelier. The sound of talk and laughter overpowers the music piped through the speakers.

Shrugging, I take one final look at the listings.

'I suppose so. I've done a thorough search of Facebook, Insta, Twitter – even LinkedIn. There are lots of people called Laurie and Malcolm Robertson, but they seem the closest match. They look in their forties or fifties, but I can't tell. I can't find anything for Malcolm, but this one seems promising. Do you recognise them?' I turn the phone round.

Eric shakes his head. 'Can't say I do. Does the profile give any more information?'

'Only that they live in Bristol.'

'Why *are* you looking, anyway? Just curious?'

Taking a sip of coffee, I sit back in the chair, contemplating.

'Well, I thought I could send them a message. Would that be weird? Would that be stalkerish?'

The look on Eric's face tells me everything I need to know.

'Hmm,' he says, his lips a straight line.

'Oh, God. It *is* stalkerish, isn't it? Tell me the truth.'

'I wouldn't go as far as that. You're not doing anything *wrong*, but maybe we should just wait until they're back from the Bahamas or the Alps or wherever it is they've gone.'

He sees me staring at the phone in my hand. My fingers hover temptingly over the 'message' button.

'Be honest,' says Eric. 'How long have you been wanting to send them a message?'

His self-satisfied smirk from across the table makes me want to hide the truth.

'OK, so it *might* have been all day.'

'All day? So *that's* why you asked me to the pub. To act as your conscience. To make sure you don't do anything rash.'

'Hey! No. I asked you out because it sounded like a fun idea.'

'Asked me *out*, did you?' He laughs again, displaying the lines around his dark eyes. He brushes a curl out of his face.

I look away.

'I don't recall . . .'

'You did. We're *out* out.'

He's teasing but, admittedly, I enjoy it.

'Be right back,' says Eric, shuffling out of his seat and heading in the direction of the toilets.

Looking down at the photo again, I wonder more about our neighbours. They have kind faces. They look happy. They look *nice*.

I go back to the profile and scroll through the photos Laurie Robertson has kept public. There are two. The smiling couple outside what looks like a blue-painted pub, a beach behind them. Then Laurie giving a thumbs up beside a heavily decorated Christmas tree.

Something catches my eye and I look away from my phone to see that Eric's has lit up with a notification. He's left it on the table and I can't resist peeking over at the photo on his lock screen that's illuminated our cosy booth.

A picture of Eric and a woman, all black-and-white and Insta-perfect, smiling as their faces touch. A sentimental kind of picture, in which Eric doesn't look like Eric; he's noticeably different. I have to squint to make sure it's him. He's clean-shaven, his hair is shorter; his dark curls aren't creeping over his forehead. His smile is wide – so wide it's unrecognisable.

I flinch and there's a plummeting sensation, as if I'm falling and I can't place why. Eric hasn't mentioned a girlfriend, only an ex. I don't know why I'm suddenly so nervous, as if the woman in the photo is staring right into my eyes, telling me to back off even though I'm not doing anything wrong.

Anyway, why am I surprised? Of course he's taken. What does it matter? My mind flicks back to Alex – the kiss we shared in the dark, his hands casually venturing up my skirt in that slow, welcome way as we waited for the Uber, as if we only had seconds left on the planet.

See? All is fine.

The photo disappears to blackness just as Eric returns to the table, swiping the phone back. He looks at me curiously, a hint of worry clouding his face.

'Oh no. You sent it, didn't you?'

'Nope! You'll be pleased to know I managed to refrain from firing off any weird messages. I'll do what we agreed. I'll wait. I'll wait for the Robertsons to come back.'

'They will,' Eric reminds me and he lets out a yawn, signalling our evening's over. 'Right, I'd better go. Are you . . .' He gestures to the door, no doubt wondering if I'll be accompanying him.

I down the cool remains of my coffee and we set off for the short walk across the street. Once again, we stop at the gates, silent for a moment, and the air is still with no Jude to interrupt us this time. Eric's hands are in the pockets of his jeans and he looks towards the house, as if searching for what to say.

And then I remember the photo. Other Eric. Loved-up Eric.

'I'll see you soon, then,' I tell him as I head up the path, keys in my grasp, the darkness of number 26 ghostlike between us.

Chapter 25

Eric

There are four boxes left in the hallway. In true Sean fashion, he's piled them one on top of the other, like a Jenga tower. I watch as the one on the top, containing books and some sports kit, teeters precariously on the verge of collapse.

Before it happens, Sean strides in through the open front door, his face flustered from carting his belongings to the back of his small car that's parked half on the pavement outside. Behind him, Kate studiously attempts to Tetris everything into the back seats. Her legs hang out of the door, boots in the air as she battles to squeeze another bag of Sean's clothing into the footwell.

'So this is it, then,' Sean says, snatching up the first box. 'The end of an era.'

I spot a couple of cookbooks from our uni days gracing the top of the pile, dog-eared and well-used.

'It is indeed. You sure you don't need any help?'

I'm currently in the limbo that is the kitchen, hovering around trying to make myself useful. I've been here practically all morning, half-dressed for work, making coffee, sitting in a living room that's now been cleared of all of Sean's stuff; his books, some family photos he kept on the mantelpiece, three of the good cushions. We're back to the bare minimum now. I'll have to buy a new wok later.

'You're all right, we've got it.'

He nods towards Kate, who gives me an enthusiastic wave. She comes in and starts taking the last of the boxes out to the car, as if she can't wait any longer.

'Sure. Well, congratulations again. You'll have to give me a tour of the new place soon.'

'Definitely, mate. This is . . . this is strange. But exciting.'

He says it with that jokey, cheeky smile of his; sarcasm mixed with pure joy. He lets out a long sigh, taking one final glance around the house he's lived in for the past few years. Despite what he proclaims, all the promises of 'you'll have to come round' and 'let's do a games night', I know it's somewhat final. Our chats and messages will descend into more snapshots of domestic bliss and more invites to things that are best done in pairs.

'Well, for what it's worth, I'll miss living with you, Sean.'

'You soppy bastard. Come here.'

To my surprise, he pulls me into a quick hug.

'Got to move on at some point, haven't we?' he says. 'Good luck with the new guy . . . Jay, wasn't it?'

'Jude.'

Sean nods and I can see the excitement on his face. With that, he passes me the key. It's warm in my hand as I watch him hurry down the path, leap into the car and leave Chapel Gardens for good. That's it – end scene.

The door clicks shut and the house is empty again. I place the key on the worktop, ready for Jude. His references checked out and he sent the deposit on the very night he turned up. He'll officially be our new housemate in a matter of days. Am I ready?

Technically, it doesn't matter whether I'm ready or not, but I can't help the feeling, the one that keeps coming back. *Everything's changing. Everything is changing, but not for me.*

I'm due to be in work in an hour, but I'm not feeling it. Right now I should be in the shower, mentally prepping for a day at the bank. Of ushering customers into the small glass-walled room while they talk to me about their lives and I gloss over, pretending I'm listening, making the right sounds at the right time, smiling at all the right moments. My jacket hangs on the door, waiting, but instead I'm standing in the hallway, unable to move, unable to think about anything but lying down and thinking. Just thinking. Thinking of all the things I could have changed but didn't.

I wander back to the bedroom instinctively and flop onto the unmade bed, staring at the ceiling, where a spider has taken residence in the corner.

I could have saved my relationship with Clarissa.

That's where it all ends: Clarissa.

Her face looms in the silence, but it's not the happy face I see. It's the one on the night it all went south. Her eyes full of hurt, followed swiftly by anger. Another thing I can never take back. It could have been different. I should have thought. I should have hugged her and told her how much she meant to me, but I didn't.

My suit hangs on the wardrobe door, but I can't move to reach it. My eyelids are heavy and the bed is too comfy. Instead, I reach for my phone and call Joshua.

'I'm not going to be in today,' I tell him, making my voice a little croaky for added effect. 'Not feeling too good, mate.'

'Oh? What's up?'

I can sense Joshua's stress levels rising on the other end of the line as he tries to quell the threat of his day tumbling down.

I'm about to tell him, to explain, but then I stop. My throat feels dry, my heart races.

'Stomach bug,' I lie.

I feel terrible, but what else can I say? That I'm not feeling it? That I can't face seeing customers today? That I can't be stuck in a glass-walled room pretending, pretending, over and over?

'Oh, God. Stay home. Get better soon, OK?'

Once he's gone, I climb beneath the duvet, encased by the warmth and the feeling of relief.

Turns out it's only temporary.

Jude arrives three days later. I notice the transit van from the living room window, parked across the road. I hear it first, the pumping seventies rock blaring from the speaker. I see the van door open and out leaps Jude.

'Hey!' I head down the path as he pulls open the back of the van.

Another man steps out of the driver's side and comes round to help. Boxes are stacked in little piles and the other man – clad in a jumper and fashionably torn jeans, even though it's freezing – begins to unload. Jude takes a bag from the back and walks over.

'Eric!' booms Jude, his voice carrying across the silent row of houses. 'How are things? This is my mate, Sam.'

The man in the torn jeans – Sam – waves.

'Need any help bringing stuff in?' I ask.

'Don't worry. We can do it! A cup of tea would be great, though. Oh, and I've brought these.' He hands me a sturdy carrier bag, which is weighty in my grip. It clinks conspicuously. 'There are some bottles in there. One's for Steph.'

'Why?'

Jude smiles with apparent delight. 'Because I felt we had a nice neighbourly connection. It's important to be a nice neighbour, don't you think? So many people are unfriendly nowadays. They keep themselves to themselves.'

'Yeah. Wouldn't want to be one of those . . .' Not at all, I think sheepishly.

'Anyway,' he continues, 'I don't know what her preference is. So I've bought some red, some white and rosé.' He pauses. 'Shit. Does she even drink wine?' He waves off the worry. 'Well, if not, I've also brought a cake, a multipack of biscuits, a huge box of teabags, some crisps and a few other bits.'

I stare blankly at the bag before taking it through to the kitchen, unpacking the contents, placing the Victoria sponge on the worktop, the biscuits in the designated cupboard. There's a thump from behind me and I turn to see Jude drop a small box on the kitchen table.

'Kitchen bits,' he explains before hurrying off again.

Flicking on the kettle, I sneak a peek inside the box, at the assortment of stuff Jude's brought. There are mugs, cake tins, pans, a generic set of cutlery . . . Sean's cleared out his personal cupboard, so most of it can go in there.

Stirring the tea in the plain red mugs that Sean left behind – no doubt starting a mug collection anew with Kate – I reach for the sugar and forget how many Jude prefers, or if he takes any at all, or whether Sam would like any. I rush on through the hallway to ask, when a vision of horror unfolds in front of my eyes.

Jude and Sam are by the van, carefully unloading what appears to be a drum kit.

A massive fucking *drum kit*.

'Erm, what's going on?'

It comes out as more of a shriek than a concerned question, just as both men are mindful of crossing the road, the precious cargo in their hands.

'What do you mean?' Jude has the good grace to look worried.

'This,' I say, pointing to the offending instrument just as Sam hurries off to gather the rest. 'You have a drum kit?'

'And a guitar.'

Sure enough, a glance behind him reveals Sam lifting a shiny black guitar from the van. He carries it over, shuffling past me and propping it against the wall. To be fair, it looks amazing. And expensive. The kind of thing I'd have loved to own when I went through my short-lived guitar phase.

'Oh, God.'

'What's wrong?'

'Please don't say you have any more instruments in that van.'

There's a flicker of fear in his eyes.

'Just a tuba, a violin and a couple of flutes. Did I not tell you? I have to practise violin at 7 a.m. every day. It's a bit screechy, but I'm sure you'll get used to it eventually. Could have sworn I mentioned it.' He turns round. 'Sam! Hold off the tuba. Change of plan.'

I can feel the colour drain from my face, just as Jude laughs uproariously.

'Mate,' he says, his hand on my shoulder, 'I'm kidding. *Kidding*. You look terrified. However, I *do* have a band. These are my instruments. Sam plays bass. And I definitely, *definitely* remember telling you.'

'You didn't.'

'I did.'

'Are you sure? I think I'd have remembered *that*.'

'Yeah! I told you I like to come home and relax with my music. Remember?' He points to the drum kit, now half-assembled in the hallway, taking up space alongside the steadily growing pile of boxes. 'See? My music. There was no room for it in my last place – had to keep most of it in the garage. And what's the good of owning these beauties when you can't play? Thanks to you, I have that freedom now.'

For fuck's sake.

'Right. So you rehearse at home? I just thought by "music" you meant . . . I don't know, Spotify?'

Jude laughs again. 'You really crack me up, you know that? Anyway, the bedroom looks big enough, but I guess we could move them to the living room some days. Plenty of space in there. My bandmates are great, you'll really like them.'

I am an idiot.

Jude's face softens. 'Look, we won't cause you any trouble. I'm not that kind of housemate. I'll always check with you before the band comes over. Besides, we mainly go over to Sam's to rehearse together. How's the tea coming along? Ah! I forgot to tell you, Sam has three sugars. I know, I know. It's grim. I'll crack those biscuits open.'

His voice trails off as he pads towards the kitchen, leaving me among the pile of cardboard and bags of clothes. As I take a box and carry it up to Jude's new room, I wonder, yet again, if I made the right choice.

Chapter 26

Steph

I should really get rid of social media.

I think about it often, as the steady light of my phone illuminates the little corner of my room. I consider stepping away – letting my thumb venture to the icon and hitting Delete.

Pros of quitting social media:

1. I could get much more work done in a day. I mean, how much time do I, do *we*, devote to endless scrolling? I could be so much more productive without the lure of my phone.
2. Better posture. Probably.
3. I'd feel less shitty, *not* wading through everyone else's brilliant lives while I'm wallowing in my crappy bed shovelling crisps into my mouth, pretending I *like, like, like* as crumbs disappear into my cleavage.
4. I wouldn't be tempted to torture myself by perusing Vikki's Instagram feed.
5. I could find new hobbies! I'd fill all the minutes I'd spend being zombielike with good, mindful things like yoga or roller skating or houseplants.

That's it: when I get to Manchester, I'll have houseplants. *So* many plants. I'll take care of them and give them names. I'll be friendly and vibrant and nurturing. I'll be one of those people with *energy*.

Yet, it feels like a special kind of sin to switch off completely and ignore the world, metaphorical fingers in ears. Would it make me ignorant?

Cons of quitting social media:

1. I want – *need* – to interact with people.
2. How will I find out what everyone's up to?
3. They'll forget about me.
4. *I have no one but them and they'll forget about me.*

I look at the Instagram icon now as I sit on the bus, gripping my coat even tighter around me because the inconsiderate twat three seats down has insisted on opening the window. It's freezing. My fingers are cold against the screen and before me is yet another grinning snap of Nat:

#MarriedLife has yet to begin, but something's telling me I'm going to love it! Woke to find these gorgeous flowers waiting for me from my wonderful man. He knows exactly how to make me feel loved and cared for! #MyLove #MyWorld #SoLucky

Would it be weird to reply with a vomit emoji?

I'm suddenly all for it. Instant deletion, that is. Until I remember all the cons.

The journey to the office is quiet, punctuated only by the sound of dance music emanating from somebody's headphones and the quiet *tap tap tap* of a laptop from the girl at the front. A vision of Eric falls into my mind, clear and immediate. I picture him typing away furiously at his laptop at night, conjuring the newest scene in his screenplay, and I find myself wondering what he looks like when he's busy working. I'm imagining him hunched over the computer, brow furrowed in concentration. Or smiling – that big, broad grin of his that only sometimes makes an appearance, which is a shame. I like his smile.

As the bell dings and the bus pulls into a stop to let off a lady with her pushchair, I wonder if this is stupid. Eric is . . . well, he's Eric. Eric from number 24. And he's taken.

Closing the app, I watch the scenery roll by outside, seeing everything with new eyes. In just a matter of weeks, I'll be in Manchester, curiously searching the view for new places, new familiarity. It strikes me that this usually boring bus ride has some significance, after all – this feels final somehow, like I have to drink in every feature, every shopfront and side street I know so well. I feel faintly solemn – will I miss this place?

I'm flustered by the time I reach the office building. Sweat sticks to me from the jog from the bus to the office but, thankfully, some angel spots my desperate sprint to the lift just in time to hold the doors.

I squeeze in silently, cringing as I spot my reflection in the shiny chrome elevator wall, tugging at my top in an attempt to cool myself down. My face is red. Sweat pools beneath my cheap blazer.

'Hey!'

Alex is a head taller than the four others in the lift and even in this tiny space with the most unflattering light imaginable, he still manages to look effortlessly gorgeous.

His suit is a dark charcoal grey today. As the door pings on floor two and everyone else steps out, it's just us, at least for another two floors until we reach Everly Cope.

'Alone at last,' he says quietly, and normally I'd wince at that line if it didn't come from him.

I laugh; Alex can get away with it.

'Going up!' the tinny elevator voice says, and Alex takes my hand and pulls me towards him, his chest against mine.

His eyes glint with mischief. I can smell the sweet scent of his aftershave and suddenly, I'm consumed with the urgent need to kiss him. His free hand travels towards the small of my back, slowly inching downwards. His lips brush against my neck and it's tempting, so, so tempting . . .

Ding goes the lift and the doors clunk into life. I jolt into the reality and we quickly separate as the doors expose us to the bright lobby of Everly Cope. Alex winks as he waits for the next floor.

'See you soon,' he says.

'Of course.'

It's my lame attempt at being all seductive and husky. Instead, it just comes out sounding like I have a sore throat.

The lift doors close, leaving me to straighten my skirt before rushing to the office, where I'm greeted by Jeff slurping his coffee and the faint hum of computers. Following the recent lay-offs, the place is not only more weirdly spacious, but there's also a quiet tension within the walls that wasn't there before.

My phone rings as my emails load. *Click click*, goes Jeff's mouse. Why is he so loud?

'Hey, Mand. You OK?'

'Steph! Did you get my messages?'

I groan inwardly, remembering the flurry of Rightmove links sent by Amanda at eleven thirty last night.

'Yep. All eighteen.'

'What do you reckon? Any that take your fancy? You'll have to move quick if you want to rent one soon, flats are getting snapped up super fast.'

Cautiously, I start flicking through, aware of Jeff's curious gaze. Not that it matters if I'm browsing Rightmove – I'm leaving, after all.

'I don't know, Mand. It's all very sudden. I need some time.'

'Exactly – and that's what I'm here for. Come on, Steph! You booked next week off, right? I'll be coming with you. I know your life's going to be hectic with all the packing and admin and whatnot, so I'll arrange some viewings for us. I can't wait!'

'Mand, you don't have to come. This is . . .' This is my responsibility, I want to say. I slump against the desk, rubbing my forehead as if to quell the stress headache that's about to form. 'Too generous.'

'Oh, I'm enjoying this, trust me. One: we get a little road trip, and two – house porn. You know I love looking around new homes. Let me help pick out your new pad. *Pleeease*?'

I click on the first link: a new-build one-bed near the city centre. White walls. A spacious living room with a balcony. Way, *way* out of my budget.

'There's a gorgeous place with an attic room,' Amanda carries on excitedly.

As she babbles on about all the hypothetical new homes in Manchester she's kindly found for me, I can sense Jeff's interest from behind the screen.

'Mand.' I cut her off, at the same time clicking through more of the listings.

As each one opens, my heart sinks even lower. There's absolutely no way on earth I can afford any of these. And then I remember – the promotion. The promotion I lied about all that time ago. Amanda thinks I'm doing way better than I actually am, which is living from pay cheque to pay cheque, just managing to scrape together enough for the move, providing the rent is small.

I can't say anything. Not in front of Jeff. As nice as it is to dream, I have to shut this down. Now.

'Can we talk about this later?' I ask.

'Sure, sure. I've requested a couple of viewings already. I'll call you.'

With a final excited squeal, she hangs up.

Even mentally reliving the lift moment with Alex can't save this broken day. In the kitchen, as I make some coffee, the kettle drowns out my sigh of annoyance. And before I realise what I'm doing, I'm opening Instagram like it's second nature, heading straight for Vikki's feed, where I'm greeted by a pair of hands, entwined.

Miles' hand, I know it anywhere – the freckle right before his thumb hasn't escaped the pretty filter. I loved his freckles. I poke at it on the screen, like I used to when we were together. I'm so lost in the memory that I almost don't notice the caption. The slew of comments and little red hearts.

The sparkling, understated diamond glistening on Vikki's finger.

#SoLucky.

Chapter 27
Eric

I think I'll add another rule to the list: don't wake Eric up at the arse-crack of dawn – especially with the smoke alarm.

'Morning!' calls Jude as I shuffle into the kitchen, almost impressed at the fact he can hear me over the sizzle of the frying pan.

He takes it from the hob, shakes it, drops it down again with an almighty *clang*. Which is why I'm out of bed at six thirty in the morning in the first place. He turns round, spotting me in the doorway.

'Bloody hell, you look knackered.'

'I am. I *am* knackered.'

Rubbing my eyes, I step into the smoky kitchen, which is alive with the sound of cooking and the wafting smell of bacon. My stomach rumbles angrily. It takes me by surprise and then I remember that I barely ate yesterday.

'Oh. Bad night?'

Jude's wearing a pair of faded grey joggers and a vest top. It's clear he works out. Or he's one of the lucky ones. Maybe I should get to the gym. It's been a while.

'Look, Jude . . . could you please try not to make so much noise at six in the morning? My room's right next to the kitchen.'

'Shit, I'm sorry. Did I wake you?' he says in surprise. He grabs another pan for the eggs – it hits the hob with another thud. 'The smoke alarm only went off once. Got to admit, that's pretty good going for me.'

There's a tinkling sound from the hallway that grows louder as Freddy struts in to greet us.

'Hey!' I say, reaching to rub his head, but he darts out of my way and straight for Jude, wrapping himself around Jude's ankles.

'Be careful, little bud!' says Jude. 'There will be plenty of food for you, don't you worry.' He turns to me. 'Great, isn't he? I love cats. This little guy's been following me everywhere.'

Gazing up, feeling nauseous with a mix of tiredness and hunger, I catch sight of the kitchen in all its glorious detail. The worktops are stacked with pans and plates. Numerous metal handles peek out of the already-full sink.

'Why are you using every utensil imaginable?'

It's meant to come out as a joke, but even I can hear the annoyance in my voice. Jude, however, is oblivious.

'I'll clean it up. Oh, and don't worry, I've got you covered.' Grinning, he shuffles a perfect fried egg onto a plate, along with some bacon and beans. 'Toast is in,' he says.

I want to hate him, I really do, but my rumbling stomach disagrees.

'Why are you so bright and . . . alive in the morning?'

Jude shrugs. 'I just am, I suppose. I'm an early bird. Like to get up and get my morning run out of the way before the day begins. You should join me!' he suggests, then catches my expression. 'Or maybe not. Your call.'

'Hmm.'

He turns his attention away from a pan of beans and focuses on me with that wry smile of his.

'Oh, I saw Steph last night as she was heading into her house. I talked to her for a few minutes and I totally forgot to give her the wine. I was thinking, why don't we have a little house-warming get-together? I'll invite Sam over, too. I'll pop round to Steph's later and ask.'

'I think Steph's out tonight.'

I have no idea why I say it, but it's the first thing to pop into my head. I don't know if Steph's out tonight. And I don't know why I'm suddenly feeling this way – this strange, almost worried way; whatever Steph *is* doing tonight, part of me doesn't want it to be with Jude. Does that make me a bad person?

'Oh! Never mind, then. Some other time.' The beans now done, he scoops them carefully onto the plate and sets it down in front of me. A big, perfect full English breakfast. 'Look, I'm sorry about the noise. I didn't realise. I think I'm just used to everyone being up at the same time.'

'I get it. Don't worry.' I tuck into a crisp rasher of bacon and all is forgiven. Almost.

I realise I'm being cruel. Jude's simply trying to be friendly. A good housemate, which is what I wanted in the first place. But while I like him, I also can't help but find him a little suffocating.

'So, what were you up to last night?' he asks.

He takes the other seat at our tiny kitchen table. The chair clunks noisily against the tiles.

'I could hear you tapping away as I went to bed,' Jude continues. 'Are you working on something?'

The question surprises me. 'Er, yeah.'

He shoots me a curious look, willing me to elaborate.

'So?' he asks. 'What is it?'

'A movie.'

Lying in bed listening to the rain – once Jude had finally ceased his drum practice – I'd managed to get another scene down. Only then to feel so uninspired that I deleted the whole thing – watched those newly curated words vanish at the touch of a button. They were no good, anyway.

'Whoa! Impressive stuff. I'd love to do something like that. Always envied people with that kind of skill.'

'Writing? Why don't you try it?'

Jude smiles. 'I'm a musician, not a writer. Shab is the lyrical genius in our band, but who knows? Maybe I'll give it a go. So, how's it all going? What's the movie about?'

I shake my head, spearing a mushroom with my fork. 'It doesn't matter.'

'You'd rather keep it hush-hush? I get it. You don't want me stealing your potentially Oscar-winning screenplay idea.'

I can't help but laugh at the mere suggestion. It's ludicrous.

'It's not that. Honestly? I think I'm about to pack it in. I was half tempted to delete the lot last night. Start afresh with something new.'

Last night, sitting on the bed as the pounding beat of Jude's drum rehearsal reverberated through the house – nothing like the Robertsons' soothing piano solos – I felt hopeless, stupid. *Where has the spark gone? What happened to it?* This is different from the usual writer's block. This feels as if all the love and excitement I'd once harboured for this project has vanished into thin air.

I don't tell Jude any of this.

'The idea's a bit shite,' I say instead.

Jude takes a sip of tea. I picture the words forming, his face full of nonchalance as he utters that well-worn phrase I can't escape from. *Can't hack it.*

It doesn't come.

'Remember, Stephen King binned *Carrie*,' he says brightly. 'He didn't think it was working, so he dumped it in the trash. Then his wife, Tabitha, fished it out of the bin. Lo and behold, we all know *Carrie*. It's bloody iconic. So, before you go and throw away any of your hard work, make sure it's the right decision. Spoiler alert: it's probably not.'

Jude's plate is empty now and I stare at it in surprise. He takes it to the sink, giving me an encouraging pat on the shoulder. Normally I'd find that odd, but coming from Jude, it's almost relieving.

'Anyway,' he says now over the noise of the dishwasher as he fills it with the dirty pans and plates. 'Is anything happening between you and Steph?'

'Why are you so enamoured with Steph all of a sudden?'

He looks away. Wow! For once Jude is quiet, if only for a second.

'Who wouldn't be? She just seems really nice, is all. Seems fun.'

'She *is* fun.'

'So why aren't you two . . .'

He nods coyly. I know what he's getting at.

'I don't know,' I admit. 'She's just my neighbour.'

Nodding, he picks up his jacket that he'd slung over the chair.

'I'm heading out now. See you later, Eric.'

Once he's gone, I pull out my phone from my dressing gown pocket with one hand as the other shovels a delicious forkful of egg and beans into my mouth. Pulling up Instagram, an app I haven't used since dating Clarissa, I hover over the search box. The photo of Steph and her sister sits in my mind – the one she showed me last night, her green eyes full of love – and I'm overcome with curiosity.

I sneakily type in the username I've committed to memory. Seconds later, there she is. Steph.

The grid unfolds like a revelation and I feel like a child sneaking a peek at a long-awaited birthday gift. I don't know much about Steph, so surely this is the place to start. To learn more, to know what she's into. Scrolling through the many photos gives me a brief, sacred glimpse I never knew I could get. One that's perfectly public yet at the same time seems completely forbidden.

There are more photos of Steph and her sister. A picture of Steph looking serenely out of a train window. Drinks. Her colleagues and friends, a vast group, posing in swanky places. Expensive drinks and posh hotels. I stop at one particular image, posted just days ago: two glasses of gin on a table. A knee, presumably hers, and a man's hand upon it. The caption, complete with a coy heart: *Great people, great night, great company . . . x*

My stomach twists, and it has nothing to do with Jude's breakfast.

I have no idea why I'm feeling this way. Steph's my neighbour. Of course she'd be seeing someone. Why wouldn't she?

Am I thinking of Steph to distract myself from Clarissa and her wonderful new life?

Steph is a neighbour. A friend. I repeat this over and over in my head.

If Steph is just a neighbour, why am I so confused?

Chapter 28

Steph

Tonight, I started packing.

It's the only sensible thing to do. While sitting at work, faced with the fact I'll be leaving *in a matter of weeks*, the thought of packing up all my worldly possessions hit me with a flutter of anxiety. Am I excited? Yes. Do I want to pack up my life?

Pros of packing:

1. Moving is exciting! Yay! #NewLife.

Cons of packing:

1. There are never enough boxes.
2. You always think you have enough time, but on moving day you're still wrapping mugs in newspaper and frantically shoving them into whatever space you can find.
3. You find a jigsaw piece. Or an important-looking screw. Where did that come from? *Is that mine?!*
4. There's always a memory somewhere, waiting for you to find it. A cup you bought on the day you moved in, a pair of trainers you wore once for a

fitness class you thought would change your life,
or a half-burned candle from a romantic home-
cooked dinner long ago, shoved in the back of a
drawer.
5. It's just bloody stressful.

But it has to be done, and tonight I'm feeling strangely
energetic. I stand in the faint warmth of my tiny home,
surveying it in all its cluttered glory. *Boxes – I need boxes.*

I have boxes; they're folded and neatly stored away in the
shed at the bottom of the garden. I put them there when
I moved in, once I'd swiftly unpacked everything, feeling
hopeful about my brand-new life.

Determined, I head out through the back door and into
the cold garden, where the grass is soon to be in danger of
reaching my knees. Technically, the garden is my responsibility, but I haven't got round to doing it – maybe Eric
would have a strimmer I could borrow . . .

It's dark and the air is bitterly cold, but I traipse down
to the shed anyway, the blades of grass tickling my legs,
using the torch on my phone to guide the way. Behind
me, the house stands tall and ghostly, and I suddenly
feel noticeably alone. There's still no light coming from
next door. I can barely see anything in the dark, let alone
past their six-foot fence. Instead, I continue to the shed,
unlocking it with a shivering hand. My face is met with
a spider's web, so I swat it out of the way, cursing myself
for not waiting until tomorrow.

I pull forth the empty boxes I'd stashed there when I first
moved in, taking as many as I can carry under both arms
and awkwardly manoeuvring back down the grassy path,
arms laden with cardboard and plastic.

The kitchen area – that's where I begin.

I pull open the cupboards, taking out everything I haven't used in a while. The bowls, the cheap champagne flutes; additional items that rarely saw any action over the past eight months. The glasses I'd stored neatly, hopefully, at the front of the cupboard with visions of bringing them out for guests. We'd sit around my living room sipping wine and laughing into the night – all the things we envisioned doing when we were at uni, playing at being adults, just an older version of playing house.

I wrap up that old dream as quickly as I wrap the glasses with old newspaper and bubble wrap I'd thankfully kept, placing them neatly in a box, being sure to snap a photo for Instagram:

A fresh start awaits – now all I have to do is pack!

Next to be tackled is the cupboard. A stack of board games sits on the top; old family favourites like Scrabble and Cluedo, their boxes faded and worn with use. I'm not tall enough to reach fully, so I grab the corner of the Scrabble box, edging it closer, closer to the end until . . .

Crash.

The boxes hurtle towards me, but I leap out of the way just in time. Plastic letters clatter to the floor.

'Shit.'

'M' is the first letter I see. I grab it, forcefully shoving it back into the little green bag with the rest, remembering the evenings spent playing this game with Mum and Amanda, and even Miles. Just thinking of Miles makes me wince – how we'd spend a night with wine and Scrabble, Miles being ever serious, me being less so as the night grew darker and the wine depleted. He's probably having a wholesome games night with Vikki right now, I tell myself begrudgingly.

Probably with their equally wholesome couple friends. Or just alone, all smug and cosy. Then they'll have great sex.

I try not to think about the sex. Miles was great at sex. I swat the mental image away like an irritating fly.

Games neatly packed, I start work on the clothes – the biggest task of the lot. There are clothes I haven't worn in a while; an endless array of garments I haven't got round to sorting. Scrutinising each one for a total of three seconds before dropping it into the box, I feel lighter. *Better*. There's something therapeutic about packing, about organising, about feeling as though you're taking ownership, even if it's just moving personal stuff from one small space into another. Feeling in control of something, for once.

I'm on a roll, high on the feeling of elation. I'm getting it done! I'm organised!

Pulling more clothing from the rail, the hangers clinking and clattering as long jackets and the odd maxi dress are tugged from the home they're so used to, I step back to admire my progress. Then I stop.

Of course, behind the curtain of clothing stand the boxes – Mum's boxes.

Now that the rail is almost bare, the boxes appear, large and looming. The writing on the top, Mum's beautiful swirly 'S' like she'd write in every birthday card, is exposed – a big reminder of what I have yet to open.

Once again, I feel compelled to run my hand along the boxes, to trace my finger along Mum's marker-pen writing, imagining her hand hovering over it. As if our hands are touching. Every time I think I miss her more than anything, something happens to make me miss her even more, and my heart is in danger of breaking all over again.

I knew I had to open the boxes someday – prise them open, cut through the packaging she'd lovingly assembled.

I already know what they contain: some of her belongings that she wanted me to have. But I don't want to revisit those things now, things that would undoubtedly take me back in time. *Not tonight*. Besides, if I open them *now*, I'd only have to seal them up again, to take them to Manchester.

Still, I can't look at them; I can't have them staring at me as I try to sleep, the outline of the boxes lurking in the shadows. So carefully, I move them, dragging them slowly towards the kitchen area. They're not too heavy, but not light, either. They can stay there for the time being.

There are some things I'm just not ready for.

The following day, Saskia's perched on my work desk, her long legs crossed as she dips a green teabag in and out of her mug as if it's taking too long. She's giving me the low-down on Caz's wedding and the choice of dress.

'Dusky pink,' she states sagely, 'simple yet classic. That's what she's going for, for the bridesmaids. Knee length. Who doesn't suit pale pink?'

'Hmm,' I say, casting my mind back to a party in which Amanda decided to wear a pale pink bodycon dress. At first glance, everyone thought she was nude.

Do I tell her?

No, I don't tell her. And this is why I need to be a better person.

'Anyway, how are things going with Alex?'

She leans in, whispering when she says his name, lest the practically empty office hears. Jeff's already done his polite conversation and left for his 9 a.m. trip to the communal kitchen for coffee, so we're safe. Jeff likes to pretend he's above office gossip. Which couldn't be further from the truth.

'Alex was talking about you the other day, you know,' she adds.

'Oh?' I'm all flustered and at that moment, my computer pings with a message from Alex himself.

I keep thinking of us in the lift yesterday. Shame we didn't have more time.

Saskia whips her head round to see. 'Ooh, is that him?'

'No. Just . . . Caz.'

Sas would be drawn to a frisky internal message like a seagull on chips. Best keep it quiet.

'Well, remember Ffion? *Really* likes him, apparently. She's found out he's into someone in our building. He didn't name you of course, but we knew. So watch out!' She throws her head back with mischievous laughter.

'What, am I going to get *Carrie*'d at the next works do?'

'Sorry?' Her brow furrows in confusion.

'Never mind.' I swat the thought, and the imminent threat, away, laughing along with forced jollity as Alex pings back:

You busy?

Then:

Sorry. I need to be careful what I say on here, but I can't help it. It wasn't a moment I'll forget in a hurry.

'Me neither xxx' is my speedy response.

'You're grinning,' says Sas. 'What's Caz up to?'

She turns to look at the monitor, but I manage to click the message away just in time.

'Wedding favours,' I say, watching Saskia's eyes light up. I lean in, like a PI divulging some top-secret news. 'Don't worry, I'll get the intel.'

With Saskia gone, my attention's back to Alex. Lovely Alex. All of a sudden I feel tingly, thinking about that moment in the elevator, how charged it was, how *needed*. And not to mention daring.

I *feel* daring now. I shoot back another message:

That was just a small taste of what's to come . . . xxx

Oh, God, did I just type that? Cringing, my head hits the keyboard in shame, wishing I could shove all the words back in. There's no undo option. *I can't undo*.

I'm half expecting some jovial 'oo-er!' response, so I'm pleasantly surprised by Alex's next move:

I'm taking you out. Let's see what the night has in store. ;)

Perfect. Xx

Turning my attention to work, I try to get into the zone. That professional place in which I normally reside from 9 a.m. right up until five. But summoning the energy is nigh on impossible today. I thought my mind was full of Manchester, but now it's full of Alex. Alex with his gorgeous suit and sandy hair. I wanted to run my hand through it as I reached for his tie, as if we were in some kind of raunchy perfume ad.

Just as I open the first email, I get a text:

Hey, Steph, it's Eric. Was wondering if you fancy lunch today. Kinda want to escape the house for a bit.

I peer down at the phone. Lunch with Eric? Right now, I have no lunch plans, so I swiftly send a reply:

Shit. I've sent him kisses, because I'm still in Alex mode. I never send Eric kisses.

Not that it matters; it's just to show I'm not being overly serious. Right?

Right.

Seconds later, my phone gives another hopeful ping.

Do you want to meet in Queen's Square at 1? x.

Sounds good! Xx

What's with 'xx'? This is new.

Shh, Eric. It was an accident. Will see you at 1!

:) xx

I go to put the phone down, but not before it vibrates in my hands. Amanda's face fills the screen. I'm popular today.

'Hey, Mand! Look, can I call you back? If this is about the flat listings you sent, I'm on it. I'm—'

Her voice wavers. She's not her usual perky self.

'Steph?' she says. 'It's not about that.'

'What's wrong? Mand, are you OK?'

'Not really,' my sister replies with a loud sniff. 'Remember Dana?'

Dana. Our childhood neighbour. Dana of hazy afternoons and playing dominoes and baking and watching old episodes of *Andy Pandy* on a VHS that she'd dug out, thinking we'd love it. We didn't, but we watched anyway, because we loved *her*. Lovely, lovely Dana.

'Of course I do.'

'Well, she passed away a couple of days ago. I've just heard. I thought you might want to know.'

Chapter 29

Eric

I wait for Steph outside the little café on Queen's Square, where we each get a chunky sandwich and a chai latte. It's not raining, so we make our way to one of benches, watching the winter mist descend as people make their way round the vast stretch of tree-lined grass, wrapped up in warm coats and scarves.

'So, what's this in aid of?' Steph asks.

She seems her usual perky self, but something seems different. Maybe she's having a bad day at work.

'You know,' she adds. 'Taking me out for lunch.'

'No reason. Well, besides wanting to get out for a bit.'

'Jeez, is Jude *that* bad?'

I sip my drink, enjoying the crisp air on my skin. 'Not really. It's just . . .' That I feel trapped, somewhat? Stuck? 'I have a week off and wanted to use it wisely. Thought being out in the cold would inspire me.'

Steph's busy unwrapping her sandwich. She doesn't need to know that I don't have a day off; my 'stomach bug' has now, allegedly, morphed into a full-blown cold. Joshua took it well, but still. Steph would think I'm skiving. She'd disapprove. That's what people do.

'I hope it's all right,' I say. 'You could have said no.'

'Why?' She tucks into the sandwich, giggling as she

realises she's taken too big a mouthful. 'That was so unglamorous,' she mumbles.

'Is it humanly possible to eat one of these glamorously?'

'No. It's like getting out of a taxi in your best dress. There's a knack to it. An art. And there's no way I'd have said no. It's actually nice to be out and . . . away from things.'

'Like what? How's work today?'

Steph lets out a long sigh, slumping against the cold wooden bench.

'It sounds stupid. But I've been thinking about next door again.'

'The Robertsons? Why?'

There's a pause. Steph is looking straight ahead, at the busy square, at the teenager who's just strode past us, backpack slung low. There's an obvious change in her demeanour.

'It sounds silly,' she begins. 'But what if they don't come back and I don't have the chance to explain? What if their pile of mail just gets bigger and bigger and suddenly there's a 'For Sale' sign outside? I'm leaving soon and it feels like I'm leaving on bad terms.'

'That's not the case, Steph. I told you – they'll be back. And we can explain everything. What's brought this on?'

She puts the sandwich down, places it on her lap.

'Today, my sister called me. Told me that someone close to us has passed away. Well, someone we were close to as kids.'

'Really? That's shit. I'm really sorry, Steph.'

'It's fine. I haven't thought about Dana in a long time. Years, even. It was only the Robertsons suddenly vanishing that made me remember all the neighbours from years ago.'

I nod. The place is quiet besides the sound of faint chatter and passing cars.

'I lived in a tower block,' Steph continues. 'So as you can imagine, we had lots of neighbours surrounding us. Dana was amazing. She looked after us when Mum was at work, and we'd always go and play games with her. She taught us to bake and she'd hang our art on her kitchen wall. Dana was wonderful.'

'She sounds lovely. You were lucky.'

'We were. We loved her. She was a great friend to my family. She was distraught when Mum died. And that's the terrible thing about all this: when Mum died, it was the neighbours who cared most. They brought round flowers and food – Amanda's house looked like a florist's – and they offered to help with whatever they could. Whereas my Auntie Grace, Mum's actual *sister*, simply slipped a sympathy card through the door.

'I hadn't seen Dana in years and then Amanda told me today that she's gone. Why didn't I keep in touch?'

'That just happens,' I offer.

Steph doesn't look at me. She stares ahead and I can see the tears forming.

'Life happens,' I tell her. 'We don't always keep in touch with everyone.'

'No.'

She shakes her head. A soft sigh escapes her and I detect a hint of uncertainty in her voice. 'We do. It's just that I'm a terrible person.'

'A terrible person? Come on, Steph. You're not a terrible person. Far from it.'

The tears are fully formed now, streaming down Steph's cheeks, flushed pink from the cold. She dabs at her eyes, smearing her make-up, but it's too late. Her shoulders shake as she sobs, muffled beneath her sleeve, and before I can stop myself, I reach for her, pulling her closer.

'Hey,' I say. 'It's OK. It's all right, Steph.'

'It's not. I had no idea. I should have known about Dana. I should have known because I should have kept in touch.

I was just so fucking stupid and selfish and wanted to leave my old life behind.'

'For good reason,' I say, and I mean it.

She moves into my shoulder, her face concealed, and I let her. I put my arm around her, feeling the warmth of her against me as I rub her shoulder in a soft, circular motion. Even though I can't bear to see her upset, the movement seems natural somehow. All I want is to keep her safe and comforted.

'No. She was family to me and I didn't keep in touch. I didn't *think*. I didn't think and I didn't care, and when I *do* care it's too late. It's way too late. And then it keeps. On. Going . . .'

'It'll be fine,' I say, then hate myself for saying it, because how can it be fine?

All the times I've hated hearing it from other people and here I am, whispering pointless missives into Steph's ears. *It'll all be fine! Don't worry, Eric, everything will be OK. Just think of everything you have to be grateful for!*

It doesn't change anything, does it?

'How do you know it'll be fine?' mumbles Steph, her face buried in my coat.

The shaking stops. My hand accidentally brushes against her hair, but she doesn't object. We're just sitting here, close, still.

'OK, maybe I don't,' I admit. 'I know things won't always be fine, but I know that they'll look better tomorrow. Things don't get better straight away, but they get easier. But listen, this does *not* make you a bad person. None of this does. I know you care about people. It's obvious.'

'You don't know that, though. You don't know me that well.'

'What if I want to?'

We sit for a few seconds, the world silent besides the noise of nature. Steph lets out a sigh, her breathing steady, but she doesn't move from my shoulder. Her hair smells like strawberries and winter air.

'Then that's just silly.'

'I know, I'm not helping.'

'You are,' she says with a hint of laughter in her voice. 'This is nice. I'm sorry for the waterworks.'

'Is this because of your mum?' I ask. 'If it is, you need to stop punishing yourself.'

When she looks up at me, her eyes tell a whole new story. This isn't the Steph I know. It's as though all of her liveliness has gone, replaced by hurt and anger. And looking into her pale green eyes, it's as if everything is unravelling.

'Maybe. I keep thinking it's my fault. Just like Mum. Could I have prevented it? Is there anything I could have done? Should I have known? Could I have helped her, made her happier?'

'Steph, there's nothing more you could have done. It wasn't your fault.'

'I could have stayed,' she says, and her voice is muffled by more tears. 'Mum was sick. She was sick, and by the time she found out . . .' She trails off and I hold her tighter. 'I should have guessed something wasn't right. I should have known that she was weaker, that she wasn't herself. She was my *mum*. And I shouldn't have gone to America.'

My head rings with all the things I could say, but I don't say a word. We stay there, clutching each other on the cold bench until the hour is up – and one thing's for certain.

I don't want to let her go.

Chapter 30

Steph

'So as you can see, the living room is spacious, with a double balcony door, additional storage space . . .'

The letting agent waves his arms around the room like an air traffic controller, pointing out all the saleable details as Amanda shuffles excitedly from foot to foot, her cardigan bright and attention-grabbing in the vast magnolia space.

'You could turn that additional bedroom into a home office,' my sister helpfully suggests. 'And some really nice curtains could brighten up the place. See? Told you this one would be perfect.' She turns to the letting agent who's accompanied us on the past four viewings. Of the three of us, it's Amanda who seems most excited. 'Is this one available now?'

The letting agent – a hopeful twenty-something called Tom in a suit that's slightly too big – releases what sounds like a sigh of relief. 'It is indeed,' he says. 'But there are more viewings lined up. If you're interested, I can take a holding fee today . . .'

I throw him my biggest, most apologetic smile. 'Maybe this is just a *little* too big,' I say.

'Too . . . big?' says Tom, disappointed. It's blatantly obvious he's getting fed up. I can't exactly blame him.

'Do you have anything smaller?'

Amanda is aghast. She shoots me a warning glare. 'Are you serious? This is like, the fourth property we've looked at. What about the last one? It was generous in terms of space.'

'The walls were bright blue, Mand. In every room. How am I meant to deal with that? Blue. *Everywhere.*'

'An underwater theme?' she says, shrugging. 'I can get Poppy to design some cardboard fish.'

Tom looks from Amanda to me, clearly unsure, as if he's weighing up his options. Get rid of us, or show us just one more? We've already wasted two hours of his day.

'I'm just looking for something a bit smaller. *Cheaper.*' I whisper the word as Amanda wanders out of earshot, marvelling at the view from the window.

Tom nods. Realisation dawns. 'I might have something,' he suggests. 'I'll have to call the office. Would you be able to give me an hour? There's a house that's just become available, so I'll see if it's ready.'

'OK,' I nod. 'We'll go and get a coffee and then meet you back at the agency. Come on, Mand!'

We shuffle out of the spacious city centre pad with its balcony and newly decorated interior and into a nearby Costa, and I feel insanely guilty. Amanda insisted on driving me all the way to Manchester so that we could have a sisterly day out, with her helping me to pick out a new home. She meticulously went through every listing, setting up a whole day's worth of viewings.

The problem? They're all way out of my budget.

I join the end of the queue while Amanda slips into a chair at the last remaining free table. I return with two mochas, topped with whipped cream, and I await the interrogation. Judging by her suddenly serious expression, I know it's coming.

'What's up with you?' she asks before I've even sat down.

'Nothing. What do you mean?'

'You're all . . . weird. And none of the flats we've looked at seem right for you. That last one was perfect. It's like you're Goldilocks – that one's too big, that one's too blue, that one is too noisy, that one was "too creepy".'

'Did you see that cellar? I wouldn't be able to sleep at night.'

'Steph.'

She attempts a serious look, only with the whipped-cream moustache – she's a sucker for the stuff, too – it just looks funny.

'What's wrong?' she asks.

I knew I'd have to tell her some time. I thought about it in the car, in the three-and-a-half-hour drive, but there was never the right moment. Not on the way, as we blasted nineties hits along the motorway, or in the services, where we shovelled down a quick McDonald's as if we were eight years old again. When is the best time to admit you've been lying for the best part of three years?

'Look, Mand,' I begin, and I stir the mocha. I've already scooped all the cream off the top. 'I didn't want to tell you, but here's the thing. I can't afford somewhere that costs over a thousand pounds a month to rent. Not yet.'

'What? But you—'

'I know, I know. I'm just not doing as well as you might have thought and—'

'So why didn't you just *tell* me?'

I look at my sister. She glares at me, those giant grey-blue eyes baring into mine, half worried, half annoyed.

'I was going to,' I lie. 'And then you arranged all this . . .'

'I thought I was *helping* you. You could have told me.'

'Why? So you'd know I was a failure?'

She puts down her mug. 'I'd never think you're a failure, Steph. Never.'

'You might. Auntie Grace does.'

'Ignore her. But on the subject of Auntie Grace, are you coming to Nat's wedding? Do you have a plus-one?'

'You do know I'd do anything but go to Nat's wedding, right? I'd rather bungee jump. Or do one of those eating challenges that go viral.'

Amanda considers this. 'But wouldn't *not* going play right into her hands? She'll think you're jealous of Nat. That's how her strange mind works.'

She's right, as awful as that might be. I can picture Auntie Grace's face as she shuffles into a pew, looking around at everyone to make sure they're teary-eyed enough for the photos. She'll be hovering like a movie director, yelling at everyone to 'gaze more lovingly!' at the happy couple so it looks better in the professional shots, a real love story. And she'll definitely, *definitely* notice anyone's absence. Including mine.

'Speaking of plus-ones . . .' There's a playful, teasing tone in Amanda's voice. 'I've seen Instagram. Who's the guy? Is that Alex?'

'Yep, that's him. It's early days so don't get too excited. I know what you're like.'

She makes me explain everything, so I do. Plenty of Alexes, I remind her – her own words – and look around as if one could walk through the door at this very moment, a perfect clone. I show her a photo I took secretly.

'Ooh!' she says, zooming in on Alex's face.

'And here's another.'

'Ooh! Take him. Take *him* to the wedding.'

I laugh it off and sigh, sinking back into the armchair. It's a little too big and it swallows me.

'OK. I still need to find a place to live, though. So, what do you suggest?'

'I'm still annoyed at you for lying. Really, Steph. You know you can tell me anything. But we'll sort it. We'll finish up here then go back and see Tom.'

We stand outside a townhouse forty minutes later; a large, newly-built terrace that's just fifteen minutes' walk from the train station.

'You might be in luck,' Tom says, rapping on the door. 'It's only gone up today.'

There's a thud from inside, heavy feet on stairs, and the door swings open to reveal a tall woman with straight black hair that reaches her waist.

'Y'all right, Tom?' she asks. And then she sees me. 'Oh, hello! Guys, they're here!' she screeches into the house, and gestures for us to follow.

Inside, the house is large, three floors. The woman with the waist-length hair introduces herself as Paula.

'Samira's moving out next week, so we need to find a new housemate,' she says, just as another two people enter the kitchen. It's vast, but there's a dining table with washing draped over the chairs, and an array of mismatched, colourful mugs on the draining board. The place looks nice. Lived-in.

'This is Liam, and Starr.'

'All right?' asks Liam. 'I take it you're here about the room? We're all super friendly, promise.'

'Do you want a tea?' asks Starr. 'Or a gin?'

Amanda and I take up the offer of a tea. Tom requests a water.

Paula leads me to the soon-to-be-vacated room, at the top of the house. There's an en suite with a shower cubicle. The room is still full of Samira's things; there's a large bed and a bookcase and a built-in wardrobe.

'Have you lived in a houseshare before?' asks Liam, appearing on the landing. I think of Eric and the recent addition to his home. How nervous he seemed at this new person moving in, sharing his space. Would these people feel the same about me?

Liam is about my height, with bleached blond hair and kind eyes.

'Only at uni.'

'Well, we're looking for someone fun but respectable. We're quite social, so if you love a pint and a pub quiz, even better.'

'She's ace at a pub quiz,' adds Amanda.

My heart swells.

They're lovely. *These people are lovely.* An hour into meeting my potential new housemates, Tom has already left, asking us to call if I want to take the room.

Of course I do. They're the friendliest bunch. Which means, if I live here, I'll have a ready-made group of friends to start my brand-new life with. I feel wonderfully optimistic all of a sudden.

'Liz is out at the moment,' Liam explains. 'She's at work, but if you want to meet her, we can video call her. She'll like you.'

It's glaringly obvious that I've found my new home. This is it. A houseshare with four amazing people.

New job. New life. New mates.

'What's your number? I'll add you to our group chat,' says Paula as I hurriedly dial Tom's number.

'I'll take it,' I tell him, and he's relieved.

Chapter 31

Steph

I head outside just as dusk descends on Chapel Gardens, the Tupperware box of cookies shuffling under my arm as I lock the flat. In the street, some of the neighbours have started putting up Halloween decorations in preparation for the weekend; windows graced with bat-shaped garlands and silhouettes, doorsteps guarded by well-carved pumpkins. Some have gone all out – the house three doors down has a fake gravestone in the garden that looks a little too real in the evening darkness and an elaborate wreath featuring a witch on a broomstick attached to the door.

It's a collective effort I feel rubbish for not being part of, so I make a mental note to at least pick up some sweets for any trick-or-treaters who might venture up the path. Maybe I'll even attempt to carve a pumpkin to leave outside. Or buy a plastic one. It would make a nice autumn-themed photo opportunity.

The fake gravestone is illuminated by a little solar light; I see it as I peek over the boundary that separates the neighbours' house from Eric's. Amusingly, the child-friendly spookiness of their Halloween theme only serves to make Eric's décor-free home – and the Robertsons', for that matter – look genuinely eerie.

Standing on the doorstep, I press the buzzer to Eric's house. Drifting out from beyond the door is music, faint music, the welcome sound of an electric guitar. A male voice is singing 'Here Comes the Sun' by the Beatles. There's a flicker of movement in the window and the door swings open to reveal Jude in a faded grey T-shirt. He grins when he sees me.

'Steph! You OK? Come on in!'

He stands aside and I step into the hallway. The guitar and the singing is no more, then I remember – Jude is the musician of the house.

'Was that you?' I ask. 'Singing?'

Jude leads me to the kitchen, giving me a playful, shy smile.

'Guilty! Sorry, was it too noisy? I didn't know you could hear me. I had the windows closed and everything. Hope nobody heard my terrible rendition of 'Jolene' earlier. Shit. That's not why you're here, is it? Because of the noise?'

Jude's mildly worried expression is amusing.

'Not at all,' I reply, holding the box of cookies aloft. 'I'm actually here to see Eric. I made him these. And for the record, you sounded fantastic.'

Jude glances curiously at the cookies in my hand and back to me.

'Eric helped me out with something yesterday, so I tried my hand at baking,' I explain.

It sounds much better than admitting to Jude how I was a blubbering wreck in front of Eric and how I've probably scared him off.

Jude nods, smiling as he leans against the kitchen worktop.

'He's just popped to Tesco for a couple of things, but he won't be long. Do you want to stay for a drink? I have some wine. Eric hasn't long left but he should be back soon. You're welcome to wait for him.'

'Are you sure I'm not interrupting anything?'

'Of course not. I was only getting in some practice.'

Jude reaches for a bottle of red on the worktop.

'This was actually for you,' he says. 'New-neighbour gift. I did tell Eric to pass it on, but he obviously didn't. He's been so busy at work lately.'

That's odd. I could have sworn Eric said he had a week off.

'That's really kind of you,' I say graciously. But also confused. 'Why did you get me this? I should be getting *you* something. House-warming and all.'

Jude laughs. 'I'm just trying to be a good neighbour. That's the downside to cities, you know? As much as I love them, sometimes people are a bit closed off. I'm a people person. Are you?'

My mind flits to my working day. I'd spent most of it on autopilot, going through complaint after complaint, trying my hardest to refrain from issuing people some very un-work-safe words. I'd managed to power through the monotony with thoughts of the new job – and, of course, texts from Alex.

'Possibly?' I reply somewhat truthfully. 'I used to be.'

'Used to be? Come on now.'

He's apparently fascinated. He leans against the worktop as if willing me to share more. He takes two glasses from the cupboard in response and pours, his eyes on me. It's like a magic trick.

'I *was* a people person. At least, I was when I was at uni. I used to want to travel. I *did* travel.'

'So you don't travel any more?'

'Not really.'

I take a sip and it's exactly what I need after a day like today. To top it off, I still have a bit of packing to do. The housemates-to-be have been texting me today, eagerly awaiting my arrival:

Room is ready for you! If you order any furniture, we can put it together for when you arrive!

Seriously, they're that great.

Jude's easy to talk to. He's that welcoming beacon of light, that man with a kind smile, probably capable of pulling out your deepest, darkest secrets without so much as a prompt.

The kitchen is chilly, so he asks if I'd rather sit in the living room. Grabbing my wine, I follow him through, absorbing my surroundings with nosey abandon. I sit next to Jude on the leather sofa as he flicks on the TV for background noise.

Just then, something brushes against my leg. I leap up, startled, catching my wine glass just in time. A little orange blur that I recognise as Freddy darts out from between my feet, his grumpy expression implying that *I* scared *him*. Jude bursts out laughing.

'Freddy!' he quips, 'you really need to stop doing that.'

'Whoa, he's fast!'

'He does that,' says Jude. 'I think it's deliberate. Just wanted to give you a fright.'

The ginger ball of fluff launches himself from the floor onto Jude's lap, where he settles down smugly. He throws me a shady glare before looking off into the distance, enjoying the way Jude is scratching between his ears, pushing himself into his hands with all the trust in the world, purring softly.

'Well, I guess I'm not moving for a while now!' Jude says. 'That's his home for the rest of the night.'

'He likes you.'

'Clearly!' Jude says brightly. 'He's not even mine. He's Lloyd's. Lloyd's gone on holiday for two weeks, so Eric and I have joint custody. He's already learning how to play us. Giving us that sad, big-eyed "I'm starving" look as if he's auditioning for an animal shelter ad. Look at him.'

Sure enough, Freddy's staring up at Jude with his huge green eyes of his, the master manipulator.

248

'Hi, Freddy!' I try, but he simply looks away, giving me the cold shoulder. 'Charming.'

Nothing about Freddy looks 'sad'. In fact, to me he seems perpetually grumpy. Or maybe it's just me he doesn't like. He might think I'm trespassing, so I'll need to get into his good books. I'm in his territory, taking up his sofa and Jude.

I reach out to smooth Freddy's silky head, feeling the soft vibrations of his purring.

'See?' says Jude. 'He's getting used to you.'

'He hasn't scratched my face off yet, so that's a good sign.' This is nice. Maybe Freddy has a sweet side, after all.

'He's loving that,' says Jude. 'You got any pets?'

I shake my head, watching Freddy, who's blissfully engrossed in his massage.

'Sadly, I'm not allowed. Landlord's orders. And I'm at work most days anyway, so it wouldn't be fair.'

'Ah.'

Jude goes to reach for his wine but decides against it, so as not to disturb Freddy. I pass it to him instead, as if we're trying our hardest not to wake a sleeping newborn.

'My family always had dogs when I was growing up. A chocolate Labrador, a springer spaniel, a tiny Yorkshire terrier . . . I miss them all. Mum's got a couple of poodles now.'

'I wish I'd had a dog,' I say almost wistfully, thinking of all the times Amanda and I had pestered Mum for a pet of our own. 'My sister and I tried everything to get Mum to agree. A full manifesto of what we were going to do, how we were going to look after it, even buy everything for it, even though we could never have afforded it with our pocket money. We'd go down to the seaside – we lived in Weston – and see all of these people walking their dogs, and we wanted one, as well. It would have been our friend.'

Pulling my phone from my pocket, I fire off another message to the housemates-to-be:

What's the pet situation?

Liam comes back straight away.

Paula has a pet hamster but don't tell anyone!

OK. A hamster. It'll have to do.

'Dogs make pretty good friends,' says Jude. 'And protectors. And running buddies. So, no luck persuading your mum, then?'

On the TV, a panel show is on, the volume low; I can just make out the faint applause of the audience. I feel lucky all of a sudden. That I'm here, indulging in wine with a friend and not alone in my flat, looking at boxes and experiencing that weird cocktail of restlessness, excitement and anxiety.

'Not at all. We lived in a small flat, and we were at school and Mum at work, so Mum had a point.'

'Fair enough. Hey, could you refill us?' he asks over the sound of Freddy's purr.

He puts one leg up on the coffee table, his feet in slippers, which look amusingly old-fashioned for the rest of Jude.

'That's better. Nice and comfy. Don't tell Eric, he hates it when I do that.'

I reach for the bottle on the coffee table, but before I can grab it, a flash of white catches my eye. Peering down, I notice something peeking out from beneath the table; the corner of a book. Reaching over, narrowly avoiding Jude's leg, I pick it up.

It's an A4 book; well-thumbed pages spiral-bound together. Small luminous sticky notes jut out from some of the pages. It looks well-read, well-loved.

'What's this?' I ask before realisation dawns.

This must be Eric's screenplay.

Jude looks, shrugs. 'Eric's. He was reading through it the other day. I have a feeling it's his film. His old draft. Did you know?'

'Know what?'

'That Eric's writing a screenplay? I think it's bloody brilliant that he's writing a film.'

I can't take my eyes off the book in my hand. I run a finger over the title page – *The Lakehouse* – as if this is some sacred document. In a way, it is.

'Have you read it?'

'Oh, no. Not yet – he won't let me. But just think . . . that, right there, could potentially be the horror film of the decade. He hasn't told me much about it but that's just him. He's one of those people who doesn't like to big up his own talents.'

The screenplay. Eric's screenplay is right here, in my very hands. I'm overcome with temptation, a sudden surge of curiosity.

It's as if the room has darkened and everything's a blur besides that book, beaming out at me invitingly.

I'm more curious than ever, my eyes refusing to leave that alluring draft. Would sneaking the tiniest peek be betraying his trust? Surely if he didn't want anyone to see it, he wouldn't leave it lying around . . .

I pull the book towards me and turn the first page. Jude's frown doesn't go unnoticed.

'Come on,' I say. 'I just want a peek. Just *one*. Eric hasn't told me much and I want to know.'

'Then ask him,' Jude replies warily.

We both look at the screenplay in my hands. I'm being incredibly careful, not wanting to get the slightest fingerprint on the cover, which makes me realise *I'm feeling guilty*.

There's a big part of me that *doesn't* want to flick through these pages. But I can't stop myself. It's as if my hands are working but it's not my mind controlling them. Here, right here, is a way of getting that little closer to Eric – something that, until now, I never realised I wanted.

Pulling my legs up onto the sofa, wine in hand, I turn the pages. Jude looks on, still running his fingers through Freddy's fur, although Freddy's turned his head to look at me, his eyes staring firmly into mine. *I know what you're doing,* he seems to say, and the flicker of guilt briefly returns before I tell myself I'm just being paranoid. Like when I'm about to go through airport security and find myself genuinely questioning whether or not someone may have slipped a gun or a giant bag of cocaine into my bag while I was checking my ticket.

Staring down at the words, I find myself engrossed. Because these words, Eric's words, are *good*. I can picture it all playing out on the screen: creepy, atmospheric, with a perfect cast of characters. There's a guy who has just gone through a break-up, the new couple who are moving in together, a student, a grieving widow . . .

I'm lost in it for what seems like hours, barely noticing Jude refill my glass. He's reading, too, over my shoulder, laughing at some of the dialogue, because not only is this creepy as hell, and unexpected, but it's funny. *Eric* is funny. And talented. This piece of work just proves it.

'See?' says Jude. 'He's great, isn't he? And . . . oh my God.'

'What?'

'He kills off the couple!'

'No way! I thought they'd at least last until the halfway mark.'

By now Eric's book is between us, balanced on our knees, and we're reading it together, even though the only person

I want to be reading this with is Eric. Freddy's still purring and we're pointing out the best scenes in genuine excitement.

It's then I hear a shuffling behind us. So does Jude. We turn round and the place is bathed in sudden silence.

Eric stands in the doorway, clutching a carrier bag, his eyes on both of us.

And I've never seen him look so upset.

Chapter 32

Eric

I want to move, but I can't.

My feet are stuck. Stuck to the stupid grey carpet. It's like they're encased in concrete as I watch the scene unfold in front of me; as though I'm directing it, watching from the sidelines. But this is real life. This is a real-life horror movie and I'm part of it. My body is rigid as Steph and my stupid fucking housemate laugh together on the sofa, all close, *too* close. They're drinking wine over what I've now noticed, with absolute soul-crushing dread, is *my screenplay*.

Steph splutters as she notices me, the glass almost tumbling from her grasp, but she catches it just in time. Her face contorts in shock as her big eyes meet mine, trying to hide the incriminating evidence by stuffing it back under the coffee table.

'All right, Eric?' Jude asks, but there's guilt all over his face.

Jude gets to his feet, sending Freddy scarpering from his lap and into the kitchen with a disgruntled meow.

'What the fuck is going on?' I hiss.

The carrier bag tumbles from my grip, tins thudding onto the carpet, but I don't care. I was only gone for less than an hour and I've returned to *this* – Jude snuggling up to Steph on the sofa, reading my work. My terrible, terrible first draft that I didn't want anyone to lay eyes on for a long, long time.

Even bloody *Freddy* was in on it, cosied up with the two of them, all smug, lying on Jude's lap like feline royalty. It took that cat three weeks to get used to me when I first moved in. Three weeks of tentative bribing to convince him I wasn't a threat, that I wasn't just some annoying bloke who'd come to steal his favourite sleeping spot on the sofa. Three weeks, yet Jude seemed to have won him over instantly.

'Hi, Eric. You startled us,' gushes Steph.

I shoot her an incredulous look.

Maybe I'm doing it wrong. Maybe this is what true horror is all about. Maybe I'm focusing on the wrong things; darkened shadows in the old, peeling hallways, figures crawling from a lake at midnight, creaking footsteps that could be your mind playing terrible tricks. Maybe, instead, it's just *this*.

Jude, with his insipid handsome grin that vanished as soon as he saw me. At least he has the good grace to look a tad remorseful. They separate quickly, like teenagers caught by an overbearing parent. Jude holds his hands up, turning to me.

'Mate, we're sorry. We just—'

'I don't want to hear it.'

'Hey,' says Steph. She gives me a hopeful smile. I don't return it.

Of all the people, I thought she could be trusted.

'We were just reading and—'

'I think you should leave now.'

Seconds pass. They stare at me as if I'm joking.

'Eric . . .'

'Can you leave please, Steph?'

My body is hot, but I can't move – it's as though I'm eight years old again, trying roller skating at the local rink for the first and only time in my life in front of my entire class at Matt Jenkins' birthday party. I'm standing at the side, gripping the bar for safety, thinking of all the various ways it could go wrong. Overanalysing in my head, taking in all the risks that only made me grasp the bar tighter as I hobbled unevenly onto the rink beneath the colourful movement of disco lights. Everyone was there – skating, moving, laughing, tumbling . . . but I didn't want to tumble. Falling would be failing. I could make out my dad's face in the sea of parents sitting in the plastic seats along the sides, watching me, giving me that 'go on!' motion. That little push.

But I couldn't move. I simply stood there, stuck, silent, furious with myself.

That fury has returned, away from the glare of disco lights. Instead, I'm facing the same rage in my living room and yet again, *I can't move*. All I feel is heat. Heat, and the need to get away, to crumple up on the floor somewhere where it's cool and quiet.

'Eric . . .' Steph tries again, softly.

She gets to her feet and moves towards me. My body manages to co-operate enough for me to step aside, avoiding her mournful look, the guilt in her face.

'Just go. Please.'

We look at each other for a moment before she finally leaves the room. Listening for the faint click of the front door as she closes it behind her, I turn to face Jude.

'I really can't fucking believe you,' I manage.

'Mate.' Jude holds up his hands in mock surrender. 'I'm sorry we looked at the screenplay. But listen, we—'

'Why the hell do you think it's OK?'

'What? Eric, calm down.'

'No!'

Jude looks at me blankly. 'What's the matter? Eric, look, we just—'

'What's the *matter*? You're asking me what the fuck's the matter? I come in to find you going through my personal stuff. Not to mention with Steph, of all people.'

He looks almost confused, like he's done nothing wrong. The absolute prick.

'Wait. I get it now. This has more to do with Steph, doesn't it?' he asks.

'You knew what you were doing.'

'What? Mate, I genuinely don't know what's got you so riled besides the screenplay. I know we shouldn't have looked at it. But it was there, and you—'

'You *know* I like Steph, Jude. You *know*. And I can't even trust you not to try to get into her knickers the moment my back is turned.'

Jude's eyebrows shoot up. He laughs. *Laughs*.

'Eric, listen. Nothing's happening with Steph. I'm not trying to get into anyone's knickers. Well, besides this one girl at work, but that's unlikely to happen. You know, Roz – the one I pointed out to you the other day? Tall, purple hair?'

'I couldn't give a shit, to be honest.'

He looks hurt.

'Right. You're angry, and I get that. Steph's lovely, but we were only chatting. She came round to see you. I asked her if she wanted to wait for you. I knew you were coming back.'

'That's it? So you just had to be all cuddled up together, drinking wine?'

I can feel the heat in my face. Jude takes a deep breath, almost frustrated. I haven't yet witnessed Jude frustrated. Until now.

'We weren't "cuddled up". You're imagining that.'

'That's not what I saw.'

'We were sat together and Freddy was on my lap – I could hardly move. What was I supposed to do when she came round, close the door in her face? She's our *neighbour*, Eric. I was only being friendly.'

'So you're "being friendly". Is that it? The excuse?'

'Eric, can you hear yourself? I bought her the wine, remember? It was *hers*. Maybe if you'd bothered to give it to her in the first place like I asked you, it wouldn't be such a problem.'

'And now it's my fault. Great.'

Jude takes a long, deep breath. He picks up the cushions from the sofa, arranging them neatly. Even the fact he's so tidy is annoying me now. I just want him out of the house.

'Listen,' he says tightly. 'Nothing happened. Is that the opinion you have of me? You actually think I'd do that? And if I did, if I *was* that monster you seem to think I am, you don't have the right to say who I, or Steph, for that matter, can talk to. If I wanted to try to "get into her knickers", as you so eloquently put it, I have every right to.'

I have the sudden urge to leap over the sofa and launch myself at this stupid man. Kick him out of the house, followed by his drum kit that takes up half the living room because it "won't fit upstairs".

But I can't – one, because I'm not strong enough, and two, I'm pretty sure that would be illegal.

Instead, I hurry towards the coffee table, snatching up my screenplay, away from any more prying eyes.

'Seeing as I can't trust you not to go through my personal stuff in the shared space, I'll be taking this. I'll be adding a new rule to the list.'

'If you want to, so be it. I don't know what I've done to anger you so much lately. You can always talk to me, you know. I don't know what's going on with you, but you can't take it out on other people. Otherwise, you'll have nobody left.'

'Forget it. I'm out.'

I'm gone before he can argue, slamming the living room door behind me.

In the quiet safety of my bedroom, his words hit me stronger, faster than any punch he could possibly swing. Within seconds, I hear his footsteps pounding up the stairs.

The screenplay crumples in my grasp and I hurl it at the wall, watching as it comes apart, a soft explosion of paper. I watch as the pages bend and flutter to the floor.

Because he's right.

He's absolutely right.

Chapter 33

Steph

It's raining, but I'm happy.

It falls like a sheet outside the window, making the lights of the harbour – tiny white orbs reflected on the water – twinkle. Alex and I are watching from the cosy safety of a warm bar. It's Halloween, but we've taken a chance on a place that doesn't seem *too* crowded with costumed drinkers, but it's still fun to spot them. I'm sporting some spider-themed earrings and dark red lipstick to give me that slightly glamorous, goth look.

Outside, people stand beneath a sea of umbrellas as a beam of moonlight dances on the water and I feel exhilarated, anew, like someone else in the presence of Alex. And then I remember, I *can* be someone else. I can be whoever I want tonight; not the usual Steph from the office, the complaints girl, obedient and quiet, getting on with things. '#Perfection' I tap out beneath my latest photo for Instagram.

Speaking of Insta, I've scrolled through it a few times while Alex has been at the bar. I've offered to get the drinks in, but he's declined. *My treat.* The girls' feeds are aglow. Saskia's posted from her at-home date night. Tamz is at the gym, her #WeddingPrep gym selfie racking up the likes. Clearly, she's touched up her hair and make-up before posting, because nobody could look that glowing and perfect after a vigorous workout. Or maybe Tamz does, because she's just that magical.

But people can be who they want to be on here, can't they? They *can* be magical, beautiful, rich, popular. It's why I've just snapped a selfie, having decided the lighting was perfect. It's obvious – social media is a sport, the perfect life always winning, and the least I can do is take part. Which might, or might not, have something to do with the barrage of questions from Saskia and Tamz at work this afternoon.

Alex is making his way back from the bar, weaving between tables full of couples. My phone pings with a message from Amanda:

Nice photo! Are you out with Alex, then?

Yes!

Aaand have you asked him about being a plus-one to Nat's wedding? The spot is open, after all.

'Hey,' he says, grinning, placing two fresh glasses on the table. 'This one's rhubarb.'

'Ooh, lovely!' I take a grateful sip, tapping out the rest of my message. 'My sister,' I tell him, fearful of looking rude, but I can't exactly keep Amanda waiting; she'll be pestering me for an answer all night otherwise.

I'm not asking him about the wedding yet, Mand. Leave me to my gin. The last thing I want to do is spring Nat on him.

Why not?

I wouldn't wish that on my worst enemy.

If HE is perfect, he'll accept you and your weird family.

I laugh. 'Sorry,' I say. 'So, we have a cousin who's getting married. She's *very* high maintenance.'

'Tell me about it,' he says with a chuckle. 'My sister was the same. I can't even begin to tell you how much *that* wedding cost. There was even a little imperfection on the cake and it was as if the world had ended.'

Well, that goes to show *he* isn't high-maintenance, so that's another plus. Although, as far as tonight is concerned, I'm totally up there. For the first time in over a year, I have *made the effort*. Like, spent-two-whole-hours-in-the-bathroom kind of effort. The shaving everywhere, body lotion, the last dregs of my expensive perfume, even plucking out rogue eyebrows kind of effort. Even those pesky white ones that for some reason are gradually increasing in number, even though my hair isn't grey yet. The hidden woes of ageing ready to pop out of you and make you *really notice* when you're prepping for a big date.

I don't know what I'm expecting with Alex. This is one of those see-what-happens kind of nights, reminding me that I'm so out of practice. On the other hand, this is also exciting. Alex is hot, extremely so, as if he could have stepped off the set of some brand-new TV show everyone's hooked on, and I am smooth and silky and wearing special underwear that I can barely feel. I'm not ready, but I'm also readier than ever. More importantly, I'm ready just to see where this goes.

Hopefully, straight into the realm of fun.

I dressed up tonight; the black dress again, only with some lace tights and accessories to make it look a little different, a little new, a little exciting.

'Sas tells me you like to travel,' Alex says now.

So far, we've covered the basics. I know he has two siblings. He broke up with his ex, Amelia, over a year ago. It was 'rather messy', but water under the bridge now. Her loss, I tell myself.

Of course Sas thinks I like to travel – and that's not far from the truth. When she interviewed me alongside Ciaran, I was all aglow with tales of America and plans and goals. Plans that never came to fruition. I've just pretended that they have.

'Do you like skiing?' he asks. 'I go every year.'

'Hmm . . .' I say, taking another sip of tangy gin.

Here's the thing, *I can't ski*. I tried once, on the dry ski slopes as a teenager on a school trip, and toppled over hilariously in front of the entire class. The thought of my legs being stuck together, my feet immovable, makes me panic. Back then, I stayed rooted to the spot, my legs entangled, thinking: how can I move? How can I run? What if this was a real slope? What if I die? And then after another two attempts, helped along by Amanda, who was equally terrible, we vowed it wasn't our thing. We'd just go our whole lives avoiding skiing, however glamorous people tell us it is.

And now here is Alex, whipping out his phone to show me photos of gorgeous snow-capped mountains and deep, fluffy virgin snow.

'Look at that,' he says. 'Verbier, Switzerland. I go every year with some friends – you should definitely come along.'

No. No, thank you.

'Maybe.'

'You'd love it,' he says.

'Would I?'

But I find myself nodding along, like a smiling mannequin with no control over my own neck.

'It does look beautiful,' I say.

I'm not wrong; it really does. But it's just not my thing. I'll stick to rainy hillsides and camping trips. Flights to sunny locations where there's wine and a poolside and books. And America. The bustling streets of New York City. The bright lights of Las Vegas. Boston's historical buildings, steeped in history. The graveyards of Salem, Massachusetts.

'Have you been to New York?' I ask.

He chuckles. 'Hasn't everyone?'

I shrug. 'Not really. I love it, though. I'd always wanted to go, ever since I was a child, and when I did, it was amazing.'

He takes another sip of his drink and we talk more about work.

'It really is a shame you're going to be leaving us,' he says, and for a second I wonder what to say.

But we can still have fun?

But I don't get the chance to speak, because Alex has leaned across the small table and his lips are on mine. Soft and slow, and I let myself fall into him, savouring the moment. He pulls me closer and I'm reminded of the elevator, and all of a sudden I want to be away from here and somewhere private.

Reading my thoughts, Alex says, 'Shall we go somewhere else after this?'

His smile is mischievous, the same kind of look he had in the lift at work, and the excitement takes over, forcing me out of the booth and into the rain, where Alex puts up his large umbrella and wraps his arm around me. His touch is electric.

'I'll book an Uber,' he says, and while he's distracted, I snap another photo.

It's a photo of Alex, candid, beneath his umbrella, standing just outside the crowd of nearby drinkers who

264

have piled out into the cool air. The photo captures perfectly the lights on the water, blurred slightly, as if Alex is the only one worth looking at. I whack on a filter, tap out a caption and post.

Alex returns. His arm snakes around my waist and I allow myself to get closer, enjoying the thrill of being here, being *his*, on such a nice night. It's as if we're on a stage and the whole city, the whole world, can see us, but I try to keep the sentimentality to a minimum.

We both know how this night is going to end. We both know what we want. This will not end in a relationship.

Just enjoy it, I tell myself.

It's only half past eight, but here in the city centre the night is still young as we weave through the bustling crowds. A man excuses himself as he squeezes awkwardly past, dressed as a giant pumpkin. A couple with a pushchair, a toddler sleeping soundly within it, passes us. The child is bundled up cosily in a woolly hat topped with a little pom-pom and a pair of matching mittens.

'Aww,' I say. 'My niece looked like that when she was a baby. Had one of those same hats.'

Alex glances over to me and smiles. 'I'm guessing you don't have any kids of your own?' he asks. 'You haven't mentioned any, so I just assumed . . .'

'I don't. Just my niece, Poppy. I love her to bits.'

'How old is she?'

'She's five.'

'So, *are* you planning on having any of your own?'

The question is surprising, but I answer anyway. 'Not really,' I reply truthfully.

'How come?'

'Personally? I don't think I'll ever be ready. Having children sounds amazing. My niece is such a brilliant kid. She's clever and bright and hilarious, and spending time with her makes me think it's something I want to do. I guess it depends on what the future brings. I'd love to have someone to share experiences with and teach all about the world and its wonders, not to mention injustices. But I can do that with Poppy. Motherhood seems rewarding, but at the same time it's hard, and exhausting, expensive, and you really have to make sure it's what you want . . .'

I trail off, looking over at the harbour. The woman and the child with the pom-pom hat have long disappeared into the distance, their space taken over by evening walkers and drinkers congregating outside the bars, faces pink with the chill and a sense of purpose.

'That's sensible,' says Alex thoughtfully. 'And refreshing, you know? So many people don't think like that. Don't think it through.'

I nod in agreement. 'It's a big decision.'

Alex continues. 'This is why you have all of these parents whining that the government isn't giving them enough money. They say, "I can't feed my kids!", like it's everyone else's fault. These women assume it's everyone else's responsibility. If they bothered to get a decent job before they popped out so many children, they wouldn't be in that position. It gets on my nerves.'

The air is suddenly cold.

'What?' I ask.

Alex laughs, pulling me closer beneath the umbrella. 'You know. Scroungers. It's all we ever hear about these days.'

'What, *poverty*?'

He shakes his head, as though the very word is awkward and vulgar and he doesn't want to hear it. 'You could call it that, I suppose.'

'I can't just *call* it that. It *is* that.'

There's a brief moment of silence. I'm lost for words. Light from a nearby street light spills into the river, illuminating the waves, and for a moment I consider jumping into the freezing water for a nice cool dip, because all of a sudden it's much more inviting than where I'm standing right now.

'So, you're happy to do it for them?' he says. His voice has taken on a serious tone. 'To pay for these people, even though it's not your fault that they chose to be irresponsible?'

My heart hammers as I look at Alex. Perfect Alex, with his great sense of humour and charming demeanour, which is hastily diminishing with every second that passes. *These women* . . .

Because it's all our fault, isn't it?

Regardless of how someone's life can go, regardless of whether you can have everything you dreamed of one moment and nothing the next, regardless of whether the life you loved crumbled when your husband walked out, barely to be heard from again . . . it's all the fault of *these women*.

I'm interrupted by another soft ping – an Instagram notification. Sure enough, Saskia's noticed, commenting beneath the photo of Alex with a row of heart emojis. It doesn't take long for Amanda to join in. 'What a catch!' she texts.

Twenty-three likes.

'Sometimes it's not as straightforward,' I manage, through a haze of newly formed anger, and rain.

It's getting heavier, distorting the path as we stand there, waiting for the Uber. I realise I'm quiet, strangely quiet, probably because my head is filled with thoughts of Mum. And I wonder what Alex sees when he looks at me. This dress feels even cheaper now, as if it's about to fall apart, as if thin, invisible fingers will pick at the seams until the fabric flutters to the floor, exposing the fraud that I am. Does he think I'm like Saskia and Tamz? Does he think I just breeze through life on a high of excitement and reliance and privilege?

I am not one of them. I will never be one of them.

Forty-one likes.

The decision is easy: I will *not* argue. I won't leap down that irreversible path, because tonight was going so well. It was meant to be fun – a bit of frivolity before I move away. When I remember that fact, I feel all right.

I can just pretend it didn't happen, brush it off and get on with things, because pretty soon I won't be seeing him again. Reluctant to text Amanda, who I picture at home watching TV with Stevie and Poppy, awaiting my updates with bated breath, to alert her that Alex is a bit of a twat – well, a lot of one – I tap out 'It's going well!' And then turn to Alex just as the car pulls up.

I wait for him to respond, to argue. 'You can't blame people like that,' I tell him. 'Not everyone's the same.'

'Fair enough,' he says, shrugging, and I'm grateful that the conversation is over.

The moment of anger has gone, swallowed into the atmosphere along with the popcorn-scented vape smoke of a passer-by.

'Do you fancy coming back to mine for a bit?'

Beep, goes my phone.

Like, like, like.

I won't have to see him again, I tell myself, trying to quell the bad feeling. What does it matter? *You need to have fun again, Steph. Fun.*

Plastering on a smile, I shuffle into the car.

Chapter 34
Steph

The car rolls to a stop outside a block of lavish new executive flats housed in an old warehouse not far from the city centre. We could have walked the distance, but Alex insisted because of the rain.

'Bought this place last year,' he explains proudly.

I don't respond, because I'm too distracted by the image of him: Alex, his light hair damp from the rain, almost falling into his eyes, clutching the umbrella as he leads me up the staircase to the second floor, his other hand in mine.

This is what I need. This is what I've been missing. The kind of company I've longed for since I've been in this city but never managed to get, even though it comes easily to everyone else; at least, it feels that way. They make it all look so simple. And here he is, giving me a playful smile as he stops outside the door with a '19' in gold lettering, fumbling for his key – and my skin tingles, brushing against his own. It's going to happen. It's going to happen *tonight*.

I've sat at work imagining just how this would go down. What I'd be wearing, where we'd be, who would make the first move. In my head, it's been me, but right now, before we've even made it into Alex's vast hallway, it's him who is leading the way. All pretence of coming in for a drink and a chat have been discarded, and it's happening. Finally, we're alone. And we're going to make the most of it.

I barely get the chance to look around Alex's flat, besides the living room; beautiful yet barely furnished, the sofa faux leather, the TV wide – the usual makings of a single man's pad. From the window I can see the lights of the river. I have no more time to be curious, because Alex's attention has turned fully to me, against the hallway wall. His lips are on mine again, pressing urgently, as though we've been apart for so long, our energy built up and waiting.

His hand is already venturing hastily up my skirt, tugging at my one decent pair of tights, and before I know it, my hands are in his damp hair and he's groaning against me. I'm enjoying every second of this. It's been so long and *I want him*. I want him so much.

I want him even more when he leads me down the corridor towards his bedroom. I want him when he pulls me onto his bed, his arms wrapped around my body, making me feel safe, needed. I want him when he's touching every inch of me and his fingers against my skin are like tiny jolts of electricity, so perfectly shocking, every touch so warm, so wanted.

Alex's touch is frantic. I let myself fall into him. Let him pull my dress over my head, move my hands, my body, all at the right moments until we're a tangle of limbs and sheets.

But it's not right. I feel detached, somehow. As if my body is moving, enjoying Alex in all his near-naked glory, but I'm not – I'm locked inside somewhere. I want to be home. Or do I? Am I thinking about it because I'm not used to this?

Alex is great. Alex is perfect and I'm lucky.

But I'm not lucky. I realise this when he looks at me. *Really* looks at me. Hungrily – and oh-so sexy – but something about this whole situation doesn't feel right. It isn't that I'm not enjoying it, or him – but *it doesn't feel right*.

He isn't right. Not for me.

'I want you,' Alex groans. 'Right now.'

His eager growl makes me melt in his grip. He's on top of me now and my body is following suit, enjoying his touch, his skin against mine.

So why does it feel so wrong?

I mean, this man is hot, and has serious bedroom talents, but this is *also* a man who thinks poverty isn't a problem. This is also a guy who, now that I think about it, would also make me cringe on a regular basis if he wasn't so attractive.

'I want you, *right now*,' he says, louder this time, as if to prove my point.

Shit.

My bra – pink, lacy and, quite frankly, itchy as hell – is in Alex's hand. He drops it to the floor, returning to my body, his hands cupping my breasts as his lips meet my neck. I'm not excited any more. This is uncomfortable.

I move to wriggle out of his grasp, but he takes this to mean I want it more. He takes my wrist and pins me to the bed, his lips against my neck, his faint stubble rubbing against my skin. *Now it's all wrong*.

'Alex, stop,' I say.

'Oh?' He pulls away, his smile naughty, then he sees my face. The intensity in his eyes diminishes. 'Why?'

'I think I need to go.'

'What did I do?'

He gets up quickly. I can't help but notice the flash of frustration on his face. The fear. What did he do? Of course, it's all about him.

'Nothing! It's not you. It's just . . .'

'What, then?'

I can sense all the reasons running through his mind. I try to come up with a good excuse, but then think, you know what? Fuck it.

'I fucking *hate* skiing.'

'*What*?'

Alex is incredulous. It's almost funny, the way he's slunk back onto the plain grey sheets, defiant and confused all at once.

'I hate skiing. I tried it when I was younger, and me and skis *do not* get on.' I'm leaping off the bed in search of my discarded underwear and dress.

'What's that got to do with anything?'

I turn to face him. 'I can't do this. You know almost nothing about me and we're just not . . . Look, this is weird. It's weird because I keep hiding things about me when I'm with you. Like skiing. Oh, and that I'm the daughter of *one of those women*. Did you know that? Is that OK with you?'

His face changes as realisation dawns. Even so, he lets out a long sigh, as though exhausted, and wills me back to the bed.

'Is that what this is about? Because I made some stupid comment? Because if so, that's silly. I apologised. Come back to bed.' He pats the sheets beside him, as if all will be forgiven and I'll crawl back to him like an obedient puppy.

'It's not just that,' I say.

'I thought we were just having a bit of fun.'

'We were.'

'O-K . . .'

He says 'OK' slowly. Like I'm a child in danger of a tantrum in public. He assumes I'll just shrug, smile obediently, agree that all is fine and continue. Because he's just that great.

But it's not fine, and he's not sorry. He's just sorry he was called out.

Alex doesn't want someone like me. If he did, he wouldn't have said those things. He thought he was dating another Sas, another Tamz. Someone undoubtedly sweet but also, often, phenomenally out of touch. He assumed I'd be impressed or, worse, that I'd be just like him. He thought I was different because I appear to fit in.

And I don't want someone who makes me lie in an attempt to impress. Someone who makes me feel the need to dress up and hide myself. Someone who makes me feel secretly inferior, so much so that I worry, and feel ashamed, and realise mid-sex that this is all so fucking bizarre.

I thought I could fit in. At the beginning, I thought it would be easy – that I could fake it. Only now, in the discomfort of my late twenties, do I notice how staggeringly, laughably naïve I was.

Pulling on my clothes in record time, I remind myself it's not his fault. He doesn't know any better.

And that, right there, is the problem.

Chapter 35

Eric

I open the door to an explosion of orange and purple and green.

'What the hell?'

'Eric!'

Jude, who's standing on a ladder in the living room, whips round to see me. He's halfway through pinning a garland to the wall above the fireplace. A row of jolly ghostlike shapes, hand in hand. It trails from his unsteady grip. As he turns, catching my disbelief, one side of the shiny foil decoration flutters to the floor.

'Dammit,' he says. 'You all right?'

'I'm good. Work was busy.'

I notice his gaze sweep over my clothes. I'm not in my work uniform. I haven't been at work for over a week, but Jude doesn't know this, even though it looks like he might suspect. It's none of his business.

Since our recent argument, he's been doing his best to stay out of my way – an arrangement I can happily get behind. Ultimately, he's been quiet, keeping his music practice to a minimum. Even in the kitchen his noise has been reduced to an almost non-existent level, as if he's sneaking around the house on tiptoe, trying his hardest to go unnoticed. The smoke alarm hasn't gone off once in the past two days.

It's bliss.

'I'm good,' I reply, stepping past a plastic bag full of white netting.

'Want to give me a hand with that spiders' web in a minute?' Jude asks brightly.

I reach in, pulling out the material, which is soft and almost sticky in my hands. As I tug the last of it from the bag, I'm greeted by a selection of weirdly realistic, massive plastic spiders.

The sofa is also taken up with Halloween decorations. There are a couple of plastic pumpkins, swathes of dark purple fabric, a tacky cardboard skeleton to hang on a door, a couple of plush black cats decked out in witches' hats and more garlands. And a mop.

'Couldn't get a broomstick?' I quip.

'Oh, that's actually for the kitchen. We really needed a replacement.'

'Right.'

Now that I really look, Jude has also placed some spooky-looking candlesticks on the mantelpiece. Then my heart sinks.

'Jude, *please* say you aren't hosting a party tonight.'

Jude steps down from the ladder, reaching for an open bottle of beer on the coffee table. He's bought beer. My mind travels to the possibility of a kitchen full of beer. And vodka. And everything else. A whole army of Jude's mates descending on the house for a loud band rehearsal-slash-Halloween piss-up.

Jude shakes his head. Looks at me as if I'm acting strangely. As if my concerns aren't valid.

'Of course not,' he says. 'Well, not for anyone else.'

'Then what's this?' I sweep my hand over the half-trans-formed room, which conveniently looks like it's being done up for a party. 'And *this*?'

'That, my friend, is a pumpkin. A jack-o'-lantern, to be precise. That's just a plastic tub, but I've got two actual pumpkins in the kitchen. I've already carved one – we can put it outside later.'

Ugh. A jack-o'-lantern. I have a rather unpleasant memory of last Halloween, kicking one of those wonderfully crafted pumpkins across a darkened street, drunk, because Clarissa dumped me.

Just looking at the pumpkin's silly, childlike, face makes me feel sick. It's not exactly a memory I cherish. I haven't touched Jack Daniel's since.

'But what's it all *for*?' I ask, bracing myself for the answer. Jude merely shrugs.

'It's Halloween! Have you not noticed? Mate, you must have walked past about five houses all kitted out in this spooky garb.'

'And?'

'You're telling me you haven't done this place up for Halloween before?'

I can't help it. I laugh. Taking in the sofa, the garland, the hope in Jude's face, it's all too much. Moving some of the plastic crap aside, I slump onto the sofa, hearing the welcoming hiss of the old leather.

'Really? Why would we?'

'Because it's fun. To be honest, compared to all the other houses on this street, this one looked a bit shit. I had some of this stuff from my old place and bought a few more things in the supermarket along with dinner. I just thought it would be a bit of a laugh. I also picked up two giant bags of those little Haribo packets, for the trick-or-treaters. We've got more than enough. If you want to help, go grab them from the kitchen and fill up those pumpkin tubs, would you?'

Sighing, I pull myself up off the sofa and pad to the kitchen, trying to ignore the mess of pumpkin innards all over the worktop, a clear sign of Jude's craftsmanship. I spot the bags of assorted sweets and snatch them up, stopping at the fridge for a beer of my own. I'm defeated. The last thing I want is to argue with Jude. For the past two hours I've been walking, wandering around Redland just to try to gain a sense of purpose, a sense of clarity, because staying in the house wasn't doing it for me. Staring at a screen, looking at the words of my screenplay blending into one another like nonsense – I only felt worse for it.

Heading back into the living room, I get a sense that something's amiss.

'Where's Freddy?' I ask. I can't see him in the living room and he wasn't in the kitchen. 'Usually, he darts out from under the hedge to come in with me, but he didn't tonight.'

'No idea,' replies Jude, making a start on the spider's web around the window. 'I haven't seen him yet. It's still early, though. Maybe he's still out, prowling.'

'Or he got scared of all this,' I say, holding up the cat plushies. Jude rolls his eyes, laughing.

'Freddy fears nothing.'

That much is true. He's probably upstairs, curled up in the warmth of Lloyd's bed, or on his favourite spot on the landing, snoozing the evening away.

'Anyway,' Jude continues, 'I was thinking we could drink, put on some classic horrors.'

'Is this all for the benefit of the neighbours?'

Jude throws me one end of the webbing and I move to the window, helping to separate it. I reach up, with him on the other end, and we attach it to each corner, spreading it across into the centre of our big bay window as creatively as we can.

'Kind of. But it's also my way of apology. For the other night.'

'I told you, I'm sorry I shouted, but you broke my trust. You *and* Steph.'

'It was pretty damn unforgivable, I know. I shouldn't have read your private draft, so your response was totally justified. I thought we could try and put it behind us and have a nice evening.'

'Sure.'

I finish up with the far corner. Our living room looks suitably creepy. Maybe we should keep it year-round.

'I love all this,' says Jude. 'My parents have always been big on Halloween. I saw all the other houses and figured, why not make a bit of effort? Even number 15 have a ghost in their window. I'm not going to be upstaged.'

'Who lives in number 15?'

'A lady called Irene. She has a cat that hisses. Just a shame about next door, though – I think number 26 is the only house in the street without a pumpkin.'

'Yeah. Maybe they'd take part if they weren't on holiday.'

'Ah well. I've got the night off, so I thought I'd indulge in a bit of Halloween spirit.'

'That's nice.'

Our spider's web is complete. We stand back to admire our handiwork, half expecting it all to fall down disastrously, but it looks fantastic.

'See?' remarks Jude. 'Looks great. But not without the spiders. You want to do the honours?' He hands me the bag then takes another swig of beer. 'What's up with you, then?' he asks. 'You seem the type who loves Halloween. Given your film collection, the screenplay . . .'

I let out another sigh as I pull spiders from the bag; two large ones and an array of smaller, more friendly-looking ones, their furry legs entangled. An entire family of smug plastic spiders staring up at me.

'I used to love Halloween. A bit more than Christmas, actually.'

'Weirdo.'

'Seriously! Always have. I used to love staying in watching movies and just eating junk all evening. Until I started going out with Clarissa . . . And then it was different. It suddenly became this big night and we'd go out.'

'Nothing beats a themed night out. Although saying that, I work at a bar. I can't exactly escape it. It's great, but it does get tiresome after eleven when everyone's pissed, the make-up's melted and the mummies have slowly unravelled. Did you enjoy it?'

'Kind of. It was mainly her friends; couples who'd host a party, or we'd go on a bit of a pub crawl. Not normally my thing, but I went anyway. She loved it.'

'Nice.'

'Until last year. She dumped me.'

'Ah.'

'On Halloween.'

'*Ouch.*'

'It wasn't the best night, I can tell you that much. I can barely remember getting into bed. So this is all just a reminder. It's reminded me that it's been a whole year and I still haven't got my life together. Right, where does this one go?'

'Hmm . . .' Jude deliberates. 'The big ones go in the corners. I'll grab some more of the candlesticks for the window, too. Look, your life isn't that bad. You make it sound like it's awful, but you've got work, and friends, and Steph. Which is why I was going to suggest inviting her round this evening.'

'What? Are you still—'

'Hear me out,' says Jude cautiously. 'As I was *going* to say, I'm sorry about the other night, but honestly, mate,

279

nothing happened. So I thought, hey, why don't we ask her to come over? I'll make myself scarce, honest. I'll stay on drink and trick-or-treat duty.'

His offer makes me want to hurl the rest of the spiders at the window. Or into the bin. He's too nice. Maybe he's a serial killer or something, trying too hard to fit in with this whole *good neighbour* act. I'll get to the bottom of it – if he doesn't kill me first, on Halloween night.

'Thanks. But I don't think Steph will be round. She's out tonight. She's seeing someone.'

'I feel I'm making your day distinctly worse. Sorry.'

'Hardly your fault, is it?'

I pull my phone from my pocket, open Instagram, showing Jude the latest pictures on Steph's feed. Her latest #DateNight selfie. The picture of a man beneath an umbrella.

'Who's he?'

'Who knows?'

Jude sighs, clicking another plastic candlestick into place.

'Well, we can drink ourselves into oblivion before some cheesy slasher flicks, if you like. That might take your mind off it. You can still ask Steph round, you know. She's still your neighbour, after all.'

'I guess so.'

'Now, where shall we put the skeleton?'

I focus on the task at hand, pinning the plastic skeleton with its grinning face to the kitchen door. Sadly, Jude is right. We're still neighbours. Even though I've spent the past few days unable to take my mind off our lunch together, reality comes hurtling back to me with a sickening thud. Steph has her own life. We're just friends.

Phone in hand, I suddenly remember to open the group chat I'd put on mute, wondering on the off-chance if one of the guys might want to join in our very minimal impromptu gathering.

Scrolling through the most recent messages, I know that won't be happening. There are pictures of my friends and all of their kids, decked out in their creepy costumes. Baby Harry is a tiny bat. Joe's daughters are amusingly dressed as the twins from *The Shining*. Top marks for that, to be fair. They're all going trick-or-treating, then heading to a kids' party hosted at Tim's.

I spot the message, an afterthought, towards the bottom of the conversation: *Feel free to come too, Eric! But it's probably not your thing!*

Just as good as being uninvited.

By half past eight, we've made it through two movies and a decent amount of booze. Our creepy window display has been successful, with plenty of children who have stopped at the door with their parents, pointing out the spiders and the bats dangling from the darkness. Jude has set up a little table, covered with the purple fabric, displaying the pumpkins and cats. It's actually awful, but people seem to love it.

Jude is at least five beers down and has tried to review the two *Nightmare on Elm Street* movies we've just watched objectively.

'What next?' he asks. 'Shall we go for *Elm Street 3: Dream Warriors* or opt for something a little more, you know, scary?'

As Jude peruses films, the doorbell rings again, the sounds of young voices travelling in from the other side.

'I'll go,' I say, grateful for the break, to stretch my legs and listen out for the tinkling of Freddy's collar.

He still hasn't surfaced and there's a dish full of food waiting for him. The posh chicken in jelly he absolutely loves. It's rare for his dish to be empty at all.

Scooping up one of the pumpkin buckets that's now only half full of Haribo, I head for the door, pulling it open to reveal a girl of about seven, dressed as a witch. It's one of those shiny costumes with a big purple hat covered in silver moons and stars. A little boy stands next to her, just as adorable in a pirate outfit, brandishing a foam sword. He must be five, tops.

'Trick or treat!' the witch yells.

A man stands at the bottom of the path.

'All right, mate?' he calls.

Proffering the bucket, I give both children a big smile. 'Great costumes,' I say, trying to emulate the perky encouragement of Jude.

The little girl leans forward, pulling out some sweets. The boy doesn't move. He just stands there, gazing up at me, suddenly terrified.

'You OK there?' I ask. 'Do you want some sweets? Or would you prefer chocolate? Take a few more, mate – you're a pirate, after all.'

He doesn't get my joke. For a second I think he's going to break down in tears. He stands there for a few moments with his sister until she trots off down the path, leaving me and the little boy staring it out.

What do I do? I'm too inexperienced for this. I'm also rather drunk.

Before I can think of what to do next, the man at the bottom of the path starts to make his way up, striding purposefully past the hedgerows of next door, almost tripping over the broken slab of pavement.

'For God's sake,' he says, grabbing the little boy by the arm. 'Are you just going to stand there or what?'

The boy is silent, tearful.

'Why did you insist on coming if you can't even take part properly? All you have to do is say "trick or treat", take a sweet and go. If your sister can manage it, why can't you? Christ. Man up.'

With that, he heads back down the path, the boy ambling behind him, looking at the floor.

And all of my resolve is gone.

'Hey!' I scream at the man's retreating back.

He turns, startled.

'What?'

'What's your problem?'

'Sorry?'

By now the little pirate is at the gate, half concealed by our wheelie bin. Anger courses through every part of me. An anger I didn't think would re-emerge, as if every ounce of fury I ever felt as a child, as a teenager, as a naïve, quiet, self-conscious twenty-something has come to the surface, merging like some kind of unknown monster.

The man glares and in his expression I see the eyes of my own dad. My dad, a man who I love so much and still do. My dad, well-meaning yet equally brutal, and in my attempt to please him I ended up feeling even worse than before. *You can't hack it. Don't worry, Eric, some people just can't do it. You're just not good enough.*

Man up.

'He's trying,' I say, angrier now. 'He's quiet, that's all. Maybe he just needs better encouragement.'

'Are you telling me how to raise my kids?'

'Not at all.'

'Are you pissed?'

'Potentially, but that's got nothing to do with it.'

At the end of the path, more parents and children congregate, peering with interest at the ruckus. They slow down, pretending they're not listening. It's probably the most interesting thing to have happened in Chapel Gardens in weeks. Suddenly, I realise just how I must look: drunk, angry, stumbling about in my garden swinging a plastic kids' bucket around in frustration. Tiny packs of Haribo fall out and litter the path.

'I'm just telling you to be nicer to your son,' I shout. 'You're just going to make him feel so much worse in the long run.'

'Are you fucking kidding me?'

Now there's an audience, but all I can see is red. I see that man's snarling face and with it, I see years, I *hear* years. Gone are the chattering parents and the man's shouting. They've faded into the air, to be replaced by the silence. So much silence. Years of staring at my bedroom door, wondering what made me so wrong, so different, so terrible. Why couldn't I do anything right?

I'm yelling. He is yelling. Until suddenly there's a hand on my arm and I'm being pulled back, back towards the house. Everything is cloudy.

'Come on,' Jude says.

I'm guided back into the brightly lit hallway.

'What was that about?' Jude asks.

I'm in the doorway now, breathing quickly, trying to calm myself.

'I wanted to punch him.'

'I could see that. Come on, try to forget about it. We'll forget about the beer – I'll make us some tea instead.'

Sinking into the sofa once more, the question reappears with such clarity. As if I'm watching a TV quiz show that only I can see. And the ultimate question: *Why can't I do anything right?*

Chapter 36

Steph

Stepping off the quiet bus and heading up the street that turns into Chapel Gardens, I pull my jacket tighter around me and wonder. How many neighbours have noticed me? How many say, 'That's Steph, from number 28?'

Since Eric and I made the pact to get to know our neighbours better, I've been trying. I've said hi to the woman walking her child to school each morning – not just a smile, but a full-on greeting.

'Hello!' she said, surprised almost, looking over her shoulder as I hurried towards the bus.

I gave her an enthusiastic wave; her daughter waved back.

'Hope you're having a good day!' I told my other neighbour, the one who takes in my parcels, who I've now learned is called Mr O'Callaghan. He's talked to me about the weather. It's a start.

In Chapel Gardens, Halloween has come and gone; the decorations have been removed, back to normality. In a matter of days, the Christmas ornaments will surface; fairy lights in every tree and hedge, decorative Santas atop chimneys, illuminated and jolly. Wreaths appearing on every front door, trees visible through the bay windows, draped in tinsel and decorated with big red baubles and lights.

I think about this as I head towards home, footsteps echoing on the quiet street. Should I put up decorations? Should I carry on Mum's love for ceiling garlands and golden candles and Christmas songs played on repeat?

It's cold out and my mind flits to the people on the bus. A dozen or so people, all engrossed in their own lives. There was the elderly lady staring out of the window, deep in thought. What was she thinking about? The teenagers at the back, clutching shopping bags that banged against the seats at every turn. The commuters, like me, silent and scrolling through phones. Headphones in, world out.

Someone must have seen me; the woman with the ponytail and pink bag who silently alights before Chapel Gardens. Would anyone notice if I stopped turning up? Would anyone notice if I wasn't there, not in my usual seat: top deck, window seat, fifth row from the front?

In the flat, I snatch up my mail and go to make myself a cup of coffee, dropping more leaflets and junk mail into the recycling. Until I spot something.

A card.

My breathing stops for all of a second. For a moment I assume it's from number 26. I tear open the little green envelope to find that it's actually from Eric – a little notecard emblazoned with a smiley face.

'I'm sorry,' it says inside, in Eric's messy handwriting. 'I was a dick. Please forgive me?'

I prop it up on the bookshelf, next to *Five People*, then open Netflix. My little studio fills with sound. I sit down, about to change into my pyjamas, when my phone vibrates with a message.

It's Eric. My heart hammers with a surge of hope. OK, he must be *really* sorry.

Steph – have you seen Freddy recently by any chance?

The hope fades. He's just asking about his cat.

Before I can tap out a reply, another message comes in, clearly typed in urgency.

I can't find him, I think he's gone. :(:(

Chapter 37

Eric

'Gone? He can't be *gone*. Eric, calm down. He's probably just hiding out somewhere. Gone on a bit of a jolly with his cat friends.'

Jude stops throwing his drumsticks into the air for all of two seconds to offer yet more wonderfully whimsical advice.

'Jude, this isn't bloody Beatrix Potter. He hasn't just popped out for a couple of days in Blackpool. Cats don't have "cat friends" that they go on holiday with. They time-share. They're very particular.'

Jude looks thoughtful. How he can sit there looking all calm is beyond my understanding. I can't, not when Freddy's missing. I'm pacing the room, trying to think of all the possibilities while at the same time *not* trying to think of all the possibilities, because some of them are too awful to picture.

'Now that you mention it, I think I watched a documentary on that once. When they stuck a camera to a cat . . .'

'You're not helping. Freddy's been missing for three days. He *never* goes missing. The longest he's been gone is less than a day. This isn't like him.'

All the terrible images whir by in my head. Freddy being stolen, Freddy being taken in by another family with a young child, who'd love him and refuse to give him back. Freddy lost, unable to find his way home. Or worse, being hit by traffic on one of the nearby roads.

So many roads.

'I'm sure we can find him. Have you checked—'

'I've checked practically every inch of the house, the garden, this street and about six more.' I've also driven around the neighbourhood, seeing if I could catch a glimpse of his bright ginger fur, or a flash of his collar. No luck whatsoever. 'I've brought out the big guns.' I point to the open pack of Dreamies treats on the coffee table – Freddy's absolute favourites – that I've been rustling in the street for forty minutes. 'I've checked everywhere, and there's no sign. I don't even want to think about how devastated Lloyd will be if we've lost his cat.'

'*We* haven't lost him. Freddy went wandering somewhere. He's a cat, Eric. They do their own thing.'

'If I ever have kids, remind me never to let you babysit.'

Before he can shoot back some witty retort, there's a knock at the door. Rushing to answer it, I see Steph. She's standing there with a worried look on her face, still in her work clothes. She must notice my dark expression, because the first thing she asks me is if I'm OK.

'I've been better.'

'I've had a scout around for Freddy, but I couldn't see him. I'm really sorry. Do you need any help searching?'

Stepping aside, I invite Steph in. Jude's face instantly brightens.

'Steph's joined the search party!' he says brightly.

'It's not a disco and buffet, Jude.'

'Fine,' he quips, 'just trying to stay positive.'

'I had a look in my garden, too,' adds Steph. 'Checked the shed, but he hasn't managed to sneak his way in there. There's an alleyway behind, do you think he could be there?

289

I can't reach the gate in my garden. It's . . . well, it's way too overgrown.'

'It's possible . . .'

Jude jumps in before I can fully respond. 'Know what? I'll go and look,' he offers. 'I'll get the torch.'

Jude pulls on his jacket. I can hear him rooting around in the kitchen cupboard for the torch before he heads to the door, sneaking me a wry smile and a thumbs up, as if this is the perfect time to think about my love life.

'Sorry for messaging you,' I say to Steph. 'I was a bit frantic. You don't have to help if you're busy.'

'Are you kidding? I love Freddy.'

'I thought you said he looked constantly grumpy?'

'He does. That doesn't mean he's not adorable.'

'He is. Very. Look, I'm so sorry about the other day. And I loved the cookies. You didn't have to go to all that trouble.'

She holds up her hands. 'I'm glad. But about the other day . . . it was my fault. I was in the wrong. It was shit of me to break your trust like that. I shouldn't have done it. I got your note, by the way. Thank you.'

She pauses. The room is quiet. I want to say something to break us out of this silence, something meaningful. Instead, she goes first.

'So, when did you last see Freddy?'

'Halloween, in the morning. He didn't come home, that much is certain – he didn't touch his food. I thought he might have just been hiding from all the noise and the people, but he didn't return. Lloyd's still on holiday. The last thing I want is to tell him his beloved cat is missing.'

Steph sits down on the sofa. 'You don't have to tell Lloyd. Not yet. Don't worry him until you know with absolute certainty that Freddy's missing. I'm guessing you've checked every possible hiding place in the house?'

'Yep.' I nod, slumping back on the sofa next to her, defeated. 'I've looked everywhere. I've also driven around the area. Nothing.'

'OK. So we'll give it until tomorrow before we start putting up posters. Try not to worry. We'll have a plan.'

Taking a deep breath, I sip the tea Jude made me. It's lukewarm, but I drink it anyway.

The front door opens and in comes Jude, brushing dirt from his jeans. For a split second I'm hopeful, but there's no Freddy trotting in behind him with his grumpy face and sleigh bell collar.

'No luck, then?' I ask.

'I didn't find him. But, well, there *is* a possibility.'

'Oh?' asks Steph.

'I managed to get into the alleyway. Couldn't see Freddy, but one of the houses has a kitchen window that's ever so slightly open. There's just enough space for a cat of his size to get through. You never know! My cousin once had this cat—'

'Jude!' I shriek. 'Not the time.'

'OK, OK! Well, I tried knocking on their door but there was no answer. And, well, it's *next* door. Number 26.'

Chapter 38

Steph

My plans for this evening may not have been grand, but they didn't involve scaling a fence in the dark in search of a missing cat. On the plus side, at least I get to spend time with Eric.

'Ready?' asks Jude.

'As ever,' I reply. Eric is quiet, focused on the task at hand.

At the count of three, Jude gives me a hoist and I'm up, clinging to the tall wooden fence for dear life before swinging my legs over to the other side. I let go and land, toppling unsteadily onto what I now realise, from the light of my phone torch, is a vegetable patch.

Eric's next to make the leap, jumping over with amusing flair. He isn't so lucky.

'Ouch!' he cries. 'I think I just squashed something,' he says sadly. 'And not just my foot.'

'Veg murderer,' I chuckle.

'I already feel terrible as it is, like we're trespassing,' he whispers, brushing dirt from his jeans. I'm grateful I wore my chunky black jumper; outside, it's freezing. If Freddy *is* trapped or lost anywhere, we need to find him, stat.

'It's OK. We're just looking for Freddy. Hopefully he hasn't found his way inside, but it's worth a look.'

Finally, Jude is last to make his attempt over the wooden fence, which doesn't seem as sturdy with a fit, fully-grown man dangling halfway over.

'Shit, *shit*,' he whispers, dropping his camping torch to the ground before making a final drop, landing with a thud in the cold, dry soil.

We find ourselves in the garden of number 26, home to Laurie and Malcolm Robertson. The garden is rather understated; there's a small patio at the front, followed by a long stretch of unkempt grass, topped off with a little area for growing vegetables. Eric staggers to his feet and heads for the house, for the dark building that towers above us.

Sure enough, the small window in the kitchen is slightly open; the perfect size for a cold, scared – or downright curious – Freddy to squeeze through. The three of us stand there in silence, wondering what we're meant to do now.

Jude heads to the back door, knocking lightly against it.

'Hello?' he calls, and knocks again, louder this time.

'Believe me, there's nobody home,' Eric says.

Shoving his hands in the pockets of his dark cardigan, Eric traipses down the garden to where Jude is standing. I feel helpless here. What are we meant to do?

'Shall we call someone?' I suggest, even though I don't have the slightest clue who we'd actually call. 'I mean, the residents haven't been home for weeks. I'm surprised they left the window open, to be honest.'

'Maybe they were hurrying away quickly. Needed to get out of the country. Oh, what if they were on the run?'

'That's what I said!' I laugh. 'Eric didn't believe me.'

'Hey,' teases Eric. 'Look, we're stuck. What if we just . . . call his name? Maybe if he's in there, he'll come. We'll hear his collar.'

Jude is already on his phone. 'We can call . . . oh, I have no idea. The council? The police? Fire Brigade?'

Eric and I stare at him. 'He's not up a tree, Jude,' Eric quips, worry creeping into his voice. 'We don't have much time. We can't wait for days until someone turns up. He's been missing for three already. What if he's stuck some-where? We can't just wait. *Freddy!*'

Jude gives the door another loud knock. 'Once more for luck.'

'Luck? Jude, this is serious, he's *gone* . . .'

'Hey!' I reach out for Eric's arm. 'Try not to panic.'

He pulls his hand from his pocket and it finds mine in the darkness. It's cold but comforting.

We stand there, calling out for Freddy, watching with curiosity as Jude gets to his knees, feeling around the door frame. Then he gets to his feet, lifting a mat by the door.

'What's he doing?' I ask Eric.

He shakes his head in wonder, pulling his cardigan closer around him, and for a moment I catch the worry in his eyes and my heart soars.

'Not a clue.'

We watch as Jude pulls back the doormat and studies the patio before returning it to its rightful place. Then he catches sight of something: a little ornament in the shape of a duck next to the door and a faded garden parasol. We observe as he pulls the duck aside and yells, 'Yes!' into the air. He turns to us triumphantly. In his hand, something small and silver glistens in the moonlight.

Eric gasps. 'Jude, is that . . .'

'Spare key!' he whispers. 'I really wish people wouldn't leave them around like this. I mean, I know it's for emer-gencies – and I won't lie, I've locked myself out *numerous* times. I even had to climb scaffolding once. But to put it somewhere so easy . . .'

Eric hurries towards the house. 'Brilliant,' he whispers. 'The only problem is, this is illegal. We'd be breaking and entering.'

'Not necessarily,' says Jude, waving the key in Eric's face. 'We have the key. Technically, we'd only be entering.'

'I'm beginning to trust you less and less.'

'Look,' I say, shivering in the freezing cold. 'All we need to do is check that Freddy isn't in there. I don't want to do this either, but can't we just pop in, take a quick look and get straight back out? We won't touch anything. Then at least it rules out this house as a hiding place.'

Jude and Eric look to each other, then to me.

'OK,' says Eric with new determination. 'Straight in, straight out.'

'Tell you what,' says Jude, 'While you're looking, I'll go and knock on some doors, let people know about Freddy. He might be cooped up in someone's shed or garage for all we know.'

'Thanks, mate,' says Eric.

'Good luck!'

Jude hurries back towards the fence, leaping over it this time with flawless precision.

'So . . . in we go, I guess?' I say, leading the way.

I'll admit, this feels wrong. This feels *terrible*. I'm a trespasser, a bad neighbour, traipsing through someone's home without their knowledge. I feel like a burglar, even though I'm stealing nothing.

'Hello?' I call as Eric turns the key and the back door opens with a noisy creak. 'Laurie? Malcolm?'

As expected, there's no answer. All I can hear is Eric's soft breathing, his footsteps as he walks in behind me, him reaching up to flick on the lights. My eyes adjust to the brightness that reveals the Robertsons' kitchen. Neat, a little old-fashioned, the place sparkling clean. Hurriedly, I rush to the window and pull it closed, just to make sure it's safe again.

'Hello?' Eric calls as he opens the door to the living room.

The entire place is bathed in silence. The air is cold. We walk slowly with trepidation, as though we're exploring a possible haunted house in the middle of nowhere, just waiting for something to jump out on us. As it happens, nothing does. 'Hello?' Eric calls again, as we head into the next room. He flicks on the light, and we find ourselves in a regular, slightly cluttered but otherwise lovely living room.

The living room is big, connected via a pretty archway to the dining room. There's a large sofa and a glass coffee table, on which are a selection of magazines. A puzzle book sits alongside a dog-eared copy of *National Geographic*. There are bookshelves at the back filled to the brim with books of all sizes and various little ornaments. Photos adorn the walls: pictures of places, of people. There are many of Laurie and Malcolm themselves, cuddled together, their smiling faces brightening the room. Their presence is enviable and I feel a pang of longing for something I never really knew I wanted.

Will this ever be me? Will I ever live in a house like this; a capsule of coupledom, our togetherness beating, heartlike, through the very walls? Will I ever be as happy as these two?

'They seem lovely,' says Eric, peering closely at one of the photos, in which Laurie and Malcolm are at another seaside destination.

There are postcards in little frames along the mantelpiece, a collection.

In the hallway, shoes stand in neat lines. Men's formal shoes, women's trainers, flip-flops, two pairs of matching wellies.

'Freddy?' Eric calls. 'Are you in here? Freddy!'

We listen, awaiting the soft jingle of a collar or tiny, delighted footsteps padding down the stairs, but nothing comes. There is no sound.

There is, however, the one thing I'm familiar with. At the very back of the room, against the wall, stands the piano.

The Robertsons' piano. The very thing that started all this, that caused me to be standing here, with Eric. I see it now, the room I always wondered about. As I waited on the other side, curled up in my broken bed after a bad, broken day, I used to imagine what it looked like in this place, this house of happiness, where music and laughter filtered through the walls, bringing me that small semblance of comfort.

'Freddy?' Eric tries again.

At the front door, the pile of mail is growing, growing, the soft pink envelope of my card almost lost within the tiny mountain of junk mail and paper.

The upright piano is tall and beautiful, its dark wood chipped and faded in places, making it even more wonderfully perfect. Propped on the stand is an open music book.

As Eric ventures cautiously to the foot of the stairs, still calling for Freddy, I look. I know I should be calling, too, but I can't help but be distracted.

When I catch sight of the book, my heart plummets.

'Sealed with a Kiss'.

I can't help it. Letting my fingers trail along the keys, feeling the satisfying, weighty tinkle of the notes, I take another look around me. The Robertsons' coats hang on the pegs by the front door. A wedding photo takes pride of place above the fireplace.

Getting up, closing the lid of the piano, I run my hand along its top, taking one final look, letting myself truly feel it. As though all the joy contained within could transfer into my own hands like magic.

My fingers brush against something. A sheet of paper. Almost instinctively, I pull it down from its place, curiosity getting the better of me.

When I look at it – *really* look – I feel sick.

'Oh my God.'

'What is it?' asks Eric.

He rushes in from the hallway, his eyes still darting frantically around for any sign of Freddy.

I hold up what I've just found. 'He's dead.'

'*What*?'

'This is an Order of Service. For Malcolm Robertson. He's dead. He's been dead for over a year. Laurie's been alone this whole time.'

Chapter 39

Eric

'Are you sure?' I ask.

Steph's face is pale and she looks in danger of falling. As if her limbs are about to fold beneath her, collapsing into herself like a marionette. She holds the Order of Service in her hands, staring at it, at the photo on the front of a smiling man. A very familiar smiling man.

Familiar because he's surrounding us, beaming out from all the pictures on the walls. So many photos of him, his arms around Laurie, his happiness emanating from behind framed glass. Everywhere we look, there they are – Malcolm and Laurie – on the beach; in front of castles and churches; standing by beautiful cliffs. And, of course, on their wedding day.

'No,' I say, remembering something. 'That can't be right. I've heard her – Laurie. She's always talking to someone. Someone else must live here.'

Steph gestures wildly around the room. 'But do you ever hear anyone reply?'

Slowly, everything falls into place. Because no, I don't – all I hear is Laurie and occasionally, the faint sound of a man talking. Thinking about it, she could have just been watching TV.

I'd always assumed a couple lived there. Just the two of them, sitting down to eat dinner. Laurie, talking in the kitchen. And someone playing the piano, with Laurie singing along.

Perhaps, after all, it was only ever Laurie.

I shake my head. 'I've heard a man's voice. But faintly.'

'Me, too. But we've only ever heard them through the wall. It always sounds like they're there, just inches away, and it feels safe. But I guess that's not the case. We really don't know them at all.'

Now, looking over Steph's shoulder at the Order of Service, it's clear how wrong I've been.

'I've never seen anyone else come to this house,' Steph says. 'Laurie Robertson has been alone for more than a year and we had no idea.'

Malcolm smiles back from the leaflet. It's crumpled slightly, as if tears have fallen onto its surface only to dry again. I prise it from Steph's shaking hands and guide her to the sofa.

'All this time and I didn't even realise. Now she's gone and I think it might be my fault.'

'It's not. We've already established that they're – well, Laurie – is probably just away for a few weeks. Don't worry, Steph.'

Steph sniffles into her sleeve, finally pulling her eyes away from the music book on the stand. She's trying her hardest not to cry.

'He's gone . . . yet everything's still in its place.'

She looks around the room as if letting this new revelation sink in, pointing out the shoes in their neat line, Malcolm's jackets still hanging on their dedicated peg.

'It's like they've both just popped out to the shops.'

Steph's voice wavers, so I sit next to her, pulling her closer.

'We weren't to know,' I tell her as she falls into me. I offer her a tissue from a box on the coffee table. 'OK, I shouldn't have done that. You use that tissue and they have our DNA. We're trespassing and they can find out we're the culprits.'

Just hearing Steph's sniffly laughter fills me with a strange sense of joy. Then I notice something. Beneath the TV, on top of Laurie's clearly old DVD player, is a number of blank plastic cases. Curious, I get up from the sofa to take a look.

'What are you doing?' asks Steph. 'Should we be nosing through more of their stuff?'

'Like I said, we're already done for.' I take the first case from the pile and pop it open. Inside is a DVD, labelled by hand: Robertson Holidays, 1998 to 2002.

There are about twelve of them, all labelled: Christmas. Camping. Wedding. Pembrokeshire, 1995 to 2019.

As I get up from the floor, the TV comes to life. Static fills the screen with a deafening hiss and I stumble backwards in shock.

'Holy shit,' I shriek.

'Er, that might have been me. I think I sat on the remote,' admits Steph.

We stare at each other, relieved yet uncertain, until Steph finally picks up the remote again. She hits Play.

'Might as well,' she says with a shrug.

Laurie's grinning face fills the screen as she sets the camera down and steps back, gesturing to the beautiful rolling hills behind her, a sunny scene. She's joined by Malcolm. He steps into the frame with a broad smile, his kind eyes from the photos concealed by a pair of sunglasses.

'Hello!' he says brightly. 'We're here in sunny Pembrokeshire.'

'You sound like a TV presenter,' Laurie quips. 'Do you want to do the weather, as well?'

'Why not? Well, as you can see, it's . . . sunny. Not a cloud in the sky! Actually, that's wrong. There are a few over there . . . and some seagulls.'

'You're hardly Michael Fish, love.' She lets out a laugh, high-pitched and beautifully contagious.

'That's him,' says Steph. with a sinking feeling. 'That's definitely the voice I've been hearing.'

'Are you sure?' But I know she's right; I've heard him too. 'Yes.'

'Judging by the footage and their outfits, I think this was originally on VHS. They must have transferred it all.'

All of their precious memories, to revisit, again and again. That's what Laurie must have been doing. Watching the videos, over and over and over. The voice we could hear through the wall wasn't Malcolm – it was Malcolm on a video, in the past.

Laurie must have watched them as she had dinner. Watched them as she settled down for the evening. Watched them before bed, after the sounds of her piano tinkled to a halt.

On the screen, the scenery changes. The video cuts to another holiday, a year later. I can barely concentrate. Laurie played the piano every night for as long as I've lived in Chapel Gardens. And all that time, she was alone.

'She was talking to him and he wasn't there,' I say.

There's more static and another scene brings the screen to life, bright and happy as the pair explore a rocky beach.

'I used to speak to my mum a lot, too,' says Steph quietly. 'It took me so long to accept that she was gone. I knew she was, of course. I knew she'd died. But after the worst of it, it took me months to *fully* accept that she wasn't on the end of a phone. You have these strange blips sometimes, where you forget, just for a moment, and when you remember again, your heart breaks. I'd go to call her, momentarily forgetting that she wouldn't answer. That probably doesn't even make sense.'

'It does. It makes perfect sense.'

'Does it? I'm probably talking gibberish. But it happened. Mum wasn't there. She wasn't at home, in her flat like she always was. I had to get used to life without her and it was *hard*. I went through a stage of speaking to her anyway. I'd have a full-on conversation with her – myself – constantly, just about mundane stuff. Until one day it hit me that there was no point, she wasn't coming back. And she can't hear me. She never will.'

'But she's still with you. Just not in the same way.'

Steph shrugs. 'Maybe Laurie's the same. A year is some time, but grief is different for everyone. My sister used to tell me that and it all makes sense now. I still tell Amanda off for going to Mum's grave all the time, still chatting to her as if she's there.'

'Why do you tell her off?'

'I guess it makes me feel uncomfortable, as if she'll never accept it. I had to, but she seems happy to keep talking to Mum and I think I just wish I could do that too. But from now on I'll stop. I feel terrible for it now. That's Amanda's way of coping, I suppose.'

I nod, feeling immensely useless for having no words, only platitudes. Steph doesn't like to hear those, I know that much. So, I say nothing, pulling her closer to me instead. This time her hand sneaks around me, accepting me, and despite the circumstances, it feels . . . nice.

The doorbell rings suddenly, its tune reverberating through the house, and we spring apart, startled.

'Who could that be?' asks Steph, leaping from the sofa.

Rushing to the front door, I push the pile of mail aside, hearing the swish as it tumbles, only to see Jude on the doorstep.

'Ta-dah!' he says proudly, and in his arms is a rather contented-looking Freddy.

'Guess who was accidentally adopted by a family up the road?' says Jude. '*This* guy. He lost his collar and they thought he was a stray. Gave them the sad eyes, by all accounts.'

Freddy lets out a guilty mew.

'Oh my God! Jude, you're a lifesaver.'

'I know. Brilliant, aren't I? So . . . you coming?' he asks, catching sight of our faces as Steph appears beside me. 'Bloody hell! You look as if you've seen a ghost. Halloween's gone, mate.'

When we don't respond, his expression changes.

'OK, let's get this little guy back to ours. Then I think a well-deserved drink is on the cards. What do you reckon?'

Chapter 40

Steph

It's a bit livelier in the Cambridge Arms tonight and I'm tucked inside in a bubble of warmth and chatter at a table by the window. I look out at the street – a street where everything feels normal. Only it isn't, because Laurie Robertson has been alone. And I didn't even notice. *We* didn't even notice.

'That's spooky,' states Jude as he returns from the bar with a tray containing two pints of cider, a large glass of red wine for me and some baskets of chips. 'And really, really sad. So you have no idea where she's gone?'

'None at all.'

Eric had decided to slip into the seat next to me. Having deposited Freddy safely in the house, complete with a full bowl of food, we headed back out to the pub, where we've just finished explaining to Jude what happened.

Jude seems shocked. Like we *should* have known about Laurie. That we should have seen her every day.

'Well, what if Laurie *isn't* the type to let everyone in on her business?' I argue, dousing my chips in vinegar.

Eric watches me, amused.

'Not every neighbour is as friendly as you, Jude,' I add.

'This is true,' he says with an air of pride. 'I remain an upstanding member of the community in whatever

305

neighbourhood I end up in. Look, Steph, don't worry. She'll come back.'

The music book. The music book was open on *that song*. I haven't divulged the entire story to Jude and right now, I don't feel like it. My head is too full of Laurie Robertson.

I just wish I could go back and change things, that night I punched the wall, shouting. The very thought of it makes me feel sick. That I shouted at someone who was all alone. That I swore, at a grieving widow.

If only she hadn't been playing *that song*.

Taking a sip of red wine, all warming and welcome, I turn back to Eric. 'What if she doesn't come back?'

'You saw her house. All her stuff is there. Even you said it looks like they've just gone to the shops. She'll return. Even if she wants to sell the place, she'll have to come back.'

'And I'll be in Manchester.'

I'd have moved away, deep into my new role, my new life, safely ensconced with the housemates-to-be, yet I know I won't be able to forget about Laurie. It'll be that final item, unchecked on the to-do list of my life.

'Does that matter? You can always come back and visit us,' Jude offers, slinking comfortably back into his seat among the chatter. 'Eric and I can stay on Laurie Watch.'

'That would be nice.'

My anxiety lifts slightly as we sink into the atmosphere of the place, calming and light, that welcome feeling of being around others. I see no reason to move from my seat, feeling enveloped in comfort, picking at the chips in the basket and talking with Eric and Jude, and in one fleeting moment, realise I'm actually going to miss them.

There's a beep from somewhere in the vicinity and Jude slides out his phone, frowning.

'Wonderful,' he says. 'Carmen's just called in sick, so I'm being asked to cover.'

'What, now?'

'It's going to be a late one.' He deliberates for a moment. 'I'll head back, get changed and get a taxi – if you fancy having a drink there, feel free to come with!' He frowns again, looking sadly at Eric. 'Actually, bad idea. You've got work tomorrow. I don't want to be responsible for any hangovers.'

Eric's expression shifts. I can see a hint of panic as he downs another mouthful of cider.

'Yeah,' he says. 'Sorry, mate.'

I look at him as he runs his hand through his curls.

'I thought you were off this week?' I ask, curious.

Eric shakes his head, a little too quickly. 'Nope. Working.'

Jude quickly finishes his drink and gets up from the table.

'Maybe another night then!' he says. 'I'll see you later.'

I feel a little sad to see Jude go. Aside from the few trips to the pub with Eric, this is the nicest evening out I've had in a long time. I actually feel like I'm part of something.

At eleven fifteen, we wander back to Chapel Gardens together, embracing the chill and the silence outside. I've had a good time, so good that I don't care about tomorrow; for once, I'm happy to wake up groggy, or risk falling asleep on the bus. Little moments can be worth it. We're quiet as we walk, but comfortably so. I'm just enjoying his company, his presence, merely walking side by side with someone after the strange evening we've had.

'See you tomorrow, then?' Eric asks at the gate.

And there it is, the awkwardness.

There's a hint of hope in his voice and I'm flushed with warmth, of the heat from the pub and the surprising feeling of sudden longing. I'm going back to the flat with Netflix

307

for company, where I'll no doubt sit sipping herbal tea, scrolling Instagram until gone midnight rather than keeping up with whatever show I decide to watch.

'Want to come in for a bit?' I ask before I can stop myself.

I want him to, because I want to tell him about how much I like his screenplay. I want to see if he's still working on it. I want to tell him about Manchester and how I'll definitely be back. I want to tell him a lot of things.

'OK.'

Eric follows me inside, eyes widening as he sees the state of the place.

'All packed, then?' he asks, surveying the perfect piles of boxes against the far wall.

I head for the kitchen to switch on the kettle. When I return to ask him if he wants any tea, I notice that Eric is staring at my now-empty clothing rail. Where, beneath it, sit the two cardboard boxes from Mum, separate from all the others.

'"For Steph,"' he reads aloud, reaching to touch them, running his finger along the stretch of tape, over the ink; Mum's curly writing, immortalised in black marker.

My stomach drops and I leap up to push his hand away.

'Please don't,' I say.

I step in front of them defensively, feeling a frayed, taped-up cardboard corner push against my leg, which only piques Eric's interest.

'What's wrong?' he says, almost laughing. He points at the boxes. 'Ah, let me guess. An ex?'

'They're not from an ex.'

'Then what's wrong?'

My defensiveness rises. 'Nothing's wrong.'

Eric takes a step back. 'Are you sure?'

I blink back tears.

'Steph?' Eric asks. 'Steph, come here.'

He takes me by the hand and guides me to my messy bed. The broken frame creaks beneath him. I always forget to make my bed in the morning and now I regret it. He pulls me down next to him.

'What's the matter?'

I don't want to tell him. Even Amanda doesn't know. The strange thing about Eric is that it's hard *not* to tell him anything. He's too kind, too comforting for me to lie to, which is a revelation in itself.

'Those boxes,' I begin. 'They're from Mum. My sister found them when she cleared out the house. Mum must have put them together before she died. She had bowel cancer.'

She was sick and I didn't know.

'So what's in them?' Eric asks softly.

'I don't know. I don't know because I never opened them.'

Eric says nothing, just stays there, next to me. Which, right now, is exactly what I need.

All I can do is look at the boxes, at Mum's lovely handwriting, until I'm back home again, transported to the living room at our old flat. The memory is vivid in colour; the deep green of the huge Christmas tree Mum would pull out from the cupboard each year. The shiny golden garlands that hung from the ceiling. Red and gold and white, our already small room transformed into a Christmas grotto, because Mum loved Christmas.

And we'd race towards our gifts on Christmas Day, Mum grinning excitedly as she handed them over. And we'd look at the labels, at the swirly writing that was recognisably hers: 'For Steph, love from Santa.' Even when we were too old to believe, she still signed them all from Santa.

I picture her sick, in that same small room but without all the decorations. I see her hands that had, at the end, become thin and frail, poised over the cardboard box.

For Steph. I imagine her pulling on the tape, lining it up perfectly. Getting it just right.

Eric speaks. 'Why haven't you opened them?'

'I can't.'

'Why?'

'I *can't*. I don't think I can bear to see what's in there.'

'How come? What do you *think* is in there?'

I know what's in there. Mum's belongings. Or at least, the ones she thought I'd want. Amanda had some, too. Amanda sorted out the house. She did it in record time. She had to; Mum lived in a council property, so it all had to be cleared as soon as possible, ready for a new family to move in and make it theirs. Another start, another life.

I know there's nothing scary in those boxes. There's no cursed object that will jump out at me or shock me, no evil-faced jack-in-the-box. Though I'd rather face one of those than what's inside – memories of Mum, ready and waiting to leap out and hit me right in the heart and remind me that I'll never see her again.

'Steph?' Eric asks. 'I can help you, if you like. I can open them with you.'

Fresh tears make their escape, spilling down my cheeks and making my eyes sting from the mascara.

I shake my head. 'Thanks, but it's OK. It's just, once I open them, I've lost all I have of Mum. The mystery's gone. It's like the very last thing I had from her will be over.'

'Not really. You have all the memories, don't you? If you hold on to this stuff, it'll only make it worse. What's in there could be comforting. You don't know until you look.'

'Would you?' I ask. 'If you were me, would you look?'

Eric nods thoughtfully. 'I'd have looked right away. But I'm impatient. Clearly, you have more resolve. The thing

310

is, your mum must have filled those boxes for a reason. It's been three years.'

'Sometimes it seems like days ago, and sometimes it feels like forever.'

'I understand,' says Eric kindly.

And yet again, he pulls me closer and I cry it out. I let all the tears spill freely and he's there, quiet, and I feel the softness of his cardigan, his quiet breathing, until I have nothing left to cry. I'm cried out and I'm tired, and I'm worried that Eric has seen me in this state more than once, but at the same time I'm too exhausted to think about it now.

Without another word, Eric helps me into the bed, pulling the duvet over me, making sure I'm comfy, and for a fleeting moment his face is so close to mine that all I want to do is kiss him.

'Need anything?' he asks.

I shake my head.

'Come round tomorrow,' he says. 'If you ever need me, I'm only two doors down.'

Seconds later, I'm asleep, dreaming of boxes, of towers of cardboard, all for me.

Chapter 41

Eric

The sound of loud knocking rouses me from sleep. I jolt upright, taking in my surroundings. My room is dark. It's early. And someone is calling my name.

'Eric?'

There it is again.

'Eriiic . . .'

Jude is calling my name.

Hauling myself out of bed, I wait for the telltale signs of an emergency – smoke, perhaps, creeping in from beneath the door, or a siren. Anything to explain why Jude's frantically knocking on my door so early. Then it hits me. *Freddy*.

Has anything happened to Freddy?

'Jude?'

I'm suddenly frantic, my tired body stumbling to the door and pulling it open to see a grinning Jude, clutching two big travel mugs. The scent of coffee reaches my nostrils and makes my stomach churn. It's only then I notice something else. Something small, four-legged and white with patches of brown on little pointed ears.

'Jude . . . what's going on? And whose dog is that? You haven't adopted him, have you?'

'Whoa, calm down,' says Jude, suspiciously perky for such an early hour.

I don't even know what time it is. All I know is I'm tired and I want to go back to sleep.

'You think I'd adopt a dog without consulting you?' he laughs.

'In all honesty? Yes.'

'Come on, mate. Of course he's not my dog. He's Sam's. I've borrowed him for the morning. Eric, meet Patch. Patch, this is Eric.'

'Wait. Sorry. You *borrowed* him?'

'Yep.'

I stare down at the little Jack Russell terrier, who's sitting calmly next to Jude, looking eagerly up at me with his big, dark eyes. In fairness, he's cute. It's difficult *not* to reach down and fuss the top of his head while I await Jude's reasoning as to why he's woken me at the crack of dawn with a dog, of all things.

'What's this about?' I ask, cautiously. 'And where's Freddy? You know he doesn't like dogs.'

'Oh, Freddy's in the living room, on the sofa, glaring like the king he is. We're not sticking around, anyway. Sam's got a hospital appointment today, so I volunteered to look after Patch for a couple of hours. Totally forgot I'd agreed to it before taking that shift last night, hence this . . .' He waves the coffee mugs. 'I thought, hey, you know who might like a trip outside? Eric. And here we are. So get dressed. I made you some coffee. Oh, and fear not' – he produces a roll of poo bags from his coat pocket – 'I'll be on poop duty.'

'That's good, because I'm going to get some more sleep, OK?'

'Wait!'

Coffee in hand, Jude shoves his body against the bedroom door to prevent me from closing it. He's stronger than me and I'm knackered, so I'm forced to give in.

'Come on, it'll be a bit of fun. Some fresh morning air works wonders.'

'For you, maybe. Look, I've got to be at work in a few hours, so—'

'No you don't.'

'What?'

Jude stands in the doorway, his face now fraught with seriousness. Patch gets to his feet, tail wagging with excitement.

'You don't have to be in work,' he says matter-of-factly.

'I do.'

'I *know* you don't, because you haven't been to work in over a week. That's fine and all, and it's not my business, but you don't have to lie to me.'

'What? Have you been spying on me or something?'

Jude doesn't move from the doorway. Anger bubbles inside me. It intensifies, just looking at this man who's standing there, watching, judging. It takes all of my tired energy not to kick the door shut in his face.

'I guessed you hadn't been at work for a while. I stopped by the bank the other day when I was in town, to see if you wanted to get a pizza, and some guy called Joshua said you were sick. Then when Steph asked you last night, it all made sense.'

'You're right. It's really not your business, is it?'

I make a grab for my dressing gown, my old trusty blue one hanging on the door. Might as well stay up now seeing as I'm awake. Really, really awake.

Jude looks at me expectantly, as does Patch, as if they're both here to give me some kind of intervention. God knows why.

'You say that, but it's *kind* of my business when I live with you. I know something's up. It's like—'

'Like what?' I cut in, annoyed.

'Like something's amiss. You're not OK. You're not *you*. I thought a walk might help, you know?'

'I don't need it. I've been going for walks practically all week.'

Which isn't a lie. I *have* been walking. Briskly round a nearby park, or the harbour. Or just sitting in my car, mulling over my thoughts. Over Clarissa. Over Steph. Trying to work through the fog of confusion and see something, anything, clearly again.

'OK,' says Jude, shrugging. He enters the bedroom, placing the travel cup on my chest of drawers. 'I wanted to give you the option, anyway. We'll be off. Sorry for waking you, mate.'

He heads out of the room, Patch trotting obediently behind him.

I don't know what it is – maybe it's spending time with Steph. Maybe it's the Robertsons. But all of a sudden I feel terrible. Just like Steph, I don't want to be a terrible person.

Quickly, I pull on jeans and a T-shirt, slipping into my trainers and coat in the hallway before I can change my mind. 'Fine!' I yell, just as they're about to leave. 'You win.'

'Brilliant,' says Jude, triumphant.

The morning air is brisk, but we've warmed up by the time we reach the Downs. Jude pulls Patch's extendable leash from his pocket and we watch as he sets off, bounding excitedly across the dew-covered grass. As much as I hate to admit it, it's been pleasant, just walking along, experiencing the misty morning when the world is quiet, talking to Jude. Who, simply by his power of conversation alone, that ability to talk to anyone, has managed to prise out more about Clarissa. Jude's wasted in his job; he should work for the FBI. It would take him mere seconds to pull a confession from a criminal.

'Would you actually *want* to get back with Clarissa, then?' Jude asks. 'I mean, if she wasn't having a baby with someone else. If she called you up and said, "Hey, do you want to try again?" Would you say yes?'

I say nothing, my eyes fixed on the path. Frankly, I have no true answer to that one.

'Word of advice, though,' he continues. 'I did it once. Got back with someone I'd split up with. Emma. We'd been seeing each other for two years and then she decided to end it. Then – God, how long was it now? Ah, must have been a year later – she called me out of the blue, wanting to get back together.'

'Did you? Get back with her?'

'Of course I did. I was twenty-five and a bit dim back then, to be honest. Thought it was the best day ever. And that it was a new start. I'd change, I'd do it all differently, yada yada. That's the kind of stupid shit we tell ourselves, and evidently, it's never real. You fall back into old habits. Emma and I did.'

'Oh.'

'Yep. Then it becomes even *clearer* why you split up in the first place. We were completely incompatible. Why did you and Clarissa split up? Did she give you a reason?'

I shake my head and sip more coffee. Of course there was a reason. I didn't care enough. We clearly had different plans. I remember those words, the anger spilling out from Clarissa, as if it were yesterday.

What's the matter, Eric, she asked. *Why didn't you answer me?*

'Ah, well,' Jude comments.

He stops reminiscing to rummage in his other pocket and retrieve a dirty old tennis ball. He throws it into the distance and it disappears into the mist, followed by Patch. A cold morning on the Downs, covered by mist, trees skeletal in their winter phase, is so atmospheric, it's inspiring.

'The thing is, I think I just wanted to get back with Clarissa because it seemed like the most logical option.'

'How is getting back with an ex who dumped you logical?'

I shrug. In the distance, Patch has befriended another dog, a small Yorkshire terrier. They chase each other in circles.

'It's not. I just *thought* it was. The guys – Tim, Joe, Luk – we've been friends for years and all of a sudden, every-thing's changing. They've got the partners, the houses, the families . . .'

'And?'

'And I don't.'

Jude lets out a sigh, looking across the fields as if the answer to everything will spring from the mist.

'What about Steph?'

'What *about* Steph?'

Jude chuckles, pulling me out of the new sense of calm I'd very nearly reached.

'There's something between you two, isn't there?'

'She's seeing someone, Jude. The guy in the photos, her hashtag-perfect-date. And she's moving away. Two reasons, right there, as to why there's nothing going on.'

Jude is quiet now. We continue along, the crisp ground crunching beneath our feet, the fresh scent of morning winter air around us. I try to let it take over, to concentrate on something else, something other than Clarissa, or Steph. Because lately, all I've been able to think about is Steph. Especially last night. Last night, with the boxes, holding her, helping her into bed as her tired eyes drifted into solid sleep. There had been a moment just before when her eyes met mine and all I wanted to do was kiss her. I was close, so close, but no. I couldn't.

'. . . need to tell them,' Jude's saying, and I realise I've zoned out. I haven't been listening.

'Sorry?'

'Work. You need to tell them the truth about what's going on.'

'About what?'

Jude stops walking. Patch darts around in the distance, safe and happy.

'Eric, I know why you're not working.'

'It was a stomach bug.'

'Like hell it was a bug. You're depressed.'

'You're a doctor now, are you? Doctor Jude and his astounding medical advice.'

'Come on, I'm not kidding. I wanted to tell you I understand. I can help.'

'Again, it seems like you're prying into my life.'

'Are you happy?'

Jude waits for an answer. He hasn't moved. A group of runners hurries past, giving us a good-morning smile.

'What sort of question is that?' I ask.

He shrugs. 'A good one? A useful one?'

The fast, fluttering feeling starts again. Right in the pit of my stomach. A fearful longing to be back home, back in my bed. Not here, out in the cold.

'No,' I answer. 'I'm not.'

He continues walking and I follow, gathering pace as Patch bounces towards us with the ball again, willing Jude to launch it.

I tell him. I tell him about Clarissa. How losing her put me right back to square one.

How it was almost behind me. How I was OK until the guys brought up the subject at Baby Harry's party.

I tell him about the house. The dreams I had that are

no longer in my grasp. Steph. Someone I finally like, who will be moving to a new city, for a new life. And the fact I'm in my thirties, still living in a houseshare, feeling like a fucking loser.

'I live in a houseshare, too,' he says. 'Does that make me a loser?'

'Of course not. Surely you have a reason to be there.'

'Yes, as do you! It's not a bad thing. I like living in a houseshare. I'll move on eventually, yes, but I like living with other people. I enjoy company. Doesn't make me a loser. Look, I think you might need to speak to someone. Someone who isn't me.'

Fear engulfs me. There's Jude, who can talk to anyone, who seems to have a personal agenda to make every wrong in the world right, and he's fobbing me off.

'What do you mean?'

'Well, you can talk to me whenever you want, obviously. I'm talking about maybe a therapist.'

'You're saying I should get *therapy*?'

'Basically, yeah.'

I stare at him, aghast. If I was feeling shit before, now it's ten times worse.

'Jude, I don't need therapy, OK? Yes, I've got some things going on, but I just need to work on them. All will be fine.'

'Not—'

'*No*,' I interrupt. I don't want to hear any more from him, not about this. 'I'll sort things out. It's a bad time. The thing with Clarissa just scared me, that's all. You think I can't deal with this?'

Amusingly, he's silent for once.

'I don't want your advice any more, Jude, OK?'

I turn round and stride back down the path towards home.

Chapter 42

Steph

When Mum died, the days that followed were a blur. A dense fog of grief that I managed to trudge through, but only just. The kind that makes you cold, makes you numb, makes your feet feel as if they're moving through mud that's waist-deep, trying everything in its power to pull you all the way in. And you're tempted to give in, only you can't. You know you can't.

Amanda was there, her outstretched arm reaching through that fog, pulling me out of it with determined force. Monday turned into Tuesday and then the days of the week seemed to blend together, a disappointing fusion of time, until I didn't know what day it was any more. Only one day mattered – the date of Mum's death – which was the only date that would register in my mind. It was the only way I could determine where time had taken me. Three days since Mum died. *Six* days since Mum died. I counted them resolutely, until the days turned into a week. Then two weeks. Two weeks and four days. A month. The calendar moved further and further away, taking Mum with it.

Gripping my sister's hand, our eyes fixed on the wooden box containing our mother, to the sad melody of 'Sealed with a Kiss', the numbness was indescribable. It took over, my movements robotic, my words few. My body ached from lack of sleep, from all the nightmares.

There was a line through my life now, thick and newly formed. I couldn't venture back across the line into my previous life, because Mum was gone. There was nothing I could do about it. I could only reach her in memory.

The boxes arrived two weeks later, hauled carefully from the back seat of Amanda's car after she'd cleared out Mum's flat. I couldn't bear to go there; I didn't want to see Mum's favourite slippers next to the sofa. I didn't want to watch as her possessions, reminders of our family, were packed into boxes. Her clothes, her perfumes, or anything she'd touched, were to be taken and boxed away. Her presence, like her body, fading and shrinking until it disappeared forever.

So I *couldn't* peel the tape off and look inside. I couldn't face looking at what Mum had left me. It was simply more confirmation that she'd gone, and I'd only disappear again, into my own little void where there are no hours and no days and, worst of all, no Mum.

'I'll get to them,' I'd told myself. 'When I'm ready, I'll open them.'

I was never ready.

Now, the boxes sit before me. This morning, I hauled them from their spot by the now dismantled clothing rail and placed them in the middle of the floor, one on top of the other, prominent and visible. I can't move without stepping round them, so the only way I can get away from them is to move them, back with the rest of my boxed-up belongings, or open them.

Eric said he would, if they were his. I remember him telling me, before I drifted off to sleep, the words going round and round in my head. I awoke this morning with a new sense of determination.

Only now I'm not so sure.

By looking inside, I know I'll have to face Mum again. I'll have to reopen a wound tinged with guilt and regret. All the regret . . . When I was having fun in America, Mum was dying. We could have spent more time together. Days. Weeks. I didn't know her time was almost up.

Am I ready for this?

Before I can stop myself, I reach for the scissors that I'd got out in preparation for this very task. I choose a fun, cheesy 2000s playlist that will remind me of her, and Amanda, the three of us, so that it'll make me sad, but in a pleasant way – a bittersweet sadness brought on by good memories. The same way that Christmas tinsel does, and birthday cake, when you take a blissful bite into the best part – that thick layer of white icing. And so I take a deep breath, and cut slowly, cautiously, through the tape.

Easing back the cardboard flaps on the first box, the first thing I see is material. Red wool with a cream-coloured pattern, folded neatly, covering the rest of the contents. The wool is bobbly and well-loved, and I recognise it immediately as one of Mum's favourite blankets, the one we used to snuggle under as kids as we sat on the sofa, bowl of snacks between us. Later, as we grew taller, bigger, Amanda and I would drape it over our legs as we sat down to watch our shows after school, half watching the TV, half watching our phones.

Lifting it from the box, I can't help but rub my face against it, feeling the softness and inhaling its scent of lavender laundry powder. Even though it's been three years, I can still smell her, I can still smell a thousand memories nestled within the fibres.

I take another look inside. No wonder this box was light; stacked beneath the blanket are clothes. I pull the items out one by one. Clothes, clearly Mum's, yet unfamiliar; there's a long coat I vaguely recall. A few pairs of shoes that are free of scuffs and scratches, unlike most of her others. There are two handbags, with the tags still on, and my heart sinks as I remember buying her one of them as a birthday gift.

Swathes of unworn fabric meet my gaze as I look inside. There's a black satin blouse, and a red one, too; a sun hat with a wide brim, which I remember her buying about ten years ago, when she was determined to go away somewhere for the summer. Gloves and shoes and costume jewellery and an unopened bottle of perfume. The box is full of clothes and accessories – why? Why didn't she, or Amanda, donate them? Mum and I were the same size in clothes, so maybe she thought I'd want them.

Slightly confused, I put the items to one side and pull the next box forwards. As I cut through the top and peer inside, something catches my eye. Something terrifying.

A small white face. Tendrils of hair that peek from beneath a lace bonnet. A pair of eyes, glassy and dark, peer blankly into mine from the confines of the box. My throat tightens.

'Shit!' I shriek, falling backwards into the pile of Mum's clothes.

Until I realise.

It's my old doll, Cecilia.

Approaching the box slowly, I take another look. Daylight streams in from the curtain and, bathed in the light, Cecilia doesn't look as scary and Annabelle-like as she did in childhood.

'For God's sake, Mum,' I laugh, and prop the doll up against my pillow. 'I think I'll hide the knife block tonight!'

This box is different, containing some of my old toys. There are photos, too; some of which I recognise from Mum's living room. Pictures of Mum with Amanda and me as children, in all our brightly coloured late-nineties glory. There are a few sets of pictures in sleeves from Mum's old camera. She'd get them developed, only to be dismayed when Amanda's thumb covered most of the images. Flicking through, I notice that these photos take place over a few summers, full of trips to the beach and the fairground. Our little weekend adventures.

There's a photo of Mum, arms outstretched, waist-deep in the sea. Mum was a good swimmer. I'd stand on the soft sand, cheering, holding Mum's clunky camera in my hand, snapping away. And Amanda would be next to me, fretting, just in case Mum went out too far. She'd picture Mum struggling, unable to get back to the shore, or a wave swallowing her up and pulling her right out to sea, so she'd never come back.

I slip the pictures back into their sleeve. Beneath them is a book. A chunky notebook with a leather cover.

It looks new. I've never seen it before. Taking it out carefully, I flick through, noticing all the pages are blank. I turn to the first page and my breath catches in my throat.

The Adventure Journal of Stephanie Higgins. A place for you to record all of your new adventures and precious memories! Love you always. Mum. Xx

The words are in pen, in Mum's neat, swirly handwriting.

She'd left this for me.

I run my hands over the leather cover, my body trembling with raw emotion, of hurt, of a kind of grief I never knew existed. Mum had left this for me. She'd left me this gift three years ago and I never knew.

With the book on my lap, unable to let it go, I take one last look in the box. Then I see it.

Tucked in the bottom, visible beneath a postcard of New York that I'd sent her, is a letter.

Chapter 43
Steph

A letter.

My heart starts racing the moment I see it. Reaching into the box to pull it out, I discover that Mum even left a kiss on the back of the envelope. *Sealed with a Kiss*, I think, shaking my head in amusement, because that's the kind of person Mum was. Funny and a bit silly, and sentimental, too. I run a finger over the mark, the shape of her lips in her favourite berry lipstick, and work on opening the letter carefully from the top so that I don't spoil it.

Taking a deep breath, I read Mum's words:

Stephanie,
By the time you've opened these boxes, I'll be gone. I know that sounds weird, especially when you say it out loud, but that's the situation I'm in. I'd always wondered if I'd know when my time was going to be up, get some warning, just like your granddad did. I thought we'd have so much more time together, but it happened sooner than I could have imagined. The pain at knowing I'll be leaving you behind is indescribable.

But there's one thing that brings me comfort, and it's that you and your sister are strong, and you have each other, and I know you'll be fine without me.

You'll get through this together. Which is why I have to say sorry, Steph.

I'm sorry I didn't tell you I was as ill as I was.

I'm sorry I didn't tell you on the phone when you were in America. I'm sorry I didn't tell you the news I'd received, that I made you believe I could beat this and that things would be OK. I pretended everything was fine when I knew it wasn't, when they told me I had a couple of months, then weeks. I kept it a secret from the both of you.

The truth is, I knew what you'd have done. I know you so well – both you and Amanda. I know you better than you could imagine, because I'm your mother, and that's a power us mothers often have. If I'd told you the truth, you'd have cut your holiday short. You'd have rushed home to be with me and not left my side. I didn't want you to do that.

I wanted you to be in America, on the trip you'd always dreamed of. You'd talked about going to New York for years. You saved for so long. You dreamed of it for so long. One of the many things I love about you is your independent spirit, your love for exploring. You were always like that.

I wanted you to live in the moment without having to worry about me. Trust me, being at home with me would not have been fun. It would have been awful, and I didn't want to see you upset. Your video calls, with your beautiful face and all the excitement in your voice, brightened each and every day. I hope you never change, that the need for adventure never leaves you.

I'm so, so sorry I never told you. I'm sorry I never admitted to you both just how little time I had left.

I've left you a journal, to make sure you keep being your adventurous self. Go on lots of holidays. See loads of new places. Meet wonderful new people who will change your life. I'll be with you, don't you worry. I'll be in your heart and I'll never leave you.

And before I go, I have one final request.

One of the boxes contains some of my belongings. Unworn clothes. Unused perfumes. A bag you bought me that was far too special to take to work every day. Books I never got round to reading. These are all things I kept 'for best'. I held on to them, kept them aside, for parties I never went to. For dream holidays that never came. I always thought the magical moment would come where I'd need to wear my best things, but I ran out of time. The truth is, every day is a 'best' day. I realised that far too late.

I wanted to show you what not to do, Steph. So wear your best clothes. Light the candles you're keeping for special days. Drink the good wine. Please never leave anything for best.

I love you and I always will. Please remember all the good, funny memories – and I know it sounds silly, but please don't spend every day upset. I'm always with you.

Until we meet again!

Mum xxx

(P.S. I always knew you hated Cecilia. Surprise!)

Tears stream down my face, falling onto the knees of my jeans, but I let them, my hands shaking as I grip the letter, trying not to let the paper get wet, smudging Mum's beautiful words.

All that time. All that time and I never knew.

Guilt has eaten away at me for three whole years. The fact I didn't know Mum was as sick as she was became a recurring nightmare after her death, inescapable. I could no longer sleep in a silent room. The night became a terrifying place. I'd spend each moment trying to keep myself awake, as if hiding from a monster that would sneak out of the shadows and tell me all the horrible things. Each time I closed my eyes, the voice would find me – my own voice, but with a sinister quality. *'You didn't spend enough time with Mum. She was dying and you didn't care. You're an awful daughter. Look at all that time you can't get back.'*

I had no idea that she'd deliberately kept it from me. I always thought she'd found out later, after I'd returned, just how long she had left to live.

I thought she would be okay. That things would have been different. That I wouldn't lose her.

Afterwards, it hurt to think that the time I spent away was time I could have had with her, my amazing, wonderful, kind Mum.

Moving my numb legs into a new position on the dusty floor, I reread the letter, wiping away more tears. Mum was right – I *would* have rushed home. Who wouldn't? Who wouldn't want to stay with their dying parent? To be fair, Mum was right ninety-nine per cent of the time. She was right when it came to fashion choices. She was right when it came to boys, hugging me on the sofa at 3 a.m. after I'd got dumped, dishing out advice which, later, I found out was spot on. So it's not surprising she was right about me.

Besides one thing: *I don't want you to be upset every day.*

Which is, evidently, the very thing I've been doing.

If I'd have opened these boxes three years ago, I'd have seen the letter. The journal. All the reasons to avoid what

I've been doing for so long: hiding away from the world. Mum wouldn't have wanted my life to stagnate; she's probably watching from above, if there *is* such a thing as Heaven, shaking her head and wondering when I'm going to get my arse into gear and actually *do* something. Maybe Manchester is a sign from her . . . Maybe that was some kind of calling.

Or, perhaps, it's something different. Some*one* different. Someone like Eric.

Relief is flooding through me, coursing like electricity that jolts me up on my feet, searching for my suitcase with the broken wheel. The first thing I pack is the journal.

Because this will be the first adventure of my new life.

Chapter 44

Eric

I must have deleted and retyped the text to Joshua at least eight times before sending it. I watch as the words appear in their finality: I'll be back in work next week. What that means for me, I'm not sure – it's not like my sick record has ever been problematic, but there's still worry, taking up space in a mind that's already full.

When the doorbell rings, I almost think it's Joshua himself, descending on the house to check up on me, but not even he's that quick.

The one person I don't expect to see so early on a Saturday morning, however, is Steph. She stands there, beaming on the doorstep next to a bright flowery suitcase.

'Why are you wearing that?' I ask, pointing to the wide-brimmed sun hat she's clinging on to for fear the wind will swipe it from her head. 'It's freezing.'

'So what? It's nice. I like it. Oh, and by the way, you were right.'

'Oh? About what?'

I step aside to let her into the hallway, the suitcase clunking behind her. It's only then it occurs to me what she's wearing: an outlandish combo of a silk blouse and a striped skirt with trainers, a sun hat and a pair of silver earrings that glimmer when they catch the morning light. This isn't jeans-and-jumper Steph, this isn't Pink Bag. This is . . . I have no idea. She resembles Moira Rose from *Schitt's Creek*.

'The boxes,' she says, by way of explanation. She leans the suitcase against the wall and slumps onto the sofa, pulling her legs up like she always does, like the Steph I know. 'You were right. I shouldn't have left it so long.'

'Wait, you opened them?'

'I did it. I finally opened them this morning. Hence the get-up.'

'I did wonder.'

'I should have done it sooner.'

She pulls out a letter from a black handbag and I can't help myself – just looking at her sat there in her sun hat when it's foggy outside makes me laugh. She doesn't seem to mind. Steph passes me the letter and I read, taking in the pretty, delicate handwriting, her mother's words.

'That letter was there the whole time,' she says once I've finished, and when I look up, there's a sad look in her eyes. 'Three years and I had no idea, because I couldn't bring myself to open those bloody boxes. I feel so stupid.'

'You're not stupid. How were you meant to know?'

'I've spent three years not living my life, pretending everything is okay when it's actually not.'

'You've been grieving,' I tell her. 'That takes time. It's different for everyone. I know I said I'd have opened them, but I can understand why you wouldn't. And judging by this' – I wave the letter in the air – 'your mum wouldn't want you to fret over it, either. She'd want you to carry on and be happy.'

Steph nods thoughtfully. She takes a deep breath and smiles. 'About Mum,' she says. 'She left me a gift. An adventure journal. And I've decided I need to find Laurie.'

'What do you mean?'

'I want to try to track Laurie down. I need to find her – I need to see her and check she's OK.'

'Steph, honestly. The fact that she left—'

'I need to say sorry,' she says. 'I need to see her in person and make things right. If I *did* upset her that night, I need to explain why. I'm not a bad neighbour and neither is she. In fact, if it wasn't for her, I . . .' We wouldn't have met, I want to blurt out, but I don't. '. . . probably wouldn't have opened the boxes. She kind of caused all this and I feel partly responsible.'

I sit next to her on the sofa, contemplating. 'Where would we even begin? She could be anywhere,' I say, defeated.

'Not necessarily. Don't give up so easily! Look . . .' Steph pulls out her phone and scrolls to the only public photos on Laurie's Facebook account. The photo of Laurie and Malcolm before a beach framed by sprawling cliffs. 'Yes, they could be anywhere, they could be in Barbados, for all we know. But that place . . . I've seen it. On framed photos in their living room. Wherever that place is, they've definitely visited it more than once. What if it's one of their favourite destinations? Laurie could have headed there.'

'Please don't suggest we go back into the house again.'

'Oh, God, no way! All I'm saying is, it might be a clue to where she's gone.'

Steph is getting excitable and I like it. Her laughter, the hope in her voice, is almost infectious. I watch as she zooms in on the photo, peering closely for any more hints, any landmarks or giveaways, and I notice something.

'Wait. That place . . . can you show me again?'

Steph hands me the phone.

'I recognise that, too. From the DVD we played. Weren't they in Pembrokeshire?'

'I can't remember,' she says.

332

At that moment, the door opens and in strides Jude, guitar in hand.

'Don't worry, don't worry,' he says. 'No practice this evening. Unless you want me to serenade you. Love the outfit, Steph.'

Steph does a mock bow. 'Why thank you! These are my mum's.'

'Good taste,' he replies. 'You guys OK?'

Steph nods. 'Kind of. You wouldn't happen to recognise this place, would you?' she asks, handing the phone to Jude.

'Steph has decided to look for Laurie,' I inform him.

'Oh?' asks Jude, interest piqued.

'Please don't think I'm crazy!' says Steph. 'Oh, God. You do, don't you?'

'Just a little,' I tease.

'I wouldn't say that at all.' Jude frowns as he scrutinises the photo.

'We think it's in Pembrokeshire,' I offer.

Steph frowns. 'And Pembrokeshire's a big place.'

Jude flashes us another of his mischievous smiles. 'Easy. Give me ten minutes.'

'He's good at this,' I explain.

True to his word, eight minutes and thirty-five seconds later, Jude leaps off the sofa and punches the air.

'Got it!' he says in triumph. 'It *is* Pembrokeshire. It's a little coastal village called Little Haven. It's by St Brides Bay.'

'Little Haven,' says Steph dreamily.

'So, what are you going to do now?' asks Jude. His eyes flit from Steph to the suitcase. 'Are you going there? Today?'

'I am indeed,' Steph replies. 'It's going to be the first adventure in my journal.' She explains the boxes, the journal, to Jude. 'I have a free weekend, so why not? I actually came by to see if Eric wanted to come with me.'

'Seriously?' I whip round to face her, half shocked, half elated. 'That's quite a journey.'

'A couple of hours,' says Jude, shrugging.

'Are you sure you want to go, Steph? What if she's not there? We don't know for certain that she is. She could be in Liverpool for all we know. Or Sweden.'

'So what? If she isn't, we come back home. Look, I know it sounds weird and a bit random, but since reading Mum's letter, I know I have to make changes. I can't keep putting things off. I miss the person I used to be, that spark of going somewhere new and wondering what I'll find. I mean, I'm going to go anyway. There's a train leaving Temple Meads in an hour, I can get us tickets. Plus, I've booked a B & B. I just wanted to ask you because, well, it's our thing.'

Our thing.

We were only brought together because of Laurie and I've enjoyed every moment, even the sad parts. Maybe Steph has a point. Without Malcolm, Laurie's been alone. We both know what it feels like to be alone.

'So, are you in?' Steph asks, eyes gleaming.

My phone vibrates with a message from Jude, who's giving me a wry smile from across the room. '*Go go go!*', it says. 'What are you waiting for? Bloody *go*.'

I'll admit, this is a crazy idea, but glimpsing the hope in Steph's eyes, I pause, trying not to let my hesitation show. Hesitation is what ruined me last time. I lost Clarissa because I hesitated.

'Fine, you win,' I say, grinning as I get up to pack. 'But how about I drive us there instead?'

'You would?' Steph says, ecstatic. 'Road trip!'

'Exactly. Let me get my things.'

'Do you trust me not to throw any wild parties?' jokes Jude. 'I promise I won't lose Freddy.'

This time, I believe him.

Chapter 45
Steph

Little Haven is in West Wales, approximately three hours away from Bristol. We hit the motorway about an hour ago, after loading up with all the snacks we could possibly need for a kind of impromptu road trip. There are bags of sweets, biscuits, sandwiches, crisps and some water on the back seat of Eric's car, not to mention the takeaway coffee. With the caffeine and the adrenaline, I'm on a high I've not experienced for a long time. Not to mention the fact I'm with Eric until tomorrow. Even if we don't find Laurie in Little Haven, I still get to spend more time with Eric.

'What are we even going to say?' asks Eric, holding his hand out for a snack.

I proffer the bag of Maltesers.

'If we see Laurie, that is,' he adds. 'Don't you think she's going to be super creeped out by this?'

'By what? That we, her doting neighbours, have driven all this way to find her?'

'OK, stalker.'

'Come on. Wouldn't you be flattered?'

'Hmm,' he says, his mouth a line of amused concern. 'I guess it depends.'

'Look, I know it seems weird, but once we explain, I think she'll be OK with it. At least, I hope so. I still feel terrible about it. Even worse when I found out about Malcolm.'

'It's not your fault, though. None of this is your fault.'

Eric keeps his eyes on the road. I can't help but admire him. Other men might have run for the hills at everything going on in my life, but no, here's Eric, the lovely guy from next-door-but-one, agreeing to go on a spontaneous weekend road trip with me. I say a silent thank you to Mum, wherever she may be, who I swear has put all of this into motion. Typical Mum.

'I know it's not, but it's still worth it to try to find out. Besides, there's a beach there. And we have a quaint little B & B. Does that help?'

'Possibly.'

Eric's doing that thing he often does; he sounds serious, but when you look at him, he's smirking, in a cute way. His dark curly hair is looking unkempt; he didn't brush it before we left and he has to drive with the window down ever so slightly, so the breeze whips in through the tiny gap. He likes to hear the sounds of the traffic, he says. It's unnerving, being totally closed off.

'Anyway,' I say smugly, 'even if we do see her, we can just say, "Oh, hi! I think we live next door to you. We just so happen to be on holiday."'

'On holiday. In November?'

'It's a very nice place, apparently. I looked it up. OK, so it may not be sunny' – I had to resign myself to this fact, leaving Mum's giant sun hat at home – 'but the sea can be so enchanting when the weather is bleak. Hey, you should have brought the screenplay! It might have been fun to work on. Very atmospheric.'

I still feel terrible for reading his screenplay, and it's still a sore subject between us, but I can't avoid it.

'Before you say anything, yes, I read your work,' I continue. 'I shouldn't have, and I'm so sorry. But the only reason I did was because I was interested and I wanted to see what comes out of that mind of yours. It's *great*, Eric.'

'Are you just saying that to flatter me because I caught you? How would you like it if I read all that terrible poetry of yours?'

Again, he's serious, but when I glance across at him, there's a hint of a smile.

'OK, OK, you can have your revenge. I'll ask Amanda if she has it. Hear me out, Eric. Jude and I loved it. You're talented.'

His cheeks flush. 'Thank you. I don't believe you, of course. I think I'm just not used to such attention.'

'Well, you deserve it. Believe me, you're a good writer.'

Eric glances across at me. His shy smile breaks into one of immense happiness. I hope, in time, he believes me about the fact he's talented. 'Look,' he says. 'I'm all for an inspirational road trip but I'm here to find Laurie too, right? We're in this together. I'm here with *you*, not for work.'

This makes me happy. Surprisingly so.

Eric looks across at me and smiles sadly.

'You'll be leaving for Manchester soon. It'll be nice to spend some proper time with you before you go.'

This, however, does *not* make me happy. All of a sudden, the elation of this morning, after the shock of Mum's letter, has disappeared like a faulty balloon, slowly deflating. Of course – I'm soon to be moving. This will probably be the last time I see Eric before I leave.

It doesn't seem as exciting any more.

It will, I tell myself; this is just a blip. This morning's events – Mum's letter, the boxes, now heading to West Wales with Eric – have thrown me off course. This weird day has nothing to do with my future; it's just a day of unusual happenings in an otherwise normal life. Right?

We don't talk much for the next hour, instead settling on a Spotify playlist that we both know so that Eric doesn't have to endure me warbling along to hours of nineties 'girl power' hits. Even though he says he doesn't mind. Still, we sing along to Bon Jovi instead, and I pass him snacks as the roads span on for miles, the surrounding fields rolling by on either side of us. Miles and miles of green, and little farmhouses way out into the distance. I've always wondered what it would be like to live in one of those. A secluded little house in the middle of nowhere. Once, that would have been a fantasy.

Now, I'm not so sure.

We're almost there. We've ventured off the motorway now and set out into West Wales.

Now, we're on the way, approaching Haverfordwest. The drive takes us through the town centre, through rows of shops and a church on a hill. I stare out of the window, watching it all roll by.

A smile creeps across Eric's face as the satnav's booming voice confirms our destination and I send up a little prayer for the place I booked last minute. It's a twin room in a little bed and breakfast overlooking the sea. Well, it's a little walk from the sea, but you can see it from the window, so that's something. It's tiny but functional, and all I could afford, and it was the only room they had. Only now, thinking of sharing the room with Eric, panic starts to build. I hope he's OK with it. He said he was, so that's fine, isn't it?

'So, when did you last go on holiday?' he asks. 'Was it America?'

'Yes. I'd planned to do so much more travelling. There's a notebook at home, packed away with all of my stuff, where I'd written a list of the places I want to go. I've been on a few beach holidays with Amanda and we planned some city breaks. Venice, Prague, Paris . . . that kind of thing, where we could really do some sightseeing. And then, well, Mum . . .' I trail off.

Eric swings into a side road that leads down a country lane. The road is winding, taking us past more fields. By now the afternoon sky is a looming grey, but I don't let it dissuade me from being here. The threat of the cold, of the rain, just makes it even more daring.

'I'm the same, really,' he says. 'I love sightseeing. Just taking a map and exploring.'

'Have you done much exploring?'

Eric shakes his head. The car slows somewhat as it fills the narrow road, flanked with trees and overgrown foliage that creeps onto the tarmac, urging us to be careful. We're away from the town now, away from the busy stores and the pretty terraced cottages and town houses that lead into the centre.

'I wanted to. Clarissa loved going on holiday. Went to quite a few places, actually – the Maldives, Miami, Cuba . . . Sadly, she didn't like sightseeing. She'd say, "I'm not traipsing round old relics, wearing those ugly walking shoes and being uncomfortable and sweaty while you take pictures."'

'Seriously?'

'I wish I was kidding. But I kind of understand, though. I mean, it was her holiday as well and she liked to spend it by the pool. She'd only take sandals and flip-flops. Funnily enough, she took more photos than I ever would have. She'd say, "Eric, can you take a photo of me jumping in the air?" and "I'm going to go over there, can you take a photo?"

339

And I'd say, "OK, smile! You're looking away . . ." And she'd snap at me, saying that was the *point*. It was meant to be as if it were a candid shot.'

I gawp at him, trying to contain my laughter. 'Wait. So you didn't get to do any of the fun stuff?'

Eric shrugs. 'It *was* fun. I think being with her was the fun part. I'm not into sunbathing, but I went along with it, just making the most of the sunshine even though I was itching to get up and go for a walk somewhere and really take it all in . . . Like go on one of those excursions. She didn't want to, so I just . . . didn't.'

'It sounded fun for her, not you.'

'Maybe. I felt a bit guilty, but then I always did. A little paranoid, too. I'd arrange a trip and I'd spend the whole time worrying that she'd be bored. Or that if I went alone, I'd miss her . . .' He trails off. 'I don't know. Sometimes I think she loved me, but other times it felt like she simply wanted me around because I was useful. We were good together at the beginning, really good. And then, well, I don't know what happened.'

'I get that.' My mind flits to Miles. 'Life changes and suddenly, things aren't the same any more.'

'It wasn't just that. *She* changed. Or maybe I did. Or maybe she was always the same and I didn't realise.'

'What makes you think that?'

'Because . . .' He keeps his eyes on the road. 'We used to be into similar things. We'd just go to the seaside some-times, or to a fairground, just get in the car and go. Then, slowly, she became less interested. Everything had to be bigger and better.

'Speaking of holidays, we once went to Portugal with a couple of Clarissa's mates. I opened my suitcase at the villa, only to discover that it wasn't my luggage. I started to fret, because clearly there'd been a mix-up.'

'Shit. Did you get yours back eventually?'

'That's the thing. I soon found out it *was* my suitcase, but all of *my* clothes were missing. There were just these . . . plain T-shirts. Polo shirts. And shorts that weren't my style. My jeans had vanished. Turns out Clarissa didn't want me wearing my usual stuff, so she re-packed my case at the last minute with clothes she'd bought.'

'Oh my God. Eric, that's . . . bad.'

'I know. I had to wear chinos the whole time. I have nothing against chinos. But they're not *me*. Clarissa expected me to thank her for it – I was so confused. I had to spend the entire holiday dressed like some other version of me, forcing smiles the whole time.'

He hasn't noticed that I'm no longer laughing. That the jollity has gone from my face. All I want to do is pull him close and show him just how fucking stupid Clarissa has been. Eric is Eric and, looking at him now, with his windswept curly hair and his faded jeans, I feel lucky. He's lovely the way he is, with his well-worn T-shirt, and the slight stubble on his chin because he didn't get time to shave this morning, because he chose to spend not just the day, but the entire weekend with me. The sudden swell of love I feel for him, likely the protective sort, fights against the rage I feel for Clarissa.

'It was like she was embarrassed by me,' he admits.

'Did you tell her how you felt?' I ask quietly, because I need to know. I need to know how anyone can think that kind of behaviour is OK.

'Of course I did, but it didn't do much. She just shrugged it off, and there wasn't much I could do. I couldn't exactly rush home and get my clothes back, could I? So I guess, like many things, it was just forgotten about. By her, anyway.'

'Eric . . .'

Was Clarissa the woman on his lock screen, that night in the pub? The beautiful woman with her arms around Eric? A different version of him. Not the Eric who's next to me in the car – the writer with the gorgeous smile who loves horror movie T-shirts and cosy nights in, whose eyes light up when he talks about his passions.

'It's not about the clothes,' he continues. 'I *know* it's not about the clothes. If only it was that simple. It wasn't the only time she pulled something like that. What hurt me the most is that I wasn't good enough for her. She obviously wanted me to be different, this different person who wears chinos and spends all day with her posh friends. She wanted me to be someone else. I know how fucking stupid that sounds. I feel silly just telling you. That's a point – why am I boring you with this? We're meant to be having fun.'

'We *are* having fun, aren't we? *I* am. OK, so admittedly, hearing what you've gone through *isn't* fun, but I like talking to you about this stuff. I'm a good listener and I have snacks. That's enough reason! Plus, you know even more than my sister does about *my* life, so that's a first. So no, Eric, you're not boring me with this.'

'If you're sure,' he says with uncertainty.

The sky is darker now, a looming, cloud-dappled blanket ready to encase us, and we talk as Eric drives down more winding country roads. Already it's feeling better here, away from the rest of the world.

'I went through years of not being good enough for my dad,' he explains, his eyes fixed on the road ahead. 'I know he loves me, but he showed it in a strange way. I think he wanted me to be more driven and career-focused, you know? Make lots of money, be successful, have a family. The life formula – everything we're *meant* to do.

'I was always more creative. I don't have any siblings, so I took the pressure. So to have Clarissa do the same – to act as if I were interchangeable, just someone she could upgrade because the previous version wasn't good enough – hit me hard. It was probably why Dad liked Clarissa so much. They're similar.'

'I can't imagine what that would feel like.'

'I envy you,' Eric says. 'How close you and Amanda are. How much your mum loved you.'

I nod, unsure how to answer, wrapped in guilt, and in the relief I feel for having that love. Even though I'd sell my soul to have Mum back, I'm grateful that the time we had was full of love. That Mum was supportive, her love unconditional. Every memory of her has been good and cherished.

There's silence now. The car is cold and I look to the darkened sky again, thinking of her.

'Look,' says Eric, pulling me from my reverie.

As the car heads slowly uphill, beneath tall trees, their near-skeletal branches waving above, the sea stands out in the distance. Beneath the dark hue of the sky, the water looks calm in comparison, its rolling waves a picture of hope. Tears threaten to surface; each time I see the sea at Weston-super-Mare, I fear it somewhat. I fear heading towards it, afraid of being swallowed up by childhood memories that I don't want to revisit for all the longing they bring. But now, my heart soars.

Mum is here, always with me, and that brings me comfort.

And there it is, on the sign we pass slowly.

'*Little Haven*'.

Chapter 46

Eric

'We're here,' Steph says. 'We're in Little Haven.'

As the horizon comes into view, the sea a sheet of grey-blue against the silver-tinged sky, I take my eyes away from the narrow, clear road just long enough to appreciate it.

According to the satnav, the B & B isn't far. Steph talks excitedly beside me about seaside memories, of sandcastles and amusement arcades and salty chips drenched in vinegar. All of my thoughts have escaped me and have trundled off down that path marked 'Clarissa'.

I wasn't expecting her to come on this journey with us, but here she is, an uninvited guest. I picture her in the back seat, big sunglasses on, arms folded as she glares into the passenger seat at Steph. For a moment I think I'm going mad, as if I'll glance into the rear-view mirror and she'll appear, phantom-like, the little frown line between her eyebrows that I once loved, growing deeper.

She'd sit like that sometimes, as if you could hear the silence, and it was loud. I'd reach out to her, one hand in search of hers, while the other gripped the wheel. Sometimes she'd take it and other times, especially towards the end of our relationship, she'd ignore it; her fingers would travel to her phone instead, scrolling through different lives as her own rushed by. I can hear her now:

Are you sure you want to wear that?

I didn't like the hotel you booked, so I changed it. It was the one Rebecca stayed in last year – it's amazing.

Noah's firm is hiring, do you want to send him your CV?

Why are you wasting hours on that bloody screenplay when you could be furthering your actual career? It's not like you'll make any money.

Her voice floats, unwelcome, through my head. It's as if these memories have remained underwater for so long, locked in a chest held firm by chains, only finally to come free and float determinedly to the surface. They're the memories I locked away all that time ago, when I'd tell myself everything was OK. When I'd give her the benefit of the doubt.

I'd locked away the memory of her scrutiny each time I'd want to wear one of my favourite T-shirts. I'd locked away the hurt when she snubbed the hotel I'd spent most of a day trawling the internet to find, making sure it would have everything she'd want for a romantic getaway. She'd shrugged it off, rebooked it as if it were nothing. As if it were something everyone did.

I'd only doubted my job because Clarissa spent so much time trying to persuade me to look for another.

I thought I wanted her back. I thought winning back Perfect Clarissa was the ticket to my perfect life, the happiness, the magic formula. In all of my efforts, I'd forgotten how much it didn't work. How we were, quite simply, incompatible.

Now, it's all so bloody obvious.

I'd been happy. I'd been happy before Clarissa, before she swooped in with all of her perfection and made me believe things that weren't true. It's nice sometimes, feeling that you're destined for more, that your own little place on this tiny earth can be much greater. And yes, we *were* happy, before the cracks began to show, before it became a competition with her friends, a transition into Clarissa's World, a performance that needed a willing participant. I was a piece of clay, yet to be moulded into something more attractive, richer, better in photos. A contest I never knew we were participating in.

Looking at the sky as the sea rolls by, whipped by the November winds, it's as if the world is clearing. I drive slowly, passing a few houses and what looks like a little holiday park, grateful. Grateful for the clarity, for the peace.

For Steph.

Glancing across at her, I take in her smiling face, her hair, slightly messy from the wind, her mum's outfit. She's searching her phone for the B & B details.

'Aha! Found the confirmation email,' she says happily. 'So there should be street parking. If we go—'

Clunk.

Before she can continue, the car shudders to an abrupt halt. The shock of it jolts us backwards, bouncing into the seat rests.

'Ouch!' says Steph.

Her phone tumbles from her grasp and into the footwell.

'Are you OK?'

'Yeah. Just a bit of a shock. Are you?'

'I'm fine. But I don't know about the car. *Shit.*'

'What happened?'

I try to start the car. Nothing happens.

Cursing under my breath, I try again, to no avail. After a fourth attempt, hope fades.

The car won't start.

We are well and truly stuck, on a country road in West Wales, in the cold.

'Fuck fuck *fuck*. This had to happen now, didn't it? Of all the days.'

There's no mistaking the worry on Steph's face.

'We'll be fine,' she assures me. 'Isn't there someone we can call to help?'

'There is, but right now we need to get this car off the road. We're blocking it. If we can just get it to the side there . . .'

We look at each other, knowing what we need to do.

'Sorry,' I say, but to my surprise, Steph bursts out laughing.

'What's funny?'

'What you said. It's typical. It happens today, of all days. OK, OK. It's not funny if your car's given up on us . . .'

'No. Please don't say that. I can't lose Christine.'

'You named your car Christine?' Steph scoffs. 'After the film?'

'Why wouldn't I? It's red.'

'It's nowhere near as gorgeous as Christine.'

I place my hand lovingly on the steering wheel. 'How dare you! She can hear you, you know.'

Steph throws her head back in laughter. Her laugh is intense and I love it. Bracing ourselves for the cold, we get outside.

'Ready?' Steph asks, and together, we manage to push the car to the side of the road, its tyres disappearing into the long grass.

I could really do with some more coffee. Anxiously, I scroll through my contacts to find the number for roadside assistance while lamenting the possible death of my car as if it's a wounded animal.

Steph's looking out into the distance, clutching her coat tighter around her. She was so excited about this trip that the last thing I want to do is ruin it.

'Right, so they'll be here in a few hours,' I tell her, waiting for the dismay to show on her face. It doesn't. 'Which means we'll lose most of the day. I'm really sorry, Steph.'

'Why? We've still got tomorrow. We can wait it out, can't we?'

I sigh, getting back into the front seat and reaching for a bag of Monster Munch from Steph's stash on the back seat, because typically, now I'm hungry. While we're stuck in what feels like the middle of nowhere. Steph slips in beside me.

'This is all going in the journal,' she tells me.

'I can't believe it.'

Steph shrugs. 'It happens. We could try to walk to the B & B. It can't be too far. Or I could look for a taxi service . . .'

'Hmm, I'm not sure. I don't want to venture too far. Actually, we did pass a caravan park not long ago. That's definitely within walking distance. They might have a reception area. Might even be some coffee. I'm desperate.'

'Good idea. Let's go.'

Steph grabs her bag and suitcase from the boot, which clunks loudly as we trundle up the hill. The wind whips at our faces, icy as we walk as fast as we can, trying to keep to one side of the narrow road. The top of the caravan park comes into view, its sign a welcome relief. 'CLIFFSIDE CARAVAN PARK', it reads, its sign tall and colourful, decorated with a picture of a sunny beach. There's a little office out front – before the path leads down towards neat rows of spacious static caravans – a small building that resembles a log cabin, decked out in colourful bunting that flaps in the breeze, but there are no lights on inside, only the ghostly shapes of a desk and a few chairs, and one of those rotating shelves full of brightly coloured tourism leaflets. The door is locked.

348

'Well, great,' says Steph, sounding defeated, which makes me feel terrible.

Even worse when, at that moment, rain starts to pelt down onto our heads. A minute later, it's heavy, pounding like bullets against the tarmac, and we huddle beneath the shelter of the office doorway.

'How about you taxi over to the B & B?' I suggest. 'I'll wait here, in the car.'

'You can't wait here alone. It'll get dark in a couple of hours.'

'Why not? I've got snacks.'

She gives me a playful nudge, just as there's a sound from behind us, the hurried creak of an opening door.

We turn to see a woman emerging from a nearby caravan, eyeing us with curiosity. She looks to be in her sixties, with a messy bun, oversized jumper and jeans, and a pair of boot-like slippers.

Her eyes travel over the both of us, taking in our faces, red from the cold, and Steph's bright suitcase.

'Hi?' she says kindly. 'You OK?'

'Kind of,' I reply, pointing in the direction of the road, even though the car is out of sight. 'We've broken down and were wondering if you had a vending machine or something up here.'

She shakes her head. 'Sorry, we don't. I'm Barbara, the site owner. Cliffside is closed during the off-season. How long have you got to wait?'

'A couple of hours.' I turn to Steph. 'You should go.'

'Go? I'm not going anywhere.'

'You wanted to find Laurie! That's a point . . .' I pull my phone from my pocket, showing Barbara the photo of the Robertsons. 'I know it's a long shot, but have you seen this woman?'

Barbara shakes her head. 'Sorry. Never seen her.'

'Eric, I'll wait with you. It's no problem,' says Steph as the rain gets heavier, blurring the sky. 'We can look for Laurie tomorrow.'

'If you're going to be here a couple of hours,' says Barbara, 'well, I know we're not open, but you can wait in one of the caravans here until they turn up. It's going to be raining all night. It'll be warm, at least. And there's coffee.'

'That would be amazing,' says Steph. 'Thank you!'

Barbara heads inside to look for the key and then leads us down the path towards caravan number seven, which stands almost lonely on the edge of the row, its pretty decking wet with rain. Barbara lets us in, pointing out the two bedrooms and living room, complete with TV and, to my utter joy – the kitchen.

'Like I said, I didn't let you in here,' she says with a wink, 'but just pop the key back on the way out.'

The caravan is cold, cold enough to see our breath on the air. Steph turns on the heating and I start on the coffee, thanks to Barbara and her kind supply of milk. Outside, the rain lashes against the windows, the noise of it loud and echoey against the walls of the caravan.

Steph collapses on the sofa as the kettle gives out a faint roar.

'I love this place,' she says.

'It's nice. Very big. I've never stayed in one of these before. Only ever went camping. This place has an *actual* toilet.'

Grinning, Steph runs her hands through her hair, wet from the rain.

'Don't you think it's weird?' she asks.

'What's weird?' I finish stirring the coffee and hand her the mug.

'Well, the car breaks down on a deserted road and we find ourselves here, on a caravan site that's just as deserted . . . it's like a horror movie.'

'Shit, you're right. Should we be scared of Barbara? Has she got it in for us?'

'But she's way too kind. I don't think she has it in her.'

'That's what we always think!' I say, laughing.

I join Steph on the sofa, just watching the rain against the window, the green of the surrounding fields disappearing into the grey haze. It's eerie, and I love it.

'The kind ones are always the most sinister,' I add. 'Or, they've got someone helping them out.'

'Why aren't you writing all this down?'

We fall against the soft cushions and talk. And we *do* write it down. Steph pulls a pen and notebook from her bag and we jot down ideas, our handwriting spindly, messy from laughter that makes us shake and giggle, as if we're children again. It's been ages since I spent time with someone just being silly, just being me, and it's freeing, as if part of me has been hidden all this time.

Steph is wonderful in so many ways and I want to tell her. I want her to curl into me, to be close, like we have been, only under different circumstances. I want her to be happy. Taking a deep breath, watching her scribble some notes for our own fun horror film, I want to tell her. The words are on my tongue. They're there, ready. I just need to let them go.

But if I do, it could ruin something good. All this fun we're having could be wiped out in an instant if I tell her. She will, after all, be leaving. Getting too close could spoil the remaining time we have left before it's back to square one.

So I say nothing.

All I can do is consider myself lucky that I'm even here with her in the first place. Which is why I want to find Laurie just as much.

*

'Sooo . . . do you want the good news or the bad news?'

'Uh-oh.' Steph looks up from the sofa, where she's playing a card game with a pack she found on the little foldaway dinner table. A card flutters off the edge as she pulls a fearful face. 'How bad is it? Can we get home?'

Quickly, I close the caravan door, fearing it'll be blown off its hinges from the weather. The rain has turned the surrounding grass to sludge. It's also drenched my clothes on the short walk to the car. Inside, it's cosy.

'Kind of. It needs work.'

'Oh.'

'But they're sending someone to repair it tomorrow afternoon, so we should be fine. We'll be home in time for Monday, at least.'

'That isn't too bad. What about the good news?'

'Well . . . Barbara has very kindly said we can stay for the night if we want to, because of the weather. She even made us some sandwiches.' I pull the foil-wrapped package from the carrier bag Barbara presented me with. 'I told her we had somewhere booked, though, so we'll probably be heading off. But the offer's there.'

Steph gathers the cards and slips them back into their little box, slowly, as if she's weighing her options. She gets off the sofa, looking around the place, taking it in for the last time as the wind wails against the structure, loud and fierce.

'They're expecting us,' she says. 'The B & B. Although it's getting darker now. And it's cold.'

'I'm really sorry,' I tell her.

'Hey, it's not your fault! I can always cancel.'

There's a twinkle in her eye and I recognise the excitement. I want us to stay. I want us to take Barbara's offer and hide out here for the night, listening to the weather and feeling safe inside.

'I'm torn,' says Steph. 'I mean, it *is* cosy here. And there's an additional bedroom . . .'

The thought hangs in the air.

'Do you want to cancel?'

Steph nods. 'Know what? I like it here. It's nice, it's warm, I'm tired, and we're already here. I reeeally don't want to move from this warm sofa. We have coffee and food and a TV. What could be better? Shall we stay?'

She's right, of course.

'In that case, I'll go and let Barbara know. I'll be right back.'

She doesn't see my huge smile as I head outside.

Later, we sprawl on the sofa beneath a duvet swiped from the double bedroom. We're tired but it's only nine thirty, and we've barely moved, besides the shuffle from the sofa to the kitchen for tea and snacks. Instead we've spent the evening playing games and just talking, sharing stories about everything that's crossed our minds: our families, memories of summer holidays and teenage loves, our school days.

'I was shy,' Steph insists.

'You were not.'

'Why is that so hard to believe? Trust me, I was the kid who hid in the toilets when the popular girls were roaming the corridors. That was, until Amanda started school and I had to put on a brave face. She was quieter than me. I at least had to act like the big protective sister.'

We face each other, Steph with her legs crossed opposite me, studying the cards she's holding.

'It's still hard to picture,' I tell her.

She pokes out her tongue over the top of her concealed cards.

'What about you?' she asks. 'Actually, let me guess. Hmm, looking at you, I'd say you were one of the lads. Actually, no. I think you were just on the periphery. I know you. You were quiet, too. Am I right?'

'Very. And you *know* me, huh?'

'I know enough to be right, clearly.'

I shrug, defeated, because she *is* right – one hundred per cent correct.

'You have me sussed. Fine, I'll admit it, I was a nerd deep down. I had a couple of best mates, we'd kind of keep ourselves to ourselves. Kept out of trouble.' Now that I say it, it's astoundingly clear how that strategy followed me to university, too: be a part of the group, fit in. 'I wonder if you'd have fancied me in Year 11.'

'Oh, definitely.'

'Lies!'

'Honestly. I probably would have, and I wouldn't have said anything. I'd have been harbouring teenage lust for you the whole school year and wouldn't have dared tell you. I'd have been writing your name on my pencil case and everything.'

'Why? I mean, why wouldn't you have said anything?'

'You might have laughed at me.'

'I'd have had the same worry. And yes, I'd have fancied you, too.'

Steph throws back her head in laughter. 'Really? You really believe that? OK, when we get back, we're digging out the high-school photos. Thank God it was all before social media was a huge thing.'

'Before everyone started to put on a big fake show about their lives, you mean?' He takes another card from the pile.

'Eric, you're just trying to distract me from this game. Nice try.'

Admittedly, this weekend has been a wonderful distraction from work, and the house; the same four walls I see each day. It's nice to be somewhere different for once, somewhere new.

Steph lets out a yawn as she pulls a card from my hand. They're spread out like a fan, in perfect order. Steph seems to have me sussed.

'Hey!' she says, going for the second-to-last one as I whip my hand away just in time. 'Let me pick.'

'Not that one!'

'Why?'

Her face is serious for all of a second before she bursts out laughing. 'Eric, I can so easily read you.'

'Are you saying I'm bad at this game?'

'Kind of. You've got all of your cards in order. I can tell you've organised them all in sections. I can see how careful you are. And that one in the middle – that's the one you don't need, that you're trying to give away.'

'How do you know that? Wait. You're cheating.'

'Because it's poking out *juuust* a little. See? It's the easiest one to pick. You've set it up that way. You think I'll automatically go for it, but I won't.'

'OK. Consider yourself the victor.' I let out a laugh and quickly reorder my cards haphazardly.

'That's better,' she says. 'Can't believe you haven't played this one before.'

'You said Amanda taught you, right? I had no siblings to teach me.'

Steph peruses her cards again. 'Sorry. I guess I had an advantage there. Amanda taught me most of the card games I know. Including poker. Which, I'll admit, she's terrible at, because her face gives it away every single time. You'd think after years she'd be more aware, but alas, no.'

The stormy weather hasn't faltered; the wind and rain is still beating against the roof of the caravan. It's haunting, almost. Just yesterday I'd never have imagined I'd be here, in an idyllic place with Steph. She's looking at her phone now that's just lit up, bright beneath the bulb of the small table lamp we're using to keep the atmosphere. 'I love how creepy it is,' she said earlier as the wind whistled and howled, though with passion rather than reluctance.

So why am I thinking about my ex?

Steph is in front of me, hair messy and frizzy from the rain – we are *both* frizzy from the rain – and she's smiling and enjoying all of this. This weird weekend in the middle of nowhere.

And yet Clarissa comes back to me Every. Single. Time.

'Speaking of Amanda, here's Wendy, her guinea pig,' she says, pulling me from the thought, showing me a reel of pictures. 'It belongs to my niece. Actually . . .' Steph moves in closer to me, snuggling against me to take a selfie of both of us. 'She'd love to see you.'

We look glowing in the picture. Glowing and happy. Seconds after receiving the picture, Amanda's video calling.

'Oh my God,' says Amanda, her face filling the screen, red hair over her shoulders. Her smile is very much like Steph's. 'Look at you guys!'

I dart out of the way, but it's no use. Steph's snuggling into me and I'm trapped, in a good way, watching as her sister's eyes light up with glee.

'Amanda, meet Eric!' she announces.

'Hey,' I say, waving awkwardly.

Amanda's red hair swishes as she moves, jolting in front of the screen. The signal out here is low. The image pixelates and Steph frowns.

'Mand? Mand! I got your messages earlier, but there's not much signal here and—'

'Where are you?'

'Pembrokeshire!'

'*Why?*'

'Long story,' I cut in.

On the screen, Amanda clearly wants to ask more but doesn't want to. Not when I'm here. So I squeeze my way out from the sofa to go and put the kettle on, leaving Steph to her conversation. I hear the words 'wedding' and 'bring him' – Amanda isn't so good at being inconspicuous.

'What's that?' I ask, taking the tea from the cupboard.

Steph fills me in on Nat, her bridezilla cousin. She explains Amanda's newly hatched plan to bring someone along, because not going would make her look, according to her aunt, 'jealous and attention-seeking'.

'I can scrub up well, you know,' I remark, giving her a wink.

Amanda giggles. 'See? Right there. That was your offer for a plus-one.'

There's silence and for a moment I think Amanda has gone, cut off in the midst of the bad weather and remote location. Yet, when I look over from pouring the tea, she's still there. Steph's face is fraught with concentration, as if she's about to deliver some bad news and is finding the right words.

Finally, Steph speaks.

'I'm not going to the wedding,' she says simply.

'What? Why?,' says Amanda. 'Come on, Steph. We were going to make a weekend of it . . . it's just one day! We can get drunk, play wedding bingo—'

'Mand. I'm not going. I'm not doing it, not any more. I think it's time to be honest about things from this point on. Mum and Grace never really got on, but that's not our fault. Why do we want to be around Grace after how she treated Mum? Would *we* ever end up like that?'

'I bloody well hope not,' Amanda says and there's sadness in her voice.

'I couldn't cope if I lost my sister like Auntie Grace lost Mum, Mand. If I lose you, I'll lose half of my world, but I'd have to deal with it, and I'd rather be alone without you than be surrounded by a hundred fake friends, or family who are just there because they feel sorry for me.'

Amanda's voice wavers, her bright, perky tone now a mumble.

'They're the only family we have left, Steph.'

'So what? People talk about toxic *relationships*, but it extends to family, as well. It works just the same. Why spend time with them when all they do is make us miserable? Why are we even pretending? I'm just so sick of it, Mand. Pretending to you, and to people at work, and everyone else that things are blissful and OK. What's the point?'

I bring the tea to the table and put it down in front of Steph.

'Maybe they love you,' I suggest, 'in their own weird way.'

Steph turns to me. 'If they do, they don't show it. They *never* did. When we needed them most, they didn't show it.'

'She's right,' says Amanda, her face frozen mid-sentence on the screen.

'You're cutting out,' says Amanda now. 'Call me when you're back, OK? I need to know everything about what you and that sexy man are up to. Love you!'

This sets Steph off laughing.

'Hey!' I tease. 'I *am* sexy, aren't I?'

She hurls a cushion at me in response.

Once Amanda's gone, the room is silent besides the tapping of the rain. I climb back beneath our duvet and snuggle closer to Steph as she blows on her tea to cool it. Her body fits so wonderfully against mine that I never want to leave this position. Steph is gorgeous and my mind is in overdrive, but right now, I'm just enjoying the warmth of her, her company.

'I know the truth now,' she says. 'I was *not* a terrible daughter. Now that I've read Mum's letter, I can accept that.'

'I admire your strength,' I tell her. 'Turning down a day of free food and booze like that.'

She shakes her head. Her damp hair rests against my shoulder.

'I'm done. I've had enough of pretending everything's all right when it isn't. I can't keep pretending to be nice and acting the part for supposed "loved ones" who don't love me back. I'm sick of saying sorry.'

The phone falls from Steph's hand and bounces onto the carpet. She's turned now, her hand on my chest, and I can't help it. Before I can stop myself, my hands are on her back and she's moving closer, closer, my lips against hers, until everything – the cards, the rain, family – is forgotten.

Except Clarissa.

I'm still thinking about her. Why am I thinking about her? *This is Steph, this is all about Steph* . . .

Steph is first to pull away, her face full of delight, as if there's more to come. We're silent for a moment, just looking at each other, studying our faces as if to etch the happiness into memory. But I can't. I don't think I can do it, because that would be something I can't venture back from. It would be unfair.

I want this, but I want more than sex, however inviting that may be. I want Steph. And I can't have Steph, because she's moving away. I don't want to ruin something nice. Not again.

'Hey,' I say, sitting up as Steph pulls away, still smiling.

'Sorry,' she says. 'I've been wanting to do that for so long.'

'Me too. It's just . . .'

'What? Oh, shit. Are you seeing someone? I had no idea. I am *really* sorry.'

She pulls away quickly, as if she's committed a terrible crime.

'I thought you said you were sick of saying sorry?'

I'm smiling, and so is she. That's good, at least.

'I am.'

'Well, don't be sorry. I'm not seeing anyone. Things have been difficult lately, that's all. My last break-up was horrible.'

'I get it. Honestly, no need to explain.'

'I do. Jude tried to talk me into getting some counselling recently.'

'He did?'

Steph's face has lost the mischief. If anything, she looks concerned. Why wouldn't she be? I've just told her I need therapy. Part of me regrets telling her, but then there's another part . . . the part that's enjoying the way her fingers softly trace along my arm, in little circles that feel so intense. At least now, she knows.

'Yeah, he did. I pretty much told him where to stick it, but I've come to realise he's right.'

'That's good! Trust me, it'll help.'

'I really hope so.'

I lie there as Steph snuggles against me again. Her lips brush against my neck. I feel her soft breath against my skin as we listen to the rain, until exhaustion consumes us. We don't move. We don't let go. In this present moment, everything feels perfect.

Chapter 47

Steph

When I step from the tiny shower room the following morning, encased in warmth and the gorgeous sensation of a fluffy towel, Eric's already dressed, fluffing up the cushions on the sofa. He's returned the duvet to the bedroom and the cups and plates are on the draining board.

We didn't even make it to the bedroom, choosing to stay put on the sofa instead. Thankfully, there was no 'who will take the big bed?' awkwardness that would usually ensue, although judging by last night, that wouldn't have been a problem.

Eric stretches and I can't resist rushing over to hug him, inhaling his scent of shower gel and shampoo.

'What's that for?' he asks, a smile lighting up his face.

'For doing the washing-up.'

'I don't believe you.'

He smiles and plants a kiss on my forehead that makes my whole body tingle.

'OK, fine. I *am* grateful for the washing-up, but it's also because I wanted to. Problem?'

'So, essentially you're saying you can't keep away from me?'

'Pretty much.'

Eric doesn't seem to mind, but I pull away, remembering what he said last night. About his ex, about the counselling. I thought things might have felt different this morning. I thought we'd wake up, feeling all shifty, sheepishly clambering over one another on the sofa as the alarm I'd set went off. Instead, I woke to the sound of seagulls screeching over the cliffs outside and Eric's soft snoring beside me, grateful I woke first so he didn't have to witness me lying there with my mouth open, drooling into my hair. Then again, what if he did? Eric isn't the type who'd actually care. Which is yet another reason why I like him so much. The list is growing by the day.

Even so, Eric clearly isn't ready for anything new yet. And that's OK, I think to myself. I want him to be happy. I want him to be happy, whether that's with me or not.

I'm moving. I'll be leaving him anyway. Now that I'm thinking about it, in the bright morning light streaming through the curtains, it makes this situation bittersweet, like it's something I'll look back on fondly one day, when I'm at my office in Manchester. My new colleagues or housemates will talk about dates, or loves that have passed them by, and I'll think of Eric. I'll open the adventure journal from Mum, read my scribbled notes and there he'll be. Then maybe I'll look him up on social media, if I haven't given it up for some annual challenge like 'No-Social September' or whatever they come up with, and find him arm in arm with someone glossy and perfect, along with the puppy they've just adopted.

It's like I can see into the future and the bleakness of it all outweighs the good.

Still, there's nothing I can do but carry on and enjoy what's left of the weekend. Last night was wonderful, even though all we did was fall asleep together, listening to the storm. I felt safe. I felt positive. As if I was allowing myself to feel good about something again. For three whole years I've been sabotaging my own life, telling myself I've been a terrible person. A terrible daughter. How can someone so fucking awful deserve to be happy?

Slipping into the bedroom, I take my clothes from my suitcase and pull them on: jeans, jumper, a pair of trainers. It's still cold outside, but the day is brightening with promise following last night's torrential weather. There's sun and the rain has cleared up at least.

'I'll quickly get dressed and then we can get going,' I yell to Eric. 'Are you hungry?'

'I'm starving. There's a pub down by the beach that does a good breakfast, according to Barbara. We could try it out if you like?'

'That sounds good.' Trainers on, I zip up the suitcase and wheel it out, muttering a thankful prayer to Barb, our saviour, who also doubles as a pretty decent tour guide.

'She said there's a coastal path that we could follow, but judging by last night's rain, it might be a bit muddy. So we can take the road. If we have no luck finding Laurie in Little Haven, then Broad Haven isn't far.'

'I guess all we can do is try,' I say. 'We have to be positive. Laurie could be anywhere. She might not even be here at all.'

'Does that mean if she's not here, we can try Barbados?'

'I wish,' I say.

The suitcase lands with a thud on the path outside and we're off.

The road down into Little Haven is long and quiet, besides the soft whoosh of the odd passing car and the rhythmic thump of my broken suitcase wheel. Every so often I have to tug at the handle to dislodge it from a dip in the road, cursing myself for bringing it with me in the first place. In my new post-Bristol life, I'll be one of those smug people who travel with barely anything. 'Told you you should have let me carry it,' Eric comments, amused.

It's a nice walk, the breeze whipping our faces as we descend the hill that leads us to the sea, dipping beneath overhanging trees and passing beautiful homes, painted in hues of pink and sky blue. Taking the coastal path would have been my first option, but we'd never have made it without getting coated in mud. Even though it's a bright, sunny morning, the ground is still wet, the long grass making damp patches on the bottoms of my jeans.

I must resemble a disappointed tourist with my bright case and parka, trundling towards a cold sea. As the road winds downwards, flanked on either side by tall trees, a row of cottages appear, pretty and idyllic.

'Wouldn't you like to live here?' I ask, as I dart to the side to avoid another passing car. 'By the sea.'

'I'd love to. It would be nice. A great view, especially in stormy weather. I'd have a little writing room, overlooking it. And maybe I'd take up surfing, or something fun like that.'

'Have you ever tried surfing?'

'Twice. Decided I didn't like it. But, who knows? Maybe I'll try again and I'll stick at it. It's one of those things you see and think, hey, that looks like so much fun, I can do that. Then five minutes in, you question your sanity.'

'That happens. I feel the same about skiing.'

'Have you—'

'Don't remind me.'

I want to broach the subject of last night, because I'm wondering how he feels, how he *really* feels. Despite the fact I'm glad he told me the truth, I don't want to get in his way. I kind of want to apologise, suddenly worried I was too forward, if I came on too strong, but then I remember what he told me.

364

I'll wait until he's ready.

We continue, following the road past more cottages until we turn into a row of pretty terraced houses. We spot the pub on the corner, The Castle, and right before us is the sea. As soon as I glimpse it, my breath catches in my throat. The sea always makes me think of home. And there it is, the beauty of it, beyond bright rocky cliffs that stand tall on either side, with what look like caverns, almost magical when the sun breaks through the clouds and bounces off the water. And there are houses atop the cliffs, beautiful houses where every day you could wake up and look out at the view. Everything is here, as if the photographs in Laurie's home have come to life.

'Breakfast first?' Eric asks hopefully as we spot the sign outside The Castle. 'Hope they're open.'

The place is indeed open, so we take a small table by the window and order a full English. While I'm waiting, I scan the area for any glimpse of Laurie Robertson. I know it's a long shot, but I have to try. A few people walk by, wrapped in hats and warm jackets, walking their dogs as they stroll past the window, but none of them resemble Laurie.

'Ordered!' Eric says, pulling out the chair opposite mine. 'So, I asked the barman.' He nods in the direction of a man behind the counter. 'He hasn't seen our missing neighbour.'

'Maybe it's just been busy.'

Eric shakes his head solemnly. 'I don't think so. This is the off-season. In the summer this place is busy. Now? Not so much.'

'That doesn't inspire much confidence.'

Eric shrugs, just as my stomach lets out a huge rumble.

'All it means is that Laurie hasn't visited the Castle. You're fretting, Steph. I know how much this means to you, but you shouldn't worry.'

'I should. I was being all hopeful until now, in the cold light of day, it's obvious I've been stupid.'

'How so? You wanted to come here and you did. Plus, I'm here. I can keep you amused, at least.'

He finally stops playing with the salt and pepper shakers and smiles at me, and my stomach does somersaults. His hazel eyes are locked on mine and he reaches over to put his hand on mine, his index finger circling my wrists. Somersaults? It's like a whole Olympic gymnastics team rehearsing in there.

'You've got a point,' I admit quietly.

'See? You wanted an adventure and the universe delivered.'

After breakfast, once we're suitably full, we head outside into the cool air. Eric wraps his coat tighter around him and leads the way towards a little gift shop to see if there have been any sightings of Laurie. Eric holds up the phone, to an apologetic shake of the head from the woman behind the counter.

'Sorry,' she says.

Leaving him at the counter to chat, I browse the shop like a child on a school trip, picking up little souvenirs and trinkets and toys. I buy a little cuddly Welsh dragon for Poppy, a notebook for Stevie and a little ornament in the shape of a daffodil for Amanda, plus some chocolates for all three. Sneakily, I also pick up a couple of keyrings – one for me and one for Eric.

I step outside, bag in hand. Eric takes the suitcase from me.

'My turn,' he says as it rolls along behind him as we head back down the road towards the sea view.

There's a walkway that leads from the top of the road towards the water and with the tide out, the sand looks beautiful and untouched. The child in me wants to whip my shoes off and stomp a path down to the sea, letting my feet sink into it, feeling the gritty sensation between my toes, even though it's the most annoying thing to deal with later. But it's too cold.

'Um, I know it's a bit cheesy, but I got you something,' I say.

I rummage in the bag, pulling out the keyring, which I present to him like some kind of majestic jewel. He looks at it and grins.

'That's perfect,' he says, running his finger over the little dragon carved into the metal. 'Thank you! I got you something, as well. But it's nowhere near as nice.'

'Oh?'

He reaches into his pocket and pulls out a little paper bag. Curious, I take it. Inside is a postcard of the Pembrokeshire coast and a little 'I Heart Wales' sticker.

'Hey, they were right by the counter and the only things I could buy without you noticing,' he says. 'Plus, I thought they'd be nice to put in the journal. I picked the best one, the one with the sea on it.'

Glancing down at the postcard, I have the sudden urge to cry, but *happy* cry. Big, happy tears. Luckily, I manage to refrain, blaming my red eyes on the cold. The gift is perfect. Eric is perfect. This moment, and everything in it, is utterly perfect.

'Thank you,' I sniff.

'Aaand,' says Eric, 'I don't think we have a proper photo yet. You'll need one, won't you?'

He turns round so the sea is behind us, pulls me in close, holding his phone aloft. I notice two elderly ladies stroll by, giving us a sweet smile, because they think we're a couple.

'Ready?' asks Eric, and we grin stupidly for the camera.

His stubble brushes against my cheek and all I want to do is kiss him, right here, right now.

We pull apart to inspect the photo. Eric looks gorgeous in it, in a way I never noticed before. I look terrible, but it's possibly one of the best photos of me ever taken.

'Where next?' he asks.

We spot another pub further up the road called The Swan, which overlooks the sea and the large cliffs that appear to lead us towards the water, the waves splashing softly against them in the winter winds. The Swan looks warm and inviting, but we save it for later and instead take the path, pulling the suitcase further and further until we're standing above the cliffs, surveying the beach below. It may be chilly, but there are still people meandering along, just enjoying the morning. A red-haired man walking his golden Cocker Spaniel, excitable on its leash in a bid to get to the waves, says a happy hello as he passes. I see figures in the distance, hair billowing in the wind, the dogs bounding and weaving excitedly between the rock pools.

Then, in the distance, I see her.

'Oh my God.'

'What?' asks Eric.

'There!'

I'm pointing to the beach, where a figure is walking along the sand. I squint to see her, but she's definitely familiar. The blonde hair that just reaches her shoulders, the slim frame. Jeans. She's walking through the waves, almost paddling in a pair of wellington boots as the foamy blue-grey water hits the shore.

Before he can say anything else, I'm running, Eric calling after me, his voice lost in the wind that whistles furiously in my ears. I'm speeding back down the path, my coat fanning out behind me in the wind as the energy warms me, making my body hot and my breathing quick. I've never run so fast in my life – maybe this is a sign to take up exercise again. Properly this time.

There she is, by the rocks. I'm getting close, close enough to see her soft footprints before they're completely washed away.

'Hey!' I call. 'Excuse me! Hello!'

The woman turns round quickly, surprise on her face as I stop beside her, panting.

'Hi,' I manage.

'Hi there! Are you all right?'

'Yeah! It's just . . . are you . . .'

I'm about to ask if she's Laurie Robertson, but when her face falls properly into view, I realise I've made a mistake. The lady before me, who's giving me a concerned smile, isn't Laurie. She's older, her blonde hair generously streaked with white, and her smile is different.

She's not Laurie.

'I'm really sorry. I thought you were someone else.'

'Oh, that's OK.' With that, she carries on walking.

I feel so stupid.

Turning back, I notice Eric walking towards me on the sand, the suitcase bobbing along behind him like a beacon. I can't help but smile as I hurry to him, shaking my head.

'Wasn't her,' I say. 'Go on, you can laugh.'

'At what? I've never seen you run so fast. I mean, I've seen you *walk* fast in the mornings, but that was impressive. No luck, then?'

Breathless, I sit on one of the jutting rocks, frankly because I want to rest for a minute and it's the most comfortable place. I don't care that there's water in my trainers, that my socks are wet, or that I'm sweating from the run, from the rush of hope.

Eric joins me. 'Look at that,' he says, pointing to the rocks behind us. 'Pretty, isn't it? I'm almost tempted to go climbing. Maybe I would if it wasn't so cold.'

I poke at the sand with the tip of my shoe, uncovering a shell. I remember trawling Weston beach with Mum when I was little, picking up all the nice-looking shells and stuffing them into my pockets. I once kept an entire collection in a jewellery box.

'You OK?' asks Eric, nudging me playfully with his shoulder. 'So that wasn't Laurie, but it doesn't matter. She'll be back next door at some point.'

'It's not that.'

'Oh? What's up, then?' He pauses. 'Is it your mum?'

'Kind of. Now and again I have these memories and it just makes me miss her even more. Like now, I'm thinking of when we used to go to the beach. Just regular stuff. After she died, I didn't want to go again. It wasn't the beach I remembered. It always looked grey to me after that, and all the waves looked daunting, like they were going to swallow me up. It was scary. *I* was scared of it.'

'Are you sure that's not just because you were feeling guilty?'

'Maybe.'

'Think about it.' He lets the suitcase go and puts his arm around me. 'You felt guilty, you said it yourself. You sort of blamed yourself for not seeing her when she was ill. Now you know the truth, though – it wasn't your fault. I think you need to try to let that go.'

'You have a point.' I lean closer, inhaling the scent of his shampoo, of his jacket, of the damp sand around us.

From my pocket, my phone gives a sudden ping. Eric pulls away. It's an email. From work. Ciaran has been copied in.

Hi Stephanie,

Just wanted to say a massive welcome to the Everly Cope team here in Manchester! We're so excited to have you on board in three weeks' time. Your copy of the contract is in the post and I've attached some info about your new office. If you ask for me at the front desk at 9 a.m., I'll come and collect you and take you to meet everyone. We're all excited to see you!

Liza Perez

HR Advisor

I slip the phone back into my pocket.

Chapter 48

Steph

On the day that Mum received her news, I was in New York. I had one day before I left for Boston. As Mum sat on the hard, unfamiliar patient's chair and faced the unknown, personified as a kind-eyed doctor, I was waking up in my hotel overlooking the sprawling, noisy city, bathed in the early morning haze of anticipation, of amazing things to come. As I descended into the subway, the humid air whipping against my skin, Mum was still trapped on that plastic seat, her heart racing, no doubt fiddling with the little charm on her bag like she always did when she was nervous or worried; twirling it round and round in a trembling hand.

By the time I surfaced in Times Square, jittery with thoughts of all the iconic places I'd visit, Mum had been told she was going to die.

The thought of Mum sitting there, getting that news alone, has haunted me.

Now, however, it feels different. *I know it's not my fault.* It's not my fault because Mum never told me. As I'd lay in bed thinking about how she died unexpectedly, the end coming at her with such spiteful force that she had to gather what remained of her life in the last few days, I'd tell myself how awful I was never to have suspected it.

Mum kept it all quiet. Even from Amanda. She didn't want the pity, or the fuss, or to watch us break down around her, missing her before she was gone. I tell Eric all of this.

'It makes me feel weak,' I say, strangely comfortable in confiding in him, and grateful he's willing to listen.

He's been listening since day one, so I'm not sure what I should have expected.

'Why?'

'I was meant to be the confident one. I've tried to keep up the pretence for Amanda and I've spent this whole time pretending I'm someone I'm not, acting like my life is better. And being with people who don't actually want to spend time with me – I'm just *there* – and then the whole thing with Alex. It's just . . . all crap. I'm a liar.'

'Alex?' Eric shoots me a curious glance.

'I'll explain another time.'

'OK. But you're not a liar, Steph.'

'Have you seen my Instagram account?'

'Doesn't everyone lie on Instagram?'

'True. So *that* can be forgiven, I guess. I just feel stuck.'

'We all feel stuck sometimes. I don't think that makes you a bad person, or weak. Hey, I told you I was going to get therapy. I've felt weak for so long. I'm only just learning it's not exactly a bad thing to admit.'

'But why?'

Eric shrugs before taking a deep breath. We're still sitting on the beach, feeling the faint rays of winter sun on our faces as it peeks through the clouds, even though it's cold and our legs are damp. We rest our feet on the suitcase.

'Well, I told you about my ex, didn't I? I guess I haven't been happy for a while. I'm convinced that my life is going nowhere. I kept thinking about my ex to the point where I thought I still loved her.'

'Oh. And do you?'

Eric shakes his head and oh, the *relief*.

'I don't. But I also felt guilty. How it ended, well, I kept replaying over and over in my head. I thought of all the things I *could* be doing, if we were still together, and all the things I'm missing out on now. You know. Marriage, kids, a place of my own . . . the things that my best friends have, that I don't. It's only now that everything is making sense. If Clarissa hadn't . . . well, it would be different, but not necessarily in a good way.'

There's that fluttery feeling again.

'What actually happened with you and Clarissa?'

Eric smiles, even though he seems sad, and I reach for his hand. He takes it as though it's a natural thing. Instinctive.

'Things were going well,' he begins. 'OK, there were a few problems, but what relationship doesn't have problems? One evening Clarissa came home from work. I was on the sofa, writing. She came in, sat down and started talking to me about one of her friends getting married.

'Then, out of the blue, she says, "Should we do it? Should we get married? Because I want to have kids soon, Eric. I want to do it before next year. Is it going to happen?"

'I just looked at her, totally flummoxed. She asked me again and all I could do was stare. I mumbled, "Umm . . ." Because it had just come out of nowhere. I didn't know what to say. And then she flipped. She got so angry.'

'Angry? Why was she *angry*?'

'Because, in her words, I didn't love her enough. I'd hesitated and I shouldn't have. I should have jumped at the chance, yelled out a resounding *yes*, and did exactly as she asked. But I was in shock. I didn't have time to think.'

'That's totally normal, though,' I say, genuinely surprised. 'Who *wouldn't* have that reaction? You needed time to consider things.'

'Not in Clarissa's world. I hesitated, and she took that to mean I wasn't certain. That I didn't want it.'

'Did you? At the time?'

'I did – at least I thought I did – but I just needed time. I spent so long after that mulling it over, wishing I could turn back time just so I could have a well-prepared answer. I've been consumed by the whole thing. It's only now I realise that we were definitely *not* meant to be together.'

'At least you know now.'

'Yeah. Clarissa was lovely when we met, but she always wanted more. She was always chasing bigger and better things. She'd drop hints to me, as well. *Get a better job. Get a more lucrative hobby.* Nearly every holiday, meal or night out would be photographed and put on show.'

I wince slightly at this, thinking of my own obsession with putting my life on display.

'I think she'd have got fed up with me down the line, because I just can't be bothered with all of that.'

'I'm glad. I like Eric. *This* one. The one who went on a road trip with his crazy neighbour.'

'The best kind of trip.'

He gives my hand a squeeze. For a moment, all the awful thoughts disappear.

'I'm glad you're going to get some counselling, though. It helped me, right after Mum died.'

'I think I've needed to for a long time. Just didn't want to admit it. I have Jude to thank, I guess. Maybe I'll get him some fudge from the shop.'

'I'm kind of surprised he didn't follow us here. He's a nice guy.'

'He certainly is. I think I owe him an apology or two. Shall we go and sit in the pub for a bit? Warm our hands on a nice cup of coffee?'

'The best idea yet.'

As we wander back up the beach towards The Swan, I retrieve my phone from my pocket and draft an email to Ciaran, my cold fingers making all the typos. I read it three times before I send it, watching it disappear, watching it go. Then I do something I've wanted to do for a long time.

I delete Instagram.

I do it before I can change my mind, watching the icon disappear. And I feel a hundred times better already.

'This place looks lovely,' says Eric as we step inside the white building with the gorgeous view.

Inside, we approach the bar and as our coffees are prepared, we ask the bartender if she has seen Laurie at all.

'This lady,' prompts Eric, showing the photo.

'She looks familiar,' she replies. 'Actually . . .' She glances past us, across the pub. 'Isn't that her, over there?'

We follow her gaze. I freeze. There, at a table in the corner of the quiet pub, reading a book with a cup of tea, is none other than Laurie Robertson.

Chapter 49

Eric

Laurie Robertson is here, in this very pub. Steph's face drops. She looks as if she's going to faint.

'Oh my God,' whispers Steph, her voice full of panic. 'There she is. What shall we say?'

'Um, I don't think we fully discussed what we'd actually do if we found her,' I whisper as we pick up our coffees.

'Oh God. This must look absurd. Laurie will think we're crazy stalkers. We *are* crazy stalkers, Eric. What do we do?'

'Don't panic, for starters.'

'Argh!'

'Confession – I didn't actually think we'd find her.'

'*What*?' Steph's eyes widen as her voice rises slightly. 'What do you mean? Didn't you trust me?'

'Of course I did! It's just that it was quite the gamble. Laurie could have been anywhere.'

She's staring at me now, concern etched into her features.

'So why did you agree to come?'

'Because I wanted to spend time with you.'

'Really?'

'Yes! I wanted to find Laurie, too, but you were going to go alone and asked me to come. And what do you do when a gorgeous woman you've liked for some time asks you on a surprise road trip? You say yes.'

'*Some time?*' she asks, but we don't have time to continue the conversation, because a few tables along, Laurie's closing her book and downing the last of her tea.

She looks exactly like she does on the photos: wavy blonde hair, her pale face slightly pink from the warmth of the pub. She's wearing a beige jacket over a striped top, and a scarf of various colours. Understated, but to us she's everything.

I throw Steph a hopeful smile. 'We have to make a move.'

Steph steps forwards first, trying to pluck up the courage. Taking the suitcase, we move towards Laurie's table, smiling as she stuffs her book – *Jamaica Inn* by Daphne du Maurier – into her shoulder bag.

'Hello!' says Steph nervously.

'Hi there. I'm just leaving,' Laurie says, gesturing to the table. 'It's the best seat.'

'Oh, that's OK!' says Steph. 'We're not actually here for the table. I'm just wondering . . . are you Laurie Robertson?'

Laurie's smile fades somewhat. Her eyes dart from Steph to me and back again, spooked. Clearly, she has no clue who we are.

'Don't worry,' I interject. 'This is going to sound strange, but we're your next-door neighbours. From Bristol.'

Laurie sits back down, just moves into the seat without looking.

'Is the house OK?' she asks with a flash of panic.

'Yes! Yes, everything's fine. We just . . . well, we wanted to speak to you about something.'

'What's this about? How did you find me here?'

'It's a long story,' I say. 'Maybe I should order us another drink.'

And then, we tell her everything.

*

Laurie Robertson sits in The Swan by a window overlooking the cliffs and sips her third cup of tea. Beside her, Steph is in awe, having explained everything from the beginning. Her mum. The song Laurie was playing on the piano that night. Our frantic search for Freddy. Of everything that followed, leading us to try to track her down on the Pembrokeshire coast.

Laurie Robertson is sweet, and smiles a lot, and has nearly cried twice. She's originally from Cornwall. She's five foot six. She's a technical writer. Her husband, Malcolm, was an engineer. They used to have a dog. Laurie Robertson is interesting in so many ways.

Laurie Robertson has lived at 26 Chapel Gardens for twenty-two years and we'd never once met her.

'I still can't believe it,' she says, looking at Steph, and I wonder if she's going to get teary again.

'I told myself – and Eric – that I'd stop saying sorry,' says Steph. 'Even though I'm going back on my word, because I'm really sorry, Laurie. I am *so* sorry if I upset you that night when I screamed and shouted. I didn't mean for you to stop playing. I love it when you play the piano. Both of us do.'

Laurie looks to me and I nod.

'She's right. It's not the same without the ten o'clock song.'

'Sometimes I sing into my hairbrush,' Steph admits.

There's a pause before Laurie laughs uproariously. She has a loud, fun laugh. I remember it from the videos. Luckily, Laurie isn't at all angry that we entered her house; in fact, she's incredibly understanding. Before we know it, we're all doing it; the whole table has erupted in laughter.

'I know,' Laurie admits. 'I'd hear you sometimes, singing. As for that night – you've got nothing to apologise for. In fact, I thought *I* was the one who needed to say sorry.'

'What?' I ask. 'Why?'

'I thought I was bringing everyone else down with me. I should be thanking you, Steph. You knocking on the wall like that gave me a wake-up call, if I'm honest.'

'No, Laurie, it was my—'

Laurie puts her hand up and offers a kind smile.

'Steph, listen, love. Do you want to know the truth?'

'Well . . .'

'I've been living alone in that house since Malcolm died. I never left. I *couldn't* leave.

'When Malcolm passed, it was a total shock. He wasn't *meant* to die. Why would he? We were both fit and healthy – I'm fifty-two, he was fifty-four. There was nothing to suggest anything was wrong. Then, one night he collapsed. He had a heart attack and didn't make it. One day my life was full, the next, it was over. Malcolm was gone. I didn't think it would ever be the same after that, and I was right.

'I stayed in the house. It's a big house for just one person. I had to adapt to being alone. I had to try to accept that he wasn't coming back, and it's difficult. It's so, so difficult. We'd never had kids. Never wanted any. We loved our freedom too much. Our friends live all over the country, and abroad: we were always so wrapped up in each other, we didn't have many close friends nearby. And then there's you two – I didn't even know you, I didn't even make the effort.'

'We're also guilty of that,' I add sheepishly.

'Malcolm was wonderful. I'd always envisioned us on so many adventures, being together until we were elderly,' says Laurie. 'Then all of a sudden, there was no Malcolm, just me. I couldn't even bring myself to pack his things away. After the funeral, I felt worse – some people say it gives you a sense of closure, but for me it was solid proof he wasn't coming home. So I carried on speaking to him.

'I'd talk to him, hoping he'd hear. I put on our old holiday videos because I couldn't bear the silence. I continued our usual routine, in the house with all of his things; I even played the piano every day at ten, like I always did. Malcolm bought me that piano. I used to play as a child and when we moved in, he surprised me with it. Told me, "As long as you play me a song every night, I'll be happy."'

Tears are coming now. They travel down Laurie's kind face and land on the sleeve of her top, dampening the white fabric. Steph has joined in, dabbing at her eyes with a napkin.

'So I kept playing. I played and played, and I watched, and I talked, and I didn't leave the house. I couldn't leave, because leaving felt like leaving him behind. And the longer it went on, the harder it became to venture out of the front door. It was my new normal. I couldn't face it. I'd much rather stay inside, where I still felt Malcolm around me, than step out and acknowledge he was gone.'

'I heard you,' I tell her. 'I'd hear you talking from the other side of the wall.'

'I know,' Laurie admits. 'I still talked to him even though he wasn't there. The night you shouted and knocked on the wall made me realise how stupid I was being. It pulled me out of the life I was living, if for the briefest moment. I thought, what are you doing, Laurie? You're annoying everyone else now. I was affecting other people and that wasn't right. The moment I heard you was the moment I knew I had to do something. I had to get out of my house.

'My cousin lives here in Little Haven. A little cottage just up on the hill. I've been coming here for years, as you know. I packed a suitcase and I left. I came here, to spend some time with Anna and her family, just to get some perspective. Some courage to return home and sort things out once and for all.

'I don't want to live like I've been living forever. I might have years left in me. I don't want to spend them locked away on my own.'

Steph exhales, letting go of the tears.

'Malcolm wouldn't want you to live like that, either,' says Steph. 'Who would?'

She's thinking of her mother's letter, tucked away safely in the journal in her bag. I can tell by the way her hand is reaching for it, protectively, as if checking the leather-bound book is still there.

'I had no idea anyone missed me,' says Laurie. 'I didn't know anyone would realise I'd gone, let alone you two. You're essentially strangers to me, and yet you've travelled for hours to get here and look for me.'

'Let me just check,' I say. 'You *don't* think we're weird?'

'Ha! Of course not. This has made my day. My year, even. Malcolm would have loved this.'

'I'm so glad we found you,' says Steph as Laurie reaches over to pull her into an unexpected hug.

She gives me one, too, and in moments we're all fighting away tears.

'You can come back with us, if you like,' I offer. 'Our car is being fixed today, so we'll be heading back to Bristol this evening, if you'd like a lift.'

'And I'm always next door,' says Steph. 'I can help with anything you need.'

'It's OK,' says Laurie. 'Thank you. I really appreciate the offer, but I'm going to stay here for another week or so. I'm enjoying the sea air – it's a bit of a novelty! But I'm going to be back, OK? Don't you worry. I'll be back next door sooner than you think, I promise.'

Chapter 50
Steph

Outside, the wind is bitter, but that doesn't matter, because it's more magical this way. It's magical because Eric is next to me, and we're watching the sea and the cliffs, absorbing the view to keep and cherish, to remember during those bad days. It's as if everything is illuminated. *Life* is illuminated, even through the gloom of a cold November day.

'I want more weekends like this,' I say, snuggling into the warmth of his coat.

The adventure journal rests in my lap, Eric's postcard tucked between its pages. I run my finger along its leather spine, this symbol of change.

'What, you'd like more weekends stalking neighbours?' he jokes. 'Laurie's lovely, isn't she? I can't believe we spent all that time living next door and never knew her.'

'And never knew about Malcolm, either. I feel terrible.'

'Don't. Laurie doesn't want you to feel bad. In a way, it's a good thing. If it wasn't for her, we wouldn't be here together. We wouldn't have met. And like she said, your response that night was a wake-up call. You helped her, Steph.'

'That's true. Doesn't disguise the fact we're shit neighbours, though.'

'Were,' Eric clarifies. 'We *were* shit neighbours.'

The morning has passed in a haze of happiness and sea air. We've been sat like this for an hour already, just chatting as we await updates about the car. The pub was snug and warm, but out here, on this wooden bench, it's more private, and I like it. I like the breeze on my face. I like listening to the sound of the waves splashing and the gulls overhead. Better still, I like Eric. His gorgeous laugh. His gentle kisses. *My God*, the way he kisses. Which is another reason we're out here and not in there, in full view of the regulars. I can't keep my hands off him.

'What I said last night,' he says now, running his fingers through my hair.

I don't tell him how nice that makes me feel.

'I didn't mean that I don't want us to be together. I just panicked. I didn't want to do anything I wasn't sure about. I've been confused lately, over Clarissa, over everything.'

'It's OK.'

'It isn't. I wanted to be sure, that's all. And I *am* certain. Meeting Laurie, hearing all about what happened, it's just made me even more certain. Can we at least spend some more time together before you leave for Manchester?'

I study his face, like I have done already many times this holiday. Those perfect features.

'Of course we can. A lot more time, actually. If you want to.'

'What do you mean?'

'I'm not moving.'

'*What?*'

He catches my playful expression and pauses, as if he can't work out whether or not I'm joking.

'I'm not going to Manchester. I emailed my boss earlier.'

'Wait. You turned it down? Why? You were so excited about that promotion.'

'Was I? I'm not so sure any more. I mean, more money would have been nice, but it wasn't right for me. I don't really want the *job*, I just wanted the next thing to tick off the list. I want to get a new job because *I* want it, not because I'm trying to fit in, doing what everyone else is doing. I like Bristol. If I moved I'd only be taking my problems elsewhere. I'd still feel the same in Manchester.'

'Speaking of which, didn't you find a new place?'

I pull a pouty face. OK, one thing I *am* sad about is the house.

'The housemates-to-be are gutted, by all accounts. Paula sent a picture of her knocking back rum and fake sobbing. But hey, they'll find someone else soon enough.'

'What made you decide? Are you absolutely certain you're not being too hasty in this decision? What if we go back, away from all the pretty scenery, and you feel different? You might regret it later.'

Shaking my head, I wriggle even closer to him. A seagull swoops down before us, stopping to rest on a nearby rock.

'I do what I always do – I made a pros and cons list.'

'And what are the pros?'

'Number one – staying would make me happy. Two – *you* make me happy.'

Eric grins. 'And what about the cons?' he whispers into my ear. 'And no, before you start – don't say there aren't any.'

'They don't matter,' I say, and I turn to kiss him again.

'At all?'

'Those pros outweigh *any* cons. I'm happy, that's the important bit. So I'm staying. You're not getting rid of me, Eric.'

'Damn,' says Eric, and he breaks out into a huge smile. 'I'm really sorry, Steph. I'm trying to be all serious about this, but I can't because I'm so bloody happy that you're staying. What are you going to do now, with your job?'

'I'll stay at Everly Cope for the next few weeks, but I'll start looking for somewhere new as soon as I get home. I want to start afresh. I'm going to try new things. Look for things that make me genuinely happy. Find *people* who make me feel the same way. Just like I found you and Jude. I'm going to take Mum's advice.'

'Speaking of happy,' asks Eric, 'do I make you happy?'

'You do. More than ever.'

'That's good to know,' he says as rain begins to fall, against our faces, against the expanse of water below.

And we don't care.

It's all part of the adventure.

Epilogue

Eric

Summer

Drinks arranged on a tray. Games in a neatly stacked pile beneath a sepia filter. 'Missing you!' she types, beneath the photo, the message just for me.

I stand at the bottom of the path, looking up at the house. Beneath the sweltering July sun, the garden looks bright, the place warm and welcoming. Clutching the bag, I walk on up, hearing the ever-familiar chimes of 'Oh My Darling Clementine'.

There's noise from inside. The door swings open to reveal Laurie, grinning from ear to ear. I hand her the bag and she pulls out the bottle of gin I'd promised her.

'Absolutely perfect,' she says, planting a kiss on each cheek. 'Steph's already here.'

Sure enough, there she is. Steph, in denim shorts and a strappy top, her hair longer now, in waves bleached slightly by the afternoon sun. She leaps up to kiss me, wrapping her arms around me before I've even had the chance to sit down.

'How was work?' I ask her.

'Busy! But fun. Remember the project I put my name down for last month? Well, I'll be leading it!'

Since leaving Everly Cope last year, Steph took a job at Amanda's children's charity. It was meant to be temporary, but Steph enjoyed it so much she decided to stay.

'How was your day?' she asks. 'How was the session?'

My last therapy session took place today. Which has, admittedly, made me feel a little anxious, yet at the same time, happy. I'm in a good place right now. I nod, smiling at her as I pull her in closer. 'It went very well. Here's to a new start.'

'Aaand?' Steph prompts.

She's awaiting my other news. I can feel the warmth in my face as I ready myself to say the words I didn't think I'd utter for a long, long time.

'It's finished.'

'Whoop!' Steph cheers, and Laurie joins in.

There's a big 'Woo-hoo!' from the dining area and in comes Jude, carrying a tray of snacks, which he places on the coffee table. 'I told you you'd do it, mate.'

'That's fantastic,' says Laurie.

'Don't get too excited,' I say, flushed, as Laurie shuffles off in the direction of the kitchen. 'I've still got so much work left to do on it. So many rewrites. It's going to take forever.'

'Eric,' Steph says, 'don't fret. You did it.'

Laurie returns with a bottle of champagne.

'I've been saving this,' she says. 'Jude, grab the glasses!'

'Come on, you don't have to do this. It's just—'

'Nonsense,' says Laurie. 'We're doing it.'

Steph pulls me in for another kiss, which prompts more whooping from Jude.

'Eric, you finished your screenplay. This is something to celebrate.'

'What if nothing comes of it? It's unlikely I'll ever sell it.'

'What if you don't? It doesn't matter. You've been

working on it for years and *you did it*. I'm liking the new version, by the way. I'm a big fan.'

'Are you sure?'

Steph nods. 'You know I wouldn't lie to you. I much prefer the setting. Empty beach, that house on the cliff, the missing neighbour . . .'

'I absolutely love it too,' says Laurie.

The bubbly is poured. We clink glasses. Watching the bubbles rise in the flute, I can't help but think how surreal this is. How much has changed in the past eight months. It's almost as if this is an alternative world and one day I'll be swept back into my old one. I worry about that sometimes. But I can't think like that any more. I left that behind. So has Steph. So has Laurie.

'I love you,' Steph whispers, clinking her glass against mine.

'Right! So, what are we playing tonight, then?' Laurie asks, cutting through our loving moment with her lively voice. 'Seeing as it's Jude's turn—'

'Monopoly,' yells Jude. 'Haven't played it in ages.'

'Ooh, just you wait,' Steph says. 'I'm brilliant at this.'

'You're on.'

Since Laurie returned from Pembrokeshire, things have been different in Chapel Gardens. The day she came back, she invited us round. Which turned into a regular thing. We now do a weekly games night on a Wednesday evening; me, Steph, Laurie and Jude, and whatever friends we'd like to bring along. All of Jude's bandmates attended last week for a night of Trivial Pursuit.

Steph helped Laurie with the house, clearing away Malcolm's things, storing them safely in the spare room; a place where she can revisit them whenever she wants, without feeling that they're surrounding her. A special place for everything. A home in which her life can continue. A new chapter.

The board is out, the pieces distributed. Laurie insists on the dog; I'm the hat. As Jude pulls the cards from the well-worn box, a sound filters in through Laurie's open windows. The sound of a van door rolling open.

'Ooh, could it be . . .' says Laurie, and we rush to the window to look.

Parked next door, outside number 28, is a removal van. Stepping out from the passenger door is a young woman in a floral jumpsuit. She stops to tie her hair back as she looks towards the door, smiling, as if all of her dreams are about to come true.

The 'To Let' sign outside Steph's old flat was only up for a couple of weeks. It'll be gone again in a matter of days.

As the boxes pile up outside the door, we all go outside to offer help.

'Just moving in?' Laurie asks.

'Yeah. I'm Allie. Nice to meet you!'

'Welcome to Chapel Gardens! Feel free to pop round. We've got a games night every Wednesday, if you're interested.'

Allie doesn't need help with the boxes, but says she'll join us next week. That's another thing that's changed in Chapel Gardens.

We're very, very nice neighbours.

Later, once Jude has headed out to work, Steph and I sprawl on the sofa, trying to get cool in the July heat.

'So, someone's moved in,' Steph observes. 'Feels weird.'

'Do you think you'll miss it?'

'Not really. I like being here.'

'Do you?'

She turns to kiss me. 'Don't you believe me?'

When Lloyd decided to move out, Steph took up my offer of the extra room, even though we spend most of the time in mine. That way, we could save for our next holiday. Our next adventure. Our future. *And* we could have a cat. At the sound of our voices, Regan scuttles in excitedly from the kitchen, her fluffy grey body leaping onto the sofa to join us. Granted, we still miss Freddy, but Lloyd still sends us regular updates of our perpetually grumpy friend.

'Shh, it's almost time.'

As we lie there, at one minute to ten, we wait. We wait until we hear the thud of the piano lid, then wait for the sound that pours in through the brick and the plaster, that makes its way from Laurie's world and into ours.

Every night, at ten o'clock, Laurie Robertson plays the piano for her husband, Malcolm. It's the one thing she'll never stop doing.

We wouldn't change it for the world.

Because every night, at ten o'clock, we know we're truly home.

Acknowledgements

Seeing a novel come together, transforming from that very first draft to an actual book, is always rather surreal. It's a magical moment that makes me want to pinch myself, but it's absolutely real, and that's all thanks to some truly great people.

First of all, huge thanks go to Rachel Neely, who saw promise in my little book idea about Steph, Eric and their mysterious neighbour, and helped me to shape it into something even more special and close to my heart. Turning this once-tiny idea into this very novel has been a wonderful experience, even though the world has been a strange and sometimes dark place recently.

To the fabulous Katie Ellis-Brown – thank you for all of your guidance, and for making my lifelong dream of being an author come true. I've learned so much on this journey thanks to you, and to Zoe Yang, Juliet Ewers and the incredible team at Orion who have helped bring the residents of Chapel Gardens to life.

As always, a massive thank-you goes to my wonderfully supportive partner, friends and family for their endless encouragement.

While I was writing the ending of this book, I lost one of my favourite people in the entire world – my amazing dad. He was always extremely encouraging, and had the ability to put a smile on anyone's face. He would have loved seeing this book dedicated to him. So here you go, Dad – thank you for being the best in the world. I miss you every day, and I always will.

And of course, to all the musical neighbours out there – this one's for you.

Help us make the next generation of readers

We – both author and publisher – hope you enjoyed this book. We believe that you can become a reader at any time in your life, but we'd love your help to give the next generation a head start.

Did you know that 9 per cent of children don't have a book of their own in their home, rising to 13 per cent in disadvantaged families*? We'd like to try to change that by asking you to consider the role you could play in helping to build readers of the future.

We'd love you to think of sharing, borrowing, reading, buying or talking about a book with a child in your life and spreading the love of reading. We want to make sure the next generation continue to have access to books, wherever they come from.

And if you would like to consider donating to charities that help fund literacy projects, find out more at **www.literacytrust.org.uk** and **www.booktrust.org.uk**.

THANK YOU

*As reported by the National Literacy Trust